NO
OTHER
SIDE

Lisa Lynch

ISBN 978-1-64458-761-4 (paperback)
ISBN 978-1-64458-762-1 (digital)

Christian Faith Publishing, Inc.
832 Park Avenue
Meadville, PA 16335
www.christianfaithpublishing.com

Printed in the United States of America

This book is dedicated to Evangelist Jekalyn Carr. The angel God placed to help deliver those who have been broken, who have lost themselves, and felt like giving up. You are the radiance of God's light. You were the light in a time of darkness for me, and for this, I am forever grateful, for you, and your ministry.

Acknowledgments

God without you this book wouldn't be possible, I wouldn't be here. I'm so glad you never gave up on me, even when I felt like giving up on myself. And thank you for loving me despite my flaws. If I had a million tongues it still wouldn't be enough to thank you.

Mother: We've been through a lot, good and bad. Thank you for being there and supporting my vision. Thank you for being there for Jaiden and allowing him to spend time with you so that I could finish this book. And thank you for your feedback with this book.

Jaiden: My prince, my twin, my smile. You're the best son anyone could ask for. I want you to know you can do anything you set your mind to. Never give up and always trust God.

Gayl Benson: My favorite aunt. Thank you. For being you, for keeping me laughing, for speaking life into me and my vision for this book, and for proof reading, giving me your honest feedback about this book. You believed in me and spoke over me at times when I didn't think this book would happen.

Daria Jones: My Fav, thank you cousin for first always giving me the truth, for being a woman who is not only creative, but full of faith. Thank you for having faith in me and this book, and for allowing me to use you in my book. Your support means the world to me.

Cora Jakes Coleman: My spiritual mother, mentor, teacher, and inspiration. Thank you for being a real woman of God, a no nonsense woman, and for coming into my life at a difficult time. You are simply amazing and I'm so grateful for you. You're one of the most gentle and caring persons I know. Thank you for all the times you took time out of your life to speak life and pour into me. And thank you for praying and covering me. Your presence in my life, and the wisdom you continuously give me has helped me to evolve into more than what I have amounted to in the past. I love you and I'll forever be grateful for you and for the humor you give. You're the greatest. The world needs more people like you. I love you mama Cora.

Kierra Sheard: My mentor, my sistHER, my inspiration. Thank you for being so real and transparent. For allowing me to enter your space and glean from you. You are such a gentle spirit. Your love for people and God is so dope, and your humor makes the world a better place. Thank you for genuinely being here for me and loving me. Thank you for the fun times and for allowing me to be me. Keeks you are so amazing and I'm so grateful God placed you in my life. I love you so much and I'm so thankful that you listened to God and birthed your vision and stepped into my life. Thank you for creating an atmosphere for me where I can come and be myself without worrying of being judged. You are a blessing and I'm so grateful for you. I got your back always. We click tight for life lol.

Ronkevia Taylor: My sister. You are so amazing. Thank you for putting up with me LOL. The sister I always wanted. Thank you for your support and for your feedback on the ideas and chapters of this book. We will forever dance together.

Azure Gabriel: My sistHer, my friend, My AZ. Thank you for being there for me when I was unsure. For being a listening ear and bringing laughter into my life. You are so amazing and I'm so grateful I can call you my sistHER. I'm so blessed that God has allowed us to enter into each other's lives. You are so dope and funny might I add. I'm grateful for your feedback on this book and thank you for helping me to make things make sense. I thank God He's allowed us to cross paths and thank you for your faith at times when I doubted.

Shamika Shaw (ShamWow) Did you ever think that your presence would have such a huge impact on others? Sham you are a breath of fresh air and a gift to the world that so many have yet to experience. You are so amazing and a light to those around you. Thank you for being a woman after God's own heart. You inspire me to push and reach for more. I'm so grateful that I was able to be in your presence and glean from you. Thank you for speaking life into me and for being there for me. I love you ShamWow and I'm so grateful that God allowed you and Ki to pair to bring life to those around you. You rock Totally, and when I say totally, I mean totally lol.

Kristal McGreggor (Red popsicle) you are such a joy to be around. We've grown from friends to family and I'm so grateful for you. Thank you for having my back and being a listening ear no matter the time of day. Thank you for being the personal trainer that gets on me when I need it the most lol. You bring spice to my life lol, and laughter to everyone around you. You are such a great person and I'm glad you're in my life. I love you Dr.

Courtney Blair (Court) My sweet country court. You're so amazing, and funny, and I love you to pieces. Thank you for being a listening ear and for giving me honest feedback on this book. I'm so grateful that God placed you in my life when He did. Thank you for being an encourager when I need it most. I'm forever grateful that you found trust in me as I have in you. I hope you never forget how much you mean to so many and the blessing you are. I love you sis.

SistHER's I'm so honored to have gotten the chance to meet you all. You all are some of the dopest females around. I'm grateful for all the talks we've had and for the trust we've found in each other. Thank you to all my sistHER's for the laughs, battles, memories, races, and fun times we've shared. I can honestly say you all have grown from friends to family and I'll forever be in your corner. We click tight for life lol. I love y'all.

Tracy Milliar: Thank you for being a real friend and for your support. You are such a blessing to know. And thank you for all the laughs and tears we've shared. You rock.

Pastor Fisher: You are a breath of fresh air. I'm so grateful God led me to your ministry. Thank you for your constant prayers and covering. Thank you for being a woman after Gods own heart and for speaking life to me. Its such an honor to know a woman like you.

Ronnie & Mary Taylor: Thank you for taking me in at a rough time in my life. And for all the wonderful food you cooked. Because of you I was able to write a lot of this book in a time when I should have been stressing over a lot. I'm so grateful for you both.

Prologue

After a lot of pleading, Lina convinced her mother to go to the service. Tina, Lina, and Ava sat next to Kelly and Amber toward the front of the church. Helen rode with Vera sitting in the back of the church, while Sam and Paul showed up grabbing two seats next to each other on the second pew. The service was huge. Some of gospels' biggest artists showed up performing together for praise and worship, while some came just to show their love and support to Pastor Andrews. With the church filled to capacity, service began, starting exactly at the time Pastor Andrews promoted it would.

The crowd seemed to come to life as praise and worship started. The musicians flowed with the singers creating an atmosphere conducive for God to come in and move. Everyone was on their feet dancing as the praise music filled the church. After two praise songs, the musicians switched the tempo from praise to worship music. The praise and worship team flowed with the musicians as God's presence flooded the church. People stood with their eyes closed worshipping God. Some stood singing with their hands lifted up, and for those who weren't used to the church setting sat listening to the voices of the singers as they harmonized perfectly together.

The congregation began taking their seats following the praise and worship part of service.

Evangelist Carr stood from her seat in the front row pews of the church, smiling, as she began walking to the podium. "I honor God for entrusting me to share this Word, which He has given me, and I thank Him for His continuous grace and mercy. I also honor the wonderful leaders of this house. I'm so grateful for this opportunity." Evangelist Carr gripped the microphone, smiling, opening her Bible to the scripture she would be using. "My question to you, how is it that a person can know the power of God, but when something comes against them, they want to give up, or blame God?" She skimmed the congregation as she turned to her notes.

Some in the congregation stared on, as others pondered the question.

"Turn with me to Job 1:8–12, I will be reading from the Amplified Bible." Evangelist Carr waited as the congregation grabbed their bibles turning to the very familiar story.

Ida, one of Evangelist Carr's armor bearers, began reading the scripture into the microphone.

> The Lord said to Satan, Have you considered and reflected on My servant Job? For there is none like him on the earth, a blameless and upright man, one who fears God [with reverence] and abstains from and turns away from evil [because he honors God]. Then Satan answered the Lord, Does Job fear God for nothing? Have You not put a hedge [of protection] around him and his house and all that he has, on every side? You have blessed the work of his hands [and conferred prosperity and happiness upon him], and his possessions have increased in the land. But put forth Your hand now and touch (destroy) all that he has, and he will surely curse You to Your face. Then the Lord said to Satan, Behold, all that Job has is in your power, only do not put your hand on the man himself. So Satan departed from the presence of the Lord.

"Now jump over to the second chapter verses one to ten." Evangelist Carr instructed.

Ida began speaking into the microphone again with loudness and authority allowing the scripture to penetrate all who heard it.

> And it reads, Again there was a day when the sons of God (angels) came to present themselves before the Lord, and Satan (adversary, accuser) also came among them to present himself before the Lord. The Lord said to Satan, From where have you come? Then Satan answered the Lord, From roaming around on the earth and from walking around on it. The Lord said to Satan, Have you considered and reflected on My servant Job? For there is none like him on the earth, a blameless and upright man, one who fears God [with reverence] and abstains from and turns away from evil [because he honors God]. And still he maintains and holds tightly to his integrity, although you incited Me against him to destroy him without cause. Satan answered the Lord, Skin for skin! Yes, a man will give all he has for his life. But put forth Your hand now, and touch his bone and his flesh [and severely afflict him]; and he will curse You to Your face. So the Lord said to Satan, Behold, he is in your hand, only spare his life. So Satan departed from the presence of the Lord and struck Job with loathsome boils and agonizingly painful sores from the sole of his foot to the crown of his head. And Job took a piece of broken pottery with which to scrape himself, and he sat [down] among the ashes (rubbish heaps). Then his wife said to him, Do you still cling to your integrity [and your faith and trust in God, without blaming Him]? Curse God and die! But he said to her, You speak as one of the [spiritually] foolish women speaks [ignorant and oblivious to God's will]. Shall we indeed accept [only]

good from God and not [also] accept adversity and disaster? In [spite of] all this Job did not sin with [words from] his lips.

"Now many of us have heard of Job being a man of faith, trusting God no matter what. We've even heard some say his wife was a foolish woman. So, I began studying the scripture. I couldn't understand why this woman who knew God, and knew how good He had been to her, her husband and family, would open her mouth to consider her husband to curse Him." Evangelist Carr scanned the crowd.

"And in my studying, it was revealed to me, it was not that Job's wife didn't believe in God, but like so many of us in the midst of trouble or whatever the situation maybe, our faith gets shaken. We feel God is smaller than what we're going through. We get tired of waiting on Him, and we start feeling like God is the reason we're going through this. Let me bring this closer to home. Sometimes, we get sick and tired of hurting or seeing our loved ones hurting, so we began to doubt God can do it, we doubt God can change our current situation because it just seems too big, and we even get mad with Him wondering, why He allowed, or, is allowing this to happen." Evangelist Carr expounded.

The congregation sat in silence as Evangelist Carr ministered. "I want you to listen to me good, and really think about what I'm about to say. Faith is the most powerful tool we can have, yet, it is the most broken." The tone in her voice intensified.

1

Monique

"God, I can't do this anymore. I can't take this! How am I supposed to live without him? How am I supposed to survive and take care of our son on my own? He vowed before you, God, till death do us part. Why is my life turning out this way?" Monique sat crying, leaning her head against her marble kitchen table with a half-drunken bottle of Hennessy and three empty bottles of oxycodone pills she had consumed. Why should I stay on this earth any longer? What is my purpose, God? I feel like I'm just a waste of breath. I'm losing everything, God. I'm losing myself! What's happening to me?"

It was now 10:33 p.m. The tender noise of Joshua snoring in his bedroom not even ten feet away from where Monique sat grabbed her attention as she got up walking into his room.

"Baby, I don't ever want you to think this is your fault or it's because you did something wrong. I really thought God would keep our family together." She sighed. "Joshua, mommy loves you with all her heart. And I want you to know I never gave up on God. People might say things like if God were real, He would have saved your mommy, but, baby, it's called freewill. It's just sometimes we get so weak and tired, we want an easy way out." Monique wiped the tears that were consuming her eyes, causing her vision to blur. "Whenever you think of me, know I will always be watching over you. Just remember, we'll see each other again one day. I love you so much, baby. Always remember that, Joshua." Monique kneeled beside Joshua's bed whispering in his ear, softly rubbing his caramel-toned cheeks and kissing his immature face before walking back to the kitchen table.

Monique believed those who tried to play God by taking their own lives didn't make it to heaven, but this was something she hoped God would give her a pass on.

"God, please forgive me for my sins, for not being strong, for not putting all my trust in You, for not giving You all my pain, anger, and burdens. I know You can fix things. I know You can do anything, but, God, I just don't see it. I don't see how I can go on any longer. I have nothing left, and my son doesn't deserve to suffer because I'm hurting. I'm broken, and it seems like no one knows my pain. It feels like I have no one to turn to. I'm slowing dying inside, and my heart hurts so badly. I put a smile on my face every day, but deep down, the pain is too much to bear. I have so much anger and hurt inside, I feel at any moment, I may explode. I'm so sick and tired of being sick and tired. I want to live, God, but… but the devil has a hold of me, and he's not letting go. I've called and cried out to You, but You're not there. I just don't understand why I'm so weak? Why is it always so easy for me to give up?" Monique wept as she sat back at the kitchen table where she, her soon-to-be ex-husband, and their son used to once sit down and eat meals together as an unbroken family. "God, I love You with all my heart. Please forgive me, please forgive me. I thought I was stronger." Monique looked at the clock on the microwave that read 12:00 a.m.

"God, please see me beyond my flaws. Please forgive me." She stood up from the table walking over to the window that was a few feet from her in the sunroom, where she and her past would stare out the window watching the sun rise each morning. "Cast your burden on the Lord, and He shall sustain you." Monique smirked before falling to the floor as the mixture of the alcohol and narcotics began taking effect in her body, causing her breathing to shallow and her stomach to bleed internally.

****

Around 6:00 a.m., Joshua awoke walking to the refrigerator as he did only on the mornings it seemed to be no school, grabbing a box of juice.

"Mommy, Mommy!" Joshua walked into his mother's bedroom. "Mommy!" He began shouting when he didn't see her in bed. "Mommy!" He walked out of his mother's room, glancing to where Monique laid on the floor in the sunroom. "Mommy, get up!" He ran shaking her trying to wake her. "Wake up." He shook her three more times before running and grabbing the house phone. It was only three days prior he learned about calling 911 in school.

"My mommy won't get up." Joshua cried loudly when the 911 operator answered the phone.

"Sweetie, I need you to calm down. What is Mommy doing right now?" The operator talked in a sweet soft voice noticing the fear and immaturity in Joshua's voice.

"She's laying on the floor and blood is there. It's on her mouth." He whimpered.

"Okay, sweetie, is there anyone else in the house with you?"

"No," he cried. "Just me and Mommy."

"Do you know your address, honey?"

Joshua gave his address to the 911 operator as he sobbed.

"Honey, the paramedics are on the way." She talked to calm him and get his mind off what was taking place in front of him.

"How old are you, sweetie?"

"I'm five in a half." He sniffled.

"You are? You're such a big boy. What is your name?"

"My name is Joshua Austin." He began to calm down, wiping the tears off his cheeks with the back of his free hand.

"Joshua, that's a nice name. What grade are you in, Joshua?"

"Kindergarten."

"Wow, you're really a big boy. Do you hear the paramedics pulling up, Joshua?" The operator talked.

"I can hear them, but they're not here. I want Mommy to wake up." He cried loudly all over again.

"Okay, honey, I need you to calm down. It's going to be okay. Can you take the phone with you to the door?"

"No, it won't go."

"Okay, sweetie, I want you to put the phone down, go unlock the door for the paramedics, and come back to the phone, okay?"

"Okay." Joshua sniffled, wiping his eyes with his hands.

"I did it." He ran back to the phone after unlocking the door, kneeling beside his mother's body. "God, let my mommy wake up."

"I'm here, honey. It's okay. The paramedics are there now. They're going to come in and help your mommy okay. I don't want you to be scared when they come inside. They won't hurt you."

"Okay, they're here now," Joshua whispered.

"Okay, sweetie, you can hang up now, and thank you for being such a brave big boy."

"Bye." Joshua tensed at the sight of the paramedics as he hung up the phone.

It took police and ambulance about eight minutes to reach Monique. Deputy Crewship, a female officer who had been with the Atlanta police force for a little over six months, also responded to the call. She walked over to Joshua picking him up, trying to comfort him as she carried him to her car.

"She has no pulse! She's gone, dude!" Sam, a newly EMT, in training, yelled to Paul the Paramedic who was training him. Paul had been in the field for seven years and was used to these types of situations.

Paramedics worked on Monique, while Deputy Crewship went to a neighbor's house to ask if they knew the family or had any numbers so someone could come pick up Joshua.

"Hi, ma'am. Yes, I have James's number. That's his father." Mrs. Shawl, an older gray-haired, dark-skinned lady who appeared to be in her mid-fifties said to the officer as she reached into her purse that sat on a table by the door, grabbing a pen and piece of paper. "Is everything okay?"

"Ma'am, they're doing everything they can for his mother." Deputy Crewship grabbed the piece of paper with James's number on it.

"Oh God! I plead the blood over her in the name of Jesus!"
Mrs. Shawl began praying out loud. She would on occasion look
after Joshua.

"Thank you, ma'am." Deputy Crewship walked back to her car
where Joshua sat with a blank stare.

After three rings, James answered the phone.

"Hi, sir, this is Deputy Crewship with the police department.
Is this James?"

He answered back with a yes that could be interpreted as who
wants to know.

"I have your son Joshua with me right now. He called 911 after
finding his mother on the floor unresponsive. We're trying to locate
relatives to come pick him up."

"Look, Deputy, I love my son, but I can't come and get him. I
can't mess up what I got going on here. I hope everything works out
because I can't be raising him in this house. Ain't no room. I have to
go." James hung up the phone before Deputy Crewship could get in
another word.

"Is Daddy coming to get me?" Joshua's eyes lit up.

"Sweetie pie, I don't know yet, but you're going to be okay."
She dialed the number to James again.

"Look, ma'am, I told you I had to go!" James yelled after picking up on the second ring before being cut off by Deputy Crewship.

"No, you look here. I don't know what the problem is and actually I could care less. This is your child, and right now, he has no one
but you to come and get him!" Deputy Crewship walked to the back
of her patrol car to prevent Joshua from hearing what was being said.

"Look, miss, call his grandma." James gave the Deputy
Monique's mother's number.

"Asshole." Deputy Crewship hung up the phone. "Oh, did I
just say that?" She covered her mouth with her hand.

After ten minutes of trying to resuscitate Monique, paramedics
wheeled her to the back of the ambulance rushing her to the hospital.

"Where is Mommy going?" Joshua cried as Deputy Crewship
buckled his seat belt.

"Your mommy is going to the hospital, so the doctors can make her feel better, and you're going to your grandma's house."

"Mommy and grandma don't talk anymore," he murmured softly, looking out the window, tears rolling down his cheeks.

2

Tina

The enormity of the situation leaves Ava and I holding each other tight under the full-sized, pink flower print blanket Daddy bought me when we were a happy family. The twin-sized bed we share is now our only feeling of protection. The sound of my mother screaming and crying, with sounds of James's fist pounding against my mother's thin body, along with things breaking lets me know my stepfather James is drunk and in a rage. The hard rain that's hitting our bedroom window does little to drown out the sound of the altercation that's going on just a few feet away from us in the kitchen. Ava is crying softly for someone to help our mother, except her cries go beyond just wanting someone to help our mother, but for our mother to help herself.

At the age of fifteen, I sit and wonder how our family went wrong; how a woman could allow herself to go through such pain day after day, feeling she needs a man to live—a man to cause her to be worst off with him than without him, a man to suck all the joy and life out of her and to make her feel she's less of a woman.

In my mind, I was rescuing my mother from the man who was slowly taking her life away, who has sucked all the color out of her and drained her of all her energy. Except my thoughts go no further than being thoughts, with the dark secret that I'm two weeks with a child from the man who is killing my mother slowly.

"James, please, please stop. I'm sorry," Tina pleaded, her voice trembling.

"Shut up, woman! You want the neighbors to hear you? Huh! You think they gone save you!" James yelled, gritting his teeth as specks of spit flies hitting Tina in the face.

"No, James. Please, baby, I love you. I'm sorry, baby." Tina whined in pain.

"Oh, you love me, huh?" James punched Tina in the stomach, causing her already bruised body to hit the kitchen floor. "Didn't I tell you to stop lying to me?" James stumbled toward Tina punching her already bruised, swollen face.

"Make him stop, please make him stop!" Ava covered her ears with her hands crying.

At this point, I can do nothing but hold my eleven-year-old sister. My reassurance of better days is nothing but words. How can I be sure of anything when I'm forced to have sexual intercourse with my mother's abuser? My fight to him is already lost. All I am capable of is being there for my sister when James beats our mother as if she's a slave who stole from her master.

I asked myself over and over why our mother stayed. What happened to her faith? Why did our lives have to be so messed up? In my questioning, I found no answers, just the sounds of yelling and crying.

"James, what did I do? Please stop, James. Just tell me, baby, what did I do?" Tina's voice squeaked as her lips split open from being hit so hard.

"What didn't you do, you trying to make me seem crazy? You tell me what the hell you did!" James grabbed Tina by the hair as she tried to get up off the floor.

"James, please." Tina tried to break free from the grip he has on her hair.

"I'll tell you what the hell you did. Didn't I tell you to pay the car insurance a week ago? Why the hell them people calling me about a damn late payment fee?" James let go of Tina's hair.

"But you—" Tina mumbled before being kicked in the ribs.

When is a woman's breaking point? In James's state of mind, he felt he was right; when in actuality, he was the one who was supposed to pay his own car insurance.

The more he strips my mother of everything that makes her a strong black woman, the more I despise his life and existence. I hear my mother pleading with a man who doesn't love her and wonder what she sees in him, why does she love him so much, why does she stay?

"Either you gone start obeying what I tell you to do, or I'm leaving. You think I like hitting you?" James stumbled toward the refrigerator, kicking Tina's legs as he goes by. "You better remember, I am the head and the tail!"

"James, I'm sorry, I promise to do better." Tina crawled to the kitchen table trying to stand to her feet as the pain from being beaten shoots through her body.

"You lucky woman, God just saved your life." He took a swig of alcohol. "I promise you I'll hurt everything you love starting with those bastards of yours." He smirked.

"Baby, I promise to be a better wife. I promise." Tina wiped her eyes as tears stream down her face.

"He's our protector, our shield from harm. He knows our troubles, danger near or far. God help me to be as You are. I need You now, more than ever before. He loves me, He cares, He holds me, He's always there." I sang softly, trying to drown out the noise of what's taking place on the other side of our bedroom door.

"I want Daddy," Ava whispered, her eyes started to swell from crying.

"I know, baby. Me too, me too." I kissed Ava's forehead.

The fact of the matter was my father was gone and would never come back. Leaving us to experience things he promised to always protect us from. Leaving us in the care of the woman I once looked up to and a man who besides was an abusive drunk was also dumb to the Word of God. The day my father left us was the day our lives started to spiral out of control and the day my mother died inside.

3

My father's name was Kevin Starr, a well-liked cop with the Atlanta PD, who also happened to be my mother's high school sweetheart and still the love of her life. He was what you considered a man after God's own heart. A God-fearing man who lived on every Word of God. He not only read the Word, but he also lived it. My father was six feet two, medium-toned complexion with dark brown eyes. He rocked a low fade, was clean cut, and loved to dress nice. His teeth were the straightest, whitest teeth, which made his smile breathtaking. My father was more than just a cop to me, he was my everything. He was what held our family together. He never showed my mother hurtful love or cussed at her but embraced her gently, cherishing the moments of holding her in his arms, smelling her sweet perfume. He never touched me or Ava in ways that hurt, instead he hugged us, never missing a beat to tell us how beautiful and smart we were.

My mother was a woman who was always smiling, full of laughter. A Proverbs 31 woman, strong, virtuous, and fearful of God and God alone. She was a strong-minded woman taking care of her family and home, never forgetting to put God first. Every morning at 5:00 a.m., she would arise to begin her one-on-one time with God. She talked about God in such a passionate way, it made you feel she had seen Him face to face. Her relationship with God meant everything to her and that was how she was raising us up. To put God first, depend, trust, love and confide in Him. To fear, respect and honor Him, and to always give Him our very best no matter the situation.

My mother worked in an upscale hair salon and was considered one of the best hairstylists in the city. Outside of work, church and family was everything to her. We lived in a two-story house with everything we could ever imagine or need. We attended the Greater Faith and Healing Church, which became a second family to us. Sundays meant Ava and I would wear matching dresses, while Momma would wear one of her many fashionable church hats.

We were a close family since the only living relative's Momma had left were her aunt Berniece who she talked to on a regular basis and cousin Kim who lived with her mother Berniece seven hours away from us. My father's family lived in California, which meant we saw them mainly during the holidays.

Usually, when Daddy wasn't working, he would have his best friend and partner, Alvin, over to our house. Alvin was about five feet four, dark-toned with a low fade. He was the funniest man I had ever met. He was the comedian on the police force and unlike Daddy, Alvin was a newcomer to Christ. He was single with no kids, so he spoiled me and Ava as if we were his own. Alvin and Daddy had been friends since high school and partners on the police force since they joined together over eleven years ago.

Alvin was my big, little uncle who had a comeback for everything, even if it made no sense. Daddy loved cracking jokes on Uncle Alvin's height and would always tell him I was starting to reach him in height. Alvin would then look at Daddy and say, "Yeah, well, that's okay. The Bible says Jesus wept, do you not realize, Kevin, that's the shortest verse in the Bible? I'm short but so is that verse, Kevin. There is power in shortness."

Everyone would look at Uncle Alvin then burst out laughing as he would stand smiling, looking around waiting on someone to take his side. He was what you would call a natural-born comedian.

4

Tina

"James, please let's just go to bed. I can make you feel good." Tina tried to strengthen her crackling voice.

"Why the hell would I want you to make me feel good? Woman, look at you, you're pathetic! You want to make me feel good, huh?" James grinned.

"Yes, baby, I'll do anything." Tina cried.

"Go get Lina out the bed so I can make her feel like a woman," James slurred his words as he took another sip from his bottle of death.

"No, James, she's only fifteen, not my baby, James." Tina looked at James, tears rolling down her swollen face.

"Didn't I tell you, you better start obeying me, woman?"

"But James, that's my baby. Do you even realize what you're saying, James? You're drunk and talking crazy." Tina wiped the tears rolling down her face with the sleeve of her shirt. "Come on, baby, let's just go to bed." She grabbed James's hand.

"Get the hell off me." He pushed Tina as he walked toward Lina and Ava's room.

"Hurry and act like you're asleep, hurry!" Lina whispered.

"Is he coming?" Ava whispered back.

"Just do what I tell you." Lina pulled the cover over their heads. "God, You're our protector, please cover us under Your wings. We can't take this anymore." A tear drops from Lina's eye.

"James, please, they're asleep. They don't need to see us like this, just go get in the bed." Tina stumbled from the pain in her body as she ran standing in front of Lina and Ava's bedroom door.

"Woman, you better be glad I have to work in the morning. God just spared you again." James turned and staggered into his bedroom, closing the room door behind him. "Tell me how that couch feels in the morning." He laughed, shouting from the bedroom.

Every hit she takes, I wonder why she allows herself to be battered when Jesus died being beaten and ridiculed for our sins, giving us the choice to be free from sin and abuse. What happened to the strong, black, God-fearing, independent woman I once knew. All I have left of my mother is the past moments we shared together as a happy family.

****

The next morning, I awoke at 7:00 a.m., after hearing James's truck back out of the parking lot. This was the Saturday Momma planned on taking me and Ava shopping.

"Good morning, baby," Tina smiled, standing at the kitchen sink with her back, facing Lina as she walked out of her bedroom, leaving Ava in bed asleep.

"Why, Momma? What's happening to you? Why do you put us through this day after day?" Lina covered her eyes with her hands as tears began rolling down her face.

"What's happening to me, huh, what's happening to me? Since when did the world start caring about what the hell is happening to me?" Tina turned facing Lina, talking through her teeth.

"You know, Momma. I started to feel sorry for you, I wondered why God was allowing you to go through this. But it's not God, it's you. You put yourself through this. You let him hurt us. You don't give a damn about us. Look at you, look at your face. All you care about is pleasing James. You sit here and complain as if the world did something to you, as if the world owes you something. If Daddy were here, you wouldn't be like this!" Lina yelled, tears running down her face.

"Don't you ever put your father in this. I love you, girls, it's just something you sometimes go through being a woman, it's called life!" She grabbed a cigarette and lighter from the shelf over the sink, shaking as tears ran down her swollen face.

"Momma, look at you. We can leave and never come back, you, me, and Ava. I can get a job and take care of us. Please, Momma. You always said, in times of trouble, God will help and give you direction. When are you going to trust God? Just let Him help you." Lina walked, hugging Tina from behind as they both cried.

"God." Tina laughed, her hands shaking while holding the newly lit cigarette. "God, don't give a damn about us. Where was God when I needed money to pay for our house, where was God when I lost everything me and your father ever worked for? Where was God when your father needed him? Where was God, huh, where was He? He wasn't there then and He ain't here now. God could care less about you or this family for that matter!" She puffed, inhaling the cigarette, releasing smoke from her nostrils.

"Do you even get what you're saying, Momma?" Lina stood, looking confused. "You know what you are, Momma. You're a sad definition of a woman. I used to admire you, but now, I hate I even came from you." Lina sniveled, letting the grip she had on her mother go as Tina turned around to face her.

"Don't you ever disrespect me again! I work too hard to keep a roof over you and your sister's head. I take too much crap from people, and I'm not about to start taking it from you!" She slapped Lina.

"You know, what the sad part is, I'm more woman than you! I'd rather live in a box than let a man cause me to lose myself." Lina held her face, crying to her room. "Where is my mom, and what happened to her?" she turned toward Tina.

I stared out the window of my bedroom. Over the last three years, our lives have been hell. The caramel complexion, hazel-eyed, curly hair woman I once knew who was always encouraged and happy is now frail and scarred up. Although it's thinned out a lot, I tried to picture her hair beautiful and bouncy the way it was when Daddy was here.

Her mind is weak, her spirit is dead. She's trapped and sees no way out. Her faith has gone, and the God she once served is not even a thought in her destabilized mind. How do you help someone who doesn't want to be helped? I am here, yet I am strong. Her depending is on man instead of on the One above. Her flesh is struggling and losing the fight to overcome, to let go of things, to move on and start over. The side I'm on is the side she's lost. Her battle, she has given over to the devil. She feels her faith failed her, but it's her who's failed in faith. No amount of makeup can cover up all the years of hurt, pain, and abuse. She's allowed James to put her through. I get lost in my thoughts, thinking about the day my mother gave up and chose to live on the other side of God.

5

June 23 had been a special day. It was not only Friday, but also Ava's seventh birthday. Tina purchased Ava a pink and white polka dot dress with white sandals to wear for her birthday dinner after school, at her favorite place to eat. Her dress also matched the colors of her vanilla and strawberry Princess castle cake, which had her picture on the windows of the castle.

At the restaurant, Kevin reserved a booth decorated with pink and purple sparkly balloons that sat around the chairs and corners of the table. As usual, Alvin was the life of the party making everyone laugh with his crazy jokes and funny expressions he made when he talked.

"Baby girl, happy birthday." Alvin reached into his pocket handing Ava a hundred-dollar bill, never looking to see what it was he were handing her.

"Wow, Ava, you can buy anything you want now." Lina grinned, staring at the crispy hundred-dollar bill.

"I hope you give me triple for my birthday considering you forgot about my birthday last year." Kevin looked at Alvin, smiling.

"Don't bring up the past, Kevin. Let's look to the future, considering everything's not about you, Kevin." Alvin smirked, cocking his head to the side, closing one eye staring at Kevin.

"Thank you, Uncle Alvin. Look, Momma, Uncle gave me a hundred dollars." Ava waved the bill in the air, grinning.

"Wait, I did?" He raised his right eye brow "That was part of my rent money. I'm gonna need that back." He pointed both his fingers toward Ava, as everyone burst out laughing.

"Princess, this is for you." Kevin reached into his back pocket, handing Ava a sparkly pink envelope. "Don't mind, Uncle Alvin, he's special." He laughed.

"Oh, Daddy." She beamed, grabbing the envelope.

"Open it already, what does it say?" Alvin smacked his hands on his thighs.

"Yay, Lina, we're going to Disney World tomorrow!" Ava's eyes began to water from excitement.

"You are?" Tina smiled, turning her head toward Kevin winking.

After everyone finished eating, they all sang happy birthday, while Tina lit the pink candles on the cake. Alvin began clapping and singing over everyone with the thought he sounded good. The truth was Alvin sang in one flat key the whole song making a good song sound bad.

Ava blew out the candles then began cutting the cake. It had a layer of fresh strawberries and glaze in the middle. The cake itself was moist, dissolving once it hit your tongue. The butter creme icing was sweet and smooth as if it has been whipped, causing your taste buds to dance. Kevin rubbed his finger over the cake then on Tina's nose putting frosting on her. She laughed, wiping her nose with her napkin as Alvin leaned his face toward Kevin to do the same to him.

"What about me, Kevin Kev?" Alvin laughed.

Kevin with a look of hilarity laughed. Everything Alvin said or did made people laugh. It was hard taking him seriously even when he was being serious because his facial expressions would tell a different story, causing you to laugh.

"Did you have fun, Ava?" Tina smiled, as the waiter came to take their dirty plates and bring the bill.

"Oh yes, Momma, I don't ever want my birthday to end." She grinned.

"I know, baby, but there will be plenty more." Tina winked, smiling at Ava who sat next to Alvin across the table from her and Kevin.

"Well, cupcake and princess, we have to get going, me and Uncle Alvin have to get ready for work." Kevin smiled.

"Daddy, please stay home with us tonight." Ava whined as her eyes lit up with the excitement maybe they would have a movie night.

"Tomorrow I promise I'll be with you for the whole weekend, no work, but I have to work tonight, princess. I have to keep the streets safe baby. I can't let Uncle Alvin go by himself, nothing would get done." Kevin laughed, pulling out his Gucci wallet, which had been a gift to him from Alvin for Christmas.

"That's right, Ava, nothing would get done." Alvin agreed before catching on to what Kevin had said. "Wait, Kevin, we all know the truth." Alvin looked at Kevin, squinting his eyes. "Tell them, tell them the truth." Alvin mouthed.

"You promise, Daddy?" Ava looked with saddened but expectant eyes.

"Have I ever broken a promise to you, princess?" Kevin stared into Ava's beautiful brown eyes.

"Nope. Daddy, I love you." She put her hand to her mouth blowing a kiss.

"I love you too." Kevin caught Ava's kiss with his hand then made the gesture as if he were putting her kiss in his pocket.

"Kevin…" Alvin blew a kiss toward him.

"Man, get out of here." He laughed, smacking Alvin's kiss away.

****

Kevin and his family arrived home around 7:00 p.m. to a package on the porch for Ava from Alvin's mother. Tina told her once she had taken a bath and gotten her pajamas on, she could open her gift. She ran to her room getting the things she would need for her bath while Lina ran the water for her in the bathroom they shared down the hall from their room. Kevin took a shower in the bathroom of their master bedroom and once out, he relaxed on the bed allowing his body to rest before he had to get going for work.

After the girls were cleaned and dressed, they ran jumping on their parent's fluffy king-sized pillowtop bed into Kevin's arms. They all laid in the bed watching cartoons until Kevin had to get up and get going.

"Daddy, we're going to have so much fun tomorrow." Ava beamed in Kevin's arms as they walked down the stairs. The excitement on her face was evident about their trip they would be taking the following day.

"I love you, cupcake and princess, make sure you say your prayers before bed." Kevin put Ava down then kissed and hugged both Lina and Ava.

"I love you, baby, be safe." Tina smiled, hugging Kevin as he embraced her like it would be his last time holding her.

"Have I told you today you're beautiful and the most amazing woman I know?" Kevin whispered in Tina's ear, then kissed her on the neck as she closed her eyes taking in every word he spoke.

"Have I told you how much I love you?" Tina held Kevin tighter. "And how you smell good?" Tina and Kevin laughed.

"I love you, baby, I'll call you in a little bit." Kevin gently squeezed Tina tighter, then kissed her one last time.

"We love you." Tina, Ava, and Lina yelled from the front door as Kevin walked to his car.

"I love you girls more." He turned, smiling. "Don't forget to say your prayers."

"Momma, we're going to have so much fun tomorrow." Ava smiled as Tina closed and locked the front door.

"Yes, we are, baby." She smiled.

Tina walked Lina and Ava to their room where they all got on their knees to say their prayers.

"Lina, you start, then Ava, and then I'll finish it." She nudged Lina in a playful way.

"Dear God, thank you for this beautiful day. Thank you for Momma and Daddy, Ava and Uncle Alvin. Please keep us safe as we sleep and keep a special protection over Daddy and Uncle Alvin. We love You so much." She smiled, eyes closed.

"God thank you for my birthday, I wish it could last forever. Thank you for loving me so much that you gave me to Momma and Daddy. Thank you for our house and my sister and Uncle Alvin too.

I'm so excited about Disney World and I love You so much. Please protect the whole wide world. Amen." Ava smiled, her eyes still closed.

"Lord, we thank you for this day You have allowed us to go safely through. I ask that You keep Kevin and the force in your hands, protect them all and let no harm come near them. I pray You will cover my girls in all they do, bless our sleep, and bless our travels on tomorrow. God, we thank you for just being You and for loving us so much. We forever give You all honor, glory, and praise in Jesus name we pray."

"Amen." Tina, Lina, and Ava said, smiling.

"Good night, girls. It's nine. Get some rest. We have a long day tomorrow." Tina tucked them in bed, kissing them each on the forehead.

"Good night, Mommy, we love you," they said as Tina closed the door, leaving it half cracked.

"I love you more," she whispered.

****

Even though Kevin and Alvin worked the night shift together riding in the same patrol car, they drove separate cars to work.

"Guys, I'm here. It's ya boy coming to save the night. I'm like the Flash. Strong, fast, and black. A beautiful black, a black that you dream about in your dreams. People call me black flash. I'm the quick one, while Kevin is the loser. I get all the work done, and I let Kevin get the acknowledgment, so he doesn't feel like the loser he is." Alvin laughed at his own comment.

"Okay, munchkin, enough with the daydreaming of how you wish life was. Get to work." The lieutenant laughed as he sat at the desk that sat at the entrance of the police substation. "And for the record, Flash is fast, not strong, or small in stature like you." He laughed.

"Well, everything isn't about size." Alvin squinted his eyes, laughing. "And everything's not about doughnuts either." He mumbled under his breath as he watched the lieutenant take a bite of a glazed doughnut.

"What was that?" Lieutenant asked as a piece of the doughnut he bit dropped on the desk. He immediately picked up the piece that dropped, putting it back in his mouth. "Five-second rule." He looked at Alvin as Alvin stood looking at lieutenant in disgust.

"Really, lieutenant, really?" Alvin shook his head, laughing.

Alvin was the type of person who could make a bad day disappear. His voice, his facial expressions, and his big imagination would have you laughing for days. And once he would get going, you were either sure to be confused or laughing at what he was saying.

"Munchkin? That hurts, Lieutenant." Alvin looked as if he wanted to cry. "It took me a minute to catch that, but I got it. That's okay, Lieutenant, I know deep down inside I'm your hero. And look who decided to finally show up for work." Alvin smiled at the sight of his best friend.

"Hey, Lieutenant, is he daydreaming again?" Kevin laughed. "This guy is funny." He joked, nudging Alvin.

"Okay, Kevin, you know what you're doing tonight, you're driving tonight. You always make me drive, and I'm finally putting my foot down. I won't let you boss me around, not one more day. And if you think you're going to make me drive, I'll just tell Lieutenant." Alvin ran out of the substation to the passenger side door of the patrol car.

"That's because you're so short. It takes a minute for you to get out the car and get steady on your feet. If we're trying to catch a bad guy, he'll get away because of you." Kevin laughed.

****

The night seemed to be going well, There wasn't much action going on and, amazingly, Kevin and Alvin only had to give out one warning to a speeding driver.

"Ah, ma'am, do you know how fast you were going?" Alvin walked up to the driver side door of the speeding car.

"Well, since you're asking me, why don't you just tell me how fast I was going." The older woman who appeared to be in her late sixties replied in a sarcastic tone.

"Well, ma'am, you were going sixty in a forty-mph zone."

"No, I wasn't, don't you tell that lie on me."

"Ma'am, I clocked you, so I know what I'm talking about." Alvin cocked his head to the side.

"Well, I'm old and I'm trying to get home, so what you gonna do about it?" The woman rolled her eyes.

"Well, ma'am, I'm just going to give you a warning this time." Alvin smiled.

"Well, that's what you ought to do. I wasn't bothering anybody, you're bothering me. I can be your grandma, little man. I ought to take you across my knee and whip your little butt." The older woman tooted her lips.

"Ma'am, ma'am, now that's not necessary. I'm a grown man." Alvin put his hand on his hip.

"You lucky I don't put soap in your mouth. You should be ashamed talking to an old lady like that." She rolled her eyes again this time, looking Alvin in the face.

"Did you just roll your eyes at me, Grandma!" Alvin stepped back from the car, throwing up his hands with the stance as if he was about to do a karate move on the lady. "How about you get out the car and whoop me then. No, I don't want to have to hurt someone so old and wrinkled. You know what answer this, what is an old wrinkled, toothless lady like you doing out this time of night? You were doing some illegal activity, huh."

"Is he serious?" Kevin watched as he sat in the driver seat, laughing. "This guy." He shook his head opening the door to get out and get Alvin.

"Ma'am, I'm sorry about that, just watch your speed and have a good night." Kevin smiled, grabbing Alvin's shoulder pushing him to the car.

"She rolled her eyes at me." Alvin nagged on. "I'm an officer!" He touched his badge.

"Just get in the car before Grandma hurts you." Kevin laughed as they opened the car doors to get in.

"Little midget!" the old lady yelled out the window as she pulled off.

"Oh, she's going down." Alvin tried reaching the gear shaft to put it in drive, wanting Kevin to pursue the lady. Each time Kevin swatting his hand away.

"I'm going to handcuff you and make you sit in the back, back seat if you don't stop." Kevin laughed.

"There's no such thing as a back, back seat." Alvin rolled his eyes crossing his arms.

"It's called the trunk." He laughed.

"Kevin, she's an undercover gangster. I know what she's hiding in the trunk, and I know she's killed a few people. I know an undercover mobster when I see one." Alvin looked up as if in deep thought.

"Man, you're crazy, you really are crazy. Your parents missed out on a check for you growing up." Kevin laughed, shaking his head. "You can't go around harassing old ladies."

"Yeah, well, she can't go around disrespecting your boss, Kevin." Alvin looked toward Kevin with a serious expression. "I'm the boss because I'm older." Alvin pointed his finger in Kevin's face.

"You better get that ashy finger out my face before I break it." Kevin said, laughing.

Besides the run in with the gangster grandma, the night seemed to be quiet as Kevin and Alvin continued patrolling their zone.

"Kevin, we need to stop." Alvin fidgeted around in his seat holding his stomach.

"And what is your reason?" He looked at Alvin. "And stop moving around like that, you're making me nervous."

"Because I need to use the bathroom." He sat back in the seat. "And you're not my daddy so stop questioning me and do what I tell you." Alvin nagged, rolling his eyes. "Please, Kevin, I'm sorry. You are my daddy." He leaned over putting his head on the dash board.

"Are you serious, man?" Kevin laughed. "Number one or number two?" He shook his head.

"Number three, now stop anywhere before I have an accident." Alvin scooted to the edge of the seat. "It was the food from that restaurant. Man, I have to go. My body's getting hot. I'm having hot flashes. Kevin, please help me." Alvin leaned, laying his head on Kevin's arm.

"Get off me, and you better not poop in this car." Kevin laughed.

Up the road sat a convenience store known to have lots of action in the parking lot. People crowded with their fixed-up cars, blaring music as if it was a spot for a car show.

"Just stop there, please, Kevin, before I call Tina and tell on you." Alvin turned his head toward the window anticipating the relief he would feel.

"That's because you messed with the wrong old lady." Kevin laughed. "Maybe we should get you a diaper."

"Maybe you should shut up." Alvin opened the car door, clenching his cheeks as he walked.

Alvin walked fast trying to hurry to the bathroom. When he walked up to the door, he did not see the store clerk at the register as he usually did.

He must be doing something behind the counter, Alvin thought. "Captain Alvin is in the building," he yelled out as he opened the door of the store. "I'll be back. I have to take care of some business," he said as he walked past the register, turning down the second aisle which held the candy. "I'm coming for you Snickers, as soon as I take a little poopy." He pointed with both hands at the candy.

Sounded like a gun shot, Kevin thought. He knew the sound all too well. Hopping out the car with his hand on his gun, he entered the store where he was shot three times along with his best friend. Alvin lay lifeless as Kevin lay in a pool of blood slipping in and out of consciousness, struggling to hold on to life.

The suspect shot at Kevin firing four rounds before fleeing the scene with cash, cigarettes, and lottery tickets in hand. One of the four bullets missed Kevin, hitting the store's front window shattering the glass. This set off an alarm alerting police something maybe going on at the store.

Two patrol cars arrived at the store within minutes, spotting one of their patrol cars in the parking lot, engine still running. Considering the officers who drove the patrol car had not responded to the call of a possible disturbance at the store, the officers immediately called for backup and entered the store with guns drawn. Before backup had arrived, one of the officers searched the store, while the other officer found Kevin and Alvin lying in a pool of blood.

"We have two officers down. We need paramedics immediately!" One of the officers radioed into dispatch. Sweat beamed off his forehead as he performed CPR on Alvin. "Come on, Alvin, breathe, come on!" He pushed up and down on his chest. "No, no, no, come on, man, you can't die, please. We need paramedics!" the officer yelled again to dispatch.

Officers also found the store clerk who happened to be the brother of the store owner, lying lifeless behind the counter. The store's surveillance system had stopped working the day prior to the robbery and was scheduled to be fixed the following Monday. So without surveillance, detectives had to piece together all they could to find a suspect.

Lieutenant arrived on scene, shaking his head. "I don't care what you have to do!" he yelled as he met with detectives and officers in the store's parking lot. "You find the bastards that did this!" His hands shook with rage, face turning red as he tried to contain his tears from falling.

****

The squeal of Tina's screams startled Lina and Ava up out of their sleep. It was 3:00 a.m. when Tina began screaming as if she were a slave being beaten for stealing from her master.

"Lina, what's going on, why is Momma crying?" Ava rubbed her eyes.

"I don't know. Stay here, I'll be back," Lina said before creeping to the top of the stairs looking to see what was going on.

"Ma'am, there's been an accident. Kevin and Alvin were involved in a shooting," a black male officer stated standing alongside his partner, a Caucasian male in the doorway of the house.

"No, no, no. Are they okay?" Tina's voice trembled.

"They're not doing so well. We need you to get to the hospital. We can take you," the Caucasian officer replied.

"Okay, okay, I have to get my girls up. I'm coming, I'm coming!" Tina said, running up the stairs leaving the front door wide open.

Lina met her at the top step sniveling. "Is he going to be okay, Momma? God can fix it right?" She began crying.

"God got them, baby, come on so you and Ava can get dressed." She hugged Lina.

Ava laid asleep resting her head on Lina's lap, while Lina cried softly on Tina's shoulder in the back seat of the patrol car. When they arrived at the hospital, Tina was met by the surgeon who operated on Kevin. Tina stood talking with the doctor while Lina and Ava stood in tears, holding hands next to the two officers who had driven them to the hospital. He informed her Kevin suffered two gunshots to the abdomen and one to the left side of his chest. He also told her he had about a 40 percent chance of recovering.

"How is he? How is Alvin?" Tina's voice squeaked.

"Ma'am, can you sit down?" the surgeon said calmly as he reached to pull a chair over for her.

"No, I didn't come here to sit. How is Alvin doing?" Tina began raising her voice.

"Ma'am, when paramedics arrived on scene, your husband's partner Alvin was found lying face down, he suffered a single gunshot to the back of the head. Paramedics worked on him but was unsuccessful in regaining a pulse. Your husband had a very faint pulse. We rushed him into surgery and worked on him for two hours removing the bullets. He's in ICU now," the doctor uttered firmly with little to no emotion.

"Oh god, Alvin!" Tina stood in shock covering her mouth with her hands. "We were all just together a few hours ago." Tears starting to form in her eyes. "I need you to take me to see my husband." Her hands began shaking.

"I don't think it's a good idea for you to see him like that. He's suffered a significant amount of blood loss." The doctor looked Tina in the eyes. "Plus, children aren't allowed on the ICU floor."

"You listen to me good. You will take me to see my husband now. This is not up for debate! I don't need you telling me what you think is a good idea. That is my husband and as God is my witness, if you don't take me now, it's going to get real ugly!" Tina's eyes grew wider and voice stronger. She was never one to raise her voice, but when she did, you knew she meant business. People in the emergency waiting room looked as Tina got louder.

"Yes, ma'am." The doctor stepped back to make a quick call to the ICU head doctor. "I just want you to be prepared. When you walk in the room, your husband will be hooked up to a breathing machine and will have all types of wires and tubes coming out of him," the doctor quickly spoke once he got off the phone noticing how Tina's demeanor began changing.

"Come on, girls." Her voice trembled.

Once on the elevator, they rode it to the third floor. Tina stood with her eyes closed holding Lina and Ava's hand praying.

"Look, girls, I want you to be strong for Daddy. We have to be strong for him. Everything is going to be okay. Daddy is a child of God, and God won't let anything happen that's not meant to happen." Tina kneeled in front of Lina and Ava once off the elevator. "Daddy is connected to a lot of tubes. I don't want you to be scared when you see him. He needs those tubes to help him get better." She wiped her eyes as tears began rolling down her cheeks. "Daddy is a strong, strong man. He's a fighter, and he'll pull through." She smiled a smile her girls could see was trying to hide the hurt and fear she felt.

"Okay, we're ready." Tina stood up facing the doctor.

"Take as much time as you need." He opened the door smiling at Tina.

"Thank you, thank you." She looked the doctor in the eyes.

They walked into Kevin's room where he laid unresponsive to his family's voice, hooked up to five different IVs and tubes. His catheter bag hung off the side of his bed, and a tube went down his throat preventing him from talking even if he were capable of doing so.

"Oh god, baby, I'm here, we're here." Tina walked over to Kevin kissing his forehead.

"Daddy." Ava walked to the side of the bed placing her hand on top of his hand crying softly.

"God, I know you can do anything. Please heal my husband. He's a good man. We need him," Tina said softly, tears rolling down her face as she held Kevin's other hand.

"No, no, no. Momma, is Daddy going to be okay?" Lina ran, pushing her head into her mother's chest crying.

"Yes, baby, yes." She stared at Kevin, talking softly. "Lina, grab Ava's other hand and you hold mines." Tina kissed Kevin's forehead again. "Bow your head, girls. If we can't do anything else, we're going to pray." She bowed her head closing her eyes.

"God, you said where two or three are gathered together in your name, you're there. We're standing together in the name of Jesus asking You to fix what's damaged and heal Kevin from the inside out. God, even though the weapon has formed, let it not prosper. You said You will strengthen us and help us. My husband really needs Your help right now. No matter what the doctors say, God, we shall believe your report. You healed the woman with the issue of blood, so please heal my husband. Please give Alvin's family peace and strengthen them for the days to come. We believe You for all things. No matter what the outcome is, I thank you for being with us through it all. We love You so much and we give You all the honor, glory, and praise. In Jesus name we pray. Amen!"

"Momma, is Uncle Alvin okay?" Lina looked at her mother with tears.

"Baby." She cleared her throat. "Uncle Alvin... well, baby, he's with God now." She rubbed Lina's cheek.

"But why, Momma? Why would He take him so soon?" Lina wrapped her arms tightly around her mother.

"Baby, always remember the Lord gave, and the Lord hath taken away. God doesn't make mistakes, baby. I don't know the answer to why God allowed this to happen, but He knows what He's doing. It's in God's hands and that's where we have to leave it," Tina said, kissing Lina's forehead. "We can't give up hope on God. He's the only one that can help Daddy now." She kissed Lina's forehead again.

"Momma, I don't want to leave Daddy by himself," Ava said softly, staring at Kevin's face.

"Baby, we're not leaving Daddy's side. He's going to be fine." Tina walked over to Ava hugging her. "God is so good, baby. Always know God is a very presence help. In times of trouble, He will help and give you direction. He has it all in His control. We just need to be strong for Daddy and have faith." She rubbed Ava's face as Ava held her arms around her waist.

"Daddy, I'm here. I'm not going anywhere, I promise. Remember when you told me God wouldn't let anything happen to his children? He won't let anything happen to you. It's okay to be scared, Daddy, but you're going to be okay. Uncle Alvin went to be with God, but now Uncle Alvin can make God laugh. I love you so much, Daddy." Lina held her father's hand, rubbing the side of his face. "Momma, can he hear me?"

"Baby, he hears you." A tear rolled down her cheek.

"I love you, Daddy. It's okay. We can go to Disney World another day. I won't be mad. Please just wake up in the morning so you can come home." Ava kissed Kevin's hand before lying on the couch that sat under the window in the hospital room.

"Momma, I'm scared what if Daddy doesn't get better." Lina looked at her mother as she walked to see who was knocking on the door.

"Baby, just pray." She looked back at Lina before opening the door.

"How is he?" Pastor Sullivan asked. He was pastor of the church Kevin and his family attended.

"Pastor, he's hanging in there, but Alvin, he's gone." Tina dropped her head. "My brother is gone."

"My wife woke me up. She was watching the news when the story of the shooting came on. Did they catch who did this?" Pastor Sullivan talked with a deep tone.

"All I know is, they were involved in a shooting. No one has told me anything. Pastor, I'm scared. I'm trying to be strong for Kevin and my girls, but what if he doesn't get better, what am I going to do?" Tina wiped her tears off her cheeks with her hands.

"Tina, let's pray," he said, grabbing her hand as he walked closer to Kevin's bedside grabbing his hand. "Creator of all, most

Gracious and Heavenly Father, we come before Your throne in need of a miracle right now. We're asking You to touch every part of Kevin's body and heal him. Lord, we command Your angels to guard all sickness and infections that may come against his body. We know all power and control is in Your hands, so we turn this matter over to You. Lord, touch Tina's mind and heart. Bring peace to her and her family right now. Touch the lives of everyone affected by this senseless crime. Help Alvin's family cope with their loss. In their time of sadness and grief, bring joy and peace to them. Help us all to lean unto You and not our own understanding. We trust You and thank you for all You're doing right now. Help us to not let go of all You've already done and what Your about to do in our lives. We release everything that is unlike You right now, every evil thought, every emotion that's affecting our thinking. And it's in Jesus name we pray." Pastor Sullivan turned, hugging Tina.

"Momma, it's okay. It's going to be okay." Lina hugged her mother after noticing her beginning to cry again.

"I know, baby, I know." She kissed Lina's forehead. "You need to get some rest, baby. It's late." She hugged Lina. "Baby, I'm so proud of you. You're being so strong for Daddy."

****

The clock above the door of Kevin's room read 5:30 a.m. when two detectives in charge of Alvin and Kevin's case knocked on the door. Pastor Sullivan sat next to Kevin's bedside holding his hand while Tina answered the door.

"Mrs. Starr, my name is detective George Hanks. This is my partner detective Amy Winston. I'm sorry about your loss. They told me Alvin was your brother. We're going to do everything we can to make sure we catch the person that did this. How is your husband doing?" Detective Hanks sounded sure of his words.

Tina stepped into the hall closing the door behind her. "He's hanging in there. How did all this happen? No one's told me any-thing," Tina spoke almost in a whisper.

"The store's video surveillance unfortunately wasn't working. But from what we've seen through surveillance from a neighboring bank is, Officer Alvin walked into the store around twelve in the morning. Seconds later, Officer Kevin was seen entering the store. The store clerk was already deceased behind the counter when Officer Alvin walked into the store. From the gunshot wound Alvin sustained, we believe he never even realized what was going on. He never had time to react. We believe your husband heard the gunshot that killed Alvin and ran into the store. He was shot and fell to the floor. He never fired a shot from his gun. The suspect, who appears to be in his mid-twenties, is seen running from the store with what appears to be lottery tickets and cigarettes. We promise we have every officer out looking for the person who did this. Once again, I'm sorry for your loss." Detective Hanks shook Tina's hand.

"Thank you." Tina looked him in the eyes.

"If you need anything, please don't hesitate to give me or my partner a call." He reached in his shirt pocket pulling out a card placing it in Tina's hand.

Tina walked back into the room falling to her knees, sobbing.

"You have to be strong." Pastor Sullivan jumped up out of the chair walking over to Tina, placing his hand on her back.

"Why? They didn't deserve this. Why did You let this happen, God? You said You would never put more on me than I could bear." Tina cried, snot running from her nose.

"Give it to God. It's okay to cry." Pastor Sullivan dropped to his knees hugging Tina. "Tina, remember the story about Cain and Abel and how Cain killed his brother Abel. Just like with Cain, God allows us to make our own choices. It's called free will. We have to be very careful about blaming God when things don't turn out the way we want, think, or feel they should. Know that Satan causes things to happen too."

"I just don't understand why God would let this happen." Tina began to calm down as she listened.

"Remember the sermon I preached a few weeks ago about free will. Sin entered into the world, so we paid for it. God gave us a choice to choose Him or not. Once again, it's called free will. Everyone doesn't choose God's side in return. We have worldly bound people living for all they think are luxuries of the world. Their decisions are works of the flesh. Tainted and corrupt. You probably won't understand why this happened, but blaming God isn't going to give you answers either. Remember sin entered the world because of man, not God!" Pastor Sullivan talked in a calm but serious voice. "Regardless of what you want it's God's will that will be done."

"God is so good to me, but I'm scared if He ever took Kevin away from me. I don't think I could love Him the same." Tina stood up from the floor sitting in the chair next to Kevin's bedside.

"There's a time for everything including losing the ones you love, but you can't take your love away from God for things that are a part of life. Even if a person's life is cut short, remember everything that happens was already planned to happen before you were born." Pastor Sullivan stood up from the chair he sat in next to Tina's. "I'm praying for you and your family. Please just trust God and hold onto His hand."

"Thank you, Pastor, for everything." Tina stood up to hug Pastor Sullivan.

"If you need anything, call me. I'll stop by around nine or so to check up on you all," he said, walking to the door.

Tina sat back in the chair next to Kevin's bedside, holding his hand as she dozed off. One hour later, she, Ava, and Lina were awakened by the sounds of alarms going off.

"Momma, what's going on?" Lina yelled, standing in a daze as doctors came rushing in the room.

"Kevin! What's going on?" Tina yelled.

"Ma'am, we need you all to get out the room." A nurse grabbed Tina's hand.

"Get your hands off me. I'm not going anywhere!" she yelled, tears running down her face.

"Code blue ICU room 6, code blue ICU room 6." The hospital speakers blared.

Lina stood in shock staring at her father as a nurse came and grabbed her.

"Daddy!" Ava tried to run to Kevin's bedside as she was grabbed by a nurse. "Daddy!" She began kicking in the nurse's arms as she reached out to her father.

"Get them out of here!" The head doctor yelled over all the commotion as they prepared to shock Kevin's chest with the defibrillator.

"Ma'am, please come with us. We're going to do everything we can for your husband." The nurse grabbed Tina's hand again, leading her to a private waiting room.

"Momma, is Daddy going to be okay?" Lina and Ava asked, tears flowing down their face.

"Baby, I don't know." Tina held Lina and Ava in her arms sobbing.

Thirty minutes later, the doctor came in to speak with Tina.

"How is he? Can I see him?" Tina jumped out her seat, relieved to see the doctor.

"Ma'am, please sit." The doctor placed his hand on Tina's back.

Without hesitation or resistance, she sat.

"I'm sorry, ma'am, we did all we could," the doctor spoke as Tina cried.

"No, please don't tell me he's not going to be okay."

"I'm sorry, ma'am, he was pronounced deceased at 7:43 a.m. We did all we could but were unsuccessful in reviving him. I wish I had good news for you. I really do. You may see him if you wish. Once again, I'm so sorry for your loss." The doctor reached rubbing Tina's back.

Tina, Lina, and Ava were escorted to Kevin's lifeless shell.

"I love you so much, baby. I don't know how I'm supposed to go on without you, Kevin. I can't do this alone." Tina kissed Kevin's forehead, leaving teardrops on his face. "Baby, we were supposed to grow old together. We were supposed to see the girls go off to college and get married together. I don't want to live without you, Kevin."

"I love you so much, Daddy. It's not fair. Why couldn't you stay with me forever?" Lina kissed her father's hand. "I'll never forget you. I'll never forget what you've taught me," Lina whispered, tears running down her face.

"I love you, Daddy. You promised you would never leave me. You said you would never break a promise," Ava said crying, kissing her father's hand.

"Ma'am, when you're ready, we need you to come with us to sign some papers," a female doctor spoke softly.

Pastor Sullivan walked into the room where Tina and her girls sat, hugging Lina and Ava. About an hour later, they walked out of the hospital with Pastor Sullivan to his car.

"God, why did you let him die?" Tina cried as they drove away. "You were supposed to protect him. What good was it to ever trust You." She stared out the car window bawling.

6

Monique

"Dude, she's gone. Let's just give up." Sam looked up at Paul as he continued doing chest compressions.

"She's not gone, and I'm not giving up until she has a heartbeat," Paul yelled as beams of sweat dripped off his forehead. He silently prayed as he took over doing chest compressions on Monique. *God, you said all you need is faith the size of a mustard seed. I know you can do it.* Paul mouthed silently.

The ambulance sirens blared as the driver hit speeds of seventy miles per hour. The hospital was thirty-five minutes away from Monique's house, but with cars on the road oblivious to the sirens, it took about forty-eight minutes to get there. The hospital staff was already on high alert a code blue, suicide was on the way. They were also informed on the type of pills found Monique possibly consumed and had the antidote ready to use.

"Paul, man, she's gone. Just give up." Sam sounded sure of his words.

"Look, you never give up. When we get to the hospital, we'll let the doctors decide when enough is enough!" Paul continued doing compressions on Monique. "What if this was your mom or sister, would you be so quick to give up? Stop being negative and help me! It's what we do. We save lives, man!" he yelled in frustration.

When the ambulance arrived at the hospital, Monique was still without a pulse. She was immediately moved to a room where she was transferred to the hospital bed, as a team of seasoned doctors and nurses stood ready to work on her. Doctors gave Monique a shot of naloxone. She was then shocked with the defibrillator. There, she gained a faint pulse. Next, they cleared her airway intubating her. She was then hooked up to an IV and given intravenous fluids, while another doctor gave her activated charcoal. This acted in the digestive tract to absorb the drug. Her stomach was then pumped to remove any remaining drug still in her stomach. After tests were run on her brain, Monique was placed in a medically induced coma to help stabilize her vitals. She was then moved to the ICU floor where she had round the clock monitoring.

Paul refused to leave since they had no other calls. He stayed until he learned Monique was alive but in very serious condition. With this type of situation Monique was in, she faced years of rehabilitation if she were to come out okay. The doctors weren't hopeful though. They said even if she were to come out of the coma, she would be a vegetable and never walk, talk, or eat again. She would have no life, and it really wouldn't be worth living.

Paul entered Monique's room before leaving the hospital with his coworkers. "God will do it for you, mistress. I know He will. Just have faith, hold on and stay strong. It's going to work out for you, and you will be a living testimony. You shall not die but live and declare the works of the Lord, and I pray God heals you and you be a witness to all, that God lives, and He can do anything." Paul touched her hand before he left the room.

"Paul bro, what made you so sure she was going to live?" Sam looked with astonishment as well as confusion when Paul walked out to the ambulance.

"I know who I serve, I know what He can do, I also have a relationship with God to where I can hear His voice, and I know what He spoke to me. I just have faith whatever God speaks will happen." Paul smiled.

"Dude, that was amazing. That woman was dead, dude. She was gone. Man, I have to get to know this God you're talking about. I didn't grow up knowing about God or religion. My family is a family that believes in luck and connecting with your inner self. They believe you're basically your own God. Bro, He seems so amazing. How does He make the dead live again? Bro, He just seems so awesome. I really want to know Him for myself." Sam smiled, excited about the opportunity to know the true and living God.

"Bro, you can come with me to bible study this week. I'll introduce you to my pastor. It's not something you will understand overnight. Just like with a relationship in the natural, you're building a relationship with God. It takes time, but if you're sincere, then God will begin to reveal Himself to you." Paul grinned as the ambulance pulled away from the hospital.

****

"Who in the devil knocking on my door, seven in the morning?" Grandma Helen complained walking to the front door in her green housecoat, peeking through the peephole. "Oh, Lord, it's the police. I ain't did nothing, I ain't seen nothing, and I ain't smelled nothing." She pushed her glasses up on her nose.

Grandma Helen was a curvy figured, medium-boned, fair-skinned woman with a few freckles on her cheeks. Her eyes were dark brown, and her hair shoulder length, silky, black, and bouncy. Even at the age of fifty-eight, she looked as if she were in her early forties; her face wrinkle free and flawless.

Often, Grandma Helen found herself pressed thinking of her late husband of thirty-two years. To cope, she turned to Mary Jane whom she told those closest to her was the only thing that brought her any kind of peace. Her husband had been her best friend, and the thought of knowing she would never see his face again hurt her to think about.

"Can I help you?" Grandma Helen spoke in a low tone.

"Hi, ma'am, my name is Deputy Crewship. I have your grandson Joshua with me. Your daughter was rushed to the hospital this morning."

"Oh yeah," Grandma Helen replied, sounding the least bit worried. "Where that sorry husband of hers?" She tooted her nose up, looking past the officer and down the street to see who were outside. Helen always felt people were snooping around her front door, always in her business.

"Ma'am, whatever the issue is between you two is really not important right now. Joshua needs someone to look after him, and your daughter needs her family right now. She had no pulse when the ambulance arrived. She was dead when they arrived at her house!" Deputy Crewship replied, frustrated after hearing the carelessness in Helen's voice.

"Well, I don't need anyone attacking me trying to be a family therapist either. What hospital is she at?" Grandma Helen said sarcastically, tooting her nose up. She was the type of person who could play the victim card very well.

"She was taken to Grace Medical Center," Deputy Crewship said before walking to her car to get Joshua. *This is one messed up bunch*, she thought as she walked down the concrete steps that led to the sidewalk.

Deputy Crewship was a slim built Caucasian woman with brown eyes and dark brown hair who didn't mind speaking what was on her mind. She was raised on the rough side of the woods. This taught her how to hold her own.

"Honey, you're going to go with your grandma until your mommy gets better." She unbuckled the seatbelt from around Joshua, grabbing his hand and leading him to the front door of his grandmother's house.

"I wish I could stay with you until Mommy gets better." Joshua squeezed deputy Crewship's hand as they walked.

"I'll come by and check on you. Okay, sweetie? You be a good boy for your grandmother." She hugged Joshua before returning to her car.

"Bye." Joshua waved as deputy Crewship pulled off.

Once in the house, Grandma Helen first made Joshua take off his shoes, then hugged him tightly in her arms.

"Baby, I've missed you so much. I don't know why your momma insists on keeping you away from me. She knows how much I love you. I'm the one that named you. Did you know you're named after your grandfather?" Grandma Helen smiled as she embraced Joshua.

"I know. Mommy told me, and she told me you were a mean, old, bitter lady after Grandpa died. What is bitter, Grandma, because I don't know?" Joshua looked up into his grandmother's big brown eyes.

"Honey, your mommy is just a little crazy sometimes that's all. That's why she keeps you from me."

"I just wish you and Mommy would be together with me like we used to be." Joshua sounded hopeful. "Is Mommy going to be okay?" His eyes began to tear up.

"Honey, I don't know. Maybe we can go see her in a little while after my friend Vera comes over. She's bringing me some pies she made, apple and sweet potato pie, then we'll go on down to that hospital to see about your momma." Grandma Helen walked over to her recliner, turning the television on. "Where your daddy been? He wasn't home when all this happened with your mother?" she asked, clueless to all that had been taking place in Monique's life.

"No, Daddy wasn't home. He doesn't come home anymore," Joshua said, drinking a juice box, watching cartoons. "Mommy cries all the time. I hug her and tell her I love her, but she still cries. She's sad, Grandma, and I don't know how to make her not sad." Joshua spoke never once looking away from the television.

"Mmmm. I tried to tell her not to marry that boy." Helen smiled at the thought she had been right about James all along.

Monique and James had been together seven years and married for five. It had been three years since Grandma Helen's husband had passed and two years since Monique and Helen stopped talking and one month since he had divorce papers served to her house.

****

Vera Reeds was a dark-toned, heavy-set lady. She had a short afro with strings of gray in it, a small gap between her two front teeth, and her face was blemish free. She and Helen had been friends for over twenty years. They had met at the church where Vera still attended, and Grandma Helen stopped attending after Joshua her husband had passed. Helen had been there for Vera when her husband Bobby passed almost five years ago. In return, Vera was there even more for Helen after Joshua had passed. Vera would always visit Helen bringing her sweets and talking about the goodness of the Lord. Vera loved God, and she could talk about God for hours and hours at a time. She wasn't the type to push God on anyone, but she loved Him and if you had a willing ear to listen, she would talk.

Vera arrived about twenty minutes after Deputy Crewship dropped Joshua off. "It's me, Helen." She spoke as she opened the front door to Helen's house. They had the type of relationship where Vera had a key to Helen's house, and Helen told her to never knock on her door. "You better just come on in." Helen would say.

"Hey, Joshua baby. I haven't seen you in a while. Do you remember me?" Vera said as she placed the freshly baked pies on the kitchen table.

"Yes, I remember you. You have all the good snacks at your house." Joshua beamed at the sight of the pies, the aroma making his mouth water.

"Vera girl, the police came here this morning and bought Joshua to me. I thought they came because somebody smelled a little Mary in the air last night, but they said Monique was taken to the hospital this morning." Helen let out a laugh from her paranoia, as she got up from the recliner walking to one of the cushioned chairs at the kitchen table.

"Why didn't you call me? I would have come and taken you to the hospital to see about her. Is she okay?" Vera sounded concerned. "What happened? And you need to stop with all that smoking. You know it's not good for you. It ain't going to help anything you're going through. It ain't gone change nothing with you, Helen." Vera shook her head.

"All the lady cop said was she had no pulse when they took her in the ambulance. You know, she come here trying to be a family therapist, trying to straighten me." Helen frowned. "And you know the Lord still working on me about this depression." She raised her right brow.

"Helen, you should be ashamed of yourself sitting here as if nothing is wrong. Do you know that means she's dead? You sitting round here like that child didn't come from your womb. How can you be so heartless toward your own child? The past is the past!" Vera shook her head. "Joshua honey, go get your shoes on. Helen, you get yours on too!" Vera ordered. "I just can't believe you, Helen. What happened between you two was never that serious. You were the one that made it more than it was. You were the one that pushed Monique away, and I don't care if you get mad at me, but you were the one that started it all." Vera yakked as they walked to her car.

Helen had a car of her own. She was just too stubborn and prideful to see about her daughter in the hospital. They all hopped in Vera's car, buckled their seat belts, and listened to the car radio as they drove almost an hour away to the major trauma hospital where the ambulance had taken Monique. Vera prayed in silence as Helen said a small prayer letting the words Vera had spoken sink in.

The Funeral

Aunt Berniece and Kim came down as fast as they could when they heard the news about the shooting. They arrived at Tina's house the next morning before the sun awakened. Berniece was a retired social worker and planned on staying as long as it was needed. Kim called her job and told them she had a family emergency and would need a couple of weeks off, so it was no rush for them to get back home. Kevin's mother Pam nearly had a heart attack after Tina called her with the news about Kevin and Alvin and was admitted into the hospital, so she wasn't expected to arrive until Friday, the day of the wake. Life seemed to go in slow motion as Tina tried everything in her to be strong for her girls. She would just lie in bed, cry, and question God. She wouldn't eat or drink and really didn't want to be bothered or see anyone but her girls. Aunt Berniece was there to tend to the girls, and Kim was there to give emotional support to her older cousin Tina. Kim wasn't the churchy type, but she did believe there was a God; and that there was a heaven and a hell.

"Tina, I love you, and I'm here for you if you need anything." Kim laid prostrate behind her cousin on the bed, wrapping her arms around her.

"Kim why? Why, why, why? Why would God take him so soon. He had a life to live. He had kids to raise! I don't want anything. I just want my best friend back." Tina cried, her mouth dry from the lack of fluids she took in and from all the crying she had been doing. Her eyes were swollen almost shut, throat sore, and nose stuffed up. "I trusted God. I trusted Him. He doesn't love me. How can He do this to me. I trusted Him, Kim." Tina whined, grabbing the sheets on the bed to keep from punching down on the bed. Her questioning became so sincere it made her feel maybe if she kept asking the question, God would perform a miracle and bring her husband back from the dead. She knew Jehovah-Jireh was a providing and powerful God who could cause the dead to rise again, and she felt He needed to do just that with her husband.

"I love you, Tina." Kim hugged her tighter as tears rolled down her face. It hurt her so much to see her cousin who she had always seen as strong and joyful hurting so badly. It damaged her even more that she couldn't take the pain away, and it also caused her to begin to question if whether this God Tina had always talked about was really everything she had confessed Him to be.

Kim had never experienced losing someone she loved deeply, and she really didn't know how to be there for Tina, or what to say to comfort her. To be honest, Kim knew there wasn't anything anyone could say or do that would take the pain away. She knew the hardest part in Tina's life was that her best friend, the love of her life and the father of her children was gone, and life was still going on around her. Bills still had to be paid, kids still had to go to school, and she would eventually have to go back to work, but the hardest part being her pain would still be there and she would have to continue life without Kevin.

Lina and Ava dealt with their father's death each in their own way. Lina wanting to be seen as the strong one cried at night when she would lie in her bed alone, away from everyone. During the day, she spent most of her time in her mother's room or next to Ava making sure she was okay. Ava would have her moments where she would cry and back away from everyone. She didn't want to watch television or talk to anyone. She would lay on the couch with one of her daddy's T-shirts in her arms staring off into space.

Aunt Berniece did all the cooking, cleaning, and arrangements for Kevin's funeral. Because of how close Kevin and Alvin were, the families both agreed to have their wake and funerals together. This would be even harder on everyone but more so on Tina, seeing two caskets filled with the ones she loved next to each other.

"Momma, we're going to be okay. You know Daddy wouldn't want us to be so sad, and he wouldn't want you being mad at God either." Lina laid in her mother's arms on her bed after Kim left out the room.

"Baby, it's just hard, but I'll be okay. Don't you worry about me. Are you okay?" Tina looked with concern in her eyes for her daughter. She knew how Lina was, and she knew Lina never wanted people to see her cry or to think she was weak. "I know it's tough, but somehow we'll make it through." She kissed Lina's forehead.

"Momma, will you please at least drink something then, at least for me? I'm not okay. I'm scared. I don't want to lose you either, Momma." Lina spoke softly, trying not to let the tears that were starting to swell in her eyes fall. At her young age, she was thought of as having an old soul and was matured beyond her years.

"Yes, baby, I will. And you won't lose me. I'm not going any-where. Go and get Ava and come back in here. I just need my girls right now." Tina's voice sounded raspy from not drinking.

As Lina went upstairs to get Ava, Berniece brought Tina in some hot tea to help soothe her throat. She sipped on the tea as she waited for her girls to come back into the room. She tried her hardest to be strong for them and not let them see her cry, but with every memory that came to her mind, and the realization that she would never touch, kiss, be held by, talk to, or just laugh with Kevin broke her down. In her mind, she thought about dying too. She thought if she died, she would be put out of her misery, she wouldn't hurt, and she wouldn't have to experience life without her husband. But in another part of her mind, she thought about her girls and not wanting them to hurt if something were to happen to her. She felt a part of her soul was missing and her heart was destroyed forever. She knew God was still God, but she felt He abandoned her prayers and allowed all of this to happen. Deep down inside, she was beginning to become bitter toward God, and she secretly felt it was no point in serving a God who couldn't keep her husband safe. Her relationship with Him was beginning to be on the rocks, and her prayer life and devotion to Him suddenly stopped. *I still love you.* A thought came to her mind but was quickly dismissed with anger that God had allowed her husband and brother to be taken within the blink of an eye. She knew God's voice but didn't care to hear from Him at all at this point. If she were to hear anything from God, it would be answers as to why He allowed this to happen.

"Mommy, I love you so much." Ava ran laying in her mother's arms when they entered the room.

"I love you girls so much." Tina kissed Lina and Ava. "Just lay here with me. I need my babies next to me." A few tears dropped from her eyes before Lina wiped them away.

Lina laid in her mother's right arm and Ava in her mother's left.

"God, please help my family, please be with us, and please comfort us. We really need You." Lina silently prayed before the three of them dozed off together.

****

The weekend had flown by and Monday had come and gone. All the arrangements for the funeral had been taken care of and the debts due for the services paid. Pastor Sullivan had been by the house almost every day since the death of Kevin to check up on the family. Tina had no desire to talk to him and kept the conversation short when she did see him. The detectives working the case had come up with a suspect and the name and license plate of the man who had claimed the lives of two of Atlanta's great officers. This man Reggie Grandoff was listed as armed and dangerous and was being highly sought after. The police department put out a reward of $100,000 for anyone who had any information leading to the arrest of Mr. Grandoff. Through video surveillance by a nearby bank, the detectives were able to get a license plate for the fugitive. He made the dumb mistake of not only parking the getaway car in the bank's parking lot that sat only a hundred yards from the store but also using his mother's car to commit the crime. They also learned the fugitive was out on bail on a home invasion charge just two months prior. He had a rap sheet, which started at the age of twelve and was known by local law enforcement for his mischievous acts in the past. Reggie was now thirty-two and seemed to enjoy the life of being a criminal.

The police force was told to be on the lookout for Mr. Grandoff and to bring him in dead or alive.

Lina and Ava were being kept home from school until the following Monday, so they could have time to cope with everything and grieve. The school's principal had the girls school work sent home and told the family to keep them out as long as it was needed. Tina made no intentions to call her boss to let her know she would be out from work. However, her boss had seen the news and stopped by to check up on her. With only $12,000 in her savings and now $3,500 left in her checking account, Tina knew she would have to go back to work before too long. She was only eligible to get a total of $12,000 from Kevin's benefits at work. Her mortgage was $2,100 a month and the car payments almost $800. She knew her bank account would be dried up in no time. Due to the fact Tina and Kevin had enrolled in a life insurance policy just a year prior, the policy had not yet matured so the money she thought she would get to cover the funeral expenses was not there. What she did get back from the insurance company was $1,100, which went toward expenses for the funeral. The police department gave $1,000 toward Kevin and $1,000 toward Alvin's expenses, which left Tina with a bill of $6,000 for her part, which she had to pay out of pocket. This put a dent on her checking account leaving her scared of her and her girl's financial future.

****

The week had crept by as if in slow motion, and the day of the wake was finally here. The plane Kevin's mother Pam was on had finally arrived in the early morning hours, and she was now fast asleep in Lina's bed with the aid of a sleeping pill. This was going to be hard on Pam being Kevin was her last son and her second son to die. Her first son died when Kevin was fourteen due to gang gun violence. This led to Kevin making the decision to become a police officer to keep the streets as clean as he could. Kevin's brother was seventeen when he was killed; he had hung with the wrong crowd trying to fit in. He went from making honor roll every report card to dropping out of high school in the eleventh grade for a life of drugs, parties, and gangs. He always told his mother he had to take care of her by any means necessary and that he was going to put her in a mansion one day. She argued with him she didn't care if she lived in a trailer; she just wanted him to stop doing what he was doing.

Pam had grown up Pentecostal but backed away from the church after she became pregnant with Kevin's brother; the church began to toot their nose up toward her, being she was pregnant and not married. She felt that she was judged enough in the streets, so she wasn't going to be judged in the one place where she should be able to go to as she was and be free. She had always said no one was perfect and the only difference between her and the folks in the church was her sin could be seen. It was a fact people knew she were having premarital sex being she was pregnant. Her sin was shown and theirs was covered. No one exposed their sins, just judged on the sins of people they could see. She felt the church was full of hypocrites who felt they were doing God some justice in pointing out her sins, when she knew better than anyone the sin she was in. She had said the only thing the church folks were doing was turning people away from the church house and from the opportunity of being fully saved and delivered.

From this time on, Pam rarely stepped foot in church. She prayed and never lost her faith in God but church folks in her mind were ignorant to the part in the Bible where it said, "Love worketh no ill to his neighbor," and "Judge not, that ye be not judged." Pam felt church folks had too much opinion and not enough of the Word. They had an opinion and a say so on everything but had no Word in them. They weren't living by the Word, just quoting scriptures and pointing fingers. And in her mind because of this, they had not enough Word. This caused her to step back from going to church functions and services. She understood although each church may be different, the church folks for the most part were all the same, all too deep and holy for their own good.

****

The wake was beautiful. There were yellow and purple-colored flowers everywhere. The choir sang songs as family; friends, and guests all got the chance to see Kevin and Alvin up close and personal. Their shells looked so peaceful and flawless as they laid in the caskets as if they were in a peaceable, unfathomable sleep.

Tina sat on the first row along with Pam and Aunt Berniece. Everyone made sure to hug Tina and Pam and give their condolences. Alvin's mom didn't stay long. She stayed just enough to kiss Kevin's forehead and rub her baby's face, kissing his cheek. The sight and recognition of seeing Alvin lying in the casket was too much for her to bear. She left the wake service with Alvin's older sister Arlene after only ten minutes. Alvin's father whom he was very close to missed the wake; he couldn't find the strength to see his only son, his baby boy in his eyes, lying in a casket. He stayed home praying God would give him the strength to prepare for the funeral.

Pam was seen going back and forth from her seat to her son's casket the whole wake. Lina and Ava both stared at their father's body and rubbed his hands. They both talked to him as if he were alive and cried knowing their father would never talk to them again. It was overwhelming for Ava to see two caskets next to each other, so Tina held her on her lap or Pam hugged her tight when she was sitting down. Tina cried over her husband's body and talked to him, begging him to wake up; she even prayed to God to perform a miracle just as He had done when He raised Lazarus from the dead. She promised God if He performed a miracle, she would do everything He asked of her. She would worship Him in a new way and seek His face like never before. She had to be helped to her seat by the chief of police and lieutenant after almost losing it and falling to the ground. The wake was just two hours, which seemed like an eternity. There were so many emotions running through everyone as people were crying and falling out. After the wake, the family went home to prepare for the big day tomorrow. The day they would say their final good-byes and the day the only vision they would have left of their father and uncle, brother and son were from pictures and memories. Tomorrow was the day everyone hoped was a bad dream they were all in—a dream they would wake from and put far behind them. It was a day that would symbolize uncertainty of what was to come.

****

Saturday morning was a morning like no other. It was the first funeral Lina and Ava would be attending and also the day everyone dreaded. Aunt Berniece got up at 6:00 a.m. to get herself ready and to get Lina and Ava up, fed, and dressed. Kim awoke around 7:00 a.m., and after getting herself ready, she went into Tina's room to help her get ready.

"Kim, I just wish God would let me die. I prayed all night. I begged and pleaded with Him to change the outcome with Kevin and Alvin. I asked Him to do this to help increase my faith. Kim, He didn't, and I can't go on without Kevin." Tears dripped from Tina's face as she rested in the bed, eyes closed crying.

"I love you, Tina." Kim laid next to her fragile cousin, putting her hands on her face and kissing her cheek. "You have to be strong. Your girls need you, and I need you too." Kim tried to find words to say that would ease the hurt Tina was going through.

"At this point, I'm no good for my girls, I'm no good for God, and I'm no good to myself. If God gave me the option right now to live or die, I would choose to die. I'm so broken and depressed. I never knew I could hurt this bad. I just want to get this day over with, so I can lie in my grave. Just promise me you'll be there for my girls if something ever happened to me." Tina spoke in a tone where her hurt, pain, and anger could be felt.

"Tina, you're such a strong, God-fearing, beautiful black woman. Whenever I'm going through, I know I can call you and you can reach God and give me a right now word. I know you're hurting right now, and I know you feel like giving up, but I need you to get into that secret place you have with God. Lean on Him and trust Him. Let Him heal your hurt. I know God didn't bring you this far for you to just give up now. Baby, I know it hurts, but life still goes on and you have two beautiful girls to live for. And I know God won't put more on you than you can bear. Promise me if you don't live for yourself or even God, that you will live for those girls. Promise me!" Kim spoke, trying to sound strong, but to the listening ear, the hurt she felt for her cousin could be heard. "Come on. Let's get you dressed so we can get going." Kim wiped her moist eyes.

****

The day everyone had wished was a figment of their imaginations was finally here. Two beautiful white limos sat out front of Tina and Kevin's house waiting for them. Sonya, Alvin's mother, father who he was very close to, sister Arlene and cousin met up at Tina's house to ride in the limos. Instead of wearing the typical black that was worn for funerals, everyone wore white. Pam said white was a sign of heaven. It represented purity and was beautiful and lively. She said that Kevin and Alvin were full of life, and they wanted to honor them knowing they made it in those pearly gates of heaven in their beautiful white robes. It was 9:30 a.m. as everyone headed to the limos to begin the twenty-minute ride to the same church where Tina and Kevin had married and were bringing their girls up in. In the first limo sat Kevin's family and the second limo sat Alvin's family. The ride to the church in both limos was soundless. No one said a word. Lina rested her head on her mother's shoulder as Ava rested her head in her mother's lap. Pam stared out the window silently praying as Kim sat next to Lina holding her hand, while Aunt Berniece sang softly to herself and prayed God gave everyone strength.

Sonya laid her head on her husband's shoulder as Alvin's sister and cousin held hands, tears rolling down their face with silent cries. They cried a cry from within their soul never making a noise.

****

The church was full to its capacity, and all that was waited for was Kevin and Alvin's family to arrive. The decorated sanctuary was beautiful; one would think they had made it in to heaven by the sight. The pews were covered in white and gold pew covers. The aisles of the floor were covered in white rose petals. White and blue-colored roses and daisies filled the isles of the church. Five big pictures of Kevin and Alvin hung. One picture with Kevin and his family and one by himself as the same with Alvin's pictures, and in the middle of those pictures was a picture with Kevin and Alvin in uniform posing together. Everyone laughed at the sight of the middle picture seeing Alvin trying to pose on his toes to make himself seem taller than what he really was. He was a natural born comic and that's what was going to be missed of him by all who filled the sanctuary. Candles and white and gold balloons filled the church along with ten white doves in two gold cages that sat by the caskets. The caskets were a pearly white color with gold trimming all around them. It was also a beautiful sight to see everyone in all white. Kevin and Alvin both wore white suits with a gold and blue-colored handkerchief in their suit pocket. The choir sang songs setting the atmosphere for the man of God to prepare to minister, as the limos pulled up.

****

I knew that death was an appointment everyone in life would one day meet. I also knew no one was exempt from it, but I always felt for my family, and all that God had allowed us to go through, that His hands were on us and we would be exempt from all that others had to go through. I never thought in a million years my family and I would be the one's sitting in the middle pews in the church. I never thought that the church would be filled with friends and family mourning over the death of someone in my family. And I never thought that the joining of all these people would be for the death of my father and uncle. Lina sat in deep reflection resting her head on her mother's shoulder.

****

God, why are you taking me through this? Tina thought as the limo pulled up to the church.

As the limo drivers parked the cars in front of the church doors, music could be heard from the opening of the car door. Both Kevin and Alvin's family lined up in front of the church doors. Pam, Tina, and Sonya held hands as Kim, Lina, and Ava held hands tightly. Alvin's father and Aunt Berniece interlocked arms with each other; Aunt Berniece helping to keep Alvin's father upright as Arlene and Alvin's cousin held hands trying to keep their composure and tears from continuing to fall. The usher signaled for the families to walk in and take their seats. The crowd of people that congregated to show their final respects to these two great men stood and praised God for the families. The church choir sang "Freedom" as the families walked to their designated pews. Pastor Sullivan wanted the home going service to be glorious giving honor to Kevin and Alvin for making it to be with the Master and King. He was saddened at their passing, but he knew they fought a good fight. They finished their course and they kept the faith. He also knew they would neither hurt nor struggle. He believed God had a great reason for allowing all this to happen, and he believed if God would have allowed Kevin and Alvin to live, their recovery would be too much for them to bear.

Finally, service was in motion; the Spirit of God rested heavy among the people who at the time neither Tina nor the rest of the family could cry. They became subject to the power and anointing of God that filled the church. The choir sang "You Deserve It" and "Goin' Up Yonder". People all over the sanctuary could be heard shouting and speaking in tongues as God's presence flooded the atmosphere. Tina broke out in a dance that could be seen throughout the church.

"Hallelujah, praise Him. He's here!" Pastor Sullivan shouted with power as angels could be seen stepping into the building by those who were in a place with God to see in the spirit realm and by those God gave a spiritual eye to see.

Pastor Sullivan joined in, leading the body of Christ into worship.

"Open up your mouths in this place. He's here. He's here. Hallelujah, we acknowledge you, Jesus. You're King of kings and Lord of lords. We bless You God." Pastor Sullivan spoke in a songful tone as the church cried out and began to worship God. "We love You, we love You, come on and worship Him. Hosanna in the highest." Pastor Sullivan began to sing, holding the mic in one hand while his other hand was lifted toward heaven.

Alvin's father began to scream and cry out to God on his knees giving his pain and anger to Him. Ava and Lina stood enraptured in God's presence, hands lifted to the King. Tina and Pam cried out, hands lifted as Sonya and Alvin's sister held each other calling on the name of Jesus, crying and thanking Him. Alvin's cousin and Aunt Berniece sat on the pew feeling the presence of God was so thick they could not find the strength to stand but to sit and worship Him. And for the first time, Kim stood hands held tightly together, eyes closed crying, feeling the presence of God and allowing Him to come into her soul and minister to her. After a few minutes had passed, she began jumping up and down arms in the air shouting and crying out, "Jesus, Jesus."

Pastor Sullivan wasn't a man who stuck to the program, whenever God moved, He flowed with Him. He began to sing "Flow to You," as the congregation worshipped God with one accord. People were so sick of all the violence and death that was happening all around them that they all came to reach God and be free from everything even if it were just for that time.

As worship ended, the people took their seats. Pastor Sullivan came from 2 Timothy 4:6–8 and Hebrews 4:1–10. The most powerful thing being said was, even though this happened, God still reigned. It was now time for the family to give reflections, followed by the rest of the congregation.

"Kevin was such a cute baby. He was always respectful from the time he learned to talk. It's so hard losing him. His brother was taken from us when he was fourteen and from then on, I clung to my baby. He was my heart. He was everything to me. He loved God so much and that makes me happy he left a strong foundation of God for his girls. When I found out the news about him and Alvin, I told God to take me too. I find myself screaming and calling his name, hoping he'll answer back. Both my babies are gone now, and I honestly don't know why God allowed the birther to outlive the birth. God knows it was hard when I lost my oldest son, and now I've lost my baby. Please y'all love your kids and let them know how much you love them, and how much they mean to you, because you never know when you won't be able to say it to them anymore." Pam fought to hold back her tears. "Thank y'all for loving my son and his family."

Pam walked to her seat as Tina, Lina, and Ava walked to the podium to say a few words.

"I want to thank you all for showing your love and support to our family. My husband was my hero, he was the true definition of a man of God, and he loved his family so much. It's so hard now, It feels like my heart has been ripped out." Tina wiped her eyes as tears ran down her face. "Even if I had eternity with Kevin it still wouldn't be enough time with him. I love you so much Kevin." Tears fell from Tina's eyes dropping on the podium. "Alvin was my brother, the comedian we all loved. I miss them both so much." She broke down crying.

Pam walked back up to the podium hugging Tina as Tina held her tightly crying on her shoulder. The congregation's eyes began to swell with tears at the sight of Tina breaking down.

"My daddy was everything to us and we love and miss him so much. We need to get our lives right with God so one day we can all see him again. He was the best daddy in the world, and I'm going to miss him so much. Uncle Alvin was like my third best friend, after Daddy then Momma. I love him, and I miss him so much." Lina spoke in a soft tone as tears fell from her beautiful immature eyes.

"I love you so much, Daddy and Uncle Alvin." Ava cried into the microphone.

As Pam, Tina and her girls walked back to their seats, Sonya and Alvin Sr. hugged Tina, letting her know they loved her and she was not alone.

"My son was so amazing, and Kevin was like another son to me. I really can't believe this happened. I miss them so much. It's just so crazy. I had just talked to them the night all this happened, and now they're gone." Alvin's father spoke as his voice cracked and tears rolled down his face. "Thank you all for loving our boys as family and thank you for the support and love you all have shown us." Alvin Sr. spoke while Sonya, Alvin's sister and cousin stood next to him at the podium. "I just want to thank you all for being so loving through this difficult time, and please keep us in your prayers."

"I love and miss those boys more than words can explain." Sonya cried. "People just don't understand. It's nothing that serious in life where you should take someone else's life like that. I just pray God will cause whoever did this to be tormented until they turn their self in or get caught. Maybe that's a selfish thing to pray, but right now, I don't care."

After the families shared memories, the rest of the congregation got the opportunity to speak and share stories and memories of Kevin and Alvin.

"I just want to say to the family of Kevin and Alvin, they were great men. They were honest men, and they didn't deserve this. Alvin would always come in with stories that would have you a little confused, but that made the night seem brighter. I remember the night this happened Alvin told me he knew he was my hero, when Kevin got to work, Alvin ran to the passenger door of the car because he said he was tired of driving all the time." The lieutenant laughed as the congregation laughed with him. "Those men will be missed dearly. Kevin was amazing. He was younger than me, but the wisdom and character he portrayed was just amazing. I never told him, but I looked up to him for that. We love you all and the entire police force is here for you." The lieutenant spoke with bass, but due to being filled with emotion at times, his strong voice shrieked.

On the ride to the cemetery, Ava talked with Pam while Lina and Tina held hands. Aunt Berniece felt it was best if Alvin's family rode in the same limo as them since it was more than enough room. They were all deeply saddened about having to see their loved ones put in the ground, but they felt a peace by God they had never experienced before. They went with knowing God would somehow give them the strength to get this done and over with.

The cemetery's service was short. The police force let out a shot from their guns in reverence to the fallen officers. The doves were released as were two white and two gold balloons. The praise and worship team sang "I'm Free", after the pastor spoke over the caskets and gave the final benediction.

"Nothing about death is easy, nothing about losing ones you love is easy, and even though the reassurance of seeing them one day is with us, death is painful. The Bible says to be absent from the body is to be present with the Lord. Why then do we grieve if we know the ones we love are with the Lord? For this life and this world we live in are only temporary. So, I charge you today to live for God. I want you to give God your all. You must love God more than you love the air you breathe. God is the only one that can really give you comfort and make your pain manageable. This day we bury two so that they can reign in heaven." Pastor Sullivan spoke as the caskets were placed in their final resting place.

8

Monique

"How can I help you?" the receptionist in the emergency room questioned Helen and Vera as they walked up to the desk.

"Hi, my daughter was transported here by ambulance this morning. Her name is Monique Austin." Helen began speaking in a panicked tone.

"She's on the ICU floor." The receptionist looked in the system then gave them visitor badges directing them to the elevator that would take them to the ICU floor.

Once off the elevator, Helen, Vera, and Joshua walked to the phone that paged the nurses on the other side of the double doors of the ICU floor, so they could go into Monique's room. A nurse came to the door that separated Helen, Vera, and Joshua from getting onto the floor where people remained in serious and critical condition.

"Ma'am, children under twelve are not allowed on the floor. There is a waiting room he can wait in just down the hall," a male nurse stated.

"His mother is here. Is there any way he can go in to see her?" Helen asked with concern in her voice.

"Since it's his mother, I can let him back at your discretion. It can be a little traumatic for small children with all the wires and noises," the nurse spoke calmly.

As they walked into the room where Monique laid helpless and fragile, tears began to fall from everyone's eyes.

"Why would she do this? Why would she be so selfish? Why would she make a mess for others to clean up?" Helen began crying at the sight of Monique.

"Helen, it's going to be okay." Vera rubbed her back.

"Mommy, I love you." Joshua walked over to Monique's bedside. "Mommy, wake up, wake up!"

"It's okay, baby. Mommy is resting so she can get better." Vera walked to Joshua, hugging him wiping his eyes. "Helen, let's pray and then me and Joshua will go on down to the waiting room."

They all joined hands as Vera began to pray.

"Our Father in heaven, hallowed be Your name. Your kingdom come. Your will be done, on earth as it is in heaven. Give us this day our daily bread. And forgive us our debts, as we forgive our debtors. And do not lead us into temptation, but deliver us from the evil one. For Yours is the kingdom and the power and the glory forever. Jehovah, we thank you for being the great I am. We thank you for being a God of holiness and righteousness. Thank you for being seated in the heavenly kingdom. God, we thank you for being a fulfilling God, and we thank you for giving up your Son Jesus Christ on the cross for our sins. We thank you for His shed blood, and we stand firm on your Word. God, we come together in the name of Jesus asking you to perform a miracle for Monique right now. We ask in the name of Jesus you heal her body completely. God, we decree she shall come out of this a living testimony by the power and hand of You. God, we know all things work together for good to those who love You, to those who are the called according to Your purpose. God, we speak life into her body. I plead the blood over her body right now in the name of Jesus. I pray You be the doctor in this hospital room. God, we believe your report, and we know by your stripes, she is healed. In Jesus name we pray. Amen." Vera turned hugging Helen. "Take all the time you need. Me and Joshua gonna go on down to the cafeteria first." Vera smiled at Helen.

As Vera and Joshua left the room, a female doctor who was placed over the care of Monique knocked on the door then walked into the room.

"Hello, ma'am, I'm Doctor Taylor." A short lady, who was mixed with Greek and African American, smiled walking into the room.

"Hi, I'm Helen. I'm her mother. Can you tell me what's going on at this point?" Helen turned toward the doctor wiping her eyes.

"She was rushed in here this morning without a pulse. Miraculously, we were able to regain a pulse on her. We had to pump her stomach and give her an antidote that counteracted the effects of the drugs she consumed. With the number of pills she took, it's a miracle she's even alive. Now there are negative effects to her taking the pills and being without oxygen to her brain. Right now, she's in a medically induced coma. We are hoping this will help stabilize her vitals, but if she is to pull out of the coma, she really doesn't have a good progression rate. You see, as of now, she has about fifteen percent brain activity. With the trauma the drugs has caused on her body, she will never eat, walk or talk again. Even if she were to pull through, she will face years and years of rehabilitation, and I'm not sure that's something she'll be up to. If I were you and I don't say this to be insensitive, but I would say my good-byes to her. Maybe she can hear you, but there is really no hope for her. At this point, it's up to you if you want to keep her alive on the ventilator or pull the plug. The ventilator is needed to help her breathe since she's in an induced coma. Once we bring her out of the coma, there is maybe a five percent chance she will make it. I'm sorry, but in all my years of practice, I have never seen a case where someone in this shape survived." The doctor looked Helen in the eyes.

"Well, Doctor, you don't seem too sure about anything, but in the name of Jesus, I speak life to her brain, and I decree it shall live. Her brain will produce activity and her brain will function at one hundred percent. You see, Doctor, I don't know you like that, but you're real negative and right now, my baby doesn't need that. I don't know if you know my God, but He's a wonder working God and this is nothing to Him. What I will tell you is when you speak of Monique Austin, you will speak life, you will not give the enemy room to move in, and you will see the powerful and almighty God move on her behalf this day!" Helen declared sternly. "You see, Doctor, this is my only baby. I lost my husband, and I'm not about to lose my baby. Do you have kids?"

"Yes, I have two." Doctor Taylor looked back toward the door.

"Okay, so I want you to think of my baby as your baby in this bed, what would you do?"

"Well I wouldn't give up because I couldn't handle losing a child. I would remain positive and hopeful."

"That's right, so from now on, I don't want to hear about what is worth living and what isn't. I don't care what medical science says, and I don't even care what your degree says. I serve a God who created the heavens and the earth. Now let's picture this, a hot sun and a heavy moon. You see it?" Helen spoke sarcastically.

"Yes, but, ma'am—" Doctor Taylor looked confused, nodding her head.

"No, no, don't ma'am me. Now if God was able to put the sun and moon in space and cause it to not fall to earth, follow me now, and He commanded the sun by saying let there be light. Now He spoke life He didn't doubt, so He spoke, and it was. Okay, so where do you think all that food comes from that you eat? Guess what if God never spoke it, you wouldn't have any food to eat. So, Doctor, I don't want to hear any more about percent chances of life and all that because God is life and He can do all things but fail. Thank you and praise the Lord." Helen turned her back on the doctor, placing her hand on Monique's hand.

"Yes, ma'am, I'll be right out in the hall if you need me," Doctor Taylor said as she walked to the door with a look of embarrassment on her face. *That lady is crazy. She didn't even make any sense*, she thought.

"Well, besides all that, I'm Ms. Dee. You did right by your baby. Don't let anyone speak that over her life. I'm her sitter while she's in here." Ms. Dee, a dark-skinned lady with a southern accent, smiled as she sat next to Monique's bedside.

"Honey, these people are crazy in this place." Helen shook her head her nose tooted up.

"God said it's going to be all right with your baby. You can mark my word. I'm a true prophet and not one-word God gives me to speak falls to the ground. You can take that to the bank. People just go through stuff sometimes, and they don't know how to express how they feel or they feel they're all alone, but God's going to do it for her," Ms. Dee spoke, looking up at the TV that sat on the wall mount.

"I believe you, woman of God." Helen smiled as she kissed Monique's forehead.

"Baby, Momma's here. It's going to be okay. I promise the God we serve is greater than this. He is, baby. Joshua is here and Mrs. Vera, we love you so much. I know I haven't said that to you in a long time, but I love you Monique, and I'm sorry all this happened. I'm sorry I haven't been there for you, and I'm sorry, baby, for being so negative." Helen rubbed Monique's hand.

Monique was created differently from her mother. She took her looks from her father's side of the family. She was a beautiful woman about five feet six. She had a good grade of hair but not that of her mother. She had natural shoulder-length hair. Her skin was smooth and blemish free, and her eyes were so dark they looked black. She was darker than her mother, a beautiful dark brown complexion. Her mother would joke with her telling her she was a dark mocha with a drop of cream. Monique had a gentle spirit and was cheerful and goofy at times. She loved life and she loved God, although she had not always committed herself to God. As a teen, she would disobey her parents from time to time and tell her mother she didn't need to go to church every Sunday to know God. It wasn't until she turned nineteen that she began to look at God differently. She wanted a relationship with Him, and He began to pull on her to get closer to Him. She knew the way and she wanted Joshua to grow up with a love for God that were pure and real and not because it was common to him.

****

"I know Mommy won't die," Joshua said as he ate a bowl of apple cinnamon oatmeal in the cafeteria.

"No, honey. Mommy won't die. God will make her all better." Vera looked at Joshua who sat across the table from her as she sipped on her hot tea.

"I know because God told me, and He told me He had to let her die to live." Joshua never once looked up from eating.

Vera spit her hot tea as she coughed. "He did? Well, when did He tell you this?" Vera was taken aback.

"He told me when I was in the car with the police lady. I knew she was dead, but God told me not to worry or be afraid." Joshua looked up, staring Helen in the eyes. "God really loves Mommy." He looked back down at his breakfast.

"Yes, baby. He does. He loves us all so much. That's something I never want you to forget. God's love is the greatest love anyone can ever have or experience. God's love is the only type of love that will ever complete you." Vera looked at Joshua as he ate.

She was shocked such a young child could talk the way he was about God. She never once doubted what he was saying though. She understood God talked to anyone He pleased. She believed Joshua was prophesying life to his mother's situation, and she also believed the scripture in the Bible that said, "And it shall come to pass afterward. That I will pour out My Spirit on all flesh; Your sons and your daughters shall prophesy, your old men shall dream dreams, and your young men shall see visions." Vera was a strong believer in the Word of God, and she knew God saved and gave chances as He willed.

****

"Baby, I love you," Helen said as she pulled out her cell phone to make a call.

"Hello." The voice on the other end of the phone sounded strong and matured.

"Yes, Pastor. It's me, it's Helen." She cried at the sound of his voice.

"Helen, I have been praying for you. I have been praying to God for the day when you would call. Helen, we have never stopped praying for you or your family. We miss and love you all."

"Thank you, Pastor. I need your prayers. My daughter is in ICU right now. I'm here with her. She tried to commit suicide. The doctors aren't hopeful. They say she only has fifteen percent brain activity. Pastor, I know I haven't been the best person, I know I haven't been to church, but I need God. We need God right now." Helen cried into the phone.

Helen's cry was sincere, and the pastor knew God was not only working on Monique's behalf, but He was drawing Helen back to Him.

"Helen, I know what the doctors are saying, but my question to you is, what do you say, and most importantly, what does your faith say?"

"I say she's healed in the name of Jesus, I say she will overcome this, and my faith says God has already healed her completely."

"Helen, sometimes God will use those you love to open up your eyes. He will use situations and even death to get your attention. But God is a healing and compassionate God. He knows your every thought and need even before you open your mouth. I'm standing in agreement with you that our heavenly father is going to not only heal her completely but that He will also allow you to see His grace and mercy and draw you closer to Him. And because of your faith, God is going to do just what you prayed. Let's pray together." Pastor Andrews smiled on the other end of the phone.

"God, we need you," Helen whispered.

"God, we thank you for being a presence help at all times. Thank you for everything You sacrificed for your people. We thank you for sitting high and looking low, and, God, we thank you for never giving up on your people. God, we most certainly thank you for being a God that doesn't treat us according to the way we treat you. God Almighty who forgives all our iniquities and heals all our diseases, this day we put on the breastplate of faith and love, and the helmet of hope of salvation. We pray You let Monique's soul live that it shall praise You, God. Your Word declares death cannot praise You but the living man, he shall praise You. We pray right now by your love and compassion toward us that You give this life a second chance, and I speak to the functioning of the brain I command you to rejuvenate and replenish in the name of Jesus. Brain you shall live, blood you shall flow, and God You will forever reign. We thank you and love you now and forever more, Amen," Pastor Andrews shouted. "Hallelujah, I see a miracle in the Spirit, and it's going to hit her body like never before!"

"Pastor, thank you so much. I'm sorry I haven't been—"

"No, Helen, it's no need to apologize. We can't dwell on the past. We can't change the past, but the future, we can. It's okay, as long as you get yourself back in a place with God, the past doesn't matter. Sometimes, life gets a hold of us and we back away from God, but the amazing thing about God is that He doesn't hold this over our heads. He loves us so much and because of His grace and mercy, we have the opportunity and chance to get back right with Him. Don't let your needing God be a convenience but let your needing God be life to you. I love you, Helen, and we are here for you." Pastor Andrews reassured her.

"Thank you so much, Pastor. I just felt so alone after my husband died. It hurt me to go to church and see so many people happy when I was miserable inside. So, I backed away. It was nothing God did or you or the church. It was just because of how I felt." Helen began to calm down.

"Helen, please I want you to get back in a place with God. One thing we as Christians or anyone for that matter must never do is move or react based on our emotions. That's why the Word says cast all your cares upon Him, for He cares for you, because when you don't, and you let your emotions dictate and guide your life, you will always certainly fail. It's going to be all right and I want you to seek God's face for yourself not because of what is going on right now. Even if you don't rush back to church seek Him."

"Thank you, Pastor, and thank you for not holding me not coming to church over my head. Thank you." Helen smiled.

"I'm here for you." Pastor Andrews smiled. "Call me if you need me, but God's going to do it for your daughter. Just hold on and have faith." He assured her with his words.

"Thank you, Pastor. I'll update you. Thank you for everything." Helen hung up the phone after they both said their goodbyes.

"God, please forgive me for not being the best I could have been, but I really do love you, and I really desire to know you intimately." Helen rubbed Monique's hand as she stood over her. "God, please give my baby a second chance." She looked up as if looking to heaven.

"Baby, I love you. I'll be back tomorrow. I'm going to go home and come back in the morning." Helen kissed Monique's forehead.

9

Tina

I t had been one week since the funeral. Pam returned to her home just two days after the funeral service. She did everything she knew to do to be there for Tina as she also tried to be there for her own self. She said it was too much for her to bear being in the same house her deceased son had lived in. While she was at Tina and Kevin's house, she spent as much time as she could with her grand-daughters and Tina. Aunt Berniece and Kim were still in town but at Tina's request, they were due to leave in two days. Tina told them they didn't have to put their lives on hold for her. She insisted she were going to be okay and they didn't need to stay any longer. It wasn't that she didn't want her family in her house; it was just she didn't want to be around anyone. She wanted to be by herself and grieve.

Lina and Ava hadn't been to school since their father was killed. They were scheduled to go back to school the following Monday. This meant they had only two days left to get their selves together before they would have to go back to school and hear the many "I'm sorry for your loss" speeches. Ava was okay with this, but Lina was not.

****

The weekend seemed to fly by. It was finally Monday morning the day reality set in, and the day life had to go on as it did before Kevin was killed. Aunt Berniece and Kim had gotten up early to help the girls get ready for school before Tina dropped them to the airport.

"I'm going to miss you girls so much." Aunt Berniece hugged Lina then Ava as they sat in their room getting ready for school.

"I wish you didn't have to leave." Ava hugged Aunt Berniece tighter.

"Baby, I will see you again. I love you so much, and you make sure you take care of your momma. It's you three now so make sure you take care of her and be good." Aunt Berniece looked Ava in the eyes.

"Auntie, I'm scared. How are we going to make it without Daddy?" Lina looked in the mirror, fixing her hair.

"Baby, just live, pray, and trust God. Never lose your faith in God. I know this is a hard time in your life, but I promise if God doesn't take the pain away, He'll at least make it manageable." Aunt Berniece walked over to Lina, hugging her. "You are so smart. God has given you a gift you have to protect at all times. Just trust Him. Be strong for your momma and sister and live." She kissed her forehead.

Kim was nervous about leaving her cousin, even though Tina had told them she would be fine, Kim could see past that and see how much her cousin was hurting. She was scared Tina would try to do something to take her own life. She knew Tina had not been herself since Kevin had passed.

"Tina, I can stay with you. It's no problem to stay a little longer." Kim laid next to Tina in her bed as Tina cried softly.

"Kim, I'm fine. I'm fine. Don't worry about me. You have to live your life and go back to work. I'll be okay, I think." Tina wiped her swollen eyes.

"Tina, it's okay to be weak, but, baby, you have to get up and live. You can't lay here and die. You have those precious girls to live for. I know you're hurting, Tina. I know, but you have to get a grip. This too shall pass." Kim rubbed Tina's back.

"Kim, every day I wake up, I get sick to my stomach. I can't explain the feeling, I don't think I will ever be able to explain the feeling, but it's torture, and I wish God would take me too. I miss him so much, Kim. I miss him." Tina covered her eyes with her hands.

"Why would a God who can do anything take my husband, why would He even say He loves us so much and He lets bad happen to the ones He supposedly loves?"

"I love you, Tina." Kim looked up toward the ceiling not knowing what to say. Kim knew little about the Word. She knew little about God, and she had not built a relationship with Him to be able to defend what Tina had said.

Aunt Berniece knocked on Tina's room door as it was time to leave to get the girls to school and them to the airport. After dropping Lina and Ava to school, Tina drove Aunt Berniece and Kim to the airport. Kim got out to get their suitcases out of the trunk as Aunt Berniece sat in the car with Tina.

"Tina, you have to be strong. If God knew death would be too much for His people to bear, I don't think He would have allowed death to be a part of life. I know it's hard. Trust me, I know, but you deal with it and you live. You can't let losing someone you love cause you to lose yourself. I love you so much, Tina. I just pray God's strength for your life." Aunt Berniece leaned over to hug Tina.

"Auntie, I'm so broken, I'm all cried out, I don't know what to do, I don't know how to think about God anymore, and I really don't care what happens to me. It's just not fair." Tina hugged her aunt tight.

"Baby, I love you and I'm just a phone call away. If you need me, I'll be here. I'll come down and see about you. Don't give up because you mean so much to so many people. We love you so much." Aunt Berniece rubbed the side of Tina's face. "You can't blame God for the bad. It's not His fault. He never intended for corruption to be in the world. You know that, you know the Word, baby. Just love on God, that's the only thing that will allow you to get through." Aunt Berniece kissed Tina's cheek before getting out of the car.

"I love you, my favorite cousin. Give me a kiss." Kim opened Tina's door trying to cheer her up.

"Get out of here." Tina laughed then hugged her cousin. "I love you and thank you for being here for me."

"I love you so much, girl. You're gonna make it. Just be strong and call me sometimes." Kim smiled as she closed the car door.

"I love you," Kim mouthed to Tina as she drove away.

10

Monique

Nurses told Helen when she reached the ICU desk, Monique had some tests ran earlier that morning; they also told her she made Dr. Taylor cry the previous day.

"Honey, that lady is stuck in her ways. She doesn't like to listen to anybody. She thinks because she has all these degrees she knows everything," a dark-skinned lady who held the title of registered nurse said when Helen walked up. "You just keep the faith. Don't let anyone tell you what it is when you know that God is really what it is." She smiled at Helen.

"Honey, you don't have to tell me twice." Helen laughed as she walked to Monique's room.

Due to the state Monique remained in, Ms. Dee was removed from Monique's room. Helen felt she was an angel sent by God to bring assurance that everything would be all right. Although she really believed things would be okay, she felt everyone could use some assurance every now and then.

"I'm here, baby. Joshua is with Mrs. Vera talking her up a storm too." Helen rubbed the side of Monique's face. "You have to be strong, Monique. You have to fight. We need you." She rubbed Monique's hand.

As Helen stood talking to Monique, there was a knock at the door.

"Um, hi, mistress. It's me, Dr. Taylor. I just wanted to apologize." She walked in the room.

"Well, well, if it ain't the devil in she form," Helen spoke in a sarcastic tone as she turned around, noticing the voice that entered the room.

"No, ma'am, I really want to apologize for how I spoke concerning Mrs. Austin yesterday. It was out of line, and I shouldn't have come to you in a negative way. I just know from my experience bad cases when I see one." She reached to shake Helen's hand.

"I don't shake hands with the devil." Helen looked at her hand. "It's not about being negative, but as a doctor, you should offer some kind of hope. Obviously, you have to be real with whatever situation is going on, but you should still offer some kind of hope." Helen turned her head back toward Monique.

"But, ma'am, I understand that, but like I said, I know a bad case when I see one," Dr. Taylor talked as if becoming frustrated with Helen's response.

"No, you don't come to someone who's worried about the life of their loved one and tell them they might as well say good-bye. Where is the hope in that? You came to me as if you were God, and you were writing her off. As long as there is still breath in her body and as long as God lives, there is hope!" Helen turned, looking Dr. Taylor in the eyes. "It's one thing to speak what is really going on, but it's another thing to speak with little to no compassion. Now as you can see, you are no longer needed in this room because the real doctor is in here." Helen smiled a fake smile.

"Ma'am, yes I'm in here, and I just came to apologize."

"No, not you, but the One who's never lost a battle, the One who gives life, and the One who has the power to heal and raise up the dead." Helen turned her head back toward Monique, rubbing her head.

There's no getting through to her, Dr. Taylor thought as she let out a breath walking out the room.

"Momma ain't no punk, and she ain't gonna push me like one either." Helen laughed.

As Helen grabbed a chair to sit next to Monique's bedside, there was a small knock at the door before it opened.

"Wow, I never knew it went like that." Helen looked at the familiar face.

Oh great, the deputy thought as she walked in. "Hi again, mistress."

"Hi, and I didn't know it went knock then open. I thought it went knock, wait for a response to come in, then come in." Helen laughed.

'How is she doing?" Deputy Crewship ignored Helen's comment.

"You know, they aren't offering any hope, but I know God."

"Would you like to pray?" Deputy Crewship who wore a pair of jeans and a T-shirt suggested.

"Prayer ain't never hurt anybody." Helen reached her hand out for Deputy Crewship to grab it.

"Amazing God, You are our strong tower. In the name of Jesus, we come to You because You are the only One that can give this weak body life. We're asking You heal her and let Gabriel bring good news as we wait on You to work things out for her. God, we trust You and we know prayer changes things. We speak to her organs, and we command them to live in the name of Jesus. God, we believe You for this miracle, and we trust You continually. Now, God, because of the enemy's laugh, perform a supernatural miracle that not even the human mind can come to comprehend. We thank you and we appreciate You for not giving up on us. In Jesus name we pray. Amen." Deputy Crewship hugged Helen.

"Thank you. She really needs positive energy and people around her right now." Helen looked at Deputy Crewship. "And what can I call you?"

"My first name is Kelly." She smiled at Helen.

"I like you, Kelly." Helen smiled back. "You tried to be a family therapist and straighten me, but I like you, and thank you for coming to see about my baby. Go ahead and pull that chair over here." Helen pointed out the chair in the corner.

"I was so worried about her all night. How is that precious little boy of hers doing?" Kelly looked with concern. "The 911 operator said he was so sweet. He really did a good job. He helped to save his mother's life." Kelly held Monique's hand. "Her husband was so rude though. He acted as if he had no care about the well-being of that child or his mother." She shook her head.

"Joshua is doing well. He's taking this entire situation well. He knows his mommy has to be here to get better. On the other hand, I never liked the man. I told her not to marry him. I knew he was trouble the first time I smelled him. He only wanted to get my baby away from me and use her. Because of him, I bet all this has happened. She was all I had left and because of him, she left me!" Helen's blood boiled at the thought of James and all the problems she felt he had caused in their lives.

"In the car, when I told Joshua I was taking him to his grandma's house, he told me you and his mommy don't talk anymore. If you don't mind me asking, what happened that you two stopped talking?" Kelly stared at Monique as she lay helpless in the hospital bed.

"Me and Monique were close. We did everything together. We got our nails done together, shopped together, and cooked together. Then she started dating old dirty James. He had a foul mouth. He cussed and drank. I asked Monique what she saw in that man and she said he had a big heart. She thought because she loved God, she could change him. I told her you can't change a man, either they change because they are tired of being the way they are, or God changes them. Anyways, she got with him and he got her pregnant. I was so disappointed in her. She knew she should have been married before she had sex with anybody, but you can't tell a grown woman what to do. Then she married the man. She went off and married that no good son of a—" Helen balled up her fist. "Lord, help me. Then my husband died. After he died, Monique wasn't there for me like I would've liked her to have been. I told her James was taking her away from me, and he was gonna end up hurting her. I started to detach myself from her." Helen's eyes began to water at the thought of all the precious time she had lost with her daughter.

"One day, I told Monique she had to choose me or James. She told me it wasn't fair I was making her choose. She said she loved me so much and I was her best friend, but she loved James and that was her husband, so she was going to stick by his side. So, I told her she was a trader and to never call me again. She cried on the phone, and I hung up in her face. I cried and cried, but every time she called me or came by my house, I would ignore her calls or knocks. I missed her, but I wasn't about to let James put things in her head about me. Eventually, the calls stopped, and she stopped coming by the house. It's been two years and the time I finally get to see her, it's a matter of life and death." Tears fell from Helen's eyes as she held Monique's hand. "I was so scared of losing my baby. I caused myself to lose her. I was so mad at her for giving up on our relationship I told God to erase her from my memory."

"Well, that's the past. I know when she wakes up, she'll be so happy to see you. I know she still loves you." Kelly walked to Helen, rubbing her back. "What matters is you make things right. She needs you more than ever right now. The most important thing is you're here for her right now in her weakest moment. You can't change the past, Momma."

"You're right. I beat myself up last night. I can't believe I let myself get so jealous and full of hate that I caused a good relationship to be ruined. I'm really not a bad person, Kelly. I know sometimes I can be stubborn and my mouth can run wild at times, but I'm really not a bad person."

"Yeah, you can be a little petty," Kelly whispered. "You know, I've learned God will allow certain situations to happen just to mend something that is broken. He also allows things to happen to open our eyes or to get us back on track. At the end of the day, life is precious and tomorrow is not guaranteed. We all have to learn to live, forgive, and love." Kelly walked back, sitting in her seat.

"You know, talking to you made me really understand the verse in the Bible that says, 'Be angry and do not sin, do not let the sun go down on your wrath, nor give place to the devil'. Because of this, I allowed him to come in and work his destruction. A relationship was destroyed, and a life could have been lost, but God said not so and because now I realize this, I know God is going to give us both a second chance." Helen stood up and kissed Monique's forehead.

"Wow, I never looked at it like that." Kelly smiled at Helen.

Helen sat back in her seat as the sounds of knocks tapped on the door.

"Come in." Helen looked at the door.

"I have some news to share. This morning, Mrs. Austin had an electroencephalogram also known as an EEG. It's a test that detects abnormalities in your brain waves, or in the electrical activity of the brain. Now in all my years, I have never seen this. Her brain activity is now at fifty-eight percent. Because of this, we're going to remove the breathing tube from her in a couple of days. We want to see how she does trying to breathe on her own. Before she is taken off the ventilator, she will have another EEG test done. Realistically, she will never be at one hundred percent brain function, but we're hoping she will have at least seventy-five percent activity. Now depending on the part of the brain that's affected due to inactivity, she may never be able to see, she may not be able to speak or function as a normal adult. It just depends on the area of the brain that is asleep as we call it, but whatever you're doing, we encourage you to keep doing." Dr. Taylor smiled before walking out of the room.

"Wow, she didn't even stay to see if you had any questions." Kelly looked shocked.

"That's because I told her this morning she was no longer needed in this room." Helen began to laugh. "I had to tell her about herself and let her know about a man named Jesus." Helen smirked.

"Oh, I see, she's met your twin." Kelly laughed. "I have to get going. I have to pick up my daughter from school. You know how teens can get if you're late, and they're the last one to get picked up. I'll keep checking up on her and tell Joshua I said hello." Kelly hugged Helen.

"You be careful." Helen clasped Kelly.

****

"God, I love you so much." Helen looked up. "You've never failed me, and You always prove the doubters wrong." Her eyes began to water. "We're so unworthy of Your blessings, yet You bless us. Thank you for fighting this battle and not letting the enemy have the last say. Thank you, God." She closed her eyes to keep the tears from falling. Reaching into her purse that sat on her lap, she grabbed her phone calling Pastor Andrews.

"Pastor, God did it. God did it." Helen beamed when Pastor Andrews answered the phone.

"Hallelujah, He's faithful Helen. God is faithful."

"Pastor, she has fifty-eight percent brain activity. They want to take her off the ventilator in a couple of days to see how she does. They're hoping her brain activity increases by the time they're ready to take her off the ventilator. I just don't know why God loves an imperfect people so much. He really loves us so much no matter how much we mess up or doubt Him."

"Helen, my daily prayer is God removes every ounce of doubt, fear, and unbelief out of me. I know how big He is, and I know what He did in the past and what He's doing in the present, and that alone is enough to trust Him. You know, it gets hard sometimes, but God always performs a miracle that shows us to never stop trusting or believing He's bigger. He can do anything," Pastor Andrews talked with sincerity.

"Thank you for your prayers, Pastor, and thank you for having faith when I didn't. I can't thank you enough." Helen lifted her hand toward heaven as she held the phone with her other hand.

"Helen, just take care of Monique right now and keep praying for a divine turn around." Pastor Andrews's voice deepened. "God bless you, Helen. Call me and let me know of any other changes, God's going to do it for her," he said before hanging up the phone.

Helen was so overwhelmed with how God was moving for Monique that she called everyone she could think too. Being she only had one person she considered a real true friend, she called her next.

"God, did it. He did it. I can't give credit to no one else but God." Helen started to cry after the voice on the other end of the phone said hello.

"What, what's going on?" Vera sounded excited and anxious. "Hallelujah, God is able," Vera shouted without knowing what is was Helen was talking about.

"Vera, God healed Monique. He did it." Helen cried into the phone.

"Is she up? How is she doing?" Vera asked.

"Oh, God, You're so worthy. Hallelujah." Helen cried. "Vera, her brain activity is at fifty-eight percent. God did it."

"Praise God. Thank you, Lord." Vera cried. "Joshua, mommy is better. God healed her just like you said." Vera hugged Joshua.

"The doctors are walking in. I'll call you back." Helen hung up the phone wiping her eyes, trying to compose herself.

"Hi, ma'am, my name is Dr. Oghenekohwo, but you can call me Dr. O. I am the chief physician here." He reached to shake Helen's hand. "As of right now, Mrs. Austin is in a barbiturate-induced coma also known as a medically induced coma. When there are improvements in a patient's general condition, we gradually withdraw the barbiturates that are used to induce a coma and the patient regains consciousness. Because of her great progression, we want to see how she does off the breathing tube and out of the coma. If she were to have trouble, we would immediately place her back in a medically induced coma. Today is just to see her progression in a natural state." His accent was deep and strong.

"Do whatever you have to do. I know God is going to do it." Helen smiled. "What about her being on that ventilator, what's going to happen with that?"

"We have been reducing the amount of oxygen we have been giving her through the ventilator. Her breathing will be okay. We're removing it today. I can tell you we serve a mighty God. I have never seen a case like this in all my years of working. We can give credit to only God. Give credit to whom it's due right." He smiled at Helen.

"You're my type of doctor." Helen smiled.

"Okay, so we'll be back in about an hour to prepare her." He shook Helen's hand again and walked out of the room.

"Baby, today is the day God's going to move on your behalf." Helen kissed Monique's head.

****

After about three hours, the medicine that was used to place Monique in an induced coma wore off. The ventilator was removed as everyone waited, hoping Monique would show improvements being in a natural state.

"Dr. O, her vitals are dropping," Dr. Taylor spoke in a panicked tone.

"Just give her body a few minutes to adjust being in a woken state." Dr. O tapped his foot against the floor.

"Her vitals are still dropping." A seasoned anesthesiologist looked at Dr. O.

"Okay, what we're going to do is place her on a noninvasive ventilator. I want her back in a barbiturate-induced coma." Dr. O gave orders. "Come with me." He turned, looking at Helen.

They exited the room where doctors were preparing to place Monique back in an induced coma, stopping at the nurse's desk that sat in front of Monique's room.

"I am very happy with what I am seeing today. I am placing her back in a barbiturate-induced coma, so her body can heal. What she needs right now is rest so she can heal completely. She will be on a noninvasive ventilator. This approach will blow air into her lungs without us having to put a tube into her trachea. What will happen is a tight-fitting mask will go over her nose and mouth. This will allow the machine to blow air into her lungs."

"But why were her vitals dropping?" Helens eyes watered.

"The trauma she went through was serious. Her body just needs a little more time to heal. To be honest with you, I have never seen someone in the state she was in come out alive and then heal at the rate she is. I am very pleased with what I saw with her today. Keep praying because it's working." Dr. O rubbed Helen's back. "Go home and rest, continue to pray and believe God will perform this miracle."

"Doctor, I respect you and I respect the God in you that I see. Please pray with me." Helen looked the doctor in the eyes.

"God, we thank You for your righteousness, holiness, sovereignty, and sacrifice of your Son on the cross. We thank You that when we could go no further, You stepped in. We command this lady lives and not dies, and by Your merciful kindness and Your grace toward us, show up and do what seems impossible. We love You and we are forever grateful and appreciative of You and all You are and represent. We love You and we will continually believe Your report. In Jesus name we pray. Amen." Dr. O hugged Helen.

"Thank you so much, Doctor. Now, I don't know how to say your name but thank you. I'm going to go on home and come back tomorrow. That's what the world needs, more faith and uh more people that will stand in the gap and stand in agreement with each other for kingdom business." Helen smiled. "We need king-dom-minded people that's what I was trying to say." Helen laughed. "God bless you, sir."

"Whenever there is a need of prayer, I am there. If it wasn't for God, I would not be here today. No matter where I am, or what profession I am in, I will never miss the opportunity to lift up the name of Jesus and come into agreement for the good of the Lord." Dr. O smiled. "In other words, God is my life. He is the reason I do what I do, and God wants us to come together in His name, and pray that others will see miracles and believe. That's why I pray continually without ceasing. I know my God hears my prayers and answers them. He really loves us." He smiled at Helen. "You know the reason I love to pray when everyone else doubts is because I know God is the author and finisher of our faith, and it's in the doubting of others that the believers rise up and God proves the doubters wrong."

11

Tina

Time had flown by. Kevin had been gone for a month and life seemed to get more and more challenging day by day for Tina. She had ignored everyone's calls and Pastor Sullivan's attempts to stop by and check up on her. She left the house only to drop her girls off to school and pick them up. She relied heavily on Lina to prepare meals for her and Ava and to get them ready for school each day. On the weekends, Lina and Ava laid up under Tina trying to comfort and console her. Tina felt God had failed not only her but her family miserably, and to her, God was just some invisible made-up hero that was brainwashed in her since a young age. She felt there had never really been a God, and that it was just practice that had become common to man passed on from generation to generation. She felt if this God she used to love were real, she wouldn't be hurting the way she was, and her husband would still be by her side. She felt God had also disrespected her by ignoring her prayers and failing at His Word.

****

Aunt Berniece had been trying to reach Tina since she had gotten home from being with her. She grew even more panicked and scared when Kim told her she too had been trying to reach Tina and could never get an answer. She knew Tina was not in her right state of mind and that she talked about wanting God to let her die too. She also knew how she felt when her husband passed shortly after

Kim was born and the things she tried to do to end her own life. She became upset with herself at the fact she listened to Tina and went home like she insisted. Aunt Berniece knew, in times like this, support was needed for someone to make it through. She knew if a person who were grieving and in the state of mind Tina was in didn't deal with their grief, their grief would deal with them. She knew depression in itself was dangerous, but when you began to rebuke God and allow yourself to fall into a pit like the enemy wanted, the only one who would be able to pull you out is God and God alone.

"Kim, I can't take this anymore. I'm calling the police so they can do a wellness check on Tina and the girls. All I can think about is what if she has done something to herself and those girls. I wouldn't be able to live with myself. I should have stayed, Kim. I should have stayed." Aunt Berniece cried.

"Momma, it's not your fault. You can't blame yourself. You know when someone is like that, you have to honor them and give them their space. All we can do is pray, Momma." Kim hugged Berniece, still nervous of the possibility that something bad may have happened.

"God, if something is wrong, I don't know what I'll do." Aunt Berniece grabbed her cell phone, calling the non-emergency number to the police department.

****

"Go away!" Tina yelled at the banging on the front door that seemed to get louder and louder instead of ceasing.

"It's the police department. Open up!"

"I said go away dammit!"

"Ma'am, just open up the door and let us see that you're okay and we'll go away." The male voice sounded sturdy.

"What, what, what! How can I help you?" Tina answered the door in a tank top and boy shorts.

"Ma'am, we're here to do a wellness check. Your aunt called and was just a little worried. She had been trying to reach you. Maybe you should check to see if your phone is off the hook." The officer smiled at Tina, glancing down toward her legs then back up her figure to her face.

"Look, I'm fine. If we're done here, you can leave!" Tina looked the officer in the eyes, annoyed at his presence.

"Ma'am, is everything okay here? Your eyes are swollen. You don't look too good." The officer put his hand on his hip as a female officer stood next to him. "Did someone hurt you?" He licked his lips, staring Tina in the face.

"Sir, I'm not okay. My husband is gone. I'm drained. All I want to do is curl up in a ball and die and on top of that, my head hurts. Now, if you're done here, please leave. I'm fine, I'm not dead, and honestly, I'm really not in the mood to be talking to you. So, are you done?"

"Sorry, ma'am, I'm just doing my job. If you have any problems, just give us a call and answer the phone next time." He smiled.

"Yea, well, if I don't then sue me." Tina slammed the door.

Tina usually spent six hours to herself crying while the girls were at school. During this time, she laid in bed thinking of different ways to kill herself. Although she tried to seem strong and not let her girls see her cry, she was weak. Tina was worried for her girls but more so concerned about dying. At times, she would cry tearless cries, and on top of that, her eyes had become so swollen she had to put cold compresses on them to help with the swelling.

****

Two hours after the officers had left, there was another knock on the front door.

"Ugh!" Tina punched down on the bed. "What do you want?" She stomped to the door opening it without looking to see who it was. She wasn't afraid of it being a bad guy because if it were, she hoped they would come in and take her out of her misery. She would even fight them to try and provoke them to kill her.

"Tina." Pastor Sullivan reached in to hug her.

"Hi, Pastor," Tina spoke with little to no enthusiasm as she returned a hug to him.

"Tina, how are you holding up? I've been coming by. I've seen your car in the driveway. I figured you didn't want to be bothered when there was no answer at the door."

"Pastor, I'm beyond broken. I've just been staying to myself." Tina walked to the couch as Pastor Sullivan followed.

"Tina, you can't isolate yourself. Don't you know that's what the enemy wants you to do? He wants you to stay stuck in this depression and grief so he can play in your mind and keep you bound. An idle mind is the devil's playground."

"Pastor, come on now. We all know there is no enemy, but the black man who killed my husband. We should be sticking together not killing ourselves off." Tina sat with her head hanging low.

"Tina, I want you to know I love you and God loves you so much more. I know it's hard but trust me when I say God will make your pain manageable." Pastor Sullivan looked at how frail Tina appeared. He could see past her outward appearance and see she was frail inside; he could see she was at a place in her life the enemy smiled upon. He knew it was vital to help her get out of this grave she had dug for herself and into the creation God had created her to be.

"Pastor, with no disrespect to you because you have always been there for me and my family and I look up to you as a father figure but…" Tina cleared her throat. "Pastor, I don't want to hear about God. I don't want to hear about how God can do this and make that manageable. I don't want to hear about God loves you or He can fix this or fix that. Pastor, I don't want to hear about God at all. I hate Him! I hate God with everything in me. I hate that I allowed myself to be brainwashed into believing He raised the dead!" The hate that Tina had bottled up inside could be felt as she spoke balling up her fist. "Pastor, I hate God so much. I hate Him! The worst thing I have done to myself and my family is believed in something that wasn't worth believing in. God doesn't love anyone. How can you say He loves when He allows us to hurt so much? How can God say He loves us so much when He took a good man away? How can God say He loves us and He couldn't even heal my husband? I hate Him, and I don't want to ever hear about God again! As far as I'm concerned, God is a made-up thing that cannot be explained. If God is so real, then where did He come from, Pastor?" Tina looked Pastor Sullivan in the face as tears dripped from her swollen eyes. "I'm tired of people saying the devil did this and the devil is the one that took your husband. Pastor, that's crap! God is the only one that can give life and take life, and I feel so stupid I ever had faith in Him!"

"Tina, I know you're hurting and you're even mad with God, but at the end of the day, you have a choice with how you react and how you respond to your pain. Never once did Job curse God because he knew at the end of the day, God was still God, and He allows everything to happen according to His will. And guess what, it does not matter how much we beg and plead, if God is going to do something, He will. He doesn't need anyone's approval or consent because He's God." Pastor Sullivan looked at Tina as she sat with her head hanging low. "It's okay to tell God you're angry with Him. It's okay to let God know you're hurting. It's even okay to tell God you don't understand why He let your husband die, but it's not okay to treat God as if He pulled the trigger!"

"Pastor, please forgive me if I come off as disrespectful or offensive when I say this. And I want you to hear me good. I don't care about your God. I don't care to hear what you have to say about God, and I'm tired of you talking about Him!" Tina looked toward the front door as if she was giving the pastor the hint that it was time for him to go.

"Tina, people who reject the Word of God are repulsive, and though you do this, I come in love and I'm not going to give up on you. I know you want answers from God, but you're going about it the wrong way. The Bible says ask and it will be given to you, seek and you will find, knock and it will be opened to you. Have you tried either of these before you go and condemn yourself?"

"Listen, I asked, I seeked, and I knocked. My husband is still dead despite doing all of that, so what do you suggest I do now? I will not go another day believing in this God who can't even live up to His Word. I don't want to hear about God anymore and next time you plan on stopping by, make sure you leave Brother Jesus and brother Holy Ghost at the door." Tina began to walk over to a medium-sized box that sat by the door. "Take this crap with you. I don't want it, and I don't need it in my house. As for me and my house, we will not discuss the Lord. Now, if you don't mind, Pastor, please leave so I can finish doing what I was doing."

"No matter how much you blaspheme God, there is something in you that is greater than this and for some reason, He still sees you as the apple of His eye. Tina, He loves you so much that He allowed His only child to be sacrificed so you could live. I love you, Tina, and I'm going to be praying for you." Pastor Sullivan walked to the door, picking up the box that sat on the floor.

"Have a great week." Tina opened the door for Pastor Sullivan.

"You are special, and you matter." He smiled at Tina as he walked out of the door.

Hate was always an ugly and hurtful word Tina taught her girls to never use. It was a word that was never allowed to be spoken in her home, and it was not something that was a part of her vocabulary. However, since the death of Kevin and Alvin, it seemed hate had become not only a word adapted into her vocabulary but an unfruitful seed that had embedded itself into her life. She no longer was a woman who produced good fruit, a woman who portrayed every fruit of the spirit, but she became a woman who now sowed in the works of the flesh. And by the looks of it, she was becoming a faithless warrior drowning in the laughter of the devil.

12

Lina

Lina did what she knew her mother would do to make sure the well-being of her, Ava and her mother were okay. She tried her hardest to show herself strong in front of her mother, but little did her mother know she cried every day at school. Since the death of her father, she hadn't been herself. The out spoken, cheerful girl was now frail, rarely speaking. She was broken and scared—scared of losing her mother as she deteriorated before her eyes. And although she was fearful of the idea of having to grow up fast, this was something she vowed to God would be done if it had to be.

At school, she found comfort in her friend Amber. Amber was well liked by everyone. Her goofy personality made it easy to put a smile on anyone's face. Amber was the daughter of a police officer who taught her to always pray. She taught her adversity would always arise, and the enemy would always try to stop her from pushing her purpose. She taught her despite everything the enemy would do to steer her away from destiny, God was bigger, and if she had faith, she would be able to overcome any obstacle or trial she was faced with.

Lina walked the halls with her head hanging low, only speaking when spoken to. She found it easiest to open up to her friend Amber. They had become friends two months prior to Kevin being killed, but the most comfort for her came from God. God had become someone she felt she was closest to. She felt God was the only one who really understood how she felt. God was becoming her comfort, her confidant, and her best friend. Lina was learning God was really the only one who knew how to ease her pain. But most of all, she loved that God was always free, with an ear, willing to listen.

"Why is this happening to my family?" Lina sat on the bathroom floor, her back against the wall covering her face with her hands crying.

Amber knew the place to seek Lina if she couldn't find her in the halls.

"Lina, I love you and I'm here for you through all of this. We're sisters." Amber kneeled down in front of Lina, moving her hands wiping her eyes.

"I'm so scared. My little sister hasn't been herself. My mom is getting worse, and if I lose my mom, I don't know what I'll do." Lina cried looking up toward the ceiling, trying not to make eye contact with Amber. "My family means everything to me."

"God, I don't know how You can make things better, but I know You can. We're Your children. Please help us. Help Lina and her family in this situation." Amber put her arms around Lina as Lina rested her head on her shoulder weeping.

"Sometimes, I wish God would have never allowed me to be born. I don't know what I'm doing. I'm trying my best to be strong. I'm trying my best to do all I can for my family right now, but it's draining me. I'm hurting so bad. I miss my daddy so much!"

"I know, Lina, I'm here for you no matter what." Amber hugged Lina tighter. "I know it doesn't take the pain away, but maybe you should think about all the good times you had together with your dad and family."

"That's what hurts the most, to see how happy we were, and to look at us now. My mother hates God, my little sister is like a zombie, and I feel like I'm the parent with two sick kids. I'm so broken inside. I just wish I could die."

"I know it's hard, but my mother taught me there's nothing more real than God's word and what He speaks. I really believe God wouldn't put more on us than we could bear. I know it doesn't look like it, but one day, it'll get better for all of you." Amber talked while Lina cried on her shoulder.

"Yea… well, I don't know. I just wish things could be different. Why would someone just take my daddy away from me?" Lina whispered as tears flowed down her cheeks onto Amber's sweater. "All my daddy ever wanted was to be there for his family and love God. Why would God let him die?" The silence in the bathroom made Lina's questions vibrate off the walls.

"It's okay, Lina. It has to get better." Amber's eyes began to water.

"I wish I could die, but I can't leave my sister and Mom." Lina sighed. "I wish we could just die together."

"I know, I know, it's going to be okay." Tears began to run down Amber's face.

"I hate death. I hate it so much! Why, Amber, why?" Lina wept. "I miss my daddy." The sound in Lina's voice shook Amber to the core.

13

Paul and Sam

Paul never stopped praying for Monique. In his spare time, he found quiet places where he could commune with the Father. There was something about this woman Monique and her situation he couldn't shake. He knew God was perfect and mighty in all His ways, and he knew God was going to perform a mighty miracle for her. He also knew it was just a process Monique had to go through, but he believed with everything in his heart God was going to bring her out. In his believing, he knew God was not a man that He should lie.

"Bro, what are you doing after work?" Sam said as he stocked supplies in the ambulance.

"I'm going to see that lady Monique in the hospital. I have to lay eyes on her and see how she's doing."

"Bro, you really are hooked on that lady." Sam looked back at Paul who stood at the door of the ambulance handing him boxes.

"Bro, I don't know what it is. Since that day, I couldn't get her out of my mind, and her son, he had to witness all of that. He was so innocent and scared." Paul touched his chin. "Look now, I'm starting to sound like you." Paul laughed.

"Bro, I don't know all those fancy prayers, but I've been praying for her. I'm connecting my faith with yours and standing in agreement with you." Sam smiled as he opened a case of needles to stock on the ambulance.

"It's not about fancy prayers that get God's attention. Really, it's about relationship and also sincerity of the prayer. You know, just let it come from the heart and mean it." Paul smirked.

"You're right. No one in the Bible I've read got all fancy. They just had a sincere heart that God saw. On the other note, did you see that hot chick the way she looked at me in bible study?" Sam grinned as a case of gloves dropped on his hand. "Whoa that hurt." His face turned red.

"Dude, you had a booger on your nose that's why she was looking at you like that." Paul laughed.

"Yeah, well, I wiped it off." He laughed. "Seriously though, bro, I'm going with you to see her."

****

"How is she doing?" Paul walked up to the nurse that sat stationed to monitor Monique in front of her room.

"May I ask your relationship to her?" The nurse smiled.

"Yea, I'm her uncle from down the line." Paul stood with a straight face.

Is this guy serious? Sam thought standing next to Paul scratching his head, a confused look on his face.

"Oh, okay, well." The nurse cleared her throat, looking at Paul as if he were crazy.

"What is it because I'm white?" Paul smiled.

"Oh no, don't mind me. She's doing better. Doctors are hoping she wakes in the next couple of days." The nurse opened the door to the room. "Take your time." She closed the door after Paul and Sam walked into the room.

"Bro, her uncle really, from down the line? You couldn't come up with anything better than that?" Sam nudged Paul.

"What? I had to say something." Paul laughed. "She caught me off guard."

"Monique, it's Paul and Sam, the paramedics that helped you. We just wanted to come by and check up on you. We're praying for you so don't give up and don't give in." Paul touched her hand.

"Bro, do you want to pray?" Sam looked at Paul.

"Go ahead." Paul bowed his head.

"Yea, well, I meant you but okay. Here it goes." Sam cleared his throat. "God, it's me again, Sam. I'm pretty sure you know that already."

Really? Paul thought.

"So, God, we're here with Monique, and we believe You for everything You are. God, we thank You for touching and healing her. We are fully convinced what You promised You are able to perform according to your Word. Your Son Jesus Christ died on the cross for our sins so with His death, we claim victory. Because He died, she will live according to Your will. So once again, we come to thank you for the miracle and the process of the miracle You are performing in her right now. Thank you, God. Amen." Sam looked up at Paul. "How'd I do?" He smiled.

"Bro, what are you talking about? You can't pray fancy prayers that was powerful, quick, and to the point?"

"I've been listening in Bible study. If you don't know what to pray, pray God's Word back to Him." Sam smiled.

"It's so sad all I ask myself is what made her get to the point of not wanting to live? Was it that bad? Did she have anyone there she could talk to, anyone to support her?" Paul stared at Monique as she lay in the bed looking helpless.

"Bro, I feel everyone has their limit in life, their breaking point. It's just not easy for some people to handle that point especially if you don't have anyone in your corner. It's either kill yourself or turn to something that will help you ease the pain. That's why some people turn to alcohol or drugs. They just want to feel numb from the pain of whatever situation they are faced with."

"I know. I just wish people knew it was a better way." Paul dropped his head, trying to comprehend it all.

14

Tina

*B*ang, bang, bang. the sound of fist pounding on the front door startled Tina.

"Who is it?" she yelled, annoyed with people coming to her house uninvited and unannounced.

Bang, Bang, Bang, the banging became louder.

"Ugh." She pushed the covers off her, feeling people had no decency or respect to leave her alone and let her grieve like she wished. "Can I lie in bed and grieve for Christ sake." She got out the bed stomping to the front door.

"What do you want?" Tina flung the front door open.

"Wow, you're beautiful." James smiled.

"Really?" Tina said in a sarcastic tone, staring James in the face. "Officer, what do you want, and why do you feel the need to bang on my door like that?" Tina put her hands on her hip.

"Ma'am, I just wanted to come by and bring you these and check up on you. I was worried about you last time I was here. I couldn't get you off my mind. You didn't look so good." James handed her a bouquet of flowers.

"What are these for?" Tina grabbed the flowers as a nice gesture, not really caring to receive anything from anyone.

"These are just to show sympathy toward you and your family."

"Thank you, but it's not needed." Tina smirked. "Sympathy won't help or change anything."

"So, are you always this mean?" James smiled, leaning against the wall.

"I'm not mean and your comments aren't needed, Officer."
Tina rolled her eyes.

"It's Officer James, and your name is?"

Tina stood in the door way wondering why this man was at her
door asking her so many questions.

"It's Tina, now are you done here? I have things to do, and I'm
really not in the mood for small talk."

"Well, actually, I was wondering if I could come in and talk
with you. It's obvious something is wrong."

"Officer, there is nothing to talk about. I'm really not in the
mood for any company." Tina let out a breath that gestured she was
done with the conversation.

"I know I'm just concerned about you, and I won't rest until I
talk to you and see what's going on with you. It's my duty to serve
and protect and to make sure the well-being of citizens is okay."

"Ugh, if it will make you leave me alone I guess." Tina turned
around, leading James to the couch in the living room. "Look, can
we make this quick? I have exactly two hours before I have to go and
pick up my girls from school."

"I understand." James sat back on the recliner. "So tell me
what's going on with you? I know I don't know you, but something is wrong and you're too beautiful to have swollen eyes." James
looked at Tina's swollen eyes with concern on his face.

"You're a cop. I'm pretty sure you've heard what happened with
my husband and brother," Tina said as her eyes began to water.

"Actually, I have no clue what you're talking about."

"My husband and brother were killed on duty. My best friend
is gone." Tears rolled down her cheeks.

"Tina, I'm so sorry. I did hear about that. I didn't know that
was your husband and brother. I didn't know them personally, but
it's devastating for us all at the job. It could've been any of us." James
rubbed his chin.

"I'm so lost. I don't know what to do anymore. I miss them
so much. It's like in the blink of an eye, my whole world is turned
upside down. It's just not fair." Tina put her hands over her face,
breaking down crying.

"It's okay. I'm here. You're not alone." James stood up walking to the love seat Tina sat on sitting next to her putting his arms around her. "I'll be your friend. You can talk to me." James smirked, rubbing Tina's back.

"I'm so sorry I look like a fool crying in front of you." Tina continued to cry.

"No, you don't. It's life and normal to hurt when you lose someone."

"I know, it just hurts so badly, and my poor babies have to see me so broken." Tina pushed back from James.

"It's okay. If you need a friend to talk to, I'm here. I just want to make sure you pull through this. If you ever need anything, don't hesitate to call me." James handed Tina a card with his personal cell number on it.

"Thank you. You know you don't have to be so nice to a mean ole lady like me." Tina laughed, wiping her eyes.

"I see you do have a kind of nice side." He smiled.

"Kind of. What does that mean?" Tina laughed.

"You know, you not rolling your eyes and hands on your hip all the time. You do have nice words in you." James laughed.

"Well, I could have told you that if you didn't get on my nerves banging on my door like that. I would say like you're the police, but you are the police so that wouldn't work, or I could say like a mad man, which I think you are." Tina laughed, smiling for the first time in two months since her husband passed.

"There's a beautiful smile." James stared at Tina's lips. "So do you work or you just stay home all day feeling sorry for yourself?"

"Excuse me." Tina rolled her eyes.

"See, I knew it wouldn't be long before your eyes cussed me out again." James laughed.

"I'm a hairstylist. I work at an upscale hair salon. Unfortunately, I have to go back to work next month. I just don't know how I'm going to do it. I'm fine one moment, the next I'm crying." Tina looked James in the eyes. "I wish heaven had a phone."

"Well, I don't mean to cut you off, but I have to get back to work." James stood up. "It was nice talking to you and seeing you smile," James said as Tina stood up to shake James hand.

"Thank you for stopping by. You weren't a pain as I imagined you would be." Tina smiled, leading James to the front door. As she closed the door behind James, she began to feel guilt that she even allowed a man who was not her husband into her home. She began to feel she was betraying her deceased husband. With this feeling of thought, she broke down crying.

James was a man who had a way with his words. He also was a man who could play on you if he saw an opportunity to. James knew the secret he kept from Tina would cause her to look at him as a liar if she knew the truth. He knew that night Kevin and Alvin were killed, he was on duty. He was the one who went to Tina's house to give her the bad news and take her to the hospital. He knew because she was so distraught she wouldn't have remembered him. James knew that night he saw what he liked in Tina and told himself she was going to be his. Although he told the truth about not knowing Kevin or Alvin personally, he had crossed paths with them on several occasions. To make matters worse, James knew Alvin had always said something wasn't right with him when he would see him.

15

Ava

"God, I'm crying because I'm thinking about what if Momma leaves me too and never comes back. Does Momma love me God?" Ava cried softly under her blanket as everyone in the house slept. The silence in the atmosphere made it easy to hear the snores of everyone in the house. "God, I miss my daddy so much. I miss uncle too, but I really miss daddy. He already left me, and now Momma is going to leave me. Momma talked more today, but it's still not the same." Ava continued to cry.

"I love you and I'll never leave you." A still small voice spoke to Ava's spirit as she smiled then drifted off to sleep.

16

Paul and Sam

Sam began to grow a bond with Paul. He started regularly attending the church Paul went to and opening up to him as well.

"Bro, I went to the doctor today. They told me I have diabetes. I'm so confused. I eat right. Sometimes, I eat a lot of sweets, but for the most part, I eat okay." Sam's worries showed as he spoke to Paul at the station.

"Sam, what is diabetes to God? If God can command dry bones to live, do you really think diabetes is bigger than death?" Paul smiled at Sam.

There was nothing no one could do to try and convince Paul God wasn't everything he knew Him to be.

"Yeah, but I'm also going through a lot at home. It's like ever since I came out to my family about my belief and faith in God, they have been giving me hell. I'm so young so you know I'm still living under my parent's roof. My sister gets on my last nerve the most. She always has something slick to say like, 'Oh, do you think you're so smart now because you believe in God?' or 'Do you really think because you read this Bible, you have all the answers to life?' She constantly says you and me both know there is no such thing as God. And my brother." Sam shook his head. "He's always like bro. I don't want to hear that Bible crap. I try to explain God to them, but they just give me hell." Sam looked down to the ground. "I don't know, man. This whole walking with God thing is just too much for me. I'm thinking about leaving the church for good and living like I used to. No beliefs, then I'll have no worries." Sam shuffled his foot around on the pavement.

"See the problem is one, God doesn't have to be explained. You have to focus on you and what God is speaking to you and doing in your life. You can't argue God because to the foolish mind, there is no getting through to it. I'm not saying your family is foolish, but they're just acting like that out of their unknown ignorance. Sam, the most important thing you have to remember is you can't live your salvation based on what others think or how they feel. The Bible says work out your own salvation with fear and trembling. And two, you can't be double-minded when adversity strikes. You love and trust God with everything in you and by doing that, others will see the God in you. All you need to do is love on your family a little harder. Love draws. You have to remember that."

"Bro, where do you get this wisdom from you have an answer to everything?" Sam laughed.

"No, I don't. I just." Paul smiled. "Hey, it comes from God. Seriously, Sam, you're going to be okay. Don't lose the faith, and don't worry about your family. They'll come around."

17

Monique

It had been a long and stressful week. Helen traveled back and forth from the hospital each day, sitting and praying for Monique. She was burned out; however, she wasn't about to give up on her daughter. Whatever it was going to take from her, she was willing to do. She made up in her mind when Monique woke up, she was going to support her and be the best mother she could be to her. She felt she had lost her once and almost completely, and she wasn't about to let anything or anyone ever get in between them again. This was also a stressful but good day. Today, doctors were going to be removing all medicines from Monique's body, hoping she woke in good health. They ran tests on her brain and vital organs including her heart to see if any damage had been caused from the dosage of pills she consumed.

Helen walked slowly up the hall leading to the elevator. Once on, she closed her eyes praying God did something to help Monique.

Ding, the elevator stopped on the ICU floor where she exited, buzzing the nurse's station.

"I'm here for Monique Austin." Helen sighed into the phone. She was hopeful yet at the same time anxious to see what would happen on this day.

"Come on in." The nurse on the other end of the phone spoke.

The ICU floor seemed to glow as the bright lights radiated causing the floor to glow brighter, giving off the effect of being wet.

Helen strolled past the nurse's station to Monique's room where she was greeted by Dr. Taylor. "Mrs. Helen, I never imagined I'd say these words, but the faith you have saved your daughter's life. I'm more than positive she will be okay." Doctor Taylor smiled before walking away.

"Ain't that something, God? The mouth of the unbeliever had to testify of You and your power." Helen smirked. "And doctor lady devil thought she was right, like things were going to turn out bad." Helen laughed.

"Hello, Mrs. Helen." The nurse assigned to Monique's room smiled. "Today's the big day." She winked.

"Lord, help her. I'm ready for this all to be over." Helen sighed, then smiled at the nurse as she entered the room.

Monique's skin glowed as she lay asleep under the medications doctors had her on. Doctors had already started the process of gradually removing the anesthetic drugs that placed her in the medically induced coma. The chief physician of the hospital made sure everything was being done to help Monique recover. Until all the medicine was free from her system, it would be a waiting game. They hoped within the next two to three hours, Monique would awake.

"Baby, Momma's here. Joshua is with Mrs. Vera. He told me to give you a big kiss and to tell you he misses you so much." Helen kissed Monique's cheek. "Baby, I can't wait to stare into your beautiful eyes." Helen stared at her only child. "You are so beautiful. I can't stop looking at you." She smiled, kissing Monique's cheek again.

"Is everything okay?" The nurse assigned to Monique's room popped her head into the room.

"Yes, baby, can you get me some juice though? I'm a little dry." Helen looked toward the door.

"Sure." The nurse smiled.

The ICU staff treated Helen well, plus they knew she would speak her mind in a heartbeat and wouldn't shut up until she got the last word out, so they did all they knew to do to avoid any confrontation.

What a friend we have in Jesus, all our sins and griefs to bear, and what a privilege to carry, everything to God in prayer. Helen began to hum as she looked out of Monique's room window.

"Here's your juice." The nurse placed a cup of crisp, cold apple juice along with a small cup of crushed ice on the bedside table.

Helen threw up a wave as she continued to hum. The day was a wet one. The sun fought against the clouds as the sun rays struggled to lightly beam through the dark clouds. Lightning could be seen in the far distance as the sounds of thunder filled the sky's air. Raindrops tapped on the window as Helen imagined the scenery to be angels in warfare against the enemy on Monique's behalf.

"Mrs. Helen." Dr. Taylor walked into the room.

Helen looked toward Dr. Taylor without saying a word.

"We're coming down in about twenty minutes to wake Monique. She's showing signs on the monitors of being close to waking up. You can leave out or stay in the room. It's your choice." Dr. Taylor smirked.

Helen nodded then stared at the peaceful state Monique was in.

****

It was now 12:15 p.m. The time of anticipation had arrived. Dr. Oghenekohwo or, to Mrs. Helen, Dr. O, the chief physician, along with Dr. Taylor and a team of anesthesiologists and nurses stood by. Helen stood on the right side of Monique's bedside; she wanted Monique to lay eyes on her as soon as she opened them. She wanted Monique to see that she had her back and was going to be by her side no matter what they had been through.

As the clock ticked to now 12:40 p.m., signs of life started to show in Monique's body. Her chest heaved slowly up and down as she slowly opened her eyes halfway then closed them shut. The cannula or NC that sat in her nose was turned on to make sure she had a steady and constant oxygen supply to her body.

"Come on, baby. Momma's here. Open your eyes, Monique." Helen rubbed Monique's forehead.

Two minutes ticked by, then four. Finally, Monique opened her eyes, turning her head slightly toward Helen staring with a confused look on her face.

"I love you, baby. I'm here," Helen spoke as tears began to fall down her face. Her hands started to shake and her heart beat faster and faster.

"Mom." Monique tried to speak as blank words come out.

"Don't speak, baby." Helen squeezed Monique's hand gently. "I'm here."

"Monique, if you can understand me, blink twice for yes, three times for no. Do you feel any pain?" Dr. O stared at Monique.

Slowly, she blinked once, then after a few seconds another blink.

"Okay, I'm going to perform an examination on you. Follow the light with your eyes." He pulled out a small pen light moving it from left to right, up then down.

Monique's eyes followed the light slowly.

"Okay good. Now squeeze my hand as hard as you can." Dr. O placed his hand in the palm of Monique's left hand.

With all her might, she gently squeezed his hand.

"Okay, I'm going to use this small pin to poke you in the hands and feet. If you can feel it, I want you to blink twice."

Everyone stood in awe at how good Monique was doing. Everyone thought when she came in, she would be leaving out on her way to the funeral home. No one believed she would pull through, and so many doctors gave up hope on fighting for her life.

Dr. O pushed the pin into Monique's left hand. After slowly blinking twice, he pushed the pin into her right hand. No matter how long it took, Dr. O was patient knowing this was nothing but a miracle. Slowly, Monique blinked twice.

Helen stood smiling as tears flowed down her face. "Thank you, Jesus," she mouthed over and over.

For the final part of the exam, Dr. O pulled the sheet from over Monique's feet. "Can you lift your legs for me?" He stared down at her ashy legs waiting for movement. "If you can't lift your legs, blink twice."

Slowly, with tears in her eyes, she blinked twice.

"Okay, can you feel this?" He pushed the pin into her big toe then the heel of her foot. "Blink once for yes, twice for no. If a little, squeeze Dr. Taylor's hand."

Softly, with all her strength, Monique squeezed Dr. Taylor's hand.

"Okay, I want a comprehensive metabolic panel done, a PT, APTT, thorough neurological exam, neuropsychological test, and an EEG. Make sure to have the results of the CT scan of the head sent to me ASAP." Dr. O ordered.

"It's going to be okay." Helen rubbed Monique's hand as nurses prepared to wheel Monique to get testing done. "Why can't she lift her legs? Why can't she move them?" Helen began to breathe fast in a panic talking to Dr. O.

"Her body has gone through serious trauma. These tests will show us exactly what is going on. She's doing amazing for all she's gone through. As soon as we have answers, I will personally give you some answers. She's a miracle." Dr. O smiled before walking out.

Helen sat in the cold room; the sound of beeping from the multimodal monitor filled the room. Helen was concerned, but she didn't let this worry her of a bad outcome. She felt deep within, everything would be all right.

"I know, God, You didn't bring her this far to leave her now." Helen began speaking quietly while grabbing a chair by the door entrance to sit in. She turned the television on that hung mounted to the wall. She dozed off for about thirty minutes only to awake to an empty room. Looking at her watch, the time read 1:40 p.m. She dozed off again for about twenty minutes before being awaken to the sounds of nurses bringing Monique back into the room.

"I love you, Monique. I didn't know if I would ever get the chance to tell you that again." Helen sighed a sigh of relief. "Joshua said to tell you he loves you and misses you so much." Helen kissed Monique's cheek.

Monique stared at her mother; she was surprised to see her crying standing next to her bedside.

"It's going to be okay." Helen pulled the chair she was sitting in closer to Monique's bedside. "Baby, so many gave up on you. They thought you wouldn't make it, but look at you. All I can hear is she'll never walk or talk again, and her life won't be worth living, and all I can think is but God." Tears of joy fell from her eyes.

Monique didn't speak; she stared at Helen then looked around the room. Still hooked up to a few monitors, she dozed off to sleep.

It took four hours for all the results from the tests to come in. Dr. O along with Dr. Taylor walked into the room, smiling. Monique awoke at the warmth of Dr. Taylor's touch.

"Monique, you are so lucky to be alive. You are truly a miracle. I have never seen a case like yours turn out for the better. Your mother is a praying woman, and I can honestly say this… if it hadn't been for your mother's prayers, honey, you wouldn't be alive today." Dr. Taylor rubbed Monique's hand.

"Mrs. Austin, Mrs. Helen, the test and blood work we ran fortunately didn't show any permanent damage. Now, because of how long the brain was without oxygen, you have weakness in your legs. And this is nothing but a miracle considering irreversible brain damage starts within three to five minutes. The good thing is over time and with rehab, you should gain full mobility back in your legs. We are referring you to a rehab center that specializes in brain injuries. There you will get the proper treatment to help you strengthen yourself and get back on your feet. Monique, with God, all things are possible, and if you can't see that in your situation, well, I wouldn't know what else to tell you. We're going to monitor you over the next couple of nights. Tomorrow, a case worker will come down and talk with you about placement in the rehab. They have an opening, so hopefully, by Monday, you should be in a bed at the rehab center." Dr. O smiled. "Don't give up." He rubbed the top of Monique's hand.

"What about her speech?" Helen looked with concern.

"The speech pathologist should be here in about an hour to check her out. The CT scan didn't show any damage to the brain in the left frontal lobe known as the Broca's area. That part of the brain controls speech, but she still has to be evaluated by the speech pathologist."

"Thank you, thank you so much." Helen looked at Monique.

****

It was now 5:23 p.m. The speech pathologist had come and gone. Her findings were: "Monique was just not ready to talk." She told Helen to just give Monique a day or two to get back to talking. The traffic of nurses and doctors had finally cleared so Helen called Pastor Andrews as well as Vera with the amazing news that was nothing short of a miracle.

Vera answered and at the news of Monique, she began shouting hallelujah all throughout the house. She put Joshua on the phone as Helen placed the phone up to Monique's ear.

"Mommy, I love you so much. I can't wait to see you, Mommy. I knew you would get better. Okay, Mommy, I'm going to eat ice cream and brownies, bye." Joshua's voiced caused tears to fall from Monique's eyes.

Since Monique awoke, Helen decided to stay the night so Monique wouldn't be alone. Vera agreed to take Joshua to school and pick him up. She loved him as if he were her own grandchild and said that it would never be a problem to keep him.

****

It was 11:43 p.m. Helen was fast asleep in the recliner chair next to Monique's bedside.

"Momma." A small voice filled the room. "Momma." It became a little louder this time, causing Helen to wake up.

"Momma." Monique looked toward Helen.

"Baby, I'm here." She jumped up, hovering her body over Monique hugging her. "Baby, I love you so much. I thought I lost you." Helen cried. "Don't you ever do that to me again. Please, Monique."

Monique said nothing; her tears absorbed into Helen's shirt. She knew why she was where she was. She felt embarrassed and was filled with guilt. She was ashamed for what she had done and part of her was mad for being in the place that she was. She was sure this life would be far behind her. And despite all of that, she was happy to be in her mother's arms.

****

The following Monday, Monique was moved to a private room at the rehab facility. They prepared her for all that would go on. It took about a week to get her registered and evaluated to make sure the proper therapy would be given to her. She wasn't too happy about being where she was and shut down on everyone in depression including her mother. In her mind, this journey she was now on was a waste of time, and she knew there was somewhere else she would rather be than where she was currently at.

18

Tina

Six months had passed since Kevin and Alvin had been killed. Still, no arrest had been made in connection to their murders. Tina was also getting behind on her bills and was in bad standing on payments for Kevin's car. She had decided to keep his car for Lina when she became old enough to drive. Tina also never fully snapped back to herself after the death of her husband. She was slacking at work and cussing more and more. She also decided to distance herself from James. She hadn't really talked to him in over a month, feeling she had started falling at his words. It confused and caused her to feel guilty for feeling the way she did. Tina didn't want anyone in her business either. She felt no one really cared how she was hurting so no one deserved to come in and have a say-so about her life. The simplest suggestion about her life made her snap.

The truth of the matter was Tina wanted to stay stuck in depression and feeling sorry for herself. She wanted a better reaction and expression out of people. She wanted them to feel her pain and see she was hurting. The problem was people knew Tina was hurting. There was just nothing anyone could do or say that would fill the hurt and void she was experiencing. There was really nothing good enough anyone could do that would take the pain away.

It was Monday morning, a little chilly but not too bad. Tina dropped the girls off to school then headed to work. She had a client scheduled for a full sew-in with color at 8:30 a.m., It was now 8:01 a.m.

The vibration of Tina's cell phone grabbed her attention. She had forgotten to turn her ringer back on from the night before. She usually turned it off when she would get into one of her depressing moods thinking about her husband.

"Hello." She tried to make her voice sound sexy at the noticing of the phone number.

"I can't hear anything, hello." James could be heard on the other end of the phone.

"Well, hello," Tina talked, trying to sound seductive. This time, her voice cracked. She coughed to clear her throat.

"Whoa, what's wrong with you?" James laughed.

"My throat got a little dry." Tina smiled.

"How about you meet me at the park? The one by the lake so I can see you," James said.

"Umm, I don't know. I have a client at eight thirty."

"Come on. It'll be quick." James's deep voice hypnotized Tina.

"Okay, but I can't stay long." She glowed, smiling.

"Don't keep me waiting. I miss those beautiful eyes." He smiled.

"Oh really, I'm on my way." Tina laughed before hanging up the phone.

The sun had already risen and was shining bright. James had beaten Tina to the park that overlooked a beautiful lake. The park was filled with river birch, white oak, flowering dogwood, and American sweetgum trees. A few ducks floated on the lake as people walked the path that traveled around the lake. The sight of the beautifully green grass made the park that much more appealing.

Tina pulled into the park spotting James's car pulling into the empty space next to him.

"Hello." Tina snuck up behind James, laying her hand on his shoulder as he sat on the bench, which sat ten feet from the lake.

"You look beautiful." James, in uniform pants and a white T-shirt, turned around locking eyes with Tina.

"You don't look so bad yourself." She smiled as James stood up to hug her.

The time was now 8:15 a.m. Tina looked at her 14K gold heart watch Kevin had bought her as an "I love you" gift. He would buy her things just to see her smile. He told her many times if he had the ability to give her the world, he would. Tina got lost staring at the watch thinking of the day Kevin had given her the watch.

"You okay?" James rubbed Tina's arm.

"Yes, I'm fine." She shook her head.

"Well, have a seat." James tapped the back of the bench.

Tina sat next to James staring out at the lake.

"So, what's up? Why did you really want me to come here?" Tina turned her head toward James.

"I just wanted to lay eyes on you." He smiled. "No, really, I wanted to make sure you were okay. I can see you've put up a wall. You're hurting and because of what you went through you've kind of hardened your heart." James began to massage the middle of Tina's back. "Look at you loosen up." He laughed.

"Who does that, who just starts massaging someone's back?" Tina smiled. Inside, she was melting and regretfully, she liked the attention James was showing her. She felt he was the only one in the world who really understood and felt her.

"Look, I don't want anything from you. I just want to be your friend. Someone you can vent to, and, you know, be with when you want to get away from everything. You've become so distant. I just want to be here for you and your girls." James looked Tina in the eyes.

"I know. I'm not trying to be distant. I'm just going through a lot." Tina stared at a lady with her dog as they walked the path around the lake.

"Tina, I don't want you to miss out on your blessing because you're trying to stay away from me. God sends people in your life for a reason so don't miss out on a great friendship trying to be so hard." He nudged Tina.

Tina let out a deep breath. It was something about James and the way he seemed to care so much that charmed her. Unbeknown to him, Tina really felt like she was falling for James. He was the complete opposite from Kevin. He seemed to have a lil thug in him, but Tina cared less about that. All she could see was his big heart and how compassionate he was.

"I'm serious, Tina, you can talk to me about anything. I'm here for you." James smiled.

"Oh goodness, my client." Tina's phone rung. "I was supposed to be at work ten minutes ago." She stood up.

"It's okay, sit down. You know, you don't want to go anyways." James grabbed Tina's arm.

"I know, but I'm doing this by myself now. I have bills." She sat down.

"That's the problem. I know what it is now. You're stressed with work and everything else." James reached into his back pocket pulling out his wallet. "How much do you charge your clients? Well, I know each style is different, but what about your client that's waiting on you? How much are you charging her?"

"For what she wants, $625." Tina combed her fingers through her hair.

"Whoa, what do you go to the horse and cut its hair for her or something?" James laughed.

"Good work and quality isn't cheap, smart guy." She laughed.

"Here, I want you to forget about work today. Go get your toes and nails done. Get a massage and some lunch. Just treat yourself so you can relieve all that stress. You deserve it." James handed Tina ten crisp one-hundred-dollar bills.

"I can't take that." Tina pushed his hand away.

"Look, I told you. Don't miss out on your blessing. I'm blessed by blessing others. It will come back to me twofold." James placed the money in Tina's hand.

"Thank you." She laughed as her phone rung for the second time.

"Look at me." James grabbed Tina's chin softly. "I want to be here for you. I care about you. I just want to make sure you're okay."

Tina locked eyes with James; his words were charming her. He was winning her over, and she was loving how she felt when she was with him. All her pain, worries or what she was going through seemed to disappear when she was with him. Somehow, the bad in her life didn't seem to matter.

"Take your girls out for ice cream or something." He went into his wallet pulling out a $50 bill.

"Oh, no. You've given me more than enough." She blushed.

"Take it. Don't hurt me like that, You not letting me be here for you hurts me." James smiled.

"Thank you so much." Tina leaned in, laying her head onto James's shoulder.

"I'm here, Tina. Don't push me away." He wrapped his arms around her, gently squeezing her tight.

Tina closed her eyes. "I love you, Kevin." She smiled. "Oh my god, I'm so sorry." Tina lifted her head up. "My husband would hold me." She looked toward the lake feeling guilty yet comfortable.

"It's okay. I understand." James pushed Tina's head back on his shoulder. "I don't want to replace him. I just want to be here for you." He hugged her tight again. "I'm going to be here for you whether you like it or not." He kidded.

"Ugh, it's my job again." Tina looked down at her phone.

"Hey, relax. Take the day to treat yourself. You deserve it. Go to the spa, do something, just focus on yourself and leave work at work." James pressed the side button on Tina's phone silencing it.

"I know I need a day of relaxation. I've been slacking at work though."

"Well, what's one more day of slack going to hurt?" James smiled, looking at his watch. "Well, beautiful, I have to get going, but I'll be expecting a call telling me how your day went." James grabbed Tina's hand kissing it.

They both stood up walking to the parking lot. James opened Tina's door then walked to his car.

"I'm here for you." He smiled, getting into the car.

After James pulled off, Tina placed her head on the steering wheel. She felt guilty she was allowing her heart to open to this man who was not her husband. She felt even more guilty for not only indulging in conversation with James but for feeling she was falling for him. James, on the other hand, knew how much Tina was hurting and was playing on that hurt to get what he wanted.

Looking at the clock on the radio, the time read 9:15 a.m.

"Well, I guess I'm going to the spa." Tina smiled, turning off her phone.

****

Tina waited in the car line for her girls. She loved the school they went to and the fact they would be at the same school until they graduated. It was a private Christian school Kevin had picked out. Tina sat in the car relaxed and rejuvenated and cared nothing about the eight voice mails from her boss. She felt the world owed her something, so she didn't bother to call her boss back or apologize to her client. Instead, she said she would go into work tomorrow and deal with it.

"I'll race you." Ava held tight to her book bag straps on her shoulder running to the car.

"You cheated." Lina ran laughing, touching the car first.

"One day, I'll beat you." Ava laughed out of breath.

"How was school today?" Tina looked in the rearview mirror at Lina and Ava in the back seat.

"It was good." Ava smiled.

"It was okay." Lina stared at her mother in the rearview mirror.

"What was your favorite part about today?"

"Lunch." Lina and Ava both spoke, laughing.

"That used to be mine too." Tina laughed.

"Really, Mama." Lina laughed.

"I'm taking you girls out for ice cream."

"Yes." Lina and Ava both smiled.

They drove fifteen minutes to the ice cream parlor. Once there, Lina ordered a banana split with extra whip cream and sprinkles while Ava ordered an ice cream cone with cookies and cream and strawberry ice cream. They sat at the table in front of the parlor.

"Mama, today we learned that sin entered the world because of man, not God. Well, people already know that, but when something bad happens, people start to blame God." Lina put a spoon full of ice cream into her mouth.

"So, God doesn't make bad people?" Ava licked her ice cream.

"No, Ava, God wants everyone to love each other. People make their own choices to be bad or good. Right, Mama?" Lina looked up at her mother.

"Honey, no matter what, God created bad people. He knows our future so He knew how people would turn out. If God hadn't allowed for them to be born, there would be no bad people in the world. We didn't come here to talk about God anyways. Let's just have a good time eating this ice cream." Tina half smiled.

Lina stared at her mother confused. She knew how her mother raised her in faith and couldn't understand what her issue was with God now.

"But, Mama, when are we going to church? We haven't been in so long." Ava looked at her mother still licking her ice cream.

"Baby, I don't know. I just don't know." Tina's eyes started to water. "Okay, girls, let's go so we can get home before we hit traffic." Tina stood up, wiping her eyes.

Once in the car, Tina's phone began to ring.

"Hello," Tina answered.

"So how was your day? I've been waiting on my call," James talked.

"Oh, it was amazing." Tina smiled.

"Who is she talking to?" Ava leaned over to Lina, whispering.

"I don't know. It sure isn't God though." Lina mumbled, looking out the window.

"I wish I could have given you a massage. I could tell how tense you were." James smiled on the other end of the phone.

"I bet you do, but I'll call you later. I have to get my babies home."

"Okay, don't keep me waiting too long, beautiful," James said before hanging up.

****

Tina cooked baked spaghetti for dinner. After, Lina and Ava took their showers and was now down stairs in the living room watching cartoons, while Tina sat in her room crying thinking about Kevin and cussing God for taking him. It was now 8:20 p.m.

"I'll get it." Lina jumped up hearing the house phone ring.

"Hey, baby, I miss you," Aunt Berniece said, hearing Lina's voice.

"Auntie, I miss you so much, when are you coming back?"

"Soon, baby. How's your sister and Mama today?"

"Auntie, it's not the same," Lina whispered as Tina walked by going to the kitchen.

"Auntie, today in school, the teacher told me I had so much wisdom from God." Lina smiled.

"Dammit, what the hell!" Tina slammed her fist down on the counter after dropping her plate of spaghetti on the tile floor.

"Baby, what's going on?" Aunt Berniece heard the commotion going on in the background.

"It's okay. Mama dropped her food," Lina whispered.

"Baby, I really want you and your sister to come live with me for a while. Your mother needs a break and time to heal." Aunt Berniece's soothing voice calmed Lina.

"Auntie, I can't. I need to stay here and take care of Mama. She really needs me."

"You know, I worry about you all. I just want to make sure you girls are okay. You shouldn't have to take care of your momma, baby. You're just a baby yourself."

"Auntie, we're fine. I love you, and I can't wait to see you again." Lina looked toward the television. "Ava's coming. She wants to talk to you," Lina said before handing Ava the phone.

"Hi, Auntie." Ava grabbed the phone.

"Hi, baby, are you doing okay?" Aunt Berniece asked.

"I'm okay. I miss you a lot too." Ava's sweet voice sounded through the phone.

"I miss you too, baby."

After finishing talking to Lina and Ava, Aunt Berniece talked with Tina.

"Tina, you will never get over your hurt if you don't deal with it." Aunt Berniece calmly talked. She was the type of woman with a voice that made you pay attention to her when she spoke. Her voice was powerful yet calming.

"Auntie, I'm trying. I'm trying to fight. I just don't know. Life and everything else seems to be against me. I'm hurting because of life and now I just don't know." Tina talked.

"Baby, I'm going to say this, and I want you to hear me good. Life doesn't hurt you, our choices do. Your choices aren't going to bring your husband back, and your choices are only hurting you. You're giving up on the One that's been there from the beginning for something He didn't even do. Vengeance is mine says the Lord. Don't fight against God for what happened. He's got it all under control."

"Auntie, if God had it under control, the man that killed my husband would be in jail. Better yet, if He had it under control, none of this would have ever happened!" Tina raised her voice in anger, yet talked low enough to where her girls couldn't hear her.

"I believe God allows some stuff to happen because if He had not, the ending result would be too much for that person to bear. Don't blame God, baby. He's never failed you yet, even though what you're going through hurts, He's still God."

"I know, Auntie." Tina rolled her eyes, not wanting to hear anything about God. "Auntie, I love you, but I have to get myself together for work tomorrow. I have a lot to deal with there. I love you, Auntie, and I hear what you're saying," Tina spoke calmly.

Before hanging up, Berniece prayed with Tina then told her she loved her.

19

Monique

U *gh, four days too long… I'm sick of this. Nobody loves me. Why do I have to do this?* Monique laid on her semi-hard mattress, thinking to herself.

Monique wasn't too happy about surviving what she thought would take her out. Besides the fact of being in the place she was in, James not picking up his phone depressed her even more. She sat every day in misery thinking of all the possibilities of what if, questioning God about her purpose, which was a purpose she gave herself. Until she was done being evaluated and registered, which took about five days, she would be resting, waiting for her rehab sessions to start. Helen visited every day without Joshua. She could see depression overtaking Monique and thought it best to wait to bring him. For four days, Monique lay in bed crying or staring up at the ceiling. She wouldn't talk or eat much; over and over, she repeated, *I'm useless and crippled*, as Helen would sit quietly praying for her daughter not wanting to irritate her.

Tomorrow would make five days in rehab; that meant the following Monday, Monique would start her physical therapy sessions. Helen promised after her first session she would bring Joshua and pleaded with Monique to pull it together.

"Baby, I'll be back tomorrow. I love you and I'm praying for you." Helen stood up, kissing Monique on the cheek before leaving.

"I love you, Momma." Monique gazed blankly toward her mother.

****

The day was beautiful; the air dry and chilly. It was the type of weather where you could put on a light sweater and still be comfortable. After dropping off Joshua to Mrs. Vera's house, Helen headed for the rehab center. She prayed long and hard the night before and felt it was time to get answers. What caused Monique to do what she did, where was James, and why hadn't he been to the hospital to see her? At 1:30 Saturday afternoon, she pulled up to the rehab center in high spirits that Monique would finally talk.

"Hey, baby, I love you." Helen walked into Monique's private room kissing her forehead. She kissed her again on the cheek. "That's from Joshua and this too." She handed a piece of white computer paper, which had a picture Joshua drew of a woman and small child with a heart, trees, and a smiling sun. "That boy cannot wait to see you. He talks my ear off about you." Helen laughed, trying to lighten up the stale mood in the room.

"I know I can't wait to see my little nugget." Monique half smiled.

"So, baby, what's going on? Why haven't James at least been to the hospital to see you?" Helen took off her sweater hanging it over the back of the chair then walked to the window opening the blinds.

"James…" She breathed hard. "James doesn't want to be with me anymore. I don't know why." Monique looked toward the window.

"What happened? When did this happen?" Helen looked confused. Last, she knew James was crazy about Monique and Monique crazy about him.

"Momma, you just don't know the half of what's been going on in my life." Monique locked eyes with her mother.

"I know we've had our differences, but I want to be here for you. Talk to me what's going on? Why did you try to take your own life?" Helen sat in the chair next to Monique's bedside.

"Momma, do you see me? This is me now. What good am I to myself or my child? I'm useless." Monique's eyes began to water.

"Baby, don't say that." Helen dropped her head trying not to let her watered eyes show.

"Momma, I wasn't working." Monique dropped her head. "James told me he wanted me to focus on nursing school. He would handle the bills. I guess he got fed up with…" Monique sat lost for words. "I really don't know what happened, but he decided his family wasn't what he wanted anymore, so he left. He told me he would pay the bills for three more months. After that, I was on my own. I had a little bit of money saved up from grants from school to pay the bills, but that wasn't enough. Momma, there were so many days I had to decide between paying for lights and water or food. Sometimes, I had no choice. We had to go without food." Monique wiped the tears from her cheeks. "Momma, some nights, Joshua would cry his stomach hurts, and it was because he was hungry." Monique wiped her eyes. "There were so many days I cried. I would sit and cry asking God what to do. I asked Him to make a way for us to have food to eat. Sometimes, my prayers went unanswered, and I started to doubt. But it's so crazy because I know how real God is. I've seen Him make ways for people." Monique stared with a serious but confused look in her eyes. "I just couldn't understand why He wasn't making a way for me. It's like everyone around me was being blessed but me. You just don't know how bad it hurt me to not be able to feed my baby. I would walk to the refrigerator knowing nothing was in it, hoping God somehow made a way for something to appear. I thought about going to the store to steal something to eat, but I couldn't bring myself to that." She cried. "He came around to lay up and make false promises," she mouthed.

"Baby, you could have called me. You know I would have been there." Helen sat next to Monique's bedside, clutching her purse as tears dripped from her eyes at all Monique was speaking. "Baby, just because God didn't do it for you that time doesn't mean He couldn't." Helen grabbed Monique's hand.

"Momma, I couldn't call you. You made it very clear." Monique silenced staring at the ceiling. "I couldn't get assistance because me and James were still legally married. They said he made too much." Monique sighed. "I've been through so much. It's hard going through and not having anyone by your side. You just don't know. I feel like such a failure to myself and my child. I feel like I'm constantly failing."

"Baby, just because you hit a rough patch in life doesn't mean you're a failure. I'm here now. You don't ever have to worry about anything like that again." Helen stood up hugging Monique.

"Momma, the day before everything happened, I got an eviction notice. It was just too much for me. James filed for divorce, and it felt like my life was crumbling into pieces. I even thought about taking Joshua out with me, but then I thought what if he died and I didn't. Sometimes, I felt like he would be better off without me, and now I'm back in the same world I was trying to run from, having to go through and deal with the same things plus more."

Helen took a deep breath, speechless at the words that came out of Monique's mouth. She could see she was hurting and how she was wearing her hurt.

"I just wish it wasn't like this. I wish I wouldn't have woken up. Why me is all I keep asking."

"Baby, why not you? We all have problems and issues, but that's only to make us strong, stronger in our faith, and it allows us to see the strength within ourselves." Helen placed her purse on the bedside table. "You can't let your issues break you, and you can't let your pain make you."

Helen and Monique both wiped their eyes at the sound of a knock on the door.

Two Caucasian males dressed in uniform walked through the door.

"Hi, I'm Paul and this is Sam." Paul reached to shake Monique's hand. Sam stood by throwing up a wave.

"Hi." Monique smiled, wondering what these men where there for.

Paul looked at Helen smiling before turning his head back toward Monique. "We're the paramedics that responded to your sons 911 call. Ma'am, I have been praying for you. I'm so happy to see you alive. No one thought you'd make it." Paul smiled.

"Thank you for your prayers and thank you for stopping by." Monique smiled.

"Monique, you're a testimony of God's mercy and grace that He gives to us even though we're so underserving. Don't stop fighting. You've come too far to quit now." Paul smiled. "Well, we have to get going, but I just wanted to stop by. I went to the hospital to see you, and they told me you were moved here. It's good to see you. Take care of yourself." Paul and Sam smiled before leaving.

"See, baby, you have so many people that care about you. You should see there's more people that love you than people that don't. Just focus on yourself so you can get better and come home. I need you, and Joshua needs you more. You know there's more than enough space at my house where you and Joshua can be comfortable."

"I know, Momma." Monique stared at the television anchored to the wall. "You and Joshua are really all I have left." She yawned.

"Those men were so nice to come by and visit. Once you're up to it, I have someone I want you to meet. She's a nice lady. She came and prayed for you when you were in the hospital. She's the deputy who brought Joshua to my house the morning everything happened." Helen gazed up toward the television.

"Momma, I'm hurting so bad. I just want my husband. I want my family to stay together. I feel like a failure, my marriage is destroyed, and I don't even know who I am anymore." Monique rubbed her eyes.

"I know it hurts, baby, but it's not your fault. The most important thing you need to know is you have a beautiful blessing from that marriage who loves you unconditionally. Everything happens for a reason, and if it's meant to be, it will be." Helen smiled, shaking her head.

20

Tina

Tina walked into work two hours late. Everyone could see she didn't want to be there by the attitude she had and the way she responded to everyone. She went off on one of her coworkers for asking her why she hadn't come in or called into work the day before. Angry that Tina cussed and yelled in front of the clients, the owner pulled Tina into the office when they both finished their client's hair.

"Look, you know you're my girl and all, but this isn't going to work. I'm running a business. You come up in here when you want to, you leave your clients head undone, and lately, you don't even show up. You're changing, Tina. I don't know what you've got going on, but this isn't you. You're not the same. I'm sorry, but I'm going to have to let you go so you can find what it is you're looking for." The owner looked Tina in her eyes.

"After all the sacrifices I've made to work here, all the time and hard work I've put in this damn place! You're just gonna fire me like that. You know like I know I've been nothing but good to you and your business!" Tears began to fall from Tina's eyes.

"That's the problem, Tina. Nobody owes you anything. You can't come in here and do what you want and expect it to be okay. No matter how you feel right now, this is my name, my reputation. They're not just saying Tina does whatever she wants. They're saying that shop is so unprofessional, those people do anything in there. Haven't you heard one bad apple spoils the bunch? I'm sorry, Tina, you've been good to me, but I have to be better to myself. I have to protect my name and if you really cared, you would feel the same way. I have to live too. I have bills and employees to pay, and I can't do that without clients."

"The hell with you, this shop, and your clients. I don't need you or this shop, you need me!" Tina slammed her fist down on the counter. "I've made this shop blossom don't forget that." Tina walked out the office slamming the door behind her.

Clients as well as the workers looked at Tina as she walked out of the salon. They heard everything that was said and couldn't believe Tina, out of all people, was acting the way she was. Tasha, who worked in the booth next to Tina, wiped her eyes as tears fell. She was hurting for Tina and knew Tina was only acting out because of all she was going through. She knew people acted out the most when they felt everything was against them, and they had no one to lean on or be there for them while going through. She had the upmost respect for Tina and cried because she knew how close Tina and Mitch the owner was.

"Who does she think she is? I'm a damn good worker. Doesn't anybody care to see that I'm hurting? I'm the one going through a hard time!" Tina yelled as she walked to her car. She opened the driver door and sat with her hands on the steering wheel. "No, no, no!" She hit the steering wheel over and over before placing her head on the wheel crying. "Why is this happening to me?"

"Tina, this isn't easy for me. You're my friend, but I have to separate friendship from business. I have to." Mitch tapped on Tina's window.

"You're supposed to be here for me. You or no one else cares about what I'm going through. You're supposed to be my friend!" Tina cried.

"I love you, Tina. You know I'm here for you. I know this isn't you. You haven't been yourself lately. I'm sorry, but this is what's best right now. Just get yourself together and when you're ready to come back, call me. You know I would never want things to end like this. Our friendship is more than this." Mitch spoke through the window as tears rolled down her face. Mitch genuinely loved Tina, but she couldn't allow her business, the one thing she worked so hard to get, to go down because of someone.

"I'm sick and tired of you and everybody else hurting me." Tina started the car, staring Mitch in the eyes.

"Tina, roll the window down. Don't be like that, You know I only want the best for you, and as someone who claims they love and respect me, you should understand where I'm coming from."

"You out of all people know what I'm up against. I'm losing everything. I lost my husband, and I don't have anyone here for me. I don't care anymore, Mitch. I don't care about this friendship. I don't care about this job, and I don't care if I ever speak to you again." Tina talked through her teeth.

"Tina, you don't mean that. Come on now. I love you. We're friends." Mitch wiped her eyes.

"Yea, well, friends don't hurt friends especially when they're already down." Tina sped off.

Mitch called Tina over and over. After Mitch's thirteenth time calling, she left a voice message: "Tina, I want you to know I love you, and I'm going to always love you. We have been friends for a long time, and I'm not going to let this situation come in between that. You know at the end of the day, I got your back just like you've always had mine. I just want you to get yourself together, Tina. You're not the same person anymore. There will always be a spot here for you. Just get a grip, Tina, please. I love you girl and I'm here. Call me whenever you want to talk. Bye, girl."

****

"James." Tina cried into the phone as soon as he answered.

"Tina, what's going on? What's wrong?" James questioned.

"I really need someone to talk to. I just don't know anymore." Tina continued to cry.

"What's wrong? Do you want me to come over?"

"Yes, but I have to go get my girls first. Can you meet me at my house in an hour?" Her voice was shaking from all the crying she was doing.

"Yes, Tina, I'm on my way. I'll wait for you if I get there before you. Do you need anything?"

"No, I just need you," Tina said before hanging up.

****

The ride home from picking up Lina and Ava was quiet. They knew something was wrong with their mother. They knew when she was in one of her moods to leave her alone and let her stay to herself. Lina was tired though. She was tired of seeing her mother hurting and tired of not being able to do anything about it. Twenty-six minutes after being picked up from school, they arrived home. James hadn't made it to Tina's yet but was on his way.

"Mama, do you want me to get you anything?" Lina hugged her mother when they walked into the house.

"No, baby, I'm okay. I love you, Lina." Tina rubbed Lina's face.

"I hate when you're hurt, Mama. You know, if I could, I would take on all that hurt you feel so you wouldn't have to hurt anymore." Lina looked up into her mother's eyes.

"Baby, I wouldn't want you to hurt. I'm okay, baby. I'll be okay." Tina kissed Lina's forehead. "Go get you and your sister a snack and get started on homework."

Five minutes later, there was a knock on the door.

"Tina, I've been so worried about you." James hugged Tina when she answered the door.

"James, I got fired. I got fired. What am I going to do now?" Tina cried in his arms.

"What happened?"

"I don't know. I guess they got tired of me slacking. What do they expect? I'm going through so much, so many emotions. No one cares how I feel and I'm sick of it." Tina wiped her eyes. "I'm sorry, come in."

James sat on the couch next to Tina. He wasn't sure if he should hold her or just sit and listen. It was eating him up inside that her daughters were home. He really wanted to be there for her more than as a friend and he wondered if his friendship to Tina went further, would her daughters accept him?

"I want you to meet my girls." Tina stood up walking to the dining room table getting her girls.

"There's someone I want you to meet," Tina said.

"Who, Mama?" Ava looked up with a piece of fruit roll up hanging from her mouth.

"My friend, I think you'll like him. He knew of your daddy. He's a police officer too."

The girls went to the living room where James sat. Lina stared at him as Ava stood next to her folding her arms.

"It's nice to meet you, lovely little ladies. You girls are so beautiful." James smiled.

"Thank you." Lina and Ava both stared at James.

"I want to be here for you girls and your mother. If you ever need anything, I will help." James looked at Tina, smiling.

"Okay, it's nice to meet you," Lina said before turning around walking back to the dining room table.

She was upset but didn't want Ava to know. She wondered why this man was in their house and why he was trying to be so friendly to them and their mother.

"Lina, why is that man here? Why is Mama with that man?" Ava sat down at the table looking over at Lina.

"I don't know. She said he knew of Daddy. Maybe he was one of Daddy's friends." Lina looked down at her homework paper.

"So, what are your plans now?" James leaned into Tina, putting his arm around her shoulder.

"I don't know." Tina began to cry again.

"Tina, whatever you need, I'm here for you." James kissed her neck.

"James, I'm already getting behind on bills. I have no clue how I'm going to make it. I have two girls that depends on me now. I don't know what to do anymore." Tina laid her head on James's chest.

"Tina, didn't I tell you I'm here for you. Figure out your bills, and I'll take care of it."

"I can't, James, you have your own things to worry about I'm sure." Tina looked up at James.

"Tina, stop. I'm good on my end, just let me know so I can help you."

"I don't know how I will ever repay you." Tina smiled, wiping her eyes.

"You don't have to repay me, just let me be here for you."

"Why do you care so much, why?" Tina looked up at James.

"Because I love you." James looked in to Tina's eyes. "You're a real woman, a queen, and I want to see you live as one."

"James… I think I love you too." Tina rubbed his face. "I want you to have me, James." She closed her eyes.

"Tina, I want you only if you really mean it."

"I mean it." Tina opened her eyes looking James in the eyes.

James sat holding Tina for twenty more minutes before leaving. He was happy he was winning her over. She was beautiful and the type of woman he could see himself being with. Whatever it was going to take, he was willing to do to as long as he could have Tina as his.

21

Tina

"Ma, you just don't know the pain I feel, the dreams I have. You just don't know." Tina looked down at the white carpet.

"Baby, we're all hurting. Trust me, you lost a part of your family, but I lost a piece of my flesh, my heart, the child of my womb. I don't think you could ever understand how bad it hurts to lose a child unless you've been in that situation. He was a piece of me, growing inside of me for nine months. Alvin was everything to me. From the moment I gave birth and laid eyes on him, I cherished him. Trust me when I say each day that goes by gets harder to deal with, but I fight and that's what you have to do to."

"I'm tired of fighting. Some days, I'm like what am I even fighting for. I'm depressed. I'm doing everything by myself, and the truth is, I don't have anyone. I'm alone. I'm just being honest." Tina stared at the picture of Kevin, her and the girls that hung on the wall. "I feel like giving up." A tear rolled down her cheek.

"Sometimes, when we're weak, we can feel like giving up, but giving up doesn't change or solve anything, baby. You'll just end up hurting those that love you and especially your girls. They need you and worry about you. Doesn't that matter to you?" Alvin's mom stood up from the recliner chair sitting next to Tina on the love seat. She wrapped her arms around her waist, pulling her into her chest as balls of tears fell from Tina's eyes. "It's okay, I love you. It's okay," she whispered into her ear.

"Why do the people I love always end up leaving me? It's not fair. Life isn't fair, man."

"Baby, this is something I've had to come to terms with. Life is very fair, no matter our upbringing and no matter our shortcomings, we all have opportunity in life. Life is very fair. It's the people in it that can make it unfair. And that's our situation right now. It wasn't life that caused us pain but the choices of another."

"It's just not fair." Tina began to cry hysterically, her body shaking.

"Baby, no one can tell you how to grieve or how long to grieve for. I cry every day, but the truth is, life is still going on, and you have to have some kind of control before your grief takes you out. I'm here for you, and although I'm not physically here in this house with you, I'm here for you praying and here if you ever need to talk." Sonya hugged Tina. Her voice was matured yet warm and stern.

"Ma, I don't want prayer! I don't want anything to do with God. If He can't bring my husband back, then I don't want anything to do with Him! Didn't he supposedly raise Lazarus from the dead? Didn't He raise the dry bones? If He did all of that, then what's the problem? Why can't He bring my husband back?" Tina pushed back from Sonya's grip. "God this, pray that. I did all that and look how it got me, hurt and messed up." Tina stood up running to the wall, punching it over and over. "I hate God! He's the reason I'm hurting. He's the reason my husband and brother are dead. He's the reason I'm losing everything. I can't take this anymore. Ma, I hate waking up. Why is God punishing me?" Tina punched the wall until her knuckles began to bleed and a small hole appeared in the wall.

Sonya, Alvin's mother, jumped up walking to Tina grabbing her. Tina dropped to the floor as Sonya dropped with her holding her.

"Baby, it's not God's fault. You have to understand that."

"I hate Him!" Tina whined as tears and snot ran down her face and lips. She fought to talk as her words were overpowered by her emotions and tears. "I just want my baby back." Tina whined, grabbing her hair then covering her face.

"Baby, giving up and going away from the God who loves you so much can prove deadly results. No matter how you feel, you have to hold onto His words."

Tina and Sonya sat on the floor as Tina cried.

"His Word is a lie!"

"Tina, if I didn't love you, I wouldn't tell you the truth. Your little feelings and emotions are going to send you straight to hell. You have allowed this to enter your heart. It's hurting me so bad hearing you talk like this. What happened to your faith? And you know what, the sad part about how you feel is, God said He would never leave you nor forsake you. You're mad at God and He's still here, loving you unconditionally despite how you feel about Him. You better get yourself together if you want to make it to heaven." Sonya looked Tina in the eyes with a stern look. "You mean to tell me you've been through church service after service, fast after fast, and consecration after consecration just to go to hell? You better think about what you say and how you feel. Don't blame God when all He's ever done is love, protect, and be with you. It hurts like hell, but at the end of the day, God thy will be done, and I don't know about you, but whatever God says, it is well with my soul," Sonya talked firmly.

"How can you say it is well? This is messed up."

"Girl, I didn't say it doesn't hurt, I didn't say I'm happy with what happened, and I didn't say I wanted them to go like that, but what can us people do? God is God, when you realize that, you'll be able to understand. God's will will always rule. It doesn't matter what we want when God has the final say."

Tina sat motionless crying. She knew Sonya was right. She knew God was the great I AM, and nothing or no one could change that. She just couldn't come to terms and understand why He would let this happen.

"I'm hurting and angry, but I will not fight against God. I will not try to understand this on my own, and I will not curse God. I'm going to love God harder. I don't know why He allowed this to happen, but He has my full attention now, and I'm going to yield to his voice and plan for my life. I want to make it into heaven when that time comes and see my baby again one day. You better think before God turns you over to a reprobate mind for good." Sonya looked at Tina. "Lean not to your own understanding, it will fail you every time."

"I just don't know anymore." Tina wiped her eyes.

"What if Kevin had survived? He was paralyzed, he suffered a brain injury from the bullet and was unable to speak." Sonya looked toward the window as she talked. "You would have your husband still, and every day you would watch him suffer. You would probably pray to God still, but because of the state your husband was in, you would slack on your relationship with Him. Would you still feel the same way? Would you really want to watch your husband suffer like that?"

"No." Tina dropped her head.

"Baby, we don't know the future. We couldn't have possibly known the outcome of that situation. That's why we must trust God has our best interest at heart. We don't know if Kevin would have been in a worse state if he would have survived. You can't blame God. His purpose may not make sense to us, but it makes sense. We just have to trust it. Baby, all I'm trying to get you to understand is, we couldn't predict the outcome and we couldn't predict if it would have been too much for Kevin or Alvin to bear had they survived."

"But it would have at least been worth seeing what the outcome would have been."

"Tina, you're being selfish and thinking only about yourself. I'm hurt, but I would never want to see someone suffer, especially someone I love." Sonya stared off. "I love my baby too much to see him suffer."

"Ma…"

"Don't ma me. You know I'm telling you nothing but truth. I love you, Tina, as if you were my own child so it's even more crucial I tell you the truth. We don't live in a predictable world and surely, we don't serve a predictable God. Get it together, baby, please get a grip." Sonya placed her hand on Tina's hand. "You know why you can make it?" She squeezed Tina's hand gently.

"To be honest, I don't feel like I can make it."

"Tina, it doesn't matter how you feel. You can make it because God is with you and in you, and because you are a strong, beautiful, faith-filled woman. I have undoubtable faith in God, and I have faith in you."

"Ma, you always find a way to get through to me. I'm hearing what you're saying, but… I just don't know. Ma, I'm in pain. My heart is hurting and I'm angry."

"I know, baby, but somehow, some way, God will make your pain manageable. Somehow, I believe things will get better." Sonya looked at Tina as she now laid her head on her chest.

"You know, you're more like a mother to me. You've been there since my mother passed. All I see is strength in you even when you're hurting. I hope one day I can be strong like you."

"Baby, I'm weak. My strength is only because of God. That's why at this moment, we have to turn to God even more. If I hadn't turned to God with how I feel, I would be locked away in my room, grieving, I probably would have lost my mind. I'm not strong, baby, God is just giving me some of His strength."

Tina closed her eyes as she listened to Sonya's heartbeat. At that moment, she felt like a baby wrapped in its mothers' arms. She breathed softly as Sonya prayed for Tina to have the strength of God.

"I love you so much, Ma." Tina blinked away the tears that were starting to swell in her eyes.

"Tina, remember it's okay to hurt, but don't let that hurt steer you away from God." She quieted. "Now, help this old lady up from the floor before you have to call 911 to help get me up." Sonya laughed followed by Tina.

"Thank you for being here." Tina stood up. "It was nice seeing you." Tina took five steps toward the kitchen.

"Wait." Sonya laughed. "You better not leave me down here."

Tina began to laugh as she turned and walked toward Sonya. "Got you, I would never leave you, old lady." Tina smiled, helping Sonya up.

"Tina, I love you and kiss my babies for me." Sonya grabbed her purse from the couch, hugged Tina, then headed to the front door. "It's gonna be okay." She smiled, walking out the door.

22

Monique

"Come on, you can do it. I don't want to hear I can't. I know you can." The physical therapist looked sternly at Monique. Mona was Columbian native with a strong accent. She was very outspoken and was not afraid to say what was on her mind.

"I just want to die. Leave me alone!" Monique cried.

"You can't die. God won't let you. It's not your time so stop moping and try." Mona held on to the pink and blue gate belt around Monique's waist.

"I can't, I can't!" Monique stood both hands on the walker shaking.

"You will never accomplish anything with that attitude. If you want me to leave you alone, then try. I'm not interested in your cant's and no's."

"Let me call my husband first." Monique whined.

"Nope, not on my time. You can call him when you get done."

"You witch." Monique rolled her eyes.

"Oh, honey, I've been called worse. Come on walk, you can do it."

Monique took five steps before falling back into the wheelchair that sat locked behind her.

"I told you, it can be done if you just try. It'll get better each day, but you have to push yourself. I don't care about what you say you can't do. Focus on what you can do." Mona leaned in hugging Monique. "I'm going to be tough on you because that's what you need right now, not someone babying you."

"What I need is for God to give me my husband back or let me die." Monique put her head down.

"Honey, God didn't take your husband. We blame Him for too much. And dying's not an option so when you think of something real good, let me know." She wheeled Monique back to her room for a ten-minute break to call her husband.

Monique was a wreck. She was unmotivated, depressed, and angry at everyone but herself. Every thirty minutes, she was away from her room. She would whine and complain to go back so she could call James, the man who she refused to believe was ignoring her calls on purpose. This man had her stuck on stupid to the fact he could care less about her situation and what was going on with her. After ten minutes, Mona went back to the private room to get Monique, so they could finish her therapy session.

After ten minutes of not getting anywhere, Monique began to whine.

"Please take me back to my room. I need to call my husband. It's important." Monique wheeled herself toward the double doors trying to leave the therapy room.

"Why do you keep calling that man? He doesn't care. You're stressing yourself out." Mona's accent made every word she spoke sound vivid.

"He's just a busy man, and I'm not doing anything until I call him!" Monique rolled her eyes, her voice increased with attitude.

"You know what, you just go. I hope you open your eyes soon." Mona's frustration with Monique's lack of concern for her own well-being grew.

Monique wheeled herself down the hall back to her private room calling James. After the fourth unanswered call, she began to cry.

"Why is he doing this to me?" Monique pushed the phone off the bedside table in a rage causing it to smash to the floor, making a loud noise that radiated the busy halls. "After all we've been through, he's gonna act like this with me." She stared at the unhooked phone on the floor.

"Somebody help me!" Monique began yelling to the top of her lungs until an aide came to assist her.

"What's wrong?" The aide rushed through the door.

"Pick up my phone before my husband calls. He should be calling soon." Monique rolled herself backward to clear the way for the aide to reach the phone.

"This lady, ugh, she makes me so mad!" Mona could be heard walking down the hall to Monique's room. "You see, you have to care about yourself. You can't get better trying to make someone care about you." Mona walked into the room. "Let's go now, back to therapy!" Mona grabbed the wheelchair handles, pushing Monique as she cried in anger.

"I just want to die. I wish I would have died!"

"So, what about your son? He needs you. I'm going to tell you something you need to hear." Mona stood in front of Monique's chair locking eyes with her. "You're the most selfish, inconsiderate person I've ever met. You placed your life in the hands of a man that doesn't love you, and you've based your happiness and health on that. If you don't want to get better and live that's fine, but don't make that baby suffer with you. Your son loves you so much, and it's so sad he loves you and you don't love him." Mona began speaking faster. "I don't care, I'm a witch, say what you want about me, but you know, I'm telling the truth!"

"You don't know me. I love my son. Don't come for me!" Monique wiped her eyes.

"Oh yeah, you love him, then start acting like it." She wheeled Monique in front of the mirror wall. "What do you see?" Mona stared into the mirror looking at Monique. "Look into the mirror now!"

"I don't know." Monique looked up then dropped her head.

"Look now, look at yourself. What do you see?"

"I see someone who's ugly and crippled." Monique stared into the mirror; tears began falling down her face, dripping on her shirt.

"What do you want to see? Look into the mirror." Mona walked to the side of Monique lifting her chin.

"I don't know." She paused, her heart pounding.

"Look, look within yourself. What do you want to see within yourself?"

"I want to see a woman that's strong… independent and loving. I want to see a woman who knows her worth and what she has to offer the world." She wiped her eyes as tears continued to fall. "I want to see a woman who loves her son more than a man, a woman who loves God and has the characteristics of God. I want to see a woman who knows there's no other side than the side of God." Monique's voice began to crack. "I want to see a woman who has the type of joy no man can take away…" She paused again. "That's it." Monique sniffled.

"That's not it. Look at yourself in the mirror. What do you see? Look into your eyes." Mona rubbed Monique's shoulder.

Monique stared into the mirror considering her own eyes. "I want mental stability. I want to see myself free. I want to be free. I don't want to see myself hurting. I don't want to see myself weak. I want to see myself smiling and loving the abilities God has given me." Monique reached toward the mirror as if to touch her reflections face. "I want to see myself as beautiful again." She dropped her head this time, sobbing.

"I see a woman who has lost herself and her way because of her own self. I see a woman who is in a battle for her life but is stuck in the middle of the fight." Mona kneeled beside Monique, rubbing her arm. "I see a woman who could have been dead, but she has so much to offer the world. I see Monique Austin. She's trapped right now, but she must believe it won't be like this always. You can fight against God and yourself, but sooner or later, you're gonna realize fighting against God won't get you anywhere and you'll come to your senses." Mona stood up hugging Monique.

"I just wish I could die." Monique continued to sob; this time, crying within silently.

"You know the only reason you want to die is because you think dying will stop the pain, and you feel dying would make everything you're going through easier to handle. But it won't do anything but hurt the ones that really love you and leave them to clean up the mess and pick up the pieces without you." Mona kissed Monique's cheek. "I'll let you sit in here and calm down. Monique, you have to believe you're an amazing person and live." Mona smiled before leaving Monique to herself.

"So, what you in for?" An older Caucasian lady slowly wheeled herself in the therapy room five minutes after Mona had left. She stopped her wheelchair next to Monique's chair. She appeared to be in her early sixties. Her eyes were mesmerizing blue, which complemented her snow white hair. Her skin presented only a few wrinkles, which helped with her appearance and fooled many to the fact she was four years shy of eighty.

"In for? This isn't jail," Monique mumbled under her breath. "I'd rather not say. I guess to get strength." Monique spoke, rolling her eyes.

"Ummhmmm, whelp." The old lady smacked her lips. "You know, I see you have a brain. You just don't use it all the time." She stared in the mirror looking in Monique's eyes.

"What?" Monique blurted out. *Should I be offended?* she thought.

Her bluntness caught Monique off guard. She knew nothing about Monique and obviously could care less about the mental or emotional state Monique was in. "I ask a question, you look at me like a deer in headlights. I don't know. If you just think and really use your brain, you'll be okay." She threw her hands up.

"Sylvia, what have I told you?" Mona's voice echoed down the hall as she walked to the therapy room.

"She's coming, quick, play possum." Sylvia the old lady dropped her head to appear as if she was asleep.

Monique looked at Sylvia like she had lost her mind. "Now you came in here telling me to use my mind." Monique stared at Sylvia.

"Sylvia, stop bugging this poor lady." Mona walked in, pushing Sylvia toward the door. "Come on, lift your feet so I can push you."

"I'm old, I'm old, and I'm blind." Sylvia blurted out. "Susie, is that you? Yoohoo, yoohoo."

"Sylvia, cut it out." Mona sighed. "Why do you always give me a hard time? What am I going to do with you? You're not blind.

You're making me go crazy." Mona pushed Sylvia to her room then went back to therapy.

"I'll give you a break today, but tomorrow, it's time to get to work." She wheeled Monique back to her room, transferring her into her bed to calm herself and rest. "You're going to make it." She smiled before leaving the room.

23

Detective Hanks was the lead on the case involving Kevin and Alvin. Nine months seemed too long for a fugitive to be out in the free world on the run. Especially for killing someone in blue. Detective Hanks as well as Detective Winston spent countless hours following up on leads that turned into dead ends. Many nights' sleep was lost, but they vowed to catch the person who was as heartless as the devil himself. Detective Hanks gave his partner the task of contacting Tina to follow up with her on the case and bring her some if any news.

It was Friday morning as the phone rung waking Tina from her sleep.

"Hi, can I speak with Mrs. Starr?"

"Yes, who's calling?" Tina spoke as the grogginess in her voice sounded. She coughed trying to clear her throat. The voice on the other end of the phone sounded somewhat familiar as Tina squinted her eyes trying to put a face with the voice.

"Ma'am, this is Detective Winston working the case of your husband and brother." There was a brief silence. "Do you have time today where we can stop by your house and speak with you?" Detective Winston paused. "I know it's been hard not hearing any news."

"Umm yes, sure." Tina quieted. "I'll call my mom over. She's Alvin's mother." Tina wiped her crusted eyes. "Lord knows, I can't handle any more bad news."

"Okay, sounds good. Detective Hanks and myself will be over around twelvish, does that work for you?"

"Yes, that's fine." Tina closed her eyes as she laid on the pillow holding the phone to her ear.

"Okay, see you then." Detective Winston smiled.

"All righty." She hung up the phone. She placed the cordless phone on her night stand, picked up her cell phone, checking the time, then laid it back on the nightstand, quickly drifting back off to sleep.

****

Around 10:37 a.m., Tina awoke. She picked up her cell phone sending Sonya a text asking her to come over to her house by 11:50 a.m. In the text, she told her she needed support for the bad news she was about to get. Sonya quickly texted back telling Tina she would be there and bring lunch for them. This also made it easier for the detectives, so they wouldn't have to make two separate stops to deliver the news.

Tina sat up in bed, rubbing her hands over her knees. She sighed as she got out the bed heading to the bathroom to brush her teeth and freshen up. She threw on a pair of jeans with a burgundy T-shirt, which read "there's power in the name of Jesus". She had gotten the shirt from a church event. Tina looked at herself in the mirror, which sat on her dresser. *I'm so sick of all of this*, she murmured then got back in the bed falling asleep.

****

Sonya arrived at 11:40 a.m. with grilled chicken and apple spring mix salad. She ordered strawberry balsamic vinaigrette to give the salad extra zest. With the dressing mixed in the salad, it was sure to have your taste buds dancing and rocking with flavor.

Sonya walked into the house calling Tina's name as she placed the bag of food on the table. "Tina, why is the door unlocked? Tina, you here?" she yelled.

"Ma, I'm upstairs. I'm coming." Tina rolled out of bed. She slowly walked down the stairs with sleep showing all over her face.

"Come on and eat before they get here." Sonya removed two containers of food from the bag.

Tina sat in the chair at the table where her food sat. It was now 11:52 a.m. and no sign of the detectives. Tina and Sonya finished their food and went to the family room turning the television on. Sonya sat in the recliner chair as Tina laid across the sectional couch.

"Ma, I'm so tired of no news. No news is as bad as bad news."

"In this situation, it is but whoever did that can't run forever." Sonya reclined the chair back.

"I wish this wasn't me. This wasn't us." Tina paused. "I wish it wasn't us going through this."

"Baby, Lord knows I wish the same thing. Lord knows." Sonya closed her eyes. She dozed off before being woken to the sound of knocking on the front door.

"I got it, Ma." Tina's body jumped at the sound of the knocking. She walked to the front door opening it.

"Hi, Mrs. Starr." Detective Hanks reached his hand to shake Tina's.

"Hello." She extended her hand shaking Detective Hanks's hand then Detective Winston. "Come on in. Alvin's mother is here too." She led them through the living room, dining room, and to the family room where Sonya sat.

"How are you?" Detective Winston walked up to Sonya shaking her hand as did Detective Hanks.

"I'm doing the best I can, taking it one day at a time."

"Please have a seat." Tina sat down looking at the detectives.

"Oh, we're okay. The reason we're here today is to let you know we've caught the person who killed your husband and brother. He was found in an abandoned house two blocks over from his mother's house. You can rest at least knowing this killer is off the streets."

"Can I see him?" Tina looked at Detective Hanks as tears began to roll down her face.

"Ma'am, if you really want to see him, I can arrange for that to happen."

"Well, did he say why he did it?" Sonya covered her mouth with her hand.

"You know, he's trying to play the hard role. He's not talking much."

"I prayed and prayed and prayed. Thank you, Jesus! I prayed to God to let the police catch the person that did this. Every night, I told God I trusted Him, and I knew He would cause the person to be caught. I'm just so happy he's in jail. Maybe we can start the healing process." Sonya cried. The hurt and pain she felt was felt through her talking.

Tina let out a sigh as she wiped her face with her hands. "I hope he rots in hell!"

Sonya sat speechless as her and Tina continued to cry. They were happy the man who destroyed their families was in jail, and even with all the bad Tina wished on his life, it didn't help in taking her pain away or making her feel any better. It made her that much madder he was still alive and her family was dead.

"When can I see him?" Tina looked down at the carpet.

"If it works for you, I can arrange for you to have a visit with him tomorrow. Whoever wants to go, I'll come by and pick you up by eleven in the morning."

"I can't, I can't. I can't face him yet." Sonya shook her head as she began to sob harder.

"That's perfectly fine. It's up to you." Detective Hanks walked over to Sonya rubbing her back. "I'm sorry we've had to come to you for this, but I'm glad he's off the streets and in jail. So, we'll come by tomorrow to take you. I hope you can start to heal for yourselves." Detective Hanks hugged Tina then Sonya. "Once again, I'm sorry for your loss."

****

Tina tossed and turned all night. She thought of every possible scenario on how the visit would turn out. She thought of what she could possibly say and how she would act. She even thought about jumping across the table and attacking the man. She knew it was going to be hard to face her husband's killer, but she wanted him to look into her eyes and tell her why. Sonya, on the other hand, was glad the man was behind bars and told detectives she would be at every court date. She decided to really leave it all in God's hands. Sonya was going to be picking up Lina and Ava for the weekend when they got home from school, so Tina could catch a break and focus on her visit to the jail. Sonya also knew how the girls noticed a change in their mother, so they hid their pain to make sure she was okay. She wanted the girls to get out of the house and enjoy being kids. She had already planned their whole weekend out. Lina and Ava's faces are what helped her to stay sane, and she loved every minute she got with them. Inside, it was apparent the girls were hurting, and that's why Sonya did what she could to take their mind off the pain they felt.

****

Tina didn't sleep much. She woke at 6:00 a.m. with no appetite. Her emotions had her going crazy, as her thoughts ran rapid. Time quickly flew, and it was now 10:47 a.m. Tina was dressed and waiting on the front porch for Detective Hanks. He had called saying he was coming up the street. A minute later, a black Tahoe pulled in the driveway. Tina stood up, jingling the door handle, making sure it was locked before walking to the car.

"Good morning." Tina smiled as she opened the car door behind the driver's seat.

"Good morning." Detective Winston looked back, smiling at Tina.

The twenty-minute ride to the jail was quiet. Tina clutched her purse tightly. She was filled with so many emotions as she tried to gather her thoughts.

"Okay, we're going to go in now. It's up to you if you want us to be in the room with you or outside the door. He'll be hand-cuffed so he can't harm you." Detective Hanks talked as they walked through security.

Once at the door that separated Tina from the man she considered to be her worst enemy, Detective Winston grabbed Tina's hand then hugged her.

"I can do this," Tina spoke softly. "I... I want to go in alone." She hesitated to get her words out.

"We'll be right here. If you need us, tap on the glass. We're watching. You can do this." Detective Winston rubbed Tina's back.

Tina took a deep breath as she stood in front of the metal door staring at it before opening it and walking in the room. She sat in the chair across from the man who had caused her so much pain. At that moment, everything she had planned to say vanished from her memory. Tina sat staring at the dark brown face in front of her. His appearance was not what she had expected it to be. She envisioned she would be staring at someone muscular and intimidating, yet the face she stared at was younger than she imagined and scared. His hair was messy, his eye was black, his face was cut up, and his lips swollen. The man before her didn't say a word. His head hung low as he tried to avoid eye contact. He had no clue who the woman was who sat before him, and he had no desire to talk to anyone.

"I tossed and turned all night. I had it all planned out what I would say to you." Tina silenced. "What's your name?" She slapped her hand on the table.

"Reggie. Aye, man, I'm innocent. The police beat me up for nothing. I ain't kill nobody." Reggie sucked his teeth.

"You're just as stupid as they say you are." Tina's anger flared. "You took my best friend away from me. You took my kids' father away from them. You took my brother away. I hope you rot. I hope you never get the chance to walk the streets again! You're trash and a waste of breath. You don't deserve to live. I hope you rot in prison!" Tears rolled down her face while she talked through her teeth. There was fire in her eyes, anger and hurt filled her face, and Tina was a second away from losing it.

"Man whatever." Reggie sucked his teeth.

"Go ahead and suck your teeth again. It's nobody stopping me from knocking the hell out of you. You're weak and you deserve every bad thing that comes to you. I hope you feel pain worse than what you've caused me to feel. I will be at every court date to make sure of it you never walk as a free man!" She pounded her fist on the table. "Why? Why? Over some cigarettes and lotto tickets or whatever it was. Tell me why dammit!" Spit flew from Tina's mouth landing on the table.

"Lady, I ain't kill nobody!" Reggie yelled.

"Shut up! It's on tape. It's all on tape. You really are as dumb as you look. I pray God has no mercy on you!" Tina wiped the tears from her cheeks. "You're worthless you bastard!"

Reggie sucked his teeth. He waved his hands trying to get the attention of the guards to take him back to his cell.

"You're mine. You ain't going nowhere. You're a reject, you've probably been one your whole life. I know your mother is ashamed you even came from her womb," Tina spoke from her anger.

"You don't know nothing, nothing about me or my family." He rolled his eyes.

"And guess what, smart ass, you will never see them again if I have something to do with it." Tina stood up, punching Reggie in his already swollen, bruised eye.

Reggie screamed out in pain, as tears began to fall from his eyes.

"I hope you cry, just like you've caused me and my family to cry. You could have just run, you didn't have to shoot them. You're a heartless coward. Now tell my why you killed them!" Tina yelled as she pounded her fist on the table over and over. The sound of her voice echoed off the walls.

"You better go in there," Detective Winston said, looking at Detective Hanks.

"No one can help you now." Detective Hanks walked in the room laughing. "You're just a scary punk, and guess what?" He leaned into Reggie's face. "I'm the only one stopping her from smacking you so I suggest you tell her what she wants to hear."

"Man, I ain't done nothing. Y'all can't do this." Reggie smacked his lips.

"I can do what I want. Look around, no one cares about you and no one cares to help you." Detective Hanks sat on the table next to Reggie.

"I hope your mother feels pain like I feel!" Tina stared Reggie in the eyes. "You have destroyed my family, and as long as I live, I will never forgive you. Your scum and I hope every day you wake up you suffer!" Tina stood up. "I'm ready." Tina looked at Detective Hanks. "You're going to rot!" Tina looked Reggie in the eyes before walking out the door.

"I'll do my bid. It ain't nothing," Reggie yelled as the door slammed shut behind Tina and Detective Hanks.

"I promise we'll do everything we can to make sure he pays for what he did. I know it won't bring back your family, but at least, he'll be off the streets getting what he deserves." Detective Hanks talked as they left the jail heading to the car.

24

"Stop, that's my husband's car!" Tina ran out the front door in a silk night gown and a pair of bedroom slippers yelling, trying to open the car door to get in the driver's seat. "Please stop! You can't take his car!" She pounded on the passenger side window after realizing the doors were locked.

It was still dark outside; the air was chilly with a slight breeze. Porch lights lit up the street, while the stillness made it evident of a sleeping neighborhood. Lina and Ava were still asleep, unconscious to their mother's shouts.

"You can't take my husband's car." She ran to the front of the tow truck. "Please, please, please, stop. Please don't take the car." She laid her hands on the hood of the truck, watching the driver's eyes as he stared unsettled behind the steering wheel.

"Why do they do this to me?" the driver of the tow truck mouthed as he sighed.

"Please, this is all I have left, please." Tina whined, as tears began forming.

The driver got on his phone calling his boss. "Jim, man, we can't do this. This lady is breaking down. Isn't their anything we can do?"

"It's a job and that's what you're there to do," he replied. "If we went around trying to help everyone, we would be out of a job. Pay your bills and you won't have these types of problems. That's what you ought to say." Jim laughed before being hung up on.

"Ma'am, I'm sorry." The driver got out the truck walking toward Tina. He handed her a card from his wallet. "You can call this number and explain your situation. They'll be able to help you. You just have to be honest with them."

She stared at the card in the man's hand.

"Ma'am, just call." He moved his hand closer toward Tina. "I'm sorry." He stared into her burdened eyes.

"Okay." Tina grabbed the card dropping her head. She sat on the step of her door crying as she watched Kevin's car being towed away. "God, are you happy now? You took my husband away. Now you're taking everything I have left," she mouthed. "You're making me look like a fool in the process."

****

A few hours later, Lina and Ava awoke to get ready for school. Lina fully dressed went to the front door peeping outside to see if she needed a jacket.

"Mama, where's daddy's car?" She walked to the kitchen table sitting in the chair next to her mother.

"Baby, it's gone. They took it. They towed it away." Tina wiped her eyes before tears could fall.

"It's okay, Mommy. Don't worry, God will take care of everything." Lina looked over, smiling at her mother.

"Tell your sister to hurry up so I can get you two to school." She smiled, dismissing the comment Lina made.

****

Besides losing her husband's truck and not having a job, the constant calling of bill collectors made it more stressful. Her credit cards were maxed out and past due. She was late on her light bill, and her phone was due to get cut off any day now. Tina was stressed and felt she didn't know which way to turn. She had given up all hope God was all His word proclaimed Him to be, and her pride or the embarrassment of how things were going downhill made her fall back from asking for anyone's help. She knew she could always talk to her aunt about anything, and now was the time she needed to talk before she lost her mind. She laid on the couch and dialed the number to the one person she felt knew her best.

"Baby, what's wrong?" Aunt Berniece talked after hearing the tiredness in Tina's voice.

"Auntie, I don't know what to do. I don't know where to go. I'm so lost, and I don't know what to do." Tina sniveled.

"Baby, what's going on? Talk to me." Her voice was reassuring as well as calming.

"Auntie, I don't have money to move. I barely have money for gas. My bank account is depleted. They took Kevin's car. I'm losing my house. I lost my job, and I'm losing my mind. I can't afford to live here especially without Kevin. I don't know what I'm going to do. I have no clue where I'm going to go. I just don't know." Tina let out a deep breath. "I can't afford to take care of myself let alone my kids. Every time I try to sit and think about what I'm going to do, I can't because I have no clue where to even start."

"Baby, you know you're always welcomed here. I would love for you and the girls to come. Your family and my home is always open to you."

Aunt Berniece was worried about Tina and hearing all that she was faced with didn't help her worries.

"I wish I knew why all this was happening to me. Why is God punishing me? I think it would have been so much better if I had never been born." Tina rubbed her eyebrows. "Sometimes, I sit and think if God doesn't help me, I might as well be dead."

"Baby, don't just sit there and die. You must fight sometimes to see something happen. And, baby, your timing isn't God's timing. Stop trying to put a time on God. He always comes through. Sometimes, it seems like He comes at the last minute—in the hour where we feel we are about to pop. But He comes through just when we need Him."

"That's the thing, Auntie. I don't have any more fight left in me. I'm so tired you just don't understand."

"Baby, I don't understand, but what I do understand is, you're a strong black woman. You don't bend or break easily. You were made tuff. You are courageous, smart, and your presence is powerful. You have God in you, with you, and for you. There is nothing too hard that He can't fix. You weren't raised to give up so easily or throw in the towel. Stop dying in your troubles and fight."

"Okay, I love you. I'll call you later." Tina agitated, hung up the phone.

I'm tired of hearing about God and what's not too hard for Him. If that was the case, then where is He now or where was He when my husband needed Him? Tina thought as she closed her eyes.

A few moments later, the phone rang as Tina began to doze off.

"Hey, beautiful." The voice on the other end of the phone made her smirk.

"Hi."

"What's wrong? Are you sick or something?"

Tina sighed loudly. "James, I don't even know where to start." She paused. "I can't afford to live in this house without Kevin. Everything is due or past due, and I have to be out of this house soon. I don't know what I'm going to do. I feel so alone. My aunt said I could live with her, and I'm thinking that may be our best move considering we're losing everything. Ugh, why me?"

"Tina, I got you. I told you I'm here for you. I can get you a place. I just want to make sure you and your girls are okay." James paused, waiting for a reply.

"James, I can't let you do that, and plus, I'm not in the predicament to pay you back. I'm sorry. I know it's really not your problem. I'm just so stressed."

"You should learn to let people bless you and stop being so mean all the time." He laughed.

"I'm not mean." Tina began to relax her worries as she let out a giggle.

"You're just a big worry head." James joked. "A mean bag of worries. All I want to do is be there for you and your girls. Can I at least do that? Can I be your friend?" James smiled on the other end of the phone.

"I'll think about it." Tina began to blush. "I'm gonna get some rest, mister, but I'll think about everything you said and call you later." Tina laughed before hanging up the phone.

She closed her eyes again in deep thought.

If I let him get me a place, does that mean I'm moving on? I feel so guilty if I move on. I mean, it's so soon, and I still love my husband. Tina felt the warm sensation of tears rolling down her cheeks. *I'm not ready to move on. Moving on means I'll forget about what me and Kevin had.*

25

"Surprise, baby." James tightly gripped the rusted look-ing door handle as he swung open the front door to an apartment.

"Umm, this it?" Tina walked in with her nose scrunched up. "It's not what I was expecting, but I guess it's okay." A forged smile glowed on her face.

"Baby, come on now." He laughed. "This what I wanted to talk to you about." He held his arm around Tina's waist as they walked through the apartment's living room.

"Wow." Tina stopped in the kitchen, spinning around. "I can see my whole apartment from the kitchen." An unpleasant look covered her face.

"Baby, I know, but this is just a start. You see, I—" James smiled before Tina cut him off.

"Wow, I can literally see the whole apartment from right here in the kitchen," she said sarcastically and a bit in shock.

"Baby, I know it's not what you're used to. I know this, but I got fired from my job two weeks ago. You know I had to take a secu-rity job, baby," James mumbled, staring at the front door.

"What! You lost your job and you're just telling me this, now?" She turned, looking James in the eyes.

"Baby, it was all just a little mix up, a little misunderstanding. Don't worry." He wrapped his arm around Tina's shoulder. "It'll be worked out in no time, then we can get any house you want." He kissed the side of her neck.

"Umm hmm." Tina stared at the kitchen cabinets. "Wow, I can see my whole house from right here." Her head shook in disbelief.

"Come on now, can a man get some credit?" He smiled.

"I'll give you an E for effortless." She smirked.

James smiled not knowing what to say toward Tina's reaction.

"Baby, I know this is unexpected. I know, but we're gonna be okay." He kissed the side of her neck. "Baby, at least I can hold you at night."

"What, wait, so..." Tina stared at the floor. "What exactly are you saying?"

"Baby, this is our home. I put both our names on the lease. I'm gonna take care of you." James smiled.

"Wow, wow." Tina stared toward the door. "Is that even legal? I mean my girls have barely met you, and now we're moving in together?" Tina paused. "I don't know, James, maybe we're moving too fast. I mean I have to protect their emotions. I don't think they've fully come to grips with their father's passing. It's just I don't know."

"Tina, let me take care of you. I love you." James gripped Tina by the waist, pushing her to the kitchen counter. "I love you so much. I love the way you smell. I love the way you look at me. I love the way you sound when you get angry." James laughed, kissing Tina's mouth. "I love everything about you, and I want to be here to take care of you and your girls." He put his hand under her shirt sliding his hand on her smooth skin up to her breast. "Let me love you." He kissed her neck again.

"James, I'm scared of moving on." Tina closed her eyes.

"Just let me love you. I don't want to take his place. I love you, Tina." He kissed her nose.

"I want you, James." Tina leaned her head back against the kitchen cabinet.

"All I want is for you to want me." He unbuttoned his pants allowing them to drop to the floor.

Tina opened her eyes, staring James in the eyes.

"It's okay, Tina. I love you." He unbuttoned Tina's pants, wiggling them down to her ankles.

"James, I don't know." She closed her eyes. The heat of the moment filled her body. She pulled her shirt up over her head leaving her body exposed. The only thing that remained was her black silk bra.

"Let me be here for you." James began sucking on Tina's neck as he lifted her on the counter, inserting his manhood into her. "I've been waiting for this moment, Tina." He began kissing her breast.

"I love you so much." Tina moaned as she kissed James on his neck.

She had finally given in and given herself to another man—a man who wasn't her husband. Her spirit now connected and became one with James and her heart slowly burned with passion for him. At this moment, nothing mattered. Kevin or the commitment she had made with him, her morals or character, nothing. Nothing she had believed about primatial sex or soul ties. At that moment, Tina became lost in the feeling of a man's touch.

26

Tina

Tina lay in bed staring up at the ceiling. Earlier in the day, she received a letter stating she had to appear in court regarding the foreclosure of her home. She was stressed about the possibility of losing the home she and Kevin worked so hard for, but the heat and chemistry she and James shared occupied her mind. She couldn't help but think of how he loved on her the day before and the way he made her feel. Because of this, she planned to skip out on court and give up on fighting for her home. She knew there was no way she would be able to get the money needed to save her home from being fully foreclosed on, and besides that, she was excited about having a warm body to lay next to each night. Even if it were possible for her to save her home, she wouldn't. She desired James and couldn't bring herself to allow him to stay in the house Kevin once lived in.

She hadn't told her girls of the surprise move they would be making. She was kind of nervous of their reaction when they found out James would be moving in with them. She planned on telling them about the move the following morning considering it was now ten at night, and her girls were sound asleep in their room. She hoped they would accept James, but she was scared they would resent him, as well as her, for falling for a man who wasn't their father. They hardly knew him and had only met him once, so this news would be somewhat of a shocker. Regardless of how they felt, she was going to make the move, so she could finally move on and live her life.

****

"You're up early." Tina walked into the kitchen, staring at Lina as she poured a glass of orange juice.

"I'm thirsty." Lina closed the fridge, placing the glass of juice on the counter, hugging her mother.

"Baby." Tina paused. "I have to tell you and Ava some big news." She hugged Lina tighter.

"What, Mama?" Lina looked up at her mother.

"Maybe I should wait until Ava wakes up."

"Mama, tell me, come on." She smiled. "Are we getting a puppy or going on vacation. Oh, wait are we going to see Aunt Berniece?"

Tina walked over to the kitchen table pulling out a chair to sit in. She looked toward the stove looking at the clock, then at Lina. Her heart was beating fast, her leg shook, she tapped her fingers on the table. *Why am I so nervous?* she thought.

"Come sit." She signaled with her hand for Lina to sit.

Lina sat smiling. The look of sleep was fresh in her eyes. She fidgeted with her glass of juice on the table. She was excited at the big news. Her heart was beating fast too, from excitement, and a grin stuck on her face.

"Lina, we're moving." Tina put her hand on Lina's leg. "Me, you, Ava, and James. He's going to help us. We're moving together." She smiled.

"Wait, what, Mama?" Her grin slowly faded, confusion covered her face. "Who's moving?" She gulped. "James? That man?" She smacked her lips. "But why he got to move with us? And why do we have to move? I love my room. I love our house." She crossed her arms sucking her teeth.

"Lina, I can't afford this house without Daddy, and God ain't gonna pay these bills, James is. It's so much going on, baby. Too much for me and too much for you to understand."

"I don't want to move, and I don't want to move with that man!" Lina's eyes watered. "If we have to move, why can't we move with Aunt Berniece?"

"Baby, it's not easy for me either, but I have to do what I have to do." Tina leaned over, hugging Lina. "It's not so bad, at least we'll have each other."

"Well, I still don't want to live with that man." She rolled her eyes. "You're smiling like I'm supposed to be happy." Her eyes rolled again. "That man!" Lina frowned. "You don't even have a job, so I don't see why we can't move with Aunt Berniece."

Ava walked in the kitchen smiling at her mother as Tina stared at Lina wanting to slap the taste out of her mouth.

"Good morning, Mommy." She sat on her mother's lap.

"Ava, we have to move with that man!" Lina shouted.

"What man? We're moving?" She looked her mother in the face.

"Yes, baby, and James is moving with us."

"He is. Why?" Ava looked at Lina.

"That man is supposedly helping mama." Lina stared at her mother. "I don't see why he can't help from his own house."

"His name is James, not that man. Don't be disrespectful, Lina."

"I'm going to my room." Lina jumped up. "Talking about some that man is moving with us," she mumbled.

Lina ran to her room as tears began to fall. She was beyond upset, for one they had to move, and two, that man as she called him had to move with them. She laid in her bed staring at the door hoping her mother didn't walk through.

"Is that man gonna sleep in the room with Mama?" Ava walked in lying on her bed, looking up at the ceiling.

"I don't know. Your mother said he's gonna help with the bills. He can do that without staying with us." Lina rolled over facing the wall, wiping her face with her cover. "He's not our dad," she mumbled.

"I wish we didn't have to move." Ava glanced over at Lina. She got out her bed and into the bed with Lina.

"I promise we'll always have each other." Lina rolled over, staring Ava in the eyes. "It won't be so bad," she whispered, knowing what she was saying was a lie. She tried to convince herself things would be okay, but she knew she was only psyching herself to make herself feel better.

"If it's going to be okay, then why are you so mad?"

"Ava, that man is not our dad. That man doesn't even know us, and we don't even know him. Momma wants to take us from our home and move with that man. I'm pissed…"

"Well, I hope he doesn't sleep in the room with Mama. He better not try to take her away from us." Ava laid her head on the pillow.

"He better not because I'll set him on fire while he's using the bathroom. I'll block the door, so he can't get out, then I'll light something and throw it in the bathroom with gasoline." Lina laughed.

"Yep, then I'll be visiting you in jail." Ava and Lina both laughed.

Lina sighed. She let out a deep breath. "New house, new school, new friends, and that man." She sighed again. "This sucks," she mumbled.

27

"Would the defendant like to say anything?" Judge Houser spoke, staring down at a stack of papers sitting in front of her.

"At this time, Your Honor, my client has no further statements."

"Would the state like to say anything?"

"Yes, Your Honor, the defendant has hurt a lot of people because of his actions. He is a danger to society and should never be allowed out on the streets again. He's a heartless monster with no regards for the well-being of others. We are seeking the death penalty."

"Does the defendant understand the seriousness of his charges? And the punishment if he is to take this case to trial and lose?" Judge Houser looked up toward Reggie.

"Your Honor, my client is aware. At this time, he has not made a decision on what he will do."

"Okay, I'm going to postpone court for another month. I want you to understand you have to decide the next court date. We can't keep pushing court back, people need to get justice and move on with their lives." The judge spoke with an attitude, telling she was tired of talking.

"Yes, Your Honor, we understand." Reggie's public defender spoke.

Tina, Sonya, a few officers from the police force as well as Reggie's mother sat in the pews listening to what was being spoken. Reggie's mother did all she could to avoid eye contact with Tina and Sonya. In her mind, her baby was being wrongly accused. He told her he hadn't done it and up until then, he had given her no reason to feel like he was lying.

The judge banged her gravel as Reggie was escorted out through a side door that took him through many halls under the courthouse and back to the jail.

"I'm so sick of this. I just want this all to be over with." Tina walked out the courtroom, clutching her purse tightly.

"I know, baby, me too." Sonya walked next to her.

"Baby, I'm taking you for lunch before I take you home." Sonya started the car.

She picked up Tina, so they could ride to court and spend a little time together. They pulled up to a pancake house fifteen minutes later, where they served breakfast all day as well as burgers, pizza, wings, fries, and whatever else you wanted any time of day.

"Mama, I have to tell you something." Tina played with the strap on her purse.

"What is it, baby?" Sonya pulled into a parking spot, putting the car in park.

"Well…" she paused. "We're moving tomorrow." She looked out the window.

"What? Moving? For what?" Sonya stared at Tina. "Where are you moving to?"

"Well, James is getting us a place together." She paused again, avoiding eye contact with Sonya. "I can't afford the house. I lost my job. I can't do this without Kevin." Tina spoke softly.

"Baby, why, why are you just telling me this the day before you're moving, and with James? Who is James because I've never met him." Sonya continued staring at Tina.

"He's a good friend whose been helping me out, you know."

"Friend my ass, Tina, out of all people you know, you could have called me. How long have you known this man? You know what, never mind. Don't answer that. You're grown." Sonya spoke sarcastically. "What happened to you trusting in the Lord? What happened to knowing God will supply your every need?"

"Trust in the Lord this, hope in that. I'm tired of doing all that. It hasn't gotten me anywhere. Mama, God, or the Bible ain't helping me or my family."

"What's your problem? What's up with you? What's your issue with God?"

"He knows my issue. The God you serve and the scriptures you read are my issue. I was naive, because of that, my husband is dead, my brother is dead, and I'm losing everything." Tina rolled her eyes.

"No, your issue isn't with God. Your issue is with yourself. You know better, your emotions and how you feel ain't getting you nowhere." Sonya turned the car off, opening her door. "You need to get a grip! I lost my baby, but you don't see me around here acting a fool and talking like one." She got out the car. "You're moving with some man you barely know, and with my babies, and you talking about God is your issue, heifer you done lost your natural black mind." Sonya went on and on as they walked into the restaurant.

28

"Why do I have to help? I'm not the one that wants to move." Lina carried a box from the kitchen to the U-Haul outside.

"Lina, please, enough with your smart mouth. Just help and lose the attitude." Tina walked behind her, carrying another box that read fragile.

She sucked her teeth. "Well, I still shouldn't have to help," she mumbled.

"Little girl, this is my last time talking to you about your smart mouth. Shut it up and get your life together before you lose it." Tina cocked her head to the side.

"Well, why can't I move with Aunt Berniece then? At least, I'll want to be there." Lina dropped the box on the ground behind the U-Haul door.

"Because I'm your mother, and you will do what I say. And don't be dropping my boxes like that cause you ain't pay for nothing in it." She eyed Lina as she walked back into the house.

"Ugh, she gets on my nerves." Lina sat at the kitchen table.

James rented the U-Haul but had to work a double shift, so he wasn't available to help move. He insisted on them moving the next day, which was Sunday, but Tina said she wanted to be held by him when he got off work. She was excited yet at the same time sad to leave the home she and Kevin built together.

Tina walked into the kitchen wrapping her arms around Lina. "I love you, Lina, and I hope you can understand why I'm doing this. This is just as hard for me, but, baby, we need a fresh start, and I can't do this and live here without Daddy." She kissed the top of her head.

"Mama, just let me and Ava live with Aunt Berniece. She would be so happy if we stayed with her. She wants us to anyways." She looked up at her mother.

"The answer is no and that's final. Now let's get the rest of this stuff moved to the U-Haul so we can get it to the new place and unpacked."

****

"We're here." Tina smiled, backing the U-Haul up toward the steps of their apartment building.

"This is it?" Ava scrunched up her nose.

"Wait, Mama, if this is it, then James could have paid for us to continue living in our house." Lina looked toward Tina.

"Lina and Ava, it's small but be grateful." Tina smiled.

Once parked, Tina led the way as they walked up the stairs to their second-floor apartment. She put the key in the knob and turned it. The lock didn't budge.

"What, I know this the right key." Tina mumbled.

"Maybe this is a sign." Lina smirked.

"Hush, girl, this ain't no sign." Tina pulled on the door knob turning the key. The door popped open. "So, the trick is to pull the door in and turn the key at the same time," she mumbled.

"Mama, this is so small." Lina walked in spinning around. "This is like a, like a, hotel room but a little bigger. Mama, I don't want to stay here." Lina complained.

"Me either. I want to stay at our house." Ava frowned.

"Girls, this is our new home. We have to make the best of it, so get used to it."

"This is not my home. I'm a prisoner being made to live here against my own will." Lina walked out the door.

"That girl is going to make me catch a case." She shook her head. "I just hope I'm making the right decision," Tina whispered to herself.

29

"I want you to understand if you go to trial and lose, you'll face a mandatory sentence of the death penalty. If I were you, I would think about this carefully," Judge Houser talked. She was an African American judge who was highly known and respected. Her tactics were fair, and she didn't play when it came to the court of law. She was blunt, to the point, and hated when people tried to beat around the bush, playing like she was stupid.

"Your Honor, I would like a few moments to go over this with my client," Eric Pines, a Caucasian man who was Reggie's public defender, stated.

"You have ten minutes," Judge Houser stated.

Eric and Reggie walked into a small room within the courtroom. Reggie's mother, Tina, Sonya, and a few of the officers Kevin and Alvin worked with sat in the pews waiting to hear the decision Reggie would make.

"I want you to really think about this. If you choose trial, you're going to lose. There's no other way to sugarcoat it. That would mean a mandatory death sentence. The best I can push for is fifty years plus anger management and a drug addiction class with five years' probation after." Eric smirked.

He could care less about the outcome of Reggie's case. He knew just as well as Reggie he was guilty, and regardless of the outcome, he would still get paid. The crazy part was Eric was in cahoots with the state prosecutors that was pushing for life without parole if Reggie decided not to go to trial. They joked and laughed outside the courtroom, but once in, they put on a facade as if they were really fighting against each other.

"I don't know, man." Reggie scratched his head. "You might as well say fifty years is a life sentence."

"You'll need to make a decision, If you choose trial, the judge will set a date. If you plead today, the judge has issued a speed sentencing and you'll be sentenced today. It's all up to you." Eric looked over some papers he had of the case findings. "It really isn't looking too good for you, I have to be honest."

****

"He was standing there looking so stupid." Tina leaned over to Sonya, rolling her eyes.

"Yea, that's how they all look when they get in front of the judge. This lady is the best in the state. I know justice will be served today." Sonya smiled.

Eric and Reggie walked from the side room back up to the podium.

"Your Honor, my client is ready to proceed." Eric stared at the judge.

"The court is ready to proceed," the reporter spoke.

"In the case of the State of Atlanta vs. Reggie Grandoff. Reggie, you are charged with one count of premeditated murder, two counts of first-degree murder on law enforcement officers, one count of first-degree robbery, one count of felon in possession of a firearm, two counts of grand theft, and one count of carrying a concealed weapon." Judge Houser sat staring down at a stack of papers concerning Reggie and the charges brought against him. "How do you plead?"

Reggie stood shaking his head. His heart pounded as if it was going to burst through his chest. He dropped his head, running his hands over his face. "Aw, man, I'm gone," he mumbled. "Guilty." Reggie looked up at the judge then back down.

"Does the defendant have anything further he would like to say?" The judge continued looking down at the papers that sat in front of her.

"I'm sorry to the families. I didn't mean for any of this to happen. I wish I could go back and change everything about that night. I just wasn't myself and now I have to live with that. I'm ready to do my bid." Reggie's eyes watered. "I'm truly sorry for hurting your families." He turned back looking at Tina as a tear rolled down his cheek. "Mama, I'm sorry. You raised me better than this." He looked toward his mother.

"Would the state like to speak?" The judge looked up and over at the state prosecutors.

"Yes, Your Honor, we're asking for the maximum sentence allowed and that would be life without parole. Mr. Grandoff is a danger to society. He has done the unthinkable over cigarettes and lottery tickets. He is unstable and can't be trusted to walk as a free man ever." The state prosecutor glanced at Reggie then back toward the judge.

"Your Honor, my client wishes to be sentenced today." Eric looked at Reggie then at the judge. "My client knows he was wrong. He was under the influence of drugs. We're asking for fifty years with anger management and a drug addiction class along with five years' probation after." Eric looked on.

Judge Houser paused for a moment. She was sharp in her work and made sure with each case she reviewed, everything that was put in front of her. "In the case of the State of Atlanta vs. Reggie Grandoff, we find you guilty of one count of premeditated murder, two counts of first-degree murder on law enforcement officers, one count of first-degree robbery, one count of felon in possession of a firearm, two counts of grand theft, and one count of carrying a concealed weapon. It's sad to see another young black man wasting his life. You can't go around like you're some kind of savage and expect leniency. There are consequences for your actions, and unfortunately, your actions have cost the lives of three innocent people. Your actions have not only impacted you but the families of those who have lost their lives," Judge Houser talked sternly. "You are hereby sentenced to life without parole. It is ordered you remain in custody until your departure to the correctional facility. I hope you can find something worthwhile to do while your serving your time." Judge Houser looked at Reggie then banged her gravel.

Reggie instantly dropped to his knees at the words of his sentencing. Tears ran down his face dripping on his shirt. He thought of the possibility of the worst but prepared himself for a fifty-year sentence. He was sincere in his apology and figured because of that, he would get some type of leniency. His mother stood up crying hysterically, as Tina and Sonya cried hugging each other.

"At this time, would the families like to say anything?" Judge Houser looked toward the pews.

"No, they do not wish to at this time," Detective Hanks spoke up.

"I would like to say something, Your Honor." Reggie's mother raised her hand.

"You may approach the podium."

Reggie's mother gripped her purse strap tightly on her shoulder. "To everyone, I'm sorry for what Reggie has done. I raised him better than that. I truly am sorry." She paused looking toward Reggie. "Reggie, you lied to me. How could you lie to me? How could you do this?" Tears began dropping from her eyes. "You are not my son. I give up on you. You are not my son. You are dead to me from this day forward!" She yelled over her tears, shaking as she talked. "You are not my child!" She turned walking out the courtroom.

"Mama, I need you please!" Reggie yelled as tears blurred his vision, snot running down his nose. He was escorted out of the courtroom to a holding cell until guards were ready to take him back to the jail.

"Thank you so much." Tina hugged the state prosecutors along with Detective Hanks and Winston. "For some reason, I still don't feel any relief," she whispered in Detective Winston's ear as tears fell. "That was so hard to witness just now."

"It takes time but now let the healing process start." She gripped Tina tighter. "No one wins in cases like these."

News reporters filled the front of the court house waiting on the outcome of the case. They bombarded Tina and Sonya as they walked out the front doors of the courthouse. Flashes from cameras invaded their space.

"Mrs. Starr, can you tell us how you feel hearing the news?" a reporter shouted.

Tina walked as she wiped her tears that seemed to never end.

"My client is happy with the news and would like some privacy so her and her family can finally start to heal." Detective Hanks looked at one of the news reporters and into their camera.

The family of the store clerk who had also been killed opted out of being at the court date. They received the news of Reggie's fate from their lawyer who attended the hearing. It was a victorious day but also a day of sorrow. The truth was, no one had won in the case. Four lives had been taken, and many other lives impacted and broken beyond repair. The sentencing of Reggie only gave a temporary fix to a lifetime of pain.

30

"Auntie, I'm still angry, even though that boy is in jail. He's cost me so much. I've lost so much. But hearing his mother and the way she yelled, the things she said. I don't know. It hurt me to witness that." Tina laid across the sofa talking to Aunt Berniece on the phone.

"Baby, that's because you still have a heart. So, what's going on with your house? And how are the girls?"

"Auntie, the girls are good. They miss you so much. Lina makes me want to kill her sometimes with her mouth. I don't know where that child gets her attitude from, but it sure isn't from me." Tina laughed.

"Baby, now I know we're not playing the 'I don't remember' card. You had a comeback for everything your mother would say. She's just going through a phase, and I know it's hard for her without her daddy." Aunt Berniece coughed. "You know that girl has an old soul."

"Yeah, well, you know." Tina laughed.

"Where are the girls?" Aunt Berniece asked.

"They're at school. The best place for Lina to be before I ring her neck. Auntie, ever since the move, she has been having the worst attitude and mouth." Tina paused. "Dang it," she mouthed.

"Move? What move?"

"I was gonna wait to tell you. You know, I was having trouble with the mortgage and I lost my job, so my friend got us an apartment."

"Us, I know you better be talking about us as in you and the girls."

"Auntie, let's not forget I'm grown now, and my friend James lives with us. He's the one paying the bills, so it is what it is."

"Girl, I will come through this phone and knock you out, talking about it is what it is. First of all, you got my babies living in the house with some man you barely know. Then you got the nerve to say you're grown." Aunt Berniece's voice deepened.

"Auntie, calm down. You know what I mean." Tina rolled her eyes.

"Girl, little woman, get it right. Ya better get it right."

"Auntie, he's a good man, and the girls are starting to warm up to him. It's new for all of us, but right now, this is what I need. I need this. I have to move on and living in that house wasn't allowing me to do that." Tina yawned. "Auntie, I love you so much, but I need to get some rest before I have to get the girls from school. They started their new school this week."

"Baby, don't worry me please. You know you can always come to my home and stay. I would prefer that instead of you living with some man you don't know." Aunt Berniece paused. "Make sure you call me later, Tina."

****

"Baby, you're home early." Tina woke to the sound of the front door being opened.

"Yeah, I had a short day today." James walked in straight to the refrigerator.

"What's wrong? You looking like you got a problem." Tina looked as James opened a can of beer. "That's a habit you need to break." She smiled.

"Tina, don't start. I've had a long day at work. I need this to deal with all the noise from your kids. You need to make them be quieter when I'm home." James plopped down in a chair at the kitchen table.

"They're kids. They're going to make noise. I don't know what to tell you. If it's a problem, I can stay with my aunt."

"You're mine now. You ain't going nowhere. You know that's not what you want. Did you forget you need me?" He smirked.

"What is up with you?" She stared at James.

"I'm not used to this that's all. I told you it's gonna take some getting used to." He swallowed a gulp of beer. "All these beautiful women in the house, it's gonna take some getting used to." James walked toward Tina, sitting next to her on the sofa, kissing her. "I love you, Tina." He kissed her lips again.

"You better, I love you too." She smiled. "I have to go get my girls." She looked at the time on her cell phone.

"Baby, let me go get them. I need to start bonding with them anyways." James grabbed Tina's hand, squeezing it gently.

"Babe, I don't know."

"How else are they gonna get used to me?" He cut her off.

"Okay, I guess." She smiled. "That's why I love you because you're so amazing." Tina laid back on the sofa, grabbing the remote, flicking through the channels.

"I'll do anything for my future wife." He laughed.

****

"Where's Mama?" Lina frowned as she opened the back door.

"She's home. She sent me to get you, so we can get to know each other better."

"For what?" Lina spit out the words before thinking.

"Lina, whether you like it or not, me and your mom are together, and you're going to be seeing me every day, so lose the smart mouth." James looked in the rearview mirror. "I'm in a house with all these beautiful women with such smart mouths." He smiled.

"Well, I don't want to live in that house with you, and I don't want to get to know you."

"Lina, hush." Ava nudged her.

"What's your issue with me, Lina?" James drove off, looking in the rearview mirror at Lina.

"I don't understand why we have to live with you. Mama said you're paying the bills, why couldn't you pay the bills at our old house? You're not my dad, and we shouldn't be living with a stranger." Lina looked out the window. Her words were innocent yet came off as foul to the listening ear.

"Baby girl, I don't want to be your dad. All I want to do is be here for you, your sister, and your mom. I'm not trying to do nothing more and nothing less." James switched lanes, looking in his side mirrors, making sure the lane was clear. "I love your mother, and I'm sorry for what you've gone through, but I can't change that. I'm here now."

"Well, I don't know." Lina closed her eyes. "I wish everything could go back to the way it was."

They drove in silence the rest of the ride home. Ava laid her head on Lina's shoulder. James occasionally looked in the rearview mirror at the girls. The ride seemed awkward from then on, and James was eager to get the two little brats as he thought of them out of his car. He turned the radio up, rolled the windows down, and drove as the wind flowed in the car.

31

Lina

The memories of how life had been up until now quickly vanished as Lina lay curled in a ball, crying in pain on the bathroom floor. Her pajama shorts drenched in blood.

"Mama, something's wrong with Lina!" Ava ran to the kitchen frantic at the sight of seeing the only person she felt protected her covered in blood.

"Lina! Baby, Oh my god. Baby, what's going on?" Tina dropped to her knees, scooping her up in her arms and rushing her to the car.

"Mama, it hurts so bad. It hurts, Mama. Make it stop." Lina whined in pain.

"Mommy's here, baby." Tina franticly put the key in the ignition.

Every bump in the road made the pain feel that much more unbearable. Every light seemed to turn red as they approached it. In Lina's mind, cars were driving slower than usual and with constant pain in her abdomen, Lina felt as if it took two hours to get to the hospital. All she could do was lay in the front seat screaming and whining in pain.

"Mama, help me." Lina cried as her mother pulled in front of the emergency room doors.

"Help me!" Tina ran into the emergency department with Lina in her arms.

Nurses rushed with a gurney within seconds whisking Lina to an exam room. Doctors felt it would be better if Lina drank contrast to get a better look in her stomach. Due to all the blood and the amount of pain she was in, they decided to do the CT scan without it.

"Try to be still," the technician uttered.

"I'm trying. It just hurts so bad." Lina cried.

After her CT scan, she was taken back to the exam room where a doctor performed an ultrasound and pelvic exam to see the damage. As Lina cried in pain, the doctor ordered she be given a type of medicine through her IV, which relieved her from the pain, causing her to go into a sleep. Within an hour, the findings were in.

"Ma'am, I don't know if you knew your daughter was sexually active, but she's having an ectopic pregnancy. Unfortunately, her fallopian tube has ruptured, which is causing her to bleed in her stomach. We have to prep her now for surgery or she could die," the doctor talked. "We're going to get started and have you sign some papers."

Tina was hurt. She was confused and thought to herself what she would do once they got home. She wondered if she would whoop Lina for having sex. She wondered if she would comfort her or if she would act as if nothing happened. She had always taught Lina how important her purity was. She taught her how to value herself and her body. She also told her she was worth waiting for and if she abstained from sex until marriage, she would be that much more valued. She told her that her first time should be special. It should be a moment between her and her husband only. She was quickly consumed with guilt at the thought of maybe she was the reason Lina ran off to a boy for comfort and to feel loved. She thought maybe she was the reason Lina was doing everything she ever told her not to. She began to feel as if she was less of a woman for allowing her kids to see how a man should not treat a woman.

After about two hours, Lina was waking up in the recovery room. She was told what happened and doctors explained depending on how she did, she would need to spend between one to two days in the hospital. She was moved to a room forty-five minutes later, where she was met by Ava and Tina.

"Lina, I'm very disappointed in you. I taught you about sex, and I told you how important your body is," Tina talked in a low voice next to Lina's bedside so Ava could not hear their conversation. She didn't want Ava to know what was going on due to her age and felt it was best if she knew nothing about Lina being pregnant. "Lina, I'm barely taking care of you and your sister. I can't afford to take care of a baby too." Tina's eyes swelled with tears.

"Mama, do you really think I would just willingly give my body to someone? I'm not you, Mama, and unlike you, I know my worth." Lina began crying, knowing she would have to tell her mother the truth. "You just don't care to see what's going on." Lina held her hand over her stomach in pain.

"Get some rest, but when you wake up, we're finishing this conversation." Tina kissed Lina's cheek.

"What's the point? It won't change anything," Lina mumbled under her breath.

****

"Mama, I'm hungry." Ava yawned.

It was 7:23 a.m. as Tina and Ava walked to the cafeteria getting breakfast before heading back to Lina's room. When they entered the room, Lina was laying watching TV, still in pain, and refusing to eat. Tina knew they had to finish their conversation. She thought long and hard about the questions she was going to ask, and the first one was going to be who was the boy who got her pregnant? She was planning on going to the boys' house when they left the hospital to tell him in front of his parents to stay away from her daughter.

"So, are you ready to talk?" Tina pulled a chair next to Lina's bedside.

"Mama, what does it matter? Things will still be the same, and you probably won't want to hear what I have to say anyways," Lina talked with attitude.

"First thing, you better watch your tone of voice when you're talking to me. I'm still your mother, and I can still knock you in the mouth." Tina cocked her head to the side.

"Yes, ma'am. I'm sorry, Mama." Lina quieted, playing with her fingers. It wasn't the feeling of Lina feeling she were grown and could talk to anyone how she wanted to, she just dreaded the fact she had to have this conversation with her mother. She felt the news would hurt her mother and possibly destroy their relationship. In a sense, she felt what had happened was her fault. She also believed if she would've told her mother what happened sooner, she would've gotten in trouble.

"So, Lina, who is this boy? And where did you find it in you to have sex with him?" Tina jumped right in.

Lina took a deep breath. "Mama." She cried, struggling to get the words out and talk about what really happened. "Mama, James did it. You and Ava were gone. I was in my bed asleep, and he came in my room cussing about how you don't do your job and how he needs a woman that will make him feel like a man. When I heard him, I jumped up, but he pinned me down." Lina cried, making it hard to understand her words.

Tina gasped, her heart pounding as her chest rose up and down.

"He hurt me so bad, Mama. You weren't there to help me, you weren't there, and I feel like you never are." Tears flowed down Lina's face. "If Daddy were here, he wouldn't let anyone hurt me." Lina stared at Tina. "I wish I would've died on the operating table. I feel so dirty. I'm not worth anything anymore." She began hyperventilating. "All I ever wanted was to be pure. I'm so dirty I don't even look at myself the same." Lina covered her face with the cover, crying.

Tina jumped up rushing to the hallway to catch her breath and grasp what it was Lina had just told her.

I know she's not a liar. I didn't raise a liar. Why would she say that? Tina thought as she paced up and down the hall. *Would he really be that nasty to do that to my baby. I mean she really doesn't like him, so she could be saying that to get us away from him. What am I saying, what is going on?* Tina began crying. After five minutes, she walked back to the room trying to compose herself in front of Lina.

"Baby, I'm going to say something to him, and I'm sorry for not being there and protecting you like I should have." Tina stared at Lina, crying. "Baby, I'm so sorry. I love you girls so much I never meant for any of you to get hurt. I'm so sorry. Please forgive me."

Tears ran down her face. "But, baby, you know we don't have anywhere to go. I can't just leave." Tina stood up walking to the hall, wiping her eyes to call James.

"What, Tina? I'm at work," James talked with aggravation in his voice.

"James, what did you do to my baby? Lina had a miscarriage!" Tina yelled into the phone.

"What the hell that got to do with me, Tina?" James yelled.

"James, she said you touched her. You sorry bastard, you touched my baby!" Tina talked in anger through her teeth.

"You stupid woman, you know that girl hot in the ass. You're gonna sit here on this phone and accuse me of doing that? You know what, you and your kids can get the hell out of my house!"

"No, baby, I was just asking." Tina lowered her voice.

"You ruined my day with this!"

"Baby, I'm sorry." Tina spoke softly so no one could hear the conversation she was having.

"I'm not doing this with you!" James hung up the phone in Tina's face.

Lina, what did you do? she thought as she walked back into the room.

"Lina." Tina looked her in the eyes. "I want you to tell me now. Tell me the truth because I know you want me away from James. I know you don't like him, and you will do anything to tear us apart. Who did you have sex with, who is he?" Anger could be heard in Tina's voice.

"I hate you, and I don't care if you never talk to me or believe me. You know, James did this to me. You're just too dumb to see it." Lina rolled her eyes, putting her head back under the covers and crying softly.

Ava sat watching television, as a bond between mother and daughter sat on the rocks at the hands of a man who could care less if mother or daughter lived.

****

Lina stayed in the hospital for two days. She was released and prescribed pain pills and told to go to her doctor in three weeks to have a checkup. It was midday and James was still at work when they arrived home. Lina went to her room to rest. Ava followed trying to comfort her from all the pain she was still in. Lina had not spoken to her mother since revealing what it was James had done to her, and although she was hurt and angry at how her mother reacted, it was killing her inside not talking to her. She loved her mother more than life itself, and all she wanted was to see her better, healthy, and happy like she used to be.

James had gotten off work at 6:00 p.m. It was now 10:00 p.m., and he was just walking through the door. Tina hadn't spoken to him since he hung up on her and since she had been at the hospital with Lina, she hadn't seen him either.

James walked through the door, rambling and cussing. He had been angry with Tina ever since she confronted him on the phone.

"James, why haven't you answered my calls and what is the reason for you acting like this?" Tina walked to the kitchen table.

James slapped Tina, causing her to fall backwards. She hit the chair, causing it to break.

Lina jumped up along with Ava running into the kitchen. "I hate you. Don't you ever put your hands on my momma again!" Lina ran toward James, punching him in the stomach. Ava ran to her mother as she laid on the floor crying in pain.

"You little bastard, you wanna act like you're a man. Imma treat you like one." James punched Lina, causing her to fly backwards into the refrigerator and hitting the floor. "Don't you ever run up on me. You trying to ruin my life, you slut?" Spit flew from his mouth.

"You worthless!" Tina screamed as Lina lay on the floor in pain.

"Shut up! Y'all can get the hell out. I'm not taking any disrespect from you or some kids that ain't even mine!" James stumbled to Tina as she stood, leaning over the kitchen table. He then grabbed her hair, preventing her from moving.

Ava crawled under the table crying in fear. "Please stop!" she screamed.

"You shut up before you get a taste of this." He looked at Ava with a death stare.

"Baby, I'm sorry. Lina, tell him you're sorry. She didn't mean it. Tell him, Lina." Tina cried, her words struggling to come out.

"But, Mama." Lina whined in pain, tears flowing down her face.

"Tell him now!" Tina raised her voice as James held a tight grip on her hair.

"I'm sorry!" Lina yelled. "I'm sorry, Mama, that you're so stupid. I'm sorry you hate us so much. I'm sorry you're so weak, and I'm sorry I tried to defend you." Lina stood up, walking to the table. She grabbed Ava before going to their room, locking the door.

"James, baby, I'm sorry. I'm so sorry."

"Yeah, then come show me how sorry you are." He kissed her neck, leaving the stench of alcohol and bad breath on her skin.

****

Lina swallowed her prescription pain pill to ease the pain she was feeling as Ava sat on the bed next to her.

"I know that Mr. James really loves Mama." Ava talked quietly.

"What? Why would you say that? Do you really think that?" Lina grabbed Ava's hands, looking her in the eyes.

"Well, I heard Mama talking to herself in the bathroom. She said he hits her because he loves her so much, and he's scared of losing her."

"Ava, Mama is not herself. That's not love. Did you ever see Daddy hit Mama or cuss and yell at her? Mama has lost her mind, and James is killing Mama mentally and physically." Lina's eyes watered.

Lina and Ava laid back on the bed staring up at the ceiling, speechless and unsure of this thing called life they were living in. Ava sighed loudly after saying a small prayer in her head. Eventually, they dozed off to sleep, holding each other tight.

****

189

At least twice a week, there was commotion going on in their house. Rarely would the week go by without any arguing and fighting. The sad part was, every time James consumed alcohol, he would get violent and angry. The demons he was battling would overpower him, putting him in an uproar. Any little thing would trigger his violent ways. If Lina or Ava laughed too loud, stared at him or showed love toward their mother, he would become enraged. James was a ticking time bomb, and Tina was a helpless, lost, and dependent soul. It seemed as if nothing or no one could get Tina to see she would be better off without James than with him.

****

Lina awoke before the sun. James had already left for work. The house was quiet and air still. The sounds of arguing and fighting could still be heard in the atmosphere in Lina's mind, as she walked to the bathroom bath towel in hand. Lina ran a hot bath filling the tub up to the point of almost overflowing.

"I can't take this anymore," Lina mumbled, staring in the bathroom mirror. "Ugh!" She scrunched up her face.

She undressed, her gown hitting the bathroom floor. Slipping in to the bath tub, Lina closed her eyes, letting out a deep breath.

"God, please forgive me. I'm sorry." She turned over onto her stomach, submerging her head underneath the water. Immediately, she raised her head up, gasping to take a breath. She lowered her head under the water again. The thought of going out by drowning herself was easier said than done. With every second she spent underwater, she couldn't find it in herself to stay under long enough to drown.

"Why, why can't I do it? I'm tired of living in this house. I'm tired of living this life." She broke down. She turned over on her back contemplating her next move on finding an easy way out.

"Lina, I need to use the bathroom." The sweet soft voice of Ava on the other side of the bathroom door brought Lina back to her senses.

"Hold on, baby, let me unlock it." Lina jumped up, wiping her face so Ava could not see she had been crying.

"I love you so much, Lina." Ava sat using the toilet as Lina laid back in the tub.

"I love you too, and I promise I'll always be here for you." Tears began to roll down her face.

"Why are you crying?"

"Because you love me so much, and I'm so happy to have you in my life." Lina wiped her cheeks. "Life without you getting on my nerves would suck." Both Lina and Ava laughed.

"Yea, well, life without you protecting me and loving me would suck even more." Ava smiled. "You're all I really have." Ava dropped her head.

"Ava, we have Momma and when she gets stronger, you'll see just how much she loves us." Lina fought to hold back her tears as they continued to fall.

32

Monique awoke with the feeling that maybe today would be a good day, better than the ones she'd been having. It was 10:15 a.m., and Monique knew she had forty-five minutes before it was time for her to go to physical therapy. She was tired of James not answering and decided to give him a piece of her mind once he did.

Monique laid with the head of the bed raised, unsure she picked up the phone calling James. After calling three times, she left him a voice message. "James, it's me Monique. I've been calling you. Anyways, I just want you to know I love and miss you so much. Baby, I need you. It's hard doing this without you. Please call me when you get this message. If I don't answer, it's because I'm in therapy, but I promise, I'll call you back. I love you so much, baby… bye." She hung up the phone.

Unsatisfied, she called him again. After the second ring, he answered the phone.

"James, baby, I've been trying to call you." Monique paused. Everything she had been thinking she would say to him quickly faded away at the sound of his strong voice.

"What, Monique? What do you want and why do you keep calling me over and over like you're crazy?"

"James, baby, I need you."

"Monique, don't call me baby. You're so stupid! You think killing yourself is going to get me back? We're done. You're not what I want anymore!" James shouted in anger.

"James, what did I do to you? What about our family? What about our son?" Monique placed her hand over her eyes as they began to water. "Please, James, let's get counseling. I still love you." Tears began to fall.

"What about our son, Monique? I'm a grown man. I don't owe you an explanation." James sucked his teeth. "I'm not going to counseling with you, Monique! You know what, Joshua can be the next man's problem."

"So, he's a problem now, James? Why are you doing this? You're divorcing me and our son! What did we do to deserve this? All I ever did was love you. I've been a damn good wife to you. I've went through hell and high water for you. How can you treat me like you don't love me?" The hurt Monique felt sounded in her voice.

"Tina! Damnit, Monique, I never loved you. I was just there for our son. I didn't know what to do when I found out you were pregnant. I felt trapped, so I married you. Look, you should worry about yourself and stop calling me. If it's not about Joshua, we don't need to talk... I've moved on and so should you."

"But why, James? Why do you hate me that much?" Monique's heart dropped at the words of the man she loved. "James, I love you so much."

"Monique, what do you want from me? You got a baby from me, what more do you want? You got what you wanted, right?"

"James, you know I've been down for you since day one. When my family told me to leave you alone, I took your side. James, please just tell me what do I have to do? I want my family together. I don't want to lose you. Please give me a chance. I love you. Don't you understand that? I want my husband by my side." Monique cried into the phone.

"Look, I don't hate you. We're just not good together. I'm sorry, Monique, it's over. I don't ever want to be with you again. What we had is dead to me."

"So, you're really gonna do this to me? All the years we've been together, you're just gonna throw it away just like that?" Monique cried. "You don't even see about Joshua. The least you could do is spend time with him or call him. And what about me? The least you could do is come see about me."

"See, there you go making it about you again."

"I'm like this because of you!" Monique cried into the phone.

"No, you're like that because you're crazy. I didn't do that to you. Maybe you should talk to your God. Maybe He can help you." James laughed.

"I can't believe you, James."

"Believe it!" he yelled before hanging up.

"Mama, what's going on?" Mona walked into the room after hearing Monique yelling and crying and the phone slamming down.

"My husband doesn't want me anymore. The time I need him the most, he doesn't want me." Monique began crying hysterically.

"Honey, you need to calm down. You're gonna make yourself hyperventilate."

"He doesn't love me. He doesn't love me." Monique bit down on her finger. "Why would God let this happen? Why would he put me through all this pain?" She moaned.

"Honey, if I were you, I would be thanking Him for opening up your eyes. Don't blame God for the actions of others. Just like God didn't make you take those pills, God didn't make that man be pathetic." Mona sat on the edge of Monique's bed. "So, what did he say?"

"I'm crazy and he never loved me." Monique's eyes now puffed from all the crying.

"What? Is he crazy? What an idiot." Mona stood up, putting her hands on her hips.

"He used to tell me he loved me so much. Now he's telling me he never loved me. What am I supposed to believe?"

"It hurts but believe what's he's telling you now. His actions show he doesn't love you, and you don't kick someone when their down."

"Mona, why won't God let me die. I'm living in a world where I'm so unhappy. I'm just tired of living. I can't remember the last time I was happy… I'm tired of waking up every day. I don't have anything to look forward to anyways. I'm just so frustrated and angry holding stuff in all the time. It's making me go crazy." Monique looked with a blank stare. "It's so many people that want to live yet they die. I want to die, and I'm suffering having to live."

"It's okay to cry." Mona leaned over, hugging Monique tight. "It's okay. Go ahead and cry, but when you're done crying, you have to dust yourself off and live. I know your purpose is great because if it wasn't, you wouldn't be here today. You have to fight for your life, fight for your joy, fight for the sake of your son, Monique. There are so many people that have passed from suicide, be grateful you have a second chance at life. Depression, suicidal thoughts, or this man isn't benefiting you, so let it go."

"I wouldn't have to feel this way if I died."

"Honey." Mona rubbed Monique's back. "If you can tell me five things being depressed, suicidal or hurt over a man has benefited you, then I'll bring you a gun to kill yourself." Mona stepped back, looking Monique into her swollen eyes.

After long thought, Monique dropped her head. "It hasn't benefited me at all." She cried.

"Exactly, and what about your son? What do you think dying will do to him? Do you see the way his eyes light up every time he comes in here and sees you?" Mona's eyes began to water. "Listen, eventually, you're gonna come to your senses and want to live. You don't want to finally have joy and start appreciating life then get hit with something that has you fighting for your life, hoping you don't die. Be careful how you speak, Monique. Life is precious, and our words have power."

"It's easy for people to say live, be happy, move on, stop complaining when it's not them." Monique rubbed the tears away from her cheeks.

"No, it's just easy for a hurting person to react based on their emotions. You know, someone once told me the weight of a tiny problem can lead to the heaviness of a big burden. I also know we sometimes would rather keep our burdens and brokenness than give them to God. You've made that man an idol whether you know it or not. Your living and life is based on if that man stays with you or not. You're willing to live if he stays with you, but if he doesn't, then you feel your life isn't worth living."

"Ugh!" Monique sucked her teeth.

"Honey, I don't care about you getting mad. You should know that about me by now. You need someone that's going to be real with you and give you the truth. At the end of the day, that man didn't give you life, our God did. It'll take time, but your heart will heal. Your emotions will get right, and you'll see life isn't so bad without him. You deserve to be happy, not the way you are now."

"You'll never understand." Monique shook her head.

"You're right, I won't because I will never let a man validate my life. No man will ever have that kind of power over me. He may leave me and of course, it may hurt. I may even cry and try to bust out his car windows. I might even show up at his house with my Taser looking for him, but at the end of the day, I will be okay. I'll heal and move on. Girl, we get one chance at life, and my life and your life is worth living," Mona talked significantly.

"Mona, but I'm so broken. I'm so hurt. My heart is destroyed. I loved him so much. He was my heart, my everything."

"Honey, that's the problem. We serve a jealous God, a God that will have no man before Him. You didn't love him, you idolized him."

"I just don't know anymore. I hate waking up every day. I hate who I've become, I hate life."

"That's because you were never really living, just existing in the shadows of someone else. Get up and live. You're a woman, one of the strongest and wisest creations God created. Live, honey, and be the queen you're meant to be." Mona pointed her finger at Monique. "Dry those tears and live, honey, it's possible. Don't try to live, just do it, find it inside of yourself and live."

"I'm just so unhappy, Mona." Monique covered her face.

"Monique, you're strong. Just live and be grateful you still have your mind." Mona walked out of the room. Quickly, she popped her head into the room. "And pull it together, your baby is coming down the hall." She smiled then walked away.

****

"Mommy." Joshua ran into Monique's arms when he entered the room. "I miss you, Mommy, are you okay?" Joshua's presence lit up the atmosphere.

"Baby, I miss you, guess what?" Monique held Joshua tight in her arms.

"What mommy?" Joshua smiled.

"I'll be coming home soon, and if you go to the nurse's station, they have a yummy treat for you." Monique kissed Joshua as he pushed back from her grip, excited to run off to the nurse's station.

As soon as Joshua left the room, tears began to fall from Monique's eyes.

"Momma, I talked to James today. He told me I'm crazy and he never loved me. He said I was better off talking to My God, maybe he could help me. He was so nasty to me. What have I done so wrong to deserve that from him?"

"Baby, I'm sorry." Helen walked over to Monique, hugging her, kissing her forehead. "Don't you worry, baby. Mama got this. That nasty thang not gonna do my baby like that. I got this, you don't worry. You just focus on getting better so you can come home to your baby. He needs and misses you so much."

Helen stayed for about five hours before Joshua began to get antsy. She told Monique they would be back tomorrow after she cooked dinner, so she could bring her some home-cooked food. She told her not to worry about James and that God would work out everything in her life. Helen, now more alert to all that, Monique had been going through with James promised better days were ahead for her. They left as Monique blew kisses to them then drifted off to sleep.

33

"I can't do this!" Monique's legs shook. Her palms were sweaty as she stood, gripping tightly on to the walker. "When I leave, he gonna have to straighten me." She took one step before stopping out of breath.

"Monique, you can do it. Come on, I'm so proud of you." Mona stood on the side of Monique, holding on to the gait belt around her waist. "I want you to get better, so you can get out of here." She smiled.

"Can we stop? I'm tired. I can't do anymore." She trembled as she forced herself to take another step.

"No, Mama, we have a goal to meet. You have to take five more steps before we can stop. You got this, Monique."

Monique was still in her feelings about James and the things he said to her. In her mind, she still wanted her husband, she wanted her family together no matter how he'd been treating her, or the things he said. But in the back of her mind, she knew her marriage was over. She knew she couldn't change him or fix their marriage without him wanting to fix it as well. She was hurt that the thing she took pride in the most was the very thing that was destroying her, and for what? She was a little embarrassed she couldn't keep her family together and wounded, with the burden she had failed in her marriage.

"I love him so much. Why is he doing this to me?" Monique took another step.

"How much do you love him?" Mona continued holding on to the gait belt.

"So much. I would do anything for him. He was my best friend." She stopped, dropping her head.

"Well, how much do you love yourself?" Mona looked at Monique.

"I, I—" Monique looked up at Mona then back down.

"Do you love that man more than you love yourself? Don't answer, just think about it. Come on, you have two more steps." Mona smiled.

Monique put one foot in front of the other slowly. She took one step then stopped to catch her breath. Slowly, she gripped the walker tighter. She took a deep breath then let it out. Slowly, again, she put one foot in front of her, then the other until she took a complete step.

"Ugh, this is hard!" Monique frowned. She plopped back in the locked wheelchair that sat behind her. "I never could've even imagined in a million years I would be in a place like this struggling to walk." Monique leaned forward as Mona removed the gait belt from around her.

"Honey, but you're here and when you leave here, you'll be wiser and stronger. This is going to let you see just how amazing and strong you really are. If you can overcome this, I know you'll be able to overcome anything." Mona placed the gait belt on her desk in the corner of the therapy room. "I'm fighting for you until you're able to fight for yourself. I believe in you, and I want to see you better." She wheeled Monique out to her room.

Mona placed the wheelchair at an angle next to Monique's bed, locking it. Monique leaned forward, grabbed the bedside rail, and pulled herself up. Mona stood in front of her as Monique slowly pivoted her feet, allowing her body to turn so she could sit on the bed.

"I'm tired of being weak." Monique slowly lowered her bottom on the bed. "All my life, I've kept how I felt and what I would go through to myself. I didn't want people in my business judging me because of how I would feel at times. I've been weak for so long. I'm tired." Monique laid back as Mona raised her legs, placing them on the bed. Her eyes began to water. "I'm not gonna be weak anymore!"

Mona moved the wheelchair, placing it in the corner next to the window in Monique's room. She walked back over sitting on the edge of the bed, noticing Monique as she started to cry. "What's wrong?" She placed her hand on Monique's leg.

Warm tears ran down her face. "All I keep thinking is I don't know what I'm going to do. I want my marriage. I want my family." She wiped her eyes with a tissue. "God, I know you didn't bring me this far just to leave me now." She closed her eyes as the tears squeezed through her eye lids, running down her face.

"The only thing you can do is give it to God. Stressing won't make it better, being angry won't make it better, crying won't change the outcome, and giving up on yourself will only hurt you, not him."

"I'm a Christian. My life shouldn't be this hard." Monique looked at Mona.

"Mama, you have it all wrong. Being a Christian is that much harder. You have people constantly judging you, looking down on you, comparing you to others. Telling you, you can't dress like this, you shouldn't listen to that kind of music, you shouldn't dance like this, then people expect you to act a certain way when you're going through things. People tend to forget you're human too. Being Christian doesn't mean your life is going to be easy, or that you'll have it all together. You know that better than me, but God is with you, and He'll help you get through life." Mona smiled. "That's about all I know. Shoot, you know more than me. I'm the beginner in this, girl." She laughed. "Relax, talk to God if you have to, leave it all in his hands." Mona stood up, walking out the room.

"I love you, Father, and I'm coming to you because I really need you. I know I messed up and now I'm looking like a fool. I don't know what to do. I want my marriage to work. I want my family. God, I'm sorry though. I keep putting this man before you, before my son, before my own self and my health. God, it hurts so bad I really love James. I just need your help. But most of all, I want you, God. I want to be in a place with you that nothing can shake me and nothing breaks me. I'm tired of feeling like I've failed, I'm tired of being weak, and I'm tired of being a disappointment to you and myself. Please help me," Monique whispered, her eyes closed. The warm sensation of tears raced down her face.

"Can I come in?" A small tap echoed off the door, an unfamiliar voice filling the room.

Monique quickly wiped her face. "Come in." She kept her eyes closed. "How can I help you?"

"Well, your mom called and said it was okay to come by and see you. I'm Kelly, the officer that responded to the call your son made to 911." She stood at the foot of the bed.

"Okay." Monique spoke without looking to see the face of the person talking.

"Can I sit with you? I just wanted to come and visit with you."

"I'm sorry, I'm not trying to be rude. Today is just not my day." Monique opened her eyes.

Kelly sat in the chair next to Monique's bed. "Your son is so precious." She smiled.

"Yes, that's my baby. He's such a smart kid. I wish his daddy was as smart as he is." Monique rolled her eyes.

"Oh, honey, that man is a jerk." Kelly looked toward Monique.

"Yes, and unfortunately, I love him." Monique laughed. "You must be the person my mom told me she wanted me to meet. I'm sorry you have to see me like this."

"At least I'm able to see you alive and talking. Your mom is something else. Bless her heart." Kelly laughed.

"That lady is, I know she can get a little crazy, but I love her so much." Monique shook her head.

They talked for an hour before Kelly left. She told Monique she would be back to visit and would be praying for her. The connection they made was likely to grow into a strong friendship, and Monique really liked Kelly's personality. Monique rested the rest of the day. She was determined to get out of the rehab, so she could figure out her life and where her and James would stand. Monique knew the only way she would be able to see James is if she popped up on him. Waiting for him to come see her was obviously not going to happen. She was determined though, either he was going to talk to her the easy way or the hard way, the choice was his.

34

I t had been a week since Kelly visited Monique. She told Amber she would be home late after her shift because she was going to visit someone in the hospital. After work, she stopped by a mom-and-pop diner grabbing salads, soup, and Cajun chicken alfredo for her and Monique. She remembered how unpleasant food can some-times be in rehab centers. She pulled up to the rehab center around six thirty still dressed in uniform.

"Come in," Monique yelled as she laid in the bed of her private room, hearing a tap on the door.

"How are you, missy? I bought dinner. I know this food ain't all that." Kelly smiled.

"Girl, you must've read my mind because I cannot with this place or this food." Monique laughed.

"So how are you, how's it going with rehab?" Kelly sat the food on the bedside tray, pulling the containers of food out the bag.

"I'm tired of this place. I miss waking up to my son. I miss my freedom. I miss being independent. I told myself I have to get better, so I can get out of here. My baby needs me, and I need to see James. I need closure or something. I'm doing a lot better, better than I have been." Monique grabbed the plastic fork, wrapping noodles and chicken smothered in creamy, buttered alfredo sauce, and stuffing her mouth.

"Yes, you need to get better, so we can hang." Kelly laughed. "I really want to see you better for real. You need to get back to your baby." Kelly sat in the chair next to Monique's bed, grabbing her salad.

"I wanted to thank you for being here for me. I know we don't know each other like that, but it helps to have someone in your corner when you're going through." Monique looked at Kelly. "And to have someone that brings you food, girl, I am blessed." She laughed.

"Yep, we all need someone. Can't go through by ourselves. Sometimes, you need the strength of the other person you know." Kelly chewed on her salad. "You're gonna be all right girl. I got you."

"So, do you have any kids, are you married?" Monique took another bite of pasta.

"I have a teenager. She's something else." She raised her eyebrows. "I'm not married. I was engaged to my daughter's father. He died a few days after he was in a car accident when she was two. It's just me and her now. Besides, I'm really not interested in dating right now. I enjoy my freedom." Kelly laughed. "Maybe one day I'll find someone and settle down, someone that can deal with my craziness."

"Tsss, I'm starting to think being single sounds better and better."

"Hello," Kelly answered her cellphone. "I told you I was coming home a little later than usual. Because I'm visiting a friend in the hospital. Little girl, you don't know all my friends. Amber, I do have friends. What do you want? Yes, I'll bring you home some food. Okay, child, I love you, bye." She hung up the phone. "My daughter told me I don't have any friends." She laughed.

"Teenagers, they swear they know everything." Monique laughed. "God knows Joshua is going to be so protective over me when he gets to his teens."

"She swears she's my mother at times. I have to put her in her place." Kelly shook her head. "But she's the sweetest and most respectful child. She makes me so proud to be her mother, and her faith and the things she says about God and the Bible is just mind-blowing."

"Well, it's getting late. I don't want to keep you and this food has given me the itis, so if you want to get home to your baby, I totally understand." Monique yawned. "Thank you so much for the food. That was the highlight of my day." She laughed. "I don't know if anyone has ever told you, but you are such a wonderful person. I'm so grateful to have you in my life now."

"Don't make me cry now." Kelly stood up, smiling. "I'm so grateful to have you in my life as well. You're a strong woman with a sweet spirit." She hugged Monique. "Here's my number. Call me anytime. I'm here for you. I promise." She wrote her number on a napkin, handing it to Monique before leaving.

35

Three Weeks Later

"Surprise." Nurses and physical therapists who worked with Monique filled her room, holding balloons, cards, and a cake.

She was startled out of her sleep. She looked around the room, rubbing her eyes. A grin appeared on her face. "Oh, thank you." She smiled.

"Mama, I want you to know I'm so proud of you. You were a pain in my you know what, but I wouldn't trade that pain for nothing in the world." Mona laughed, showing her pearly, white teeth. "I'm going to miss you. Now I don't have anyone to fight with." She smiled.

"Aww, come here." Monique smiled, sitting up in bed. "You know you're my girl." She hugged Mona. "I'm going to keep in touch with you. I promise."

Mona placed the cake on the bedside table, cutting it into big triangle pieces. It was a marble cake with butter creme icing, which read, "Congratulations on your new journey". They all took their slice of cake, taking turns hugging Monique and handing her cards.

"It my birthday and it's not even my birthday." Monique laughed.

"Can you believe you're finally getting out of this place tomorrow?" Mona sat at the edge of Monique's bed, putting a chunk of cake in her mouth.

"I know. I'm so ready to go." Monique took a plate of cake.

"So, what are you going to do? Where you gonna live when you get out of here?" Mona looked at Monique.

"Well, my mom packed up my place while I was in the hospital and moved everything to her house. She has a big enough house, so me and my baby will be staying there."

"That's good. That lady loves you so much. Family will be good for you." Mona smiled. "Have you heard from the ex?"

"No, he doesn't pick up for me anymore. The hell with him, right?" Monique took a bite of cake.

"Hey, that's his loss, not yours." Mona finished up her cake. "Let me go get Silvia. She's going to hate me." Mona looked at her wrist watch.

"Mona, I'm serious. I'm going to keep in touch with you. You're my girl." Monique smiled.

"You better or I'll come find you." Mona laughed, walking out the door. "You know I'm crazy like that."

Monique called Kelly, telling her she would be leaving the rehab tomorrow and wanted a nice meal and to hang when she got out. Kelly told her she was off from work and would whip up something for her.

"So, I don't know if you're up to it, but I have an extra ticket to see Daria Jones in concert next weekend." Kelly talked in the phone.

"Girl, yes, I'm up to it. I've been in hospitals and rehabs for too long. I need to get out and breathe, have a little fun." Monique laughed. "That's enough time to prepare myself. That gives me a week and four days to be exact to prepare for this concert." She grinned.

"Okay, so I'll see you tomorrow and be ready to eat," Kelly spoke.

"Well, what's on the menu?" Monique questioned.

"I'll make baked mac and cheese, green beans, yellow rice, yams, barbeque ribs, corn bread, and my secret sweet tea. Oh yea and a homemade strawberry cake with homemade butter creme icing," Kelly spoke. "And I can't forget about my famous potato salad."

"Girl, let me find out you a black woman in a white woman's body." Monique laughed.

"Girl, it gets real in this kitchen." Kelly laughed. "Well, let me get going. I guess I better make it to the grocery store before I have to pick up Amber from school. She hates shopping with me." Kelly laughed.

"Okay, I'll see you tomorrow."

"And make sure you bring your mom and Joshua. Amber will love him," Kelly said before hanging up the phone.

She smiled as she dialed her mother's number.

"Mommy, I'm officially coming home tomorrow. I'm all cleared, I'm stable on my feet, and Kelly is cooking us a big dinner tomorrow." Monique smiled.

"Thank you, Jesus. Finally, I'm so happy, baby. I'm happy for you. Now what she making?" Helen asked.

"Well, she's throwing down baked mac and cheese, green beans, yellow rice, yams, potato salad, barbeque ribs, corn bread, sweet tea, and homemade strawberry cake with butter creme icing."

"Potato salad? Umm, baby, she making the potato salad? You know I don't eat everybody potato salad." Helen scrunched up her nose. "You know how I am about eating folks' potato salad."

"Mommy, really?" Monique laughed.

"Baby, I have to call Pastor and tell him the good news. He's been so worried about you," Helen talked.

"Okay, Mommy. I'll call you later. I love you so much." Monique smiled.

"I love you too, baby." Helen hung up the phone.

****

"Pastor, my baby coming home. All tests came back normal. She can walk without a cane. She's good." Helen talked as soon as the pastor's voice sounded on the phone.

"Praise God. That's good news. I'm so glad to hear that," Pastor Andrews spoke.

"Pastor, thank you for all your prayers. It means a lot to me and my family. Not sure how I could ever repay you. but I'm so grateful for you."

"Well, I'm having a program coming up. It's going to be big. I have a powerful woman of God bringing the word. I would love for you to bring your family and for you to spread the word. I'll keep you updated with the date."

"I'm there, Pastor." Helen smiled. "I have to go see my dear friend Mary right now, just wanted to call and give you the news." Helen pulled Mary from her stash.

"Okay, Helen, tell your friend Mary I said hello," Pastor Andrews said before hanging up the phone.

Helen hung up the phone, grabbing her lighter and blunt. She walked to her back porch, lighting the blunt. She inhaled until the tip of the blunt was lit. Slowly, she exhaled, blowing smoke from her mouth. "Mary, Mary, you've been so good to me, ole Mary, Mary, you've been good to me." Helen sung as she continued to inhale on her blunt, lying in the recliner chair she had on the back porch.

36

The aroma of fresh candied yams, sweet, tangy, tender, barbeque ribs, sweet, fluffy, golden homemade cornbread, and sweet strawberry cake with fresh butter creme icing filled the air as Kelly opened the front door.

"Oh my god, your home is so nice." Monique walked in, hugging Kelly. Amber stood next to her mother, smiling, along with Lina and Ava.

"Ladies, this is Mrs. Monique, her mother Mrs. Helen, and Joshua." Kelly hugged Mrs. Helen as Joshua hugged on his mother's leg.

"You're so cute." Amber talked in a funny voice, reaching for Joshua after she hugged everyone.

"And you girls are so beautiful." Monique Hugged Lina and Ava. They smiled as Kelly walked around them closing the door.

She gave a small tour of her 3,400 square-foot home, and then after, she led everyone to the living room.

"The food will be ready in about ten minutes," Kelly yelled from the kitchen where she and Monique sat at the table, talking.

"I'm so happy to be home. You just don't understand." Monique took a sip of iced tea.

"I know you are." Kelly stood up, walking to the oven, grabbing an oven mitt before taking out the mac and cheese. "Have you heard from James? Has he attempted to come by and see you yet?" Kelly placed the foil pan of hot mac and cheese on the counter.

"Girl, that's another story. He still hasn't picked up the phone or attempted to come by." Monique rolled her eyes.

"So when did you get home?" Kelly looked at Monique.

"I got home around nine this morning. Took a long, hot bubble and Epsom salt bath, did a little shopping with my mom, went home took a nap, then surprised Joshua after my mom picked him up from school. He was so happy to see me he cried." Monique smiled, taking another sip of tea.

Kelly took the top off the green beans mixing it, steam quickly rose from the pot. It had smoked neck bones, bacon, butter, onions, and pinch of fresh garlic in it.

"Girl, that smells so good." Monique looked at Kelly.

"Yassss." Kelly covered the greens, laughing. "Can you let everyone know they can come sit at the table?"

Monique walked to the living room, gathering everyone. All the kids ran to the kitchen table, leaving Helen behind. They took their seats as Kelly placed all the food in her, only comes out on holidays, dishes. She placed them all on the table along with the proper utensil next to each bowl. After, she took her seat, handing everyone a plate.

"When I jingle these keys." Helen held the keys in the air, mouthing to Monique as she sat across the table from her. "If this potato salad nasty, this jingle means it's time to go."

"Are you okay, Mrs. Helen?" Kelly asked. She sat next to Amber who sat between her and Mrs. Helen.

"Baby, who taught you how to make potato salad?" Helen scrunched up her nose.

"Momma, really?" Monique laughed, shaking her head.

"Well, my next-door neighbor when I was younger. Her name was big momma. I would stay the night at her house when my mom picked up extra shifts." Kelly grabbed the spoon next to the bowl of potato salad, spooning out a chunk of it.

"Okay..." Helen tooted her nose. "Imma kill you if this is nasty." She looked at Monique, mouthing.

"Momma, stop," Monique mouthed, trying not to be seen.

Helen spooned a small chunk of potato salad. She continued with the other dishes before sticking her fork in the yams, taking a bite.

"Momma, we ain't gonna say grace?" Monique looked at Helen.

"Oh yes." Helen sarcastically sat her fork on her plate. "Hell, I'm hungry." She blurted out.

Lina, Amber, and Ava laughed as they closed their eyes.

"You are so embarrassing," Monique mouthed before closing her eyes.

Monique said grace, followed by everyone digging in their plates. Helen cleared her plate, leaving the potato salad for last. She slowly put some on a fork, easing it to her mouth.

She slowly chewed, then looked at Monique. "She aight," Helen mouthed.

They all sat around the table, laughing. After dessert, everyone packed to-go plates before leaving. Kelly left the same time as Monique, dropping Lina and Ava home. She was so happy to see Monique out and smiling, and she loved the fact Joshua loved her and the girls.

****

Helen, Monique, and Joshua arrived home around 9:00 p.m. Monique decided to keep Joshua home from school the following day, so they could have a movie night. She ran Joshua's bath, filling the bath tub with bubbles and toys. She sat watching Joshua play as he talked to her about ninja turtles and slime. She smiled and laughed at the funny stories he told, which made no sense. Being able to look at her baby and have her mind in a new space was what she had been missing for a while.

"Joshua, I love you so, so, much." Monique leaned, kissing Joshua on the forehead.

"Mommy, I love you so much, a million, billion, ninja years more." Joshua smiled, wrapping his wet, soapy arm around his mother's neck. "And I'm going to love you forever, even when you get elderly and wrinkled." Joshua laughed.

37

"Hello," Tina answered the phone, sleep still in her voice.

"Yes, I'm looking for James," the voice on the other end of the phone spoke with anticipation.

"May I ask who's calling? My husband is at work." Tina rolled over in bed, pushing the cordless phone to her ear.

"Excuse me, did you just say husband?" Helen smacked her lips.

"Yes, who's calling?"

"Maybe I have the wrong number. Is this the number for James Austin?"

"Yes, it is. How can I help you?"

"I knew it. I knew he was a dog." Helen rolled her eyes. "Um lady, ma'am, there's no way you can be married to James. He's already married." Helen's voice deepened. "At least not legally," she said sarcastically.

"Excuse me, who is this and what do you want with my husband?" Tina sat up in bed, confused.

"No, baby, he's not your husband. He's my daughter's husband and the father to her five-year-old son."

"What! Who is this?" Tina's heart dropped to her stomach, her juggler vain pulsating faster and faster.

"Look, baby, James is married and has been for five years." Helen shook her head.

"But," Tina mumbled. "He has a child?"

"Let me introduce myself. My name is Helen. My daughter is Monique Austin. You know, the wife to James. I don't know what's going on, but I have been trying to get a hold of him since his wife's been in the hospital. I know he knows what's going on. The officer told me she spoke to his rude butt," Helen spoke sternly. "And his son misses his sorry butt."

"Oh my god." Tina sighed. "Is this a joke? How did you get my number?"

"Baby, listen to what I'm telling you. He's already married. Now I need you to be honest with me." Helen looked over her shoulder, making sure Monique or Joshua wasn't around listening on this good Saturday morning.

"He, we." Tina stumbled over her words. "He never told me anything about a family. He never talks about having a wife or child. He never brings him around. H-he," Tina stuttered. "He got, we live together. We've been together for almost three years now. I don't understand how, I mean why? Oh my god, what is going on?" She breathed heavily. "I'm so confused."

"Mmmm, that's 'cause he's a dog. Look, baby, James is a dirty dog. An old dirty dog at that." She rolled her eyes. She slammed her palm against her kitchen table. "I don't know what he's been telling you. I really don't care at this point. I'm just trying to figure out what tricks this dog is playing. Unfortunately, my daughter met James when they were younger. He has a son who misses him. My daughter has been going through a lot because of him. He hasn't called to check up on her. He hasn't checked up on his son. Hell, he hasn't done anything to help financially." Helen quieted. "I mean it's not much to say. He's out here tip'n an dip'n and married with a whole family. I tried to warn her about that man. How did you meet him anyways?"

"We met after my husband was killed. They worked for the same company. He came on to me. It was never my intentions. I can't believe he has a family." Tina held her hand over her forehead. "I should've known, man, I should've known something. He lost his job and that's when he moved us in together."

"Whatcha say? He lost his job too." Helen cut her off, speaking sarcastically.

"He never told me anything about his family. I believed he was who he portrayed himself to be." She balled her fist. "I would never... I would never have dealt with him had I known."

"I never liked him, and this is why. He's a manipulating bastard. He abandoned my baby when she needed him the most. Where is he?"

"He's at work right now. I can't call him. He won't want to talk. I'm just trying to wrap my brain around this. He's married, but we've been together for almost three years and living together for two. How in the world is this possible? I should've known!"

"My daughter said he stopped by every now and then. He stayed the night a few times. Besides that, he's been MIA. He wants a divorce after all this time. He should've been, did that, wasting my baby's time. I can't stand him. Don't worry, Imma take care of him. He hurt my babies." Helen took a sip of soda. "Imma get that dog. When you see him or talk to him, whichever is first, tell him Helen is angry and she wants to talk ASAP. My baby don't need to be stressing over how she gonna handle taking care of Joshua on her own. He gonna pay up and do for his child, enough is enough!"

"This is too much. What is going on, why would he keep that a secret?" Tina closed her eyes, taking a deep breath.

"Because he's a professional liar, make sure you tell him what I said," Helen spoke before hanging up the phone.

"Lord, I cannot tell Monique this right now. She can't take no more hurt from that man," Helen whispered.

38

"Mama, where you going?" Ava lay on the couch, looking as Tina walked to the front door fully dressed.

"I'll be back. I'm just going for a walk." She turned the top lock on the door to the left, unlocking it.

"I wanna come." Ava sat up.

"No, baby, I need to cool off. I'll be back." Tina opened the door, walking into the brightly lit day. The day was perfect. The sky was blue, the sun was shining, it wasn't too hot or too cold.

"How could he, why would he? All the hell he takes me through, He knows I love him. I'm gonna burn all his clothes and set him on fire for playing with me. He'll have to choose what life he wants to live," Tina mumbled as she walked down the sidewalk, hoping her walk would calm her enough to have this conversation with James. "I need to get out of this relationship. Look at me." Tina looked up at the blue sky. "Why would he lie, why would he keep this from me? I thought I knew him. Now I see why he wouldn't marry me. He's already married. Bastard!" She rolled her eyes. "God, I hate him so much for hurting me. I'm tired of people hurting me!" Tears fell from her eyes. "It's going to be okay, Tina. You can work this out. It'll be fine. I can work things out with James, I need him," she mumbled on and on. "This is not so bad. I know he really loves me. This is something we can get past." She continued walking down the street.

"Aye lady, you all right?" a man spoke from his front porch as Tina walked past.

"I don't know," she yelled. *I really need a cigarette*, she thought to herself, wiping her face with the sleeve of her shirt.

Two blocks away from her house sat a convenience store. She walked into the store, giving a half smile. She was known by the store workers as a regular. They knew what cigarettes she wanted before she even opened her mouth. She would also buy James's beer from time to time there. She bought her cigarettes, opening the pack as she walked out the door. Lighting the cigarette, she inhaled until the tip was bright red.

Smoke flowed from her nostrils as she continued walking. "Who am I? What am I doing, where am I going in life? I've messed up so much and now I don't know what to do. I'm so unhappy within myself. I'm unsure of who I am. I'm just so tired of me, myself, and I. My ways, my thinking and being trapped and unsure. I'm not happy at all. God. if you're still here for me and if you can hear me, please help me. I know I've let you down and hurt you so bad. I know I've been nasty, real nasty to you, but, God, it's me, and I don't know what else to do. I need you. I don't have anyone else to turn to," Tina talked under her breath. She threw the cigarette butt down, grabbing another one out the pack. "What am I saying? I know I'm the last person God wants to hear from. I've ruined that relationship. I just don't know where to turn." She walked a few more feet to a bus stop and sat on the bench, lighting her second cigarette.

"James, we really need to talk, it's an emergency and I need you to come home asap." Tina sent a text to James's phone.

Within seconds, he texted back. "What's so important that it can't wait until I get home, Tina?"

"James, I just really need to talk to you," she replied.

"It better be important. I'll take my break early. I'll be home in about an hour," he replied.

Tina stared at the text message. Her eyes swelled with tears as she blinked to keep them from falling. "Once again, I'm looking stupid." She stood up to walk back to the house.

It only took Tina a few minutes to walk home. Ava was still on the couch watching television when she walked back in the house.

"Baby, go wake up your sister. I need you two to go to Amber's for a little while." Tina sat on the couch next to Ava, kissing her forehead.

"Can we do something with you today, Momma?" Ava smiled.

"Yes, but Mommy has to take care of something first. After I pick you girls up, we can do whatever you want." She rubbed her face. "Now, go wake up Lina."

****

James walked into the house in a good mood. He walked up behind Tina as she stood washing a few dishes in the sink. "What's going on?" He kissed the back of Tina's neck.

"I love the name, Monique. What about you, baby? Tina rolled her eyes.

"What? I asked you what's going on, what's the emergency?"

"So, he really gonna act like he don't know who name I just said," Tina mumbled under her breath. "When are you going to call your wife? And your mother-in-law is angry with you." Tina turned the water off, turning around facing James. "You have a damn child, you're married, and I knew nothing about it!"

"What?" He stood with a confused countenance.

"So, you want to play this game? Did you not hear what I said? Who is Monique, who is Joshua, and when were you planning on telling me you're married? I've spent three years with you, and for what? You've wasted my time and put me through hell!" Tina bawled her fist. "You know damn well if I would've known you were married, I would not have given you the time of day. You're not even that cute!"

"Woman, shut the hell up." He stepped back. "Don't question me about something that doesn't concern you!"

"Doesn't concern me, have you lost your mind? I've given my body up to you. I've shared things with you that I've never told anyone but Kevin. I've let you into my life, my kid's life. You don't have a right to tell me this doesn't concern me! You're married! What part about that do you think is okay to not let me in on? That fact you're married or the fact you have a child that I've never heard about!" Tina jumped in James's face. "You round here stressing how you such a man, yet you have a child you do nothing for. And I'm the one looking like a fool!"

"Tina, this is my last time telling you, don't question me about something that doesn't concern you. Now I came here with a good attitude, but you're about to really piss me off!" James pushed Tina in the chest.

"You, sorry bastard, you're a liar, and a dead beat!" Tina punched James in the face. "I hate you!" She cried.

"Mind your damn business!" James punched Tina, causing her to hit the stove then fall to the floor. "I'm the best thing that's ever happened to you, and you want to question me about something that has nothing to do with you. I'm married, so what!" He stood over Tina, punching her over and over.

"I loved you so much," Tina squealed as she balled up to protect her face and stomach as much as she could from James's hits.

"You ain't nothing but trash, ain't nobody ever gonna want you. You can't make it without me!" He grabbed Tina by the neck, making her sit up.

"Every time I asked you about us getting married, you said the timing wasn't right. It wasn't right because you're already married. James, you wasted three years of my life. I'm messed up because of you. I never asked for this relationship." Tina tried to speak as her tears, emotions, and the pain she was now in overpowered her.

"Tina, what does it matter? I'm here with you, right?" James took his hands from around Tina's neck.

"Why do you hate me so much?" she screamed, as she sat on the floor, leaning against the stove.

"Shut up!" James slapped her in the face twice.

Tina screamed in pain; her cheek stung and instantly turned red. The sting took the words out of her mouth, leaving her holding her face, crying. The force of the slap made it feel as if she had a heart beating in her cheek.

"All I ever did was love you. What did I do? What did I do that was so wrong? I don't understand why you hate me so much."

James raised his fist to hit Tina again. He stared into her eyes then paused as he shook his head. "I can't love. I can't love anyone."

He smirked. "I'm incapable of loving. God messed up when He created me. You did this to yourself." He grabbed his car keys and walked out the door.

Tina sat against the stove, crying as she watched James leave out the front door. Once she heard the door lock, she stood up and limped to the bathroom. She looked in the mirror at her face then dropped to the floor bawling. "God, please help me. I'm so sorry for hurting you. I'm sorry for robbing you. I'm sorry for blaming you and cursing you. I'm sorry for turning my back on you." Tina wiped the snot from her nose. "God, I'm sorry for putting everything in my life before you. I'm sorry for not trusting you. I'm sorry for not loving you. I'm sorry for treating you bad. God, I need you. I don't know what else to do. I'm sorry, God, I'm sorry for falling short and going against everything you've taught me. I'm a mess, God, please help me. I can't do this anymore. I'm tired of fighting against you. I'm tired of running." Tina sat up, leaning against the wall. "God, all I can think about is how my relationship was with you back then, how close I was to you, how much I could hear you speaking to me, and how you allowed me to see through your eyes. And I look at where I am now. I hate who I've become. I'm nothing like I used to be. God, I don't know if I can ever make it right with you again, but I need you. I'm tired of this life, and I'm tired of hurting you. You've been there for me from day one. You've never done anything to hurt me or cause me to fall. I'm sorry, God, and if you can hear me, please help me. I need you." Tina stood up, walked to her room, and got in the bed under the covers. "God, I'm sorry. I'm sorry for all that I've done to you and to my family." Tina sighed then closed her eyes. "I don't want this life anymore. I can't do this. I want to live for you, please help me. Kevin, I'm sorry for letting you down. I'm sorry for letting you and our girls down."

****

"Why you look so bothered?" Amber looked at Lina as they sat on the couch, watching television.

"Something is up with my mom. She had Ava wake me up, so we could come over here." Lina rolled her eyes. "She gets on my nerves. I know it has something to do with James."

"Yeah, but you don't know if that's the real reason why she had you come over. What if she has a big surprise for you when you get back home." Amber smiled.

"I know my mother too well. I know it has something to do with him."

****

Ava sat at the kitchen table with Ms. Kelly and Monique eating freshly cut mangoes and pineapples.

"Ava, go ask the girls if they want some before I put it away." Kelly smiled.

Ava stood up, walking with a piece of mango in her hand. "Do you want some pineapples and mangoes before it gets put up?" Ava talked as she bit into the juicy, ripened mango.

"I do." Amber stood up. "Come on, Lina." She grabbed her hand.

"No, I'm okay. I don't want any." She stared at the TV.

Amber and Ava walked to the dining room, sitting at the table.

"Is Lina coming?" Kelly looked across the table at Amber.

"No, she's not feeling too good," Amber said as she reached into the bowl of fruit.

"What's wrong with her?" Monique looked at her.

"I can't say." Amber looked down.

"I'll go check on her." Monique smiled then stood up from the table, walking into the living room, sitting next to Lina on the couch.

"So, what's going on with you?" She rubbed Lina's hand.

She let out a sigh. "My mom, I'm just worried about her that's all." Lina stared at the television.

"Baby, you can talk to me about anything. You can't hold on to stuff. It'll eat you up inside."

"My mom." Lina paused. "My mom is with this man. She makes us tell people he's our stepfather, but they're not married. I hate him. He's done nothing but ruin our lives and hurt my mother. She's so messed up over him." Lina stared into Monique's eyes.

Monique gulped. "Why do you say she's messed up?"

"Any woman that lets a man beat on them and hurt her kids is messed up. She thinks she needs him, but she doesn't. I can see that and I'm only fifteen. I just wish she could see that."

"Wow," Monique mouthed.

"She met him after my father died and since then, our lives have been hell." Lina shook her head. "I'm sorry for cussing, but there's no other way to say it."

"Oh, honey, I understand about your life being hell because of someone else." Monique squeezed Lina's hand gently. "You know, the only one that can open your mom's eyes is God. I know you probably don't want to hear that right now, but I'm not telling you something I've heard. I'm telling you from experience."

"She doesn't believe in God anymore. She hates Him."

"Well, it's sad that you're a child and you have to be the adult in this situation, but you have to stand in the gap for your mother right now and keep her in prayer. Pray until God moves and trust me, He will. Sometimes, God will allow us to go through our own mess so that when He brings us out, we'll only be able to give Him the glory. Believe it or not, God gets tired of us wallowing in our mess, and when He says enough, she won't have a choice but to come out."

"I know God can do it. I'm just scared if He doesn't help her soon, it'll be too late. Then me and my sister won't have a mother." Lina's eyes watered.

"Oh, honey." Monique pulled Lina into her chest, wrapping her arms around her. "God, this is your baby. This thing has become a weight to her. I'm asking in the name of Jesus that you move in this situation and allow her mother's eyes to be opened. God, move sooner than later and help this family. In Jesus name I ask this, Amen."

"Amen." Lina began to cry. "Thank you." she whispered.

****

Tina beeped her horn as she sat in Kelly's drive way. It had been four hours since Lina an Ava were at Kelly's house. The girls came running out racing to the front seat. Lina sat in the front seat and Ava in the back seat.

"Mommy, I love you so much." Lina smiled at Tina, noticing the bruises on her face and swollen lip.

"I love you too." Tina smiled.

They stopped at the gas station along the way home, so the girls could get a few snacks. Once home, Ava went to her room taking a nap as Tina and Lina sat at the kitchen table.

"Momma, I'm praying for you, and I'm sorry you have to go through this." Lina looked into Tina's eyes. "I know you're stronger than this, and I know God is going to help you see again. Because even if you don't feel it or think it, God loves you so much."

Tina began to cry. She thought about when she was sitting on the bathroom floor just a few hours earlier crying out to God. She believed her daughter was confirming God was still with her, and that He had heard her cry.

"Baby, I'm so sorry for everything I've allowed you and your sister to go through. I don't ever want you to grow up to be like me." Tina talked as emotions overtook her.

"Mommy, I wouldn't want to be like anyone else but you. You've shown me no matter what, hold onto your faith. It's okay that you've gone through a small defeat, but you're coming out of this battle. You might have a few scars and wounds, but you're coming out alive." Lina stood up, walking to her mother, wrapping her arms around her, leaning her face against her mother's.

"Baby, you don't understand what your words mean to me right now." Tina sobbed. "I don't know how, but I'm leaving James. If I don't, I'm going to die mentally and emotionally." Tina paused. "I can't take this anymore, and I can't put you girls through this anymore."

"I don't know how either, but I'll do whatever I have to to make sure we're okay." Lina let go of her mother, wiping the tears from her mother's face. "I love you so much, Mommy, and I'm sorry if I've done anything or said anything in the past that hurt or disrespected you." She kissed her mother's cheek.

"Baby, I'm sorry for everything. I have to make this right. I have to."

Tina and Lina went into the room with Ava squeezing in the bed with her. Lina wasn't sure if her mother was serious, but she believed God was there, and He was going to move in their situation. Even if it took months from now, Lina was determined to keep praying until her mother was strong enough to follow through with her promises. In the meantime, she vowed to protect her mother and sister as much as she could, and to do whatever she had to, to get them out of the situation and house they were in.

39

"Lina!" Amber shouted, running down the hallway to her locker. "Lina, guess what?" She smiled, breathing heavily out of breath.

"Girl, what is wrong with you?" Lina stood with a confused look. "I heard you all the way down the hall." She laughed while straightening out her locker.

"I know but—" Amber said, trying to catch her breath. "Guess where we're going this weekend." She grinned.

"I don't know. We as in who?" She turned, looking at Amber.

"Well, me, you, Ava, my mom, and Mrs. Monique." Amber put her right hand on the locker next to Lina's. "Just guess where we're going." She put her left hand on her hip.

"Well, I don't know because I didn't know I was going some-where this weekend." She laughed.

"Since you want to be so difficult, I'll just tell you." Amber paused. "Wait for it, and we're waiting." She laughed.

"Just tell me already." Lina nudged her.

"We're going to see Daria Jones in concert." Amber grinned from ear to ear.

"Oh… my… god! Are you serious, oh my god." Lina screamed, smiling. "I can't believe this. I love her." Lina's eyes began to water. "Are you serious or just playing?"

"I'm so serious. I have to figure out what I'm going to wear." Amber smiled. "And guess what else." Her eyes lit up.

"What, just tell me." Lina placed her hands on Amber's shoul-ders, gently shaking her.

"We have VIP experience tickets. We get to meet her and take pictures with her, and talk to her, and hug her." Amber beamed. "I'm so excited. She's so amazing. Her songs give me so much life." Amber giggled.

"Oh my god," Lina shouted, causing people who were passing by to stare at her. "I hope she sings 'Smile', that's my song. I can't believe this, I love her so much. Oh my god, oh my god." She jumped up and down. "I'm going to cry. This is the best thing that's happened to me in a long time. She's my inspiration." She smiled, wiping the tears from her eyes.

"Saturday is going to be here before you know it, so you need to figure out what you're wearing. You and Ava can just come over after school Friday and stay the night. My mom already said it was okay. I can't wait this is going to be so litty." Amber hugged Lina.

"Yep, and Ava is going to flip when I tell her who we're going to see." Lina jumped up and down, grinning.

****

Amber and Lina paced back and forth in Amber's bedroom, anticipation was killing them. They had two hours left until it was time to leave for the concert and couldn't keep still from eagerness. They hardly slept the night before, excited about how their VIP experience would be. They talked all night about what they would say to Daria, and the things she would possibly say back to them.

Kelly had told Monique to be at her house around 1:30 p.m., so they could chat before the concert. Joshua would be staying with Mrs. Helen, so they could have a full girl's day. Monique was also excited about meeting Daria Jones. She was new to her music but fell in love with how pure and real her lyrics were. She felt each lyric spoke to her brokenness and built her back up. She loved even more how Daria sang from her soul, making her music that much more interesting. With every word sung, a picture was painted right before your eyes. Her music came to life, transforming the atmosphere.

"Girl, if this time doesn't hurry up and come on, I'm going to lose my mind." Amber bounced on her bed.

"I know, man. This is crazy. Time is moving so slow." Lina bit her bottom lip, staring at the clock. "Ava, are you excited?" Lina looked at Ava as she sat playing a game on Amber's computer in her room.

"Yes," she said, without breaking stare from the computer. "And you know, time moves the same every day. It's just because you're so excited that it seems to be moving slower."

"Okay." Lina looked at Amber before they both busted out laughing.

"Well, all I know is Daria is my best friend. She just doesn't know it." Lina and Amber laughed. "I just wish my mom would come so she could get out the house." Lina looked at the clock on the wall again. "I know if she just heard her music and got the chance to talk to her, it would help her." She laid back on the bed, staring up toward the ceiling.

"Things will change for her. They have to." Amber laid back on the bed. "I think I hear Mrs. Monique talking." She jumped up, running out the room to the front door.

"Hi, sweetie." Monique reached, hugging Amber.

"Hi, you look so pretty." She wrapped her arms around Monique.

"Lina, Ava, Mrs. Monique is here," Amber yelled.

"Hi." Lina walked up to Monique, hugging her as did Ava.

"You girls are so beautiful." Monique smiled. "You get prettier by the day."

"Thank—" Lina started to speak.

"Mom, is it time to go yet?" Amber asked, cutting everyone off.

"You. Thank you." Lina laughed.

"I guess." Kelly looked at her wrist watch. "This girl has been on twenty, aggravating my last nerve about this concert." Kelly looked at Monique, shaking her head.

"Girl, I been on go all morning too. I can't wait for this concert." Monique laughed.

Everyone grabbed the things they would be taking with them and headed to the car. The concert started at four, but they needed to be at the concert hall by two thirty in order to participate in the VIP backstage experience.

****

"About time, finally, we're here." Amber smiled, staring out the car window.

The concert hall's parking lot was packed. Lines wrapped around the building with people waiting for the doors to open to get their seats. Amber and Lina led the way as Kelly, Monique, and Ava followed behind them. They walked to the front of the building where a small line for the VIP experience entrance was. After a short wait, they were in. They were led to a medium-sized room, which held about forty people who were waiting on Daria to arrive. Noise filled the room as people talked, laughed, and smiled, excited to meet such a huge but humble star.

Daria Jones walked in about ten minutes later, wearing a black fitted jump suite with a shimmery gold blazer. She wore black heels with gold and red designs on them. Everyone stood up, clapping as she walked in the room.

"Stop, aww, thank you." She smiled. "Thank you for coming and sharing this special moment with me. I'm so grateful to all of you, and forever grateful for your love and support." She walked around the room, hugging everyone, smiling.

Daria Jones was a powerhouse in her own right; her voice was amazing and captivated those who heard it. Her strong foundation in God gave her the mind-set of humbleness and kept her grounded. Most of all, she had a heart for people, which drew people to her. Her style and the way she sung was groovy, soothing, euphoric, and eclectic. When she sang, it made you feel as if you were in a utopia. But most of all, when she sang, it was from the heart. Daria's music was labeled as R&B/soul/inspirational. She didn't want to box her music into one category, feeling her music wasn't based off just one genre. She was different from the norm and felt it robbery to consider just one type of style for music when she had a love for it all. She wanted people to get a message from her music, whether it was to feel inspired, love, hope, comfort, or to know they weren't alone. Her goal through her music was to make the world a better place, even if it only reached one person. And her love for people is what kept her going. The faces of people in the audience inspired her to keep going and doing what she was doing in music, which was her first love. She knew people were counting on her, and she knew her voice and talent was a gift from God to help others. She was effective when she sang, and people made sure she knew how much joy she brought them through her music.

The guest at the VIP experience were amazed at how vibrant, funny, and down to earth Daria was. She joked with everyone, took pictures, and laughed, allowing others to see that just because you're a huge star, you don't have to be bigheaded, snobby, or uptight. You could have fun and be you. Her main goal was to remain true to herself in all she did and to show people that it's okay to be you and love who you are. She made sure after every concert, she spoke to the crowd telling them to love themselves, spend time with themselves, and be the best you that you could be.

Daria walked to the corner area where Kelly and Amber stood.

"Hi, you're so pretty." She hugged Lina.

"Hi." Lina hugged her, speechless as her eyes watered.

"Aww, don't cry." She stepped back from Lina, holding her chin up.

"I can't believe I'm finally meeting you. You're so amazing. I love you." Lina grinned, wiping her eyes.

"Aww, thank you." She smiled.

"Girl, you give me life over and over again." Amber hugged Daria.

"You're so crazy." She laughed as she hugged Amber back.

Daria's fans appreciated her and made her feel appreciated. When she felt like giving up, she knew it was her fans that kept her on her game and making music. She was excited to meet the ones who supported her and allowed her ministry to make a difference. After going around the room personally meeting everyone, Daria walked to a small stage where she stood to answer questions.

"What is your favorite song from one of your albums and why?" Someone in the crowd raised their hand.

"Well, I would have to say 'Smile', because it brings me to a happy place. It reminds me no matter how dark things may seem, it's not always about me and if I put a smile on my face regardless of what I'm going through or how I feel, and the fact that I never know what someone else is going through, if I put a smile on my face, I know it will bring joy, and my smile could help someone else get through their day. A smile can really take you a long way." Daria smiled.

"What would you say to someone who has felt like giving up on God?" Lina raised her hand.

"Don't give up. It can seem as if God has forgotten you, but He hasn't. Sometimes, we're in places where we have to just trust Him, even if we don't see or feel him. And enjoy the process whether it hurts, enjoy every moment because it's all going to work out for your greater good. Also, your story isn't your own. It's definitely for someone else. So, to answer your question, remember, God loves you so much. Sometimes, our circumstances can cloud our mind, judgment, and even our faith, so you have to ask yourself, is it really worth giving up on someone who has never given up on me? Someone who pushes me to be the best I can be, someone who gave up so much for me, and someone who's there for me even when I don't feel like being there for myself. Don't give up." Daria looked on at others as they raised their hands.

"What would you say to someone who has been hurt from past relationships whether it be from a relationship, friendship, or church?" Kelly raised her hand.

"I would say life goes on. While that situation may seem like it's the worst possible thing that could ever happen to you and this may be true, there's always someone worst off than you. We tend to forget that. Encourage yourself to know it's not your fault. Some things that happen to us aren't always our fault depending on the circumstances. Don't beat yourself up for what may have happened. It happened, but you don't have to be the victim of holding onto that hurt. You can be free and move on. Also, you have to guard your heart and yourself to not let it happen again. Be wise." She smiled.

People asked a few more questions before Daria and her team handed out special gift bags to let her fans know how much she appreciated them. She walked around taking more pictures and talking with people before leaving the room, allowing everyone to get their seats before the doors were opened for the people outside.

"She touched my face." Lina chuckled. "I'm never washing my face again." She smiled, talking to Amber.

"Well, I'm never washing my hand or my shirt." Amber laughed.

"Oh, you're washing your face, crazy girl." Kelly nudged Lina in the back, laughing.

****

The music blared through the speakers. Daria's voice filled the room as people stood up; some dancing; some recording with their phones; some sitting, crying as the words of the songs touched them in their situations; and some singing along.

Lina stood between Monique and Amber.

"I hate I have to go back home tomorrow. James Austin drives me crazy. I wish he would disappear so me and my family could have peace," Lina talked.

"I know, and I keep saying it. Better days are coming for you and your family. You have to focus on that because if you focus on the bad, it will drive you crazy." Amber grabbed Lina's hand.

"Ugh, just the thought of hearing his voice is making me sick." Lina looked toward the stage.

Did she just say James Austin? Monique mumbled. *I know it can't be more than one James Austin.*

"We're actually here watching Daria Jones." Amber looked at Lina. "Let's enjoy this time and worry about James later." She smiled.

The concert lasted for two hours. Daria ended the show with a song she had written called "Chances". At the sound of the beat, the crowd went crazy.

Monique closed her eyes, singing along as she swayed side to side, dancing with her hands. "This is my song." She opened her eyes, smiling. "You better sang that song!" she shouted.

****

Monique sat in the passenger seat pondering in thought. She wanted to ask Lina about the James she had mentioned to Amber but was unsure of how to go about it. For thirty-five minutes, she thought over and over what to say to Lina.

"Can I talk to you alone?" Monique turned in the seat, looking at Lina as they pulled into Kelly's driveway.

"Sure." Lina stared out the window.

Everyone went inside leaving Monique and Lina on the porch.

"I don't mean to intrude or be nosy, but I overheard you mentioning a man named James Austin to Amber." Monique looked into Lina's eyes.

"Ugh." Lina sighed. "Yes, that's my mom's boyfriend. She tries to make me and my sister say he's our stepfather but he's not, and he will never be a father to me or my sister." Lina dropped her head. "I hate that man."

"What does he look like? If you don't mind me asking."

"He's dark skinned, has a low haircut, and he used to be a cop until he got fired." Lina smirked.

Monique's heart skipped a beat. She knew there was no coincidence of there being two men named James Austin who were police officers. "So, you don't like him?" Monique asked, her voice shaking.

"Like isn't even a word I would use to describe it. My family hasn't been the same since he's been around. Three years too long." Lina looked up toward Monique.

"Three years? You've known him for three years?"

"Yes, he's been with my mother for three years, ever since my father passed, he's been in the picture."

Monique looked away, blinking fast trying to blink her tears away. She began to put two and two together. James had started acting funny with her, staying out all times of night and telling lies that he was working extra shifts. Eventually, he moved his stuff out without a reason as to why and came by every now and then to sleep with Monique. She figured something was going on but wasn't sure what it was. She wanted to dig in deeper but didn't want to make Lina feel uncomfortable.

"Does he have any children?" Monique looked toward the car in the driveway.

"Nope, I've never seen or heard about any kids of his."

Monique shook her head. She could feel her temperature rising from anger. She stood up brushing off her shirt. "Honey, go on inside. I'm going for a little walk." She smiled, walking toward the road. *I should call that bastard and tell him about himself. It's one thing to deny me but to deny your own flesh and blood*, she thought. She walked a couple hundred feet down the road then made her way back to Kelly's house. Without saying goodbye, she got in her car and left.

40

"Momma!" Monique ran busting through the front door. "Momma!"

"Monique, what's wrong, baby?" Helen jumped up from the couch.

It was now ten at night. Joshua was sound asleep in his bedroom, unaffected from his mother's yell.

"Momma, James." Monique fell into her mother's arms, resting her head on her breast, crying. "James was cheating on me. He was cheating. That's why he stopped coming around. He doesn't even acknowledge he has a child. He's with a woman who has two daughters. Momma, why, why?" She sobbed.

"Baby, it's okay. Imma handle him." Helen kissed Monique's forehead. "I love you and Joshua. He has the best mother in the world. It's on James. He's the one missing out on watching Joshua grow up." Helen walked with Monique to the couch. "Baby, sit down. It's something I have to tell you."

Helen and Monique both sat. She held Monique in her arms as she continued to cry.

"Momma, I don't understand why, what was so wrong with me that he decided to just up and leave and get a new family? I gave him all of me, I loved him so hard, I waited on him hand and foot," Monique talked in a whisper. "I look like an even bigger fool now."

"It's nothing wrong with you, baby, nothing at all. He didn't realize the diamond he had. It's his stupidity and his loss." Helen squeezed Monique tighter in her arms. "You didn't know, baby, you don't look like a fool. He does."

"When I see that lady!" Monique sniffed the snot back up. "He has a damn wife, and she's sitting here with my husband, my son's father, playing wife."

"Baby, I called James. He…" She paused. "Baby, I talked to the lady James is with. I'm sorry, baby, I couldn't tell you right then and there. I knew it would hurt you to the core if you found out. I just wanted you to be able to focus on yourself and get better." Helen stroked Monique's hair. "Baby, that lady knew nothing about you or Joshua. She didn't know he had ever been married. She was shocked and hurt when I told her. You can't blame her because she didn't know." Helen kissed Monique's forehead again.

"I hate him so much! I don't give a damn about me but to deny or not even acknowledge your own child. He's innocent. He didn't ask to be in this world or to have him as a father. How can you abandon your own child like that?" Monique continued to cry. "I guess I'm just more hurt to know that my marriage is really over and to know my son is going to be the one that gets hurt from this."

"Baby, he's not going to hurt. He has people that love him and will do anything for him." Helen stared down at Monique. "I'm going to do whatever I have to do to protect his heart and innocence. He's not going to hurt at all. And if James doesn't want to man up and be around, then that's his loss." Helen kissed Monique on the head. "Now you, I want you to be okay. Let that man go, baby. That's the best thing you can do for yourself, your child, and your health. Find your peace and let him go."

"Mama, it's hard but I'm trying. I've been home now, and he still hasn't called or answered my calls. It's like I don't even exist to him." Monique wiped her eyes with her mother's blouse. "I guess it's finally time to let go and move on," Monique whispered. "I just don't know how."

"Baby, trust me. When you finally free yourself from that man and break the soul tie you have with him, your life is going to be less stressful, and your heart will be free to really love again." Helen gently squeezed Monique. "Baby, I promise I got you and I'm going to walk through this with you. I love you so much, baby." Helen rocked back and forth as she held Monique in her arms.

"I love you too, Momma." Monique closed her eyes. "You smell like pine cones." Monique laughed through her tears.

"Just breathe it in, baby." Helen laughed along with Monique. "I love you and don't you worry." She stroked Monique's hair. "Just wait until I talk to that fool," Helen mumbled.

41

"You look rough on this beautiful Sunday." Black laughed. She was a girl who ran with a crowd known to be mischievous, always in mess. Black was two months shy of eighteen, but due to so many absences, she was missing credits, which caused her to be considered a sophomore/junior in high school. This caused her to be partly in the same grade as Lina.

"Black, shut up!" Lina rolled her eyes as she walked to the mailbox to check the mail, which hadn't been checked in almost a week.

"Everybody knows ya stepdaddy be beating ya mom's ass. He must've gotten to you too." Black licked her lips, walking behind Lina.

"If you ain't helping me…" Lina paused. "Girl, shut up! God gonna make a way for us to get out of that house with James." Lina rolled her eyes.

"Girl, you sound dumb as hell. All this bad stuff happening in the world and you sitting here talking about God will make a way. You dumb as hell if you sit here and think waiting on something or someone invisible is gonna change your life." Black rolled her eyes.

"It ain't like God the one making all this bad stuff happen. He's not telling people to do the bad and ignorant stuff their doing. If you had any sense, you would know it's called freewill. It's like how your parents tell you to go to school. You have a choice to go to school and do what you're supposed to do, or to do what you want and not go. It's freewill. And just because God isn't stopping all the bad in the world doesn't mean He can't. But that's another story, something you wouldn't understand." Lina smirked.

Black was known to be a little rough around the edges. She was also known to have money and the latest pair of name brand shoes to come out. Her hair stayed done and her hustle or whatever it was she did kept her looking fresh. At least, that's what people thought. Her father was into selling drugs and was the one who kept her looking the way she did.

"I got you only if you're serious." Black stood, looking, as Lina turned the key in the mailbox.

"Man, I'll do anything to get my mom and sister away from that man. I want him out of our lives for good." Lina pulled two envelopes from the mailbox before slamming it shut.

"Oh yeah, what happened to God will make a way." Black laughed.

"Girl, please don't start. You can't expect God to move if you don't do your part." Lina rolled her eyes.

"Oh, trust me. God ain't in this." Black smirked. "I got something in mind, but you have to be serious. I don't have time for games." She smiled.

People couldn't understand why Black was the way she was. She was a beautiful chocolate complexed girl. Her parents were still together married and did everything they could to make sure Black, whose real name was Brianna, had what she needed. All she had to do was go to school and makes good grades while they handled everything else.

"This something I have to do." Lina smirked, trying to hide the nervousness she felt inside. Deep down, Lina was scared. On the other hand, she felt she couldn't sit around any longer to wait for James to kill her mother. "I'm about this." Lina smiled.

"The saying goes, I'm about that, not I'm about this." Black laughed. "This Friday night, gonna be lit so get ready." She smiled.

****

"I have to tell you something. Promise me you can keep this secret." Lina leaned against the lockers as Amber rummaged around in her locker.

"Since when did you start having secrets to keep?" Amber slammed her locker shut to keep all the junk she had in it from falling out.

"So…" Lina paused, biting her lip. "I have a plan to get me and my family away from James."

"A plan, what plan?" Amber stood in front of Lina, smacking on a piece of gum.

"I'm going with Black. I don't know where yet, but it's gonna get me the money we need to get our own place and pay the bills up for a couple of months."

"Are you talking about Black, as in Brianna?" Amber stood with a confused look on her face. "Lina, are you crazy? You know how that girl rolls. She's nothing but trouble and this already sounds like a bad idea."

"I'm not crazy. I'm desperate. Amber, I hate the life me and my family living. It's like no one cares to do anything about it but me. I'm my sisters' keeper, and I can't allow her to keep going through what we deal with. I want my family back, and I'll do whatever I have to do to make it happen." Lina stared into Amber's eyes.

"But what about God, don't you think He'll make a way? A way for you and your family to be happy?"

"Amber, God is taking too long. Like how long does He expect us to sit and suffer?"

"Maybe it's not God taking too long. Maybe it's your mom taking too long to listen to what God is saying."

"Well, even if that's the case, I have to have faith for all of us right now, and faith without works is dead, right?"

"Yea, well, I don't think that's the kind of works the book of James was talking about." Amber sucked her teeth. "Look, I know I can't tell you what to do especially when you have your mind set on something, but I can tell you whatever you're going to do isn't worth hurting God or your relationship with Him. He's been there for you this whole time and you know it. You're the image of God your mom sees right now, and we both know it's not because of your own works."

"Amber, just let me do me. I don't need anyone judging me right now. Especially when you're not the one in my shoes. You can't tell me anything 'cause it's not you." Lina lowered her head, rolling her eyes.

"I'm not judging you. Just promise me you'll stay in contact with me the whole time you're wherever you are."

"I promise." Lina smiled. "Now, let's get to class before we're late."

****

Amber felt uneasy about the whole situation with Lina. She knew it was out of character for Lina to do whatever it was she was planning to do. She also knew Lina and Ava were going through hell in the house with James. What she couldn't understand is why Mrs. Tina allowed herself and her girls to go through everything Lina told her they went through. An even though her mother was a cop and could get Lina and Ava out that house, Lina begged Amber not to tell anyone especially her mother the things she shared with her. She knew DCF would probably get involved and take her and her sister away from their mother, possibly even splitting them up and arresting their mother for child neglect, feeling she neglected to care about their safety, keeping them in the house.

"What's wrong, baby?" Kelly asked as Amber sat at the kitchen table in a daze.

"I don't know. It's this girl who has trouble in her home with her family and..." Amber paused as her eyes began to water. "She thinks doing bad stuff will change her family's situation."

"Aww, sweat pea." Kelly walked over to Amber, kissing her forehead, rubbing her back. "It's okay, baby, we—"

"It's not, Mom. Why is it some people have life so good and some have it hard?" Amber cut her mother off.

"Sweetie, I wish I knew the answer, but I don't. I think having a hard life for some helps you to appreciate things even more. In a sense, it gives you the fight to want more out of life. But all you can

do is encourage those who are going through and pray for them."
Kelly wrapped her arms around Amber's shoulders.

****

Black texted Lina to meet her by the mailboxes around 7:10
p.m. She told her they were going to a hotel and men were going to
be there. She also said to wear something that would show some skin.
It was now 6:23 p.m., so Lina hopped in the shower to freshen up.

"God, what am I doing? What am I doing? This isn't me," Lina
whispered as beads of water hit her back. The steam from the shower
covered the walls and mirror in the bathroom. She closed her eyes,
soaping up her face. "I can do this, anything for my family. I just
want us to be happy again," she whispered as she turned her body,
allowing the hot water to flow on her face, rinsing the suds. "Why
does it have to be like this?" She washed her body and then rinsed
off. She turned the water off and reached around the shower curtain,
grabbing her towel off the sink. She patted her face dry before covering her face with the towel, letting out a silent scream.

"I wish I knew what I was doing, I'm scared but I can't back out
now, plus my family needs this," Lina texted Amber once she was out
the shower and dressed.

"What did you tell your mom?" Amber texted back.

"Me and Ava are staying the night at your house. I'm not leaving my sister here. We'll drop her off to your house before we go, I'll
come over after," Lina replied.

"I can't believe you're actually doing this, just make sure you
text me and let me know where you are," Amber immediately replied.

The time was now 7:03 p.m., Lina and Ava walked into their
mother's room to hug and kiss her and to let her know their ride
was out waiting. Lina told her mother Ms. Kelly was picking them
up so she didn't have to drive them. Tina trusted her girls at Kelly's
house and thought of Amber as a respectful and well-mannered girl.
And Kelly was okay with Lina and Ava staying the night since she
picked up an extra shift and would be working late. She didn't like
for Amber to be home alone even though she taught her how to use a

gun and showed her where she kept her extra gun in case something ever happened.

"We'll be back tomorrow, Mama. We love you." Lina smiled as her and Ava walked out the front door.

"Girl, that's what you call showing some skin?" Black laughed as she rolled down the passenger side window. Her parents rented her a car, which happened to be a black on black Camaro since hers was in the shop. "Come on, get in." She unlocked the doors.

"This is all I had." Lina lifted the lever on the front seat, moving it up so Ava could get in the back seat. Lina wore a red spaghetti strap shirt with a pair of white skinny leg jeans and gold sandals.

"Okay, so the plan," Black said before Lina interrupted.

"Wait until we drop my sister off," Lina whispered. "She doesn't need to know what's going on."

Once they pulled up to Amber's house, Lina got out to let Ava out the car. She hugged her and told her she loved her and would be back in about two hours. Amber and Ava walked to the porch, waving as Lina and Black pulled off.

"So, this is the plan." Black smiled, pulling out a blunt from her purse. "It's a dude named Rico and his homeboy Dread. They trap out of their hotel room. My cousin chills with them and said they keep at least $30,000 in a shoebox under the bed. I'll grab the money. All you have to do is keep Dread occupied." She lit the blunt, hitting it four times before passing it to Lina.

"I don't smoke." She pushed Black's hand away. "Occupied?" Lina tooted her nose up, cocking her head to the side.

"Yes, occupy. And, girl, hit the blunt. Trust me, it's gone ease ya mind." Black leaned her hand toward Lina again.

"How do I occupy a man who has the ability of occupying his own self?" Lina rolled her eyes, grabbing the blunt, hitting it and immediately coughed like she was coughing up a lung. "I'm…" She coughed twice. "Done." She coughed four more times.

"I don't know. Figure out something. Anyways, when I get the money, I'll come out and tell you I'm feeling sick or something. That's gonna be the signal for us to leave before they figure out what's going on." Black reached under her seat, grabbing a small bottle of Hennessy and two small Styrofoam cups.

"Ummm, I don't drink." Lina looked at the bottle.

"Yeah, well, you don't smoke either but look at you." Black put the bottle between her legs, opening it. "Trust me, once you drink a little of this, you'll be cool, calm, and collective to get the job done." She poured some in each cup. "Look under your seat and get that can of Coke, pour it in the cups." She looked at Lina then back at the road.

"Girl, how do you even get alcohol, you're not even twenty-one?" Lina cracked open the soda can.

"Who said you had to be twenty-one to get alcohol? That's what the government wants you to believe. I got the connect." Black laughed.

"I knew this was a bad idea. I knew it," Lina mumbled but did as told. "So, when they find out what we did, they'll come looking for us. I don't know, Black, this sounds dangerous." Lina turned, staring at Black.

"You worrying about the wrong thing right now. We gotta get this money. Just chill, we got this. Don't get scared and back out now." Black turned the radio down, grabbing her cup and taking a sip. "Drink your drink and calm ya nerves, girl."

"I'm... I'm not scared. You just better be right about your plan." Lina's voice cracked as her stomach began to turn in knots. She grabbed the cup, taking a gulp. "Oh my god, this is disgusting. You can't possibly like the way this taste." She grabbed the can of Coke, taking a gulp from the leftover soda in it.

"It ain't all that, but it makes me feel hella good." Black laughed.

Lina sipped on the drink to calm her nerves while Black drove with the music blasting. It took about forty minutes to get to the hotel where Rico and Dread were. Once in the parking lot, the sight of the place looked a bit rundown. It was a two-story building with about thirty rooms between the first and second floors on each side of the building. Lina thought to herself either the rooms inside looked really nice, despite the outer appearance, or the rooms were really cheap to stay in. Despite the many potholes in the parking lot, it was packed with cars and people making all kinds of noise. People filled the pool area, drinking and loud talking while some women danced around the poolside. Black parked four parking spaces away from the entrance. She wanted to be as close to the entrance as she could in case they had to make a quick getaway.

"Try not to look so scared. Loosen up and breathe," Black talked as she used the rearview mirror to put on some red matte lipstick. "Do you want some?" Black puckered her lips together.

"First off, this ain't no hotel. This is what you call a motel, and no, I don't want no lipstick. Yes, I'm nervous. I don't belong here, oh Jesus." Lina began to talk fast. "My momma gonna kill me if she finds out. Oh my god, I can't breathe." Lina began huffing fast.

"Here, take a shot." Black poured some Hennessy in both their cups, gulping hers down.

"Ugh, this is so nasty." Lina gulped hers down, scrunching up her face.

"Calm down. You can't go in there acting all nervous talking all fast. They're gonna figure out something is up, or they're gonna think you're crazy or on something. Just chill." Black opened the car door, stepping out.

They got out the car as Black locked the doors. They walked slowly through the parking lot heading to the stairs, which took them to the room that sat on the second floor. Men whistled at them calling them sexy and thick. They shouted for them to come where they were, so they could get to know them. Lina was nervous but ready to do what they came to do, so they could get as far away from this place as possible.

"OMG, this place is a dump, and these grown men are whistling at us. I'm freaking out inside. OMG." Lina pulled out her phone, texting Amber.

Within seconds, Amber texted back. "Where are you?"

"I'm at Swim Inn Motel, second floor. We're going to room 237. Pray for me..." Lina replied.

"Lina, please text me and let me know what's going on..." Amber texted.

"Ok we're knocking on the door, I'll text you," Lina texted then put her phone on silent mode.

Black knocked on the door twice. "They need to come on," she mumbled as Rico opened the door.

"Hey, beautiful, come in." Rico smiled.

Black and Lina walked in sitting on the sofa. Lina looked around the room, shaking inside. The room, which happened to be a suite, was a small room with a tiny kitchenette and sitting area. The bedroom sat off to the corner of the sitting area with the bathroom adjacent to the bedroom. The room had a musty smell mixed with the smell of marijuana and alcohol. The air conditioner rattled, which made it obvious it had problems because the walls sweated. Broken up blunts laid on the coffee table along with gar guts, which covered the coffee table and floor. The room was foggy from all the smoking Rico and Dread had been doing. Open bottles of alcohol sat on the table and counter in the kitchenette area with a few dirty glasses on the table.

"So, what's yo name, sexy?" Rico smiled, looking at Lina as he walked over to Black, grabbing her hand.

"Umm." Lina stared at the television. *My mom's gonna kill me*, she thought.

"Her name is Mya." Black nudged Lina.

"Man, let her talk for herself. She knows her name." Rico laughed. "You look nervous, shawty. Imma get Dread out here to calm you down." Rico smiled then yelled for Dread to come from the room.

"Just chill." Black leaned over to Lina, whispering.

"Hi, beautiful." Dread, a dark-skinned man who had a mouth full of golds and about ten thick dreads, who looked to be in his mid-twenties walked from the room, sitting in the recliner chair next to the chair Lina sat in. He puffed on a blunt as he talked.

Lina sat staring at the television, scared. Her heart was racing, and her throat was beginning to get dry.

"You wanna hit the blunt?" Dread reached over to Lina, trying to hand the lit blunt. "It'll calm ya nerves."

"Um, no, thank you. I don't smoke." Lina looked at Black.

"Girl, you just hit the blunt in the car." She mouthed to Lina.

"Well, we going in the room so you two can get to know each other." Rico laughed as he lit up his own blunt. "Bruh, you got ya hands full." He laughed again.

Black and Rico went into the bedroom while Lina sat on the couch, feeling out of place. Dread stood up, walking over to the couch Lina sat on, scooting his body close to hers.

"You don't have to be so tense. I just want to get to know you. Loosen up." Dread placed his blunt in the ashtray on the coffee table. He leaned back. moving in to kiss Lina's neck.

Lina moved her head away, hoping he got the gesture she was not interested.

"Calm down, sweetie." Dread placed his hand on Lina's thigh, moving his head toward her neck, trying to kiss her again.

"Have you ever had bumps on your mouth or cold sores, because I'm not trying to catch anything?" Lina blurted out.

"Man, you trippin, just chill." He laughed.

"I need to use the bathroom." Lina looked at Dread. She stood up waiting for him to direct her where to go. She was disgusted with the fact this man who she knew nothing about and vice versa thought it was okay to kiss her.

"It's the door right there." He pointed to a dingy brown-looking door.

Once in the bathroom, Lina texted Amber.

"OMG... Their smoking weed, and he tried to kiss me. I want to leave! p.s. I did smoke a little weed and drink just a tad bit on the way here..."

"I can't believe you out here smoking and drinking now!!! Where's Black?" Amber texted back immediately. She kept her phone by her waiting for Lina's reply.

"She's in the room with some boy, I'm sitting in the bathroom, but it's a boy waiting in the sitting area for me. I'm so uncomfortable."

"Just leave, tell Black your mom found out you aren't at my house," Amber replied, she began to worry.

"I don't know, I'll text you in a few," Lina replied.

Lina stood, leaning against the wall, rubbing her face with her hands. "God, I don't know what I'm doing. I don't want to be here. This isn't me. This isn't what I do," she whispered. She flushed the toilet and turned the sink on to make Dread think she had used the bathroom. She turned the water off and walked to the recliner, sitting down, trying to avoid eye contact with Dread.

****

The only lighting in the room came from the television. Rico made sure to turn the volume up enough in case things with him and Black were to happen. He had one thing on his mind and by the way, Black was looking he was sure he was about to get what he wanted.

"You looking all good." Rico smiled, showing his golds as Black laid back on the bed, her feet still on the carpet.

"So why you wanted me to come chill with you?" Black bit her bottom lip.

"I get lonely." Rico laughed.

"Stop playing. I'm pretty sure girls be all up on you."

"They do, but I got my eyes on somebody."

"Oh yea." Black laughed. She knew of Rico but had never talked to him up until a week ago, when her cousin put her on about Rico and his business.

"I just want to spoil you." Rico rubbed Black's bare skin on her stomach, moving his hand up to her breast. He laid his body on top of hers as they began kissing.

"We can't do anything without a condom." Black pushed Rico on the chest.

"You serious, man." He jumped up, fumbling in his pant pockets. "I ain't got none." He looked at Black, hopeful she would change her mind.

"Well, you're outta luck then." Black rolled her eyes.

Rico walked to the sitting area to ask Dread if he had any protection. "Man, you really gonna make me go all the way to the store for a condom?" He walked back to the room.

"Did you think I was playing? I'm not doing anything without protection."

"Girl, you tripping. I'll be back. Don't go nowhere, man." Dread grabbed his car keys, stepped into his Jordan slides, and left the room.

Black waited ten minutes to be sure he was really gone. She silently walked to the room door locking it, then started looking under the bed for the money. After moving a black duffle bag that contained a couple guns, she found the shoebox. She opened the box and seen what her cousin had been talking about. The box contained fifty and one-hundred-dollar bills. She grabbed the money, making sure she left nothing behind and placed it in a small black backpack she had worn. She sat on the bed thinking of what it was she was going to say to leave without bringing any suspicion to them.

****

"Aye, bro, I'm running to the store. I'll be back in a few." Rico walked past Dread and Lina, and out the door.

"So, you gonna act all shy and sit over there or come over here?" Dread smiled at Lina.

"I'll sit right here." Lina looked at Dread, becoming frustrated at how hard he was trying to get her to fall for him.

"Why you acting like that?" He stood up, walking to the chair where Lina sat. "I just want to be your friend." He placed his hand on top of Lina's.

"I need to use the bathroom." Lina jumped up walking fast to the bathroom. "I have diarrhea," she yelled before closing the door shut.

"This boy is making me feel so uncomfortable," Lina texted Amber.

"Just leave, I'll call my mom to come get you," Amber replied.

"I can't, your mom would tell my mom and she would kill me, she already thinks I'm a liar, I can't have her knowing I'm not really at your house," Lina replied.

Black walked out and sat on the couch, asking Dread where Lina was.

"Man, ya home girl been tripping all night." He shook his head.

"She's a good girl, that's why." Black laughed.

Black sat watching television on the couch when Dread's phone began to ring.

"Bruh, where you at?" Dread lit up his blunt.

"Aye, Taye, coming to get five racks? Give him that. He should be there in about ten minutes." Rico talked loud enough that he could be heard over the phone.

"I'm on it, aye, bruh, bring me back a peach soda." Dread said before he hung up the phone.

Dread walked into the room, closing the door behind him. Black jumped up, running to the bathroom, trying to get Lina, so they could hurry and leave before their plan was known.

"Lina, let's go." Black began tapping on the door as she began to panic. "I got it. Let's go now!" She talked loud enough only to be heard by Lina.

Dread looked under the bed, pulling the shoebox from underneath the bed. He opened it, immediately calling Rico.

"Bruh, where you put it at?" Dread asked, thinking Rico had moved the money.

"Dummy, man, don't play with me. It's in the gray shoebox under the bed."

"Rico, it ain't there. Ain't nothing in it." Dread threw the box on the bed.

"Bruh, I'm on my way. Don't let Black leave!" Rico hung up the phone.

As Lina was opening the bathroom door, Dread ran out of the room with a gun.

"Where the money?" He put the gun to Black's head.

"What money?" She tried to play it cool.

Lina immediately slammed the door shut, locking it. She pulled her phone out from her pocket to text Amber.

"OMG, this is bad. He has a gun, and he's yelling at Black asking where's the money," Lina texted as her hands shook.

"What are y'all gonna do?" Amber replied as she cried, panicking, trying to figure out what to do.

"I don't know he's banging on the door. I'm scared help," Lina texted as she began to cry.

Lina could hear Dread yelling at Black to take off everything she had on. He continued to bang on the door and jingle the door handle, trying to get the bathroom door open.

"Oh my god, the other boy is back," Lina texted Amber as she heard Rico walking through the door, yelling.

"You got two seconds to give me my money or I'm killing you and your friend!" Rico yelled in Black's face.

"I don't know what money you're talking about." Black kept her composure, ignoring the commands of Dread to take off everything she had on.

"Amber, he's gonna kill us, he said he's gonna kill us." Lina shook nervously as she texted Amber, crying.

"Lina, stay in the bathroom, I'm calling someone," Amber texted back.

"You better come out the bathroom before I bust the door open. You got two minutes to get out here!" Dread yelled, banging on the door.

Lina turned to the wall, pounding her head softly against it, trying to figure out what to do. Dread began kicking the door, trying to bust it open.

"Amber, I have to go, if I don't he's gonna kill us. I love you and let my family know I'm sorry and I love them so much," Lina texted Amber before walking out the bathroom. She had seen what happened in movies to people who were in her situation. She knew from the sound of Rico and Dread's voice, and Black playing dumb, the outcome for them wasn't going to be good.

"Tell ya friend to give me my money or Imma hurt both of y'all. We can play this however you want to!" Rico yelled. "That's the only reason you came here!" Split flew from his mouth as he got in Black's face.

"Bruh, she got it, shawty was in here with me." Dread looked at Rico.

"But since that's ya friend, Imma have to kill both of y'all. I suggest you tell your friend to give me what belongs to me." Rico pulled out a gun, waving it in the air, staring at Lina.

"I don't know what you're talking about. I just want to go home." Lina cried.

Black stood next to Lina by the bathroom door quietly. She figured if she showed fear, they wouldn't let them go.

"Look, homie, we ain't got ya money, so chill." Black smirked.

"Oh I see, you wanna act like a lil smart ass? Imma show you what a smart mouth gets you." Dread shoved his gun in Black's face. He snatched the book bag she had on, causing her to fall to the floor. He opened the bag where all the money sat. "So, this how we doing it now!" He laughed.

"Can we please leave? You have your money." Lina begged.

"Y'all ain't going nowhere. See, I can't let you take what's mine and when I get it back, you think you're going to leave just like that. I wish I could let you go, sweetie, but then I know you would run to the police and we can't have that." Rico rubbed his chin. "Man, I hate to do this to a good girl, but I gotta kill ya."

Black and Lina began to cry. Lina was worried more about what would happen to her sister and the things she would have to go through being in the house with James. She also thought how much her death would destroy her already destroyed mother. Black felt bad she had gotten Lina involved in all of this and began apologizing over and over to her. She knew Lina was really a good girl and wanted nothing more than to see her family happy.

"Get on ya knees." Rico pointed the gun at Lina while Dread pointed his gun at Black. "Imma give y'all five minutes to think about your actions." He laughed.

Lina held Black's hand and began to pray. She asked God to forgive them for their wrongdoings. She asked Him to protect their families and to help them heal from what was about to happen to them. She asked God to really guide Ava and send someone in her life who could help steer her in the right direction, and then she asked God to have mercy on Rico and Dread's soul. Black held Lina's hand tight, begging God to help them. She promised God if He did, she would change her life and stop all the bad she was doing.

"Times up," Dread spoke quietly.

At that moment, the room door flung open.

"You sorry, little wannabe thugs! You have two seconds to back away from them. The cops are on their way, and I'm going to make sure of it you two never see the light of day. Besides the fact you have a minor in your room, you're imprisoning the daughter of a police officer! Now act stupid if you want to!" Monique pulled her gun out, pointing it at Rico. "Lina and you, get up, get your stuff and go now!" Monique looked at them. "Your messing with a woman who's been broken, and I ain't scared of taking my anger out on you! If you ever mess with them again, Imma make sure of it your family won't be able to ID your bodies!" Monique hit her gun against the wall in anger, causing a small hole to appear.

"What minor? Man, we ain't know she was a minor." Rico shook his head as two police officers ran up the stairs with their guns drawn. "Naw, man, I can't go back to jail. They gonna send me to prison." Rico's voice cracked.

Dread stood with his arms raised in the air at the command of the officers. He knew once they discovered all the drugs, money, and guns they had in the room, they would be headed to prison for a long time.

Sirens filled the night's air as dozens of police cars filled the parking lot, lighting it up with red and blue lights. And as full as the parking lot had been, it seemed to clear up at the sound of police sirens. Once outside, Monique hugged Lina as she cried. The officers took statements from Lina and Black and allowed them to be released in the custody of Monique. They walked Black to her car, making sure she was okay emotionally to drive home.

"Lina, this is crazy," Monique said as they walked to her car.

"I," Lina said as she dropped to the ground, immediately laying on her stomach.

Instantly, Monique dropped to the ground as well, looking at Lina. "What happened?"

"I thought that was a gunshot." Lina looked around, realizing the sound she heard was Dread kicking the door as he was escorted out of the room.

"Girl, get up. You got me out here on this ground looking crazy." Monique laughed as they both got up. "You know how us folks do. We be right with you without even knowing what's going on. One take off running, we all running." Monique laughed. "Seriously, Lina, what were you thinking? You could have gotten hurt or killed. I know this isn't you." Monique talked calmly as she turned the engine on. Le'Andria Johnson's "Jesus" played over the radio.

"I know, but it's hard when you feel like you have no one there for you, no one pushing you or encouraging you, cheering you on. All you have is a messed-up situation, and I'm sick of it. I just wanted to get some money to get me and my family away from James." Lina laid her head against the passenger side window.

"Lina, God can make a way." Monique glanced over at her. She could see she was shaken up, but she could also see she was really hurting inside. Monique also knew how it felt to feel trapped and alone, so in a way, she could understand how Lina felt.

"I thought God would have helped us by now, I don't know. I don't hear His voice anymore. All I hear is James in my head, and I hate it." Lina sighed.

"Honey, God works on His own time, not ours. I know God won't let his children suffer and not do anything about it. I'm confident things will change for you and your family. I know God will allow you to have real joy and peace again." Monique looked at Lina. "You're not alone. I'm here for you, and you can always call and talk to me no matter what time of day or night it is. You're an amazing young lady, and God has so much for you." Monique reached her hand over, laying it on top of Lina's. "It's going to be okay." Monique gently squeezed Lina's hand.

"How can you say that?" Lina cried.

"Honey, because I know. I'm not telling you nothing I think. If you only knew my story and seen the things God did for me." Monique's eyes began to water. "If He did it for me, trust me, I know He'll do it for you."

Lina began to cry harder. She started to feel what she hadn't felt from her mother since her father's death. She felt this lady who barely knew her really cared for her. She started to look up to Monique as she once looked up to her mother.

"Honey, calm down. It's going to be okay. Trust me on this." Monique squeezed Lina's hand again.

Lina wiped her eyes as she calmed down. "How did you know I was there?" She grabbed a tissue from the cup holder, wiping her nose.

"Amber called me and told me everything."

"I'm sorry I got you involved in this. You're not going to tell her, Ms. Kelly, are you?" Lina looked at Monique. "She would tell my mom, and my mom would kill me and probably wouldn't let me spend the night at Amber's anymore. She already thinks I'm a liar"

"Lina, promise me you won't do anything like that again."

"I promise." Lina dropped her head.

"I want to share something with you that I've never shared with anyone." Monique let go of Lina's hand to put her signal on to switch lanes. "I can honestly say I regret my decisions in life up until now. I regret I didn't take advantage of school. I should have been in someone's college on their track or softball team. I regret I missed the opportunity to become successful. I don't regret my child, but I regret the fact I let myself get wrapped so tight around a man, and I didn't pursue what God had for me. I'm saying this because I don't want you to grow up with regrets. I know you're in a terrible situation right now, but make the most out of life, make the most out of being a child, and make the most out of having the opportunity to become more than what you're going through." Monique glanced at Lina. "Don't do something that will put you in a predicament of regretting, because it's an awful feeling when all you can do is look back, wishing you could change things you did in the past."

"I regret what I did tonight, but I thought the plan would work. I thought God would bless it because He knows what we go through." Lina looked up at Monique.

"Lina, this is something I've had to ask myself. When are we going to start caring about how God feels? We can't say we trust God and have our own agenda of how we're going to get things done. God isn't in mess, and He surely doesn't bless it." Monique laughed. "Baby, take what I'm saying and listen."

"I never looked at it that way." Lina smiled.

"My mother used to pray this prayer with me. Is it okay if I pray it with you?" Monique turned the music down.

"Yes."

"God, grant Lina the serenity to accept the things she cannot change, the courage to change the things she can, and the wisdom to know the difference. And, God, create change in her life and keep her from evil that she may not cause pain. Amen." Monique smiled, turning the radio back up.

"Amen." Lina smiled. "Thank you for coming and for under-standing me." She smiled again. Lina leaned her seat back, staring up at the stars through the front windshield.

It took about forty-five minutes to get back to Amber's house. Amber and Ava sat on the porch watching YouTube videos, waiting for Monique and Lina to pull up.

"Lina, I'm so happy you're okay. I was so scared." Amber ran to Monique's car, opening the door, hugging Lina. "I don't know what I would have done if something happened to you. Have you heard from Black?" Amber held tight to Lina's neck.

"I was going to text her once I took a shower and laid down. I was so scared I thought I would never see my family again. But Mrs. Monique is crazy." Lina began to laugh. She was still shaken up over the whole situation but found a little humor when she thought about Monique and the way she came busting through the door. "You didn't tell Ava what happened, did you?" She looked toward the porch where Ava sat glued to videos.

"No, she doesn't know anything. I didn't want to scare her." Amber let go of Lina's neck.

"You girls have to understand God is a comforter. When you feel like things are too much, seek Him and spend time with Him even more. I'm speaking from my own experiences, you have to trust Him with all that's going on. It's the only way you'll be able to deal with life and the things that are going on in your life," Monique talked quietly. "I love you, girls, and I'm here for you if you ever need me, if you ever need to talk or anything. Don't take matters into your own hands because God will allow you to do so, but He'll also show you it won't work," Monique talked as Amber and Lina listened. "Now, I have to get home to my baby before he goes to sleep, but I want you girls to know I love you and I'm really here for you."

Amber and Lina waved as Monique backed out of the driveway and made her way down the street. They stared down the road until her tail lights were no longer visible.

"I gotta see my baby." Lina ran to Ava, hugging her tight, telling her she loved her so much.

They all went inside the house, preparing the living room for a movie night.

"I'm gonna go take a shower first." Lina walked into the kitchen as Amber popped popcorn. She went into Amber's room, grabbing her night clothes. Once in the bathroom, she sent black a text asking her, "Was she ok and had she made it home?" She undressed and got in the shower. She stood under the hot water thinking about everything that had happened and how God had spared them. She began thanking God and telling Him she loved Him so much and was sorry for not trusting Him with everything.

After getting out the shower, everyone snuggled in their blankets on the couch watching a movie. Once Ava fell asleep, Lina told Amber everything that had happened. In the process, Black texted back and said she was home and was laying down. She told Lina she was thankful for her and wanted to change, but she didn't know how or what it would require. Lina texted Black, telling her she knew a lady she could talk to and gave her Monique's number.

"Lina, you're my best friend, and I never want you to forget that. If I loss you, it would be like losing a piece of me." Amber said.

Eventually, the hour got the best of them, and they fell asleep as the movie played.

42

"Daddy, I don't understand why we have to take the car back. What am I supposed to drive?" Black rolled her eyes, sitting in the passenger seat.

Her father kept quiet as he shook his head rubbing his hand on his head.

"This is so unfair!" Black stomped her foot on the floor.

He turned the music up a little louder as he got in the right turning lane. They were about ten minutes from the car rental place.

"Dad! It's not fair, my car isn't even fixed yet!" Black turned the car radio down.

"Brianna, who the hell do you think you are? Better yet, what do you think you are?" He turned right, continuing down the road.

"Dad, why are you so angry?" Black looked at her father.

"Brianna, what did you do last Friday? Where were you? Did you go to the movies with your friends like you told me?" He looked at her with anger in his eyes.

"Yes." Black hesitated. She could tell her father was mad but hadn't yet put two and two together.

"So, you lying now? You ain't no damn ghetto, hood chick. Is that what you wanna be? You out here trying to rob and steal like you ain't got what you need at home! I give you every damn thing. Your mother works her ass off to make sure you good!" Her father turned the radio off.

"But I didn't," Black said before he cut her off.

"You did! Don't lie to me. You think people ain't out here talking? Did you forget the streets talk!" He slammed his fist down on the dash board, swerving the car a little. "I'm out here in these streets, Brianna, me!"

"But, Daddy, I—" Black cried.

"Shut up, you don't get to talk. You ain't grown, you ain't going to school, you out here pretending to be something you not, and now you tryna rob people!" Spit flew from his mouth as he banged his fist against the dashboard again. The car swerved a little more before red and blue lights flashed in his rearview mirror.

"Daddy, the police." Black looked scared.

"Shut up, you don't get to talk. Now I gotta go and fix this mess. Do you not understand people want your head? They blaming you and your friend saying y'all the reason them boys locked up!" He pulled the car over on the side of the road, turning the engine off. "You my child, you don't need for nothing. What's up, man, what you thinking?" Black's dad continued to yell as two Caucasian officers walked up to the car.

"Sir, I need to see your license and registration," one of the officers said as he held his hand on his gun, the other officer walked to the passenger side of the car.

"Ma'am, are you okay? Did he do anything to hurt you?" The officer looked at Black.

"No, I ain't hurt her!" he yelled. "Don't you talk to them!" he yelled, looking at Black.

"Ma'am, I need you to step out the car." The officer on Black's side drew his gun.

"She ain't stepping nowhere that's mine." He reached into the center console, grabbing his license.

"Sir, step out of the car and walk to the hood of the patrol car!" the officer on the driver side yelled.

"Daddy, don't." Black cried. "Don't get out."

Black's father stepped out the car walking to the patrol car as instructed. Before reaching the trunk of his car, he stopped, turned, and walked to the window of the driver side door.

"We gonna talk about this after. I love you, it's okay," he said to Black before turning to face the officer and walk to the patrol car.

Pow… Pow… Pow… Pow… shots ranged from the gun of the officer who stood between his car and Black's father's car.

"Daddy! Daddy! Daddy!" Black yelled, trying to open her door to get out the car and get to her father.

"Ma'am, don't move!" the officer on the passenger side of the car yelled, kicking her door shut.

"That's my daddy. Why did you shoot him? Why did you shoot him?" she screamed as snot and tears covered her face. "You shot my daddy, why? He didn't do nothing, you shot my daddy! Daddy, get up! Get up!" She tried crawling to the driver side seat.

"Ma'am, don't move, don't move!" the officer on the passenger side yelled.

"That's my daddy. He's dying, you shot him for no reason! Daddy, get up!" Black yelled, sitting back in her seat. "You gonna shoot me too? Go ahead, shoot!" Black screamed at the officer by her door. "That's my daddy. Let me get to my daddy please."

"Don't move!" he yelled. "This is my last warning, don't move!"

"Let me call my mom then. Do something, he's dying. Do something. Daddy, get up!" She cried.

"We need paramedics, shots fired," the officer on the passenger side yelled in his headset to dispatchers. "What happened, what happened? I can't believe you shot him," he yelled to the other officer.

"I don't know I got nervous. Why did he go back to the car, why did he go back to the car?" the officer yelled. "I thought he grabbed something, what did I do?" he yelled, pacing.

The officer on the passenger side stood at Black's door preventing her from getting out of the car until other police arrived.

"That's my daddy. Let me get to my daddy!" Black yelled as police arrived checking for a pulse.

Paramedics arrived three minutes later confirming he was dead. Black was able to call her mother and was released in the custody of her mother when she arrived fifteen minutes later.

"What happened, baby?" Black's mother wiped her eyes as tears continued to fall.

"Mama, they shot him for no reason. He didn't do anything wrong. He didn't say anything wrong. They shot for no reason, Mama." Black cried, hugging her mother tight.

The scene was now a crime scene, which prevented anyone from getting close to the body or the car. They stood around until the head of the police came and talked to them. Eventually, they left with little information on why this had happened.

"It's all my fault, it's all my fault." Black cried as her mother drove away. "I should have never," Black mouthed. "They wouldn't even let me touch my daddy. They shot him for no reason." She cried.

"Baby, that's the price you pay for being a black man in America." Her mother cried.

Black's mother had a strong dislike for the police since a small child. At the age of ten, she and a couple of friends were harassed by a police officer. At the age of fifteen, they watched their friend get beaten by police; once he was on the ground, they watched as an officer allowed his K9 dog to attack him. At the age of sixteen, she watched as police harassed her father, later to be found wrong; the chief of police was sent out to their house to apologize. Black's family had a history of bad experiences with law enforcement and although they knew not all cops were bad, they felt all cops had an intention, and that they didn't trust.

"They shot my daddy for no reason." Black held her head down as they continued driving. "He didn't do nothing at all." She cried.

43

"I'm so glad it's almost Friday. These classes are killing me." Amber fidgeted with the lock on her locker.

"Tell me about it. So, have you seen Black around?" Lina opened her locker, grabbing the textbook she needed for her trigonometry class.

"Nope, I hope she's okay, though I haven't seen her. I mean it's not like we see her all the time anyways, but at least we see her at lunch." Amber laughed. "Want some gum?" She pulled a new pack of sweet watermelon flavor from her locker, taking the clear wrapper off the pack.

"For real, I really love Mrs. Monique. I'm so glad I've met her." Lina laughed. "She is crazy." She reached her hand to take a piece of gum.

"She really is." Amber laughed. "Look who's here coming down the hall." Amber tapped Lina. "I'm surprised to see her at school for second period." Amber slammed her locker shut, placing the lock back on it.

"Hey, Black." Lina smiled as Black walked toward them.

"What's up?" she spoke with no emotion.

"Did you get the chance to call Mrs. Monique?"

"For what, what am I calling her for?" Black pulled on the straps of her backpack.

"Well, you said you wanted to change. You just didn't know how. She knows all about God and going through stuff." Lina looked at her.

"Girl, I ain't got time to be hearing nobody's stories or listening to some talk about God." Black rolled her eyes.

"Dang, what's your problem?" Amber butted in.

"Ain't yo mama the police, yea, aight then, you can't say nothing to me." She rolled her eyes at Amber. "And last time I checked, I never told you I wanted to change. I told Lina, so mind ya business."

"Okay… Rude." Amber leaned against the locker.

"You the one said you wanted to change," Lina talked. "Ain't no need to get an attitude."

"Look, Lina, my daddy dead because of me, and I ain't see God there helping him when he got shot by the police. Ain't nobody stories gone help me, so leave me alone about Monique and God. I really don't care about nothing, and I don't care about changing or hearing this lil white girl talk."

"I'm sorry, but what does my mom being a police officer have to do with your dad?"

"I hate the police, and you ain't nothing but a privileged white girl whose mother is a cop. You will never understand how it feels to feel like it's a crime to be black, or to feel like police look at your race like they're trash." Black balled her fist. It was evident of how much she disliked the police by the demeanor of her body as she talked.

"Okay, let's be real. You can't treat all police or white people like we think like that. My mom is nothing like that and neither am I."

"Amber, just chill." Lina put her hand on Amber's shoulder.

"So, you taking her side now?" Amber looked at Lina.

"Amber, this is something that's real, and you could never understand, so stop please."

"Exactly, so you don't speak to me, and I don't want to hear nothing none of y'all have to say." Black walked off.

"I haven't heard anything about her dad dying." Lina looked at Amber. "I hope she's okay." Lina watched as Black walked until she disappeared in the crowd.

"That's messed up for real, for her to think that every white cop or white person is like that." Amber shook her head.

"I just think she's speaking from the hurt and anger she feels from losing her dad like that, then to look at the world and to see all these people being killed by police brutality and nothing being done can make you have strong hate in your heart."

44

"Hello," James answered the phone. "Hold on," he spoke before the person on the other end of the phone could get a word out. "Yeah, I heard they hiring. My buddy told me they make a lot of money in construction there. I think I might go down there sometime this week." He talked to a man standing next to him.

"Hello, I'm still here," Helen said sarcastically.

"Sorry about that, who's calling?" James said into the phone.

"Fool, don't act like you done forgot my voice. You've forgotten about your wife and son and now you tryna play dumb like you don't know who this is," Helen talked. She sat on her back porch, smoking on a freshly rolled blunt.

"What do you want, lady?" James let out a deep breath.

"Don't call me lady, you fool. You know what I want. Why haven't you seen your child or cared to at least call him, send money, anything? And why haven't you checked up on your wife? Your real wife, not the one you round there playing house with." Helen inhaled then exhaled, letting out smoke through her nostrils and mouth.

"Look, I'm a grown man. Don't question me about stuff that don't concern you." James turned the volume down on the side of his phone. "Now, your daughter is not my problem, and I'm not doing anything for Joshua until she understands its over between us."

"You look here you big, nasty, dirty, useless, ignorant fool. My daughter doesn't need you and if you think you're hurting her by not doing anything for Joshua, you're mistakenly wrong. That is your child, not just hers. Now I'm not gonna make a grown man take care of his responsibilities but what you not gonna do is use him as a pawn in your game. Either you gonna be in his life or you not. Make it clear cause we ain't got time for games. I will not let you hurt my grandbaby nor will I let you come in and out of his life when you feel it's convenient for you. He's a real person with a heart and feelings, and if I have to take you to court to protect him, that's what I'll do. Now you can go ahead and get back to your underpaid job with your raggedy." Helen paused. "I'm trying to change so get back to work with your unintelligent, raggedy self." She hung up the phone.

"That's what he not gonna do." Helen inhaled again, then exhaled the smoke. "And I ain't gonna tell Monique she gonna have to see for herself. You can't make a man care about his child." She put out her blunt laying the butt in the ashtray on a small plastic table next to her chair.

****

"Grandma." Joshua ran with his bookbag on, hugging Helen as she watched television in her recliner.

"Mama, why you up so early?" Monique walked in the living room.

"I had a phone call I had to take. Now I'm up." She smiled.

"Yeah, and you smell just like pine cones." Monique squeezed her nose.

"Mama, grandma smells like pine cones? The ones the squirrels eat?" Joshua scooted a chair out from the kitchen table.

"Yes, baby, the ones squirrels eat." Monique laughed. "I think they eat pine cones," she mumbled. "If they do, they sure don't eat these kind of pine cones," she mumbled, grabbing a bowl out of the cabinet, filling it with Capt'n Crunch cereal and milk. "Joshua, eat so we can get going for school." She placed the bowl in front of him.

"Why you all dressed up?" Helen looked at Monique.

"I have to go somewhere after I drop Joshua off." She walked to the sofa, plopping down on it.

"You want me to drive you? I can throw on some clothes, and we can do breakfast after." Helen turned the TV volume down.

"No, Mama, but we can do lunch when I get back. Your treat." She looked at her mother, smiling.

"I guess, I mean I was hoping you said okay to breakfast. I got the munchies." Helen laughed.

"Mama, Imma pray for you. You need Jesus." Monique shook her head.

"You ain't never lied." She laughed.

****

"Joshua, Mommy loves you so, so, so, so much. I want you to know you're amazing, you're smart, you're blessed, you're a king, you were fearfully and wonderfully made. God is in you, and God is with you. You are prosperous, you are anointed, you are loved, and you can do anything you set your mind too. Have a wonderful day, and I pray God's love, peace, and protection over you." Monique bent down, giving Joshua a kiss.

"Mommy, you're the best mommy in the world, and I love you so, so, so, so much too." He wrapped his arms around her. "I love you, Mommy. See you later." He smiled as he walked into his classroom.

"Aww, I wish my son said that to me. All he says is, can I bring him a snack when I pick him up?" a parent, who was dropping her son to Joshua's class, said. "He's such a good boy." She smiled.

"He really is." Monique giggled at her comment about the snack.

****

She pulled into the parking lot. Her heart was beating fast, her palms sweaty. She was nervous of the reaction she would get and even more nervous of embarrassing herself. She still had so much love in her heart despite the hurt she had been experiencing. She looked in the rearview mirror, rubbing her edges, making sure they were good. She put on a light brownish, gold, lip gloss. She opened her purse, grabbing her bottle of endless weekend body spray from Bath

& Body Works, spraying her shirt and bottoms. She let out a deep breath and opened the car door.

"Oh my god, I hope this goes well," she mumbled, stepping out the car.

The parking lot was full for the time of day it was. She had done her research and found out James worked at a mall as a security guard. The stores in the mall hadn't yet open, but the mall itself was open. She shut the car door and headed for the doors by the food court entering the mall. She also knew James usually stayed by the food court until the mall officially opened.

"Hi," she spoke low as she walked up behind James.

"Hello," he spoke as he turned around, smiling. His smile quickly faded. "What are you doing here, Monique?" His demeanor changed.

"Now, we're not going to make a scene because I would hate for you to lose the job you have, that you don't use the money from, to support your son." Monique clutched her purse strap.

"Monique, what do you want? I told you I don't want to be with you." He looked Monique in the eyes.

The man who stood before her was not the same man she married. His countenance was different. His eyes looked tired, his face had gotten a little smaller as if he had lost weight, and his hair wasn't freshly cut as he always kept it. Despite the way James had treated her and Joshua, she still loved him.

"You know, I love you so much. All I've ever done is love you. Our son loves you. He misses you and forgive me for wanting my family. I'm willing to put the past behind us, James. I'm your wife for god sake." Monique felt her eyes beginning to water. She blinked until she felt the tears disappear.

"Monique, I have someone and I'm happy."

"You never even gave me an explanation for why you just up and left. What did I do?" Monique talked as she fought to hold back her emotions.

"Monique, I'm a grown man. You coming to my job with this foolishness. You about to piss me off." James balled his fist. "You need to leave. This isn't the time or place."

"Well, when is the time? You don't answer my calls, you've ignored me. When is the time, James?" Monique got loud as tears rolled down her face. "Forgive me for caring so much, James. I love you, and all I wanted is for my family to be together. That's all." She pointed her finger in his face. "I know about your lil friend you playing house with and her kids." Monique pushed his forehead with her finger.

"Monique, don't make me put my hands on you." He yanked her out the door to the mall's parking lot.

"Get your hands off me." She punched him in the chest.

"Monique, I'm not doing this with you. It's over between us. Get that through your fat head. And until you understand that, don't expect me to come around for Joshua. I'm not doing this with you right now so leave!" he yelled.

"You know what?" Monique looked him in the eyes as she wiped tears from her cheeks. "I've been crying because of you. I love you, and I will always love you, but what I'm not going to do is beg you to love me back. If this is what you want, then fine. Live your life and be so-called happy, but you're gonna regret you let a good woman like me go. Good-bye, James." Monique turned to walk to her car.

"Man, you been knew it was over between us." James laughed.

"James, go to hell." Monique walked down the side walk through the parking lot and to her car.

She opened her car door as her emotions got the best of her. She started the ignition, locked her doors, turned the AC on and cried. She knew in her heart seeing James today most likely wasn't going to end well, but she hoped for different results. She sat in the car for five minutes before opening the glove compartment, grabbing the small pack of wipes, cleaning her tears away. She was hurt but also a little relieved to be able to start the process of finally moving on.

When she returned home, she went straight to her room, dropping to her knees.

"God, I honestly don't know how I'm going to do this. I want to be over James all the way. I'm tired of hurting. I just want to be free. Please help me." She got up, laying in the bed. She turned the television on, surfing the channels before falling asleep.

****

"Hello, hi, Pastor," Helen answered the phone.

"How are you, Helen?" Pastor Andrews spoke.

"I'm good, hungry. I tried to get Monique to wake up, so we can go to lunch, but I'm still home." Helen shook her head.

"Well, I was just calling to let you know about the service I told you about. It's really going to bless people. We have some amazing and anointed people coming. The program is next month on the nineteenth. That's a Saturday at 6:00 p.m., so let everyone know. I'm trying to bring the whole city out." Pastor Andrews laughed. "It's gone be lit, fire, epic, as the young folk say." He laughed.

"Okay, Pastor, you know I'm there long as we ain't in church for ten hours." Helen laughed. "I'm kidding, but I'm serious." She coughed. "Okay, okay, I'm there."

"Okay, Mrs. Helen, I'll save you a seat on the front row."

"You pushing it." Helen laughed.

"All right now, see you soon." Pastor Andrews laughed before hanging up.

45

News about the service Pastor Andrews was having spread around the city fast. He advertised every place one could think to, even the places where most people judged him for going. His goal was to win souls no matter if he had to go on street corners, areas known to drug dealers, strips where prostitutes hung, or in poor parts of town. He wasn't the typical preacher who lived based on the rules and laws of religion. He moved as God told him and purposed his life on relationship rather than religion.

"Hey, Black." Lina smiled as Black walked to a table where she sat at lunch.

"Hey." She sat down, biting on a french fry.

"I'm sorry about everything that happened with your dad. I know you miss him. I miss mine so much." Lina opened a can of grape soda.

"Yeah," Black said, pulling out her phone from her pocket.

Amber walked up sitting next to Lina. "Have y'all heard about the service Jekalyn Carr gonna be at? It's here next month."

"Yeah, I'm gonna try and talk my mom into going, but you know how she is." Lina bit into the cheeseburger Amber bought her from the student grill.

"If you go, we can sit together." Amber bit into her chicken strips.

"Black, you should go too. I think it would help you with what you're going through." Lina looked at her.

"Look, I ain't here for this. I'm good." Black chewed on her fries.

"I think you should go, God is the only one that can help with how you feel." Amber smiled.

"Aye, I'm good. That ain't for everybody. God and church ain't my thing. And right now, how I'm feeling, God, church, or some program is the last thing on my mind." Black stood up from the table. "And stop talking to me about God." She rolled her eyes before walking out the cafeteria.

"Dang, something is wrong with that girl." Amber rolled her eyes.

"She's just hurting Amber, and you can't force God on anyone." Lina continued eating her food.

"I know you're right 'cause if it wasn't for my momma, I don't think God would be my type of stuff either." Amber flicked a straw wrapper off the table. "I can't wait though."

"'Cause it's gone be lit," Amber and Lina said at the same time then burst out laughing.

46

Evangelist Jekalyn Carr

Evangelist Carr gripped the microphone tightly. "When I say faith is the most powerful tool we can have, yet, it is the most broken, the story of Job is a perfect example of that." Evangelist Carr smiled. "Isn't it funny how we can be so quick to blame God when things get rough? Sometimes, we can even blame God for the situations we put ourselves in." Evangelist Carr took a sip of water, placing the bottle back on the table next to the podium.

"I believe the test was partly for Job, but because God knew his heart, his intentions, and he knew he could trust Job, I believe the real test in this story was for those around Job, especially his wife and friends. Sometimes, God allows those connected to us to see how we're tested in order to increase their faith, because sometimes, we're the only God people may see. He allows those who are supposed to be our support system, our mentors, our friends, or those in our lives that seem as if they're so strong, to see how we'll react toward Him in times of adversity." Evangelist Carr skimmed the crowd. "Don't fight the process even when you don't understand, because when you fight the process, you're fighting against God. We don't always understand things that happen in our lives, but we must always remember to hold onto God's unchanging hand," Evangelist Carr spoke with boldness and authority.

"When you are deeply rooted in the right foundation as Job was, your situation may shake you, it may bring you to your knees, it may even cause you to resent the day you were born, but it will never allow you to curse the one that makes all things new. Job understood

God did not promise adversity would skip over him, so when adversity hit, his faith began to speak. Understand my faith is tied to my heart, character, and identity. Some of you may be wondering how so? When I'm going through, what's really in my heart has to come out. I can't say I believe and when adversity hits, what's in my heart says otherwise." Evangelist Carr paced the pulpit. "When you're deeply rooted in the right foundation, your faith in God and obedience to Him produces a character that doesn't line up with what you're going through, but with what you believe God and His Word to be. That's why people often wonder, how is she praising God and her lights just got cut off, or how is he dancing, and he just found out his son is strung out on drugs, or how is she still worshipping God when she's just been diagnosed with stage three cancer?" She walked back behind the podium looking at her notes.

"The mistake in this story is the devil did not know the true identity of Job. Satan did not understand. My identity is not based upon stuff, it's not based upon my possessions. My identity isn't based on my children, or the love I have for them. And if the devil cannot attack your character, he will try to attack your identity. You have to understand when you lose your identity, you lose your purpose," Evangelist Carr spoke. "I believe Job's wife did not know her true identity. Sometimes, we can get wrapped up in what we feel our purpose is, that we mistake our purpose to be our identity."

People sat glued to the pulpit as some recorded the message with their phones.

"I asked the question, how is it that a person can know the power of God, but when something comes against them, they want to give up, or blame God? You have to understand it's not that one does not know the power of God, our minds become manipulated by the enemy. Many thoughts and questions flood our minds, along with our emotions. Your emotions and how you feel will mess you up each time. It's in this state we tend to not so much as rely on the power of God, but instead drown in our worries and feelings. With this, there are two choices a person can make. You can one, run deeper into your problems, or emotions, feeling giving up is the best option, or, two, we can run straight to God, meaning despite the fact that my spirit is so troubled, and I don't feel like praising you, despite the fact I feel like the walls are crumbling around me, and, God, to be honest, I'm angry with you. Despite everything the enemy is throwing at me and telling me, despite all of that. God, I trust you for the process, and I'll still run to you. We can see this with Job," Evangelist Carr spoke.

"But in our weakened state, we can feel like God's not there. We may even feel like God doesn't care, or we're not hearing from Him. Allowing us to feel giving up is the best choice. As we saw this with Job's wife and friends. You must know God will not put more on you than you can bear. Realize no amount of money can bring you out, no man, no pastor, no teacher, friend, nobody but God can bring you out. Clearly, God is testing you to see if everything were against you, would you still trust Him?" Evangelist Carr pointed out in the crowd. "God has given us the power to overcome everything the enemy throws our way. The power to heal and the power to speak things into existence. I don't care what it looks like, I don't care what it feels like. I don't care whose left you or hurt you, I don't even care about what you feel you may lack, God has given you the power, and you must tap into that. Don't lose your identity because of life or what it throws at you." Evangelist Carr closed her Bible. "Tonight, God is asking, can you really trust me when all else fails, when things don't go your way, when you lose the ones you love, when you can't see a way out? When you've been used, when the devil has touched everything you love. When people try to persuade you otherwise. Can you still trust me?"

Some people sat while others stood in amazement at the wisdom coming from Evangelist Carr's mouth. This was something that drew the pastors of this house to her. Jekalyn Carr was more than a gospel artist. She was a powerful, anointed woman of God. A preaching machine, preaching each time, as if her life depended on it. The way she talked about God and worshipped Him let people know she was serious about God's business and had a personal relationship with Him. She was pure in heart, a woman after God's own heart, obedient to his Word. She embodied the character of God and was no nonsense when it came to God and the things of God. She lived and breathed the Word, and His light and radiance shined through her. She was full of wisdom, wise beyond her years, speaking with power and authority. And each time she opened her mouth, the presence of God showed up mightily.

"It's one thing to hear God is bigger than anything you're going through or could ever go through. But it's another to know Him for yourself to be and do mighty things. When we fully come to the realization of how big He really is, the small stuff that's portraying itself to be goliaths won't be able to faze you." Evangelist Carr smiled.

"We have to trust and believe God is bigger than sickness, suicide, depression, hurt, or anything we could ever go through on this earth. We serve a God who conquered death!" Evangelist Carr ministered as the power of God flowed through her. "We know God is bigger than all of this, He's proven that time and time again, yet when adversity hits us, when life's problems and situations hit our lives, or even better, when people hurt us and let us down, God seems smaller than everything. I stopped by to remind you God is still bigger! You ought to speak and tell the devil, you may have had my mind, you may even have taken some things away or stopped me from moving forward, but I stand in the bigness of God, and I'm taking it all back! I want you to shout no matter what, God, you're still bigger. That's it, shout one more time. God, you're still bigger!" Evangelist Carr smiled toward the crowd as they all shouted.

"It's something about when God preserves your life, you could be trying to commit suicide and you may even try and carry out the plans and instead of God allowing you to die, He allows you to have a setback in order for you to live and see His hand over your life." Evangelist Carr closed her notes, handing her Bible and notes to her armor bearer.

"If there are any of you who feel this message was for you, or you're in need of prayer, come to the altar. There are some who may feel they've lost track and want to get back in a place with God, or you feel you've messed up so bad that God doesn't love you, if that's you, come up here. If you've been hurt and gave up on God, come up here. If you're dealing with unforgiveness and there are still some things you haven't let go of that's hurting you mentally and emotionally, and you know by now it should not have a hold on you like it does, then come. If you feel you've failed not only yourself but also God, then come up here." Evangelist Carr walked back and forth on the pulpit.

"Many of you may be stuck in a place of unsureness. You get out of one situation just to find yourself right back in the same situation. God is freeing you tonight, the Bible declares, 'Where the Spirit of the Lord is there is liberty'. God is here. All you have to do is let Him work out every kink and problem you may be in the midst of. You see, the devil has placed in your mind God isn't there, that your situation is bigger than God, and if you bow down and serve him, He will give you peace. But I stopped by to tell you on tonight the devil is a liar. God gave you power over the enemy and if you just activate your faith, God will show up and show out on your behalf!" Evangelist Carr spoke as people began to line up at the altar.

"I want you to come up here with everything you need God to do in your life, everything that has caused you to be sorrowful in spirit and begin to make your requests known to God. Cry out and let God work in you and for you. The Bible declares when Hannah spoke in her heart, only her lips moved, but her voice was not heard, because she was bitter in soul and wept in anguish. She was a woman of sorrowful spirit, and she poured her soul out before the Lord that God granted her petition. I stand in agreement with you that God will grant your petitions on tonight."

As the people stood lined up in front of the altar, Evangelist Carr walked down the line of people at the altar. Some people stood with their hands lifted high, eyes closed. Some stood with their eyes open while they cried and mouthed words to God, and some stood standing still not knowing what to expect. Evangelist Carr walked down the line of people as God led her.

She stopped in front of Monique. "You really are a living testimony to just one of the small things God can do. It's a miracle you're even alive right now. Doctors gave up on you. They said you wouldn't make it. They even said your life wouldn't be worth living, but God said not so. Isn't it amazing when God throws a but where everyone else has placed a period." Evangelist Carr waved her hand in reverence to God's presence. "God is restoring every broken piece in your life. He created you as an overcomer. He never created you to depend on man. You've had so many disappointments in your life. So many people have turned their back on you and hurt you, but tonight, God says He's filling every place in your life where you feel a void, every place where you've been hurt and have uncertainty. Now on the count of three, I want you to open your mouth and cry out to God. God says there's a releasing in you that's going to take place, all the anger, pain, frustration, and hate you've been dealing with, I want you to let it all out. One... two... three!" Evangelist Carr shouted into the microphone. "Open up your mouths in this place and praise Him with her. That's it. Come on, open up your mouths," she declared boldly.

"God, I bind up every negative thought, every controlling spirit, every spirit of dependency on man. God, I annihilate every spoken word and thought the devil has placed in her mind. I command her spirit man, her mind, and her life to line up with the Word of God. In the name of Jesus, I command Michael to go forth and war for her in the spirit. God, release your power on her and wipe out every negative thing in her life!" Evangelist Carr spoke as the power of God flowed through her. "The bible says, 'You are of God, little children, and have overcome them, because He who is in you is greater than he who is in the world.' Woman of God, because you're an overcomer, because you made up in your mind that the devil can no longer have control over your mind and life, because you made up your mind that for God I live and For God I die, and because of the Holy Spirit that lives on the inside of you." Evangelist Carr placed her hand over Monique's heart. "I prophesy over your life that you have the ear and the attention of God, and whatever you can even think of that you want, it shall be released into your hands! Woman of God, heaven is at your assistance, supplying every one of your needs."

Monique stood with her hands in the air crying, taking in everything God was speaking through His prophet.

"Woman of God, the battle's not yours. It belongs to the Lord. There's a releasing, just open up your mouth and praise Him," Evangelist Carr shouted before she was led by the Spirit with the utterance of tongues. "The deliver is here, open your mouth and cry out to Him, cry out to Him, We refuse to live without You," Evangelist Carr spoke in a songful tone. "As you cry out to Him, He's shaking off every generational curse. I command every thought, every action, and your DNA to line up with the Word of God! It's not God's desire for you to suffer with hurt. The devil is a liar. God, touch her mind right now! And God says because you're under this anointing every crooked place in your life is being made straight, God is taking you over!" Evangelist Carr began to shed a few tears as she stepped back from Monique, lifting her hands under the power of God.

"Woman of God, I want you to listen to me good." Evangelist Carr stepped up to Monique again, placing her hand on her shoulder. "God says He allowed you to go through what you went through. He says when you died naturally, you died to everything that held you bound. He had to strip you of everything you knew including life itself in order to give you life. God says from the day He breathed breath back into your nostrils, your mind-set changed, your lifestyle changed, your faith changed, and your heart changed, and because of this, you will only be able to say God did it. No longer will man have power over you, no longer will you see your problems, situations, past hurt, and failures as big, but you will look to the Father and say your bigger than this, your bigger than that. If you could bring me back from death, what is this or that to you, that you can't fix it! Woman of God, don't let bitterness, or your emotions be the death of you," Evangelist Carr spoke with such force, power, and wisdom from the Holy Spirit that those in the pews could do nothing but stand in awe at how God used those He chose.

"God says the reason He allowed you to live is because His hands has always been on you, even when you gave up on yourself, He never gave up on you. He says because of your emotions, you were headed for a path of destruction, and the only way He could get your attention was by allowing you to go through a process. It's in the midst of a process, we find ourselves. It's in the middle that God is able to get our attention, and in the process, we are strengthened, and our faith increased."

Monique began to mouth the words, "Thank you, Jesus. God, I love you."

"God Almighty, we thank you right now for the process, we thank you for having Your hand upon us, and we thank you for never giving up on us. God, we know that in you, there is life, peace, and joy. We thank you for your unfailing love and for being a God that is true to your Word. God, I command right now that she will have the vision and the mind of you. And, God, I pray You will use her and continue to reveal Yourself to her. I pray right now that never again will she lose sight of the purpose and destiny you have given her. I speak to the wiring of her mind and I command, God, by your power, you rewire her to be a strong woman of God!" Evangelist Carr prayed as she placed her hand on Monique's forehead. You shall live, and you shall fight!" Evangelist Carr spoke as the power of God arrested Monique, causing her to fall to the floor in a peaceful manner.

As Monique laid on the floor speaking in tongues, crying under the power of God, Evangelist Carr moved down the line laying hands on those she was led to. People were falling to the floor slain under the power and hand of God as Evangelist Carr walked by laying hands on them.

"Man of God, lift your hands." Evangelist Carr stopped in front of Sam. "God says diabetes will not overtake you. By His stripes, you are healed, and I speak to every cell in your body, I speak to your pancreas, and I speak to your blood. In the name of Jesus, I call out diabetes and we dry you up. I curse you diabetes, and I serve you notice this day God has erased you! Man of God, God says because you chose to serve Him, because you chose life, and you realized there's no other side you'd rather chose than God's side, He's going to reveal Himself to you. God says He's erasing every past hurt in your life, He's giving you peace at home and because of you, your family will be saved. Man of God, I can tell you from my own experience, God is everything you could ever want or need. I want you to know everything you need is in God. There's nothing too big for Him, you serve a faithful God." Evangelist Carr looked Sam into his eyes. "God says don't get too comfortable in the position you're in. I see you working ministry, stay focused and watch God." Evangelist Carr looked as if she had tunnel vision walking to those God directed her to.

"I need some prayer warriors to open up your mouths all across this room and pray." Evangelist Carr declared as she signaled for Ida and Roxy, her assistants, to come and stand on each side of Tina holding her hands, praying. Ida stood on Tina's right side as Roxy stood on her left.

Tina stood with her eyes closed silently pleading with God. "You have to change me, God, I can't leave this altar the same way I came. God, please forgive me and change me from the inside out. God, I need you to fix me." Tears rolled down Tina's face.

Evangelist Carr placed her hand over Tina's heart. "God says you're at a point of death, you're spiritually dead, you're emotionally dead, you're dead to yourself, and if it weren't for your kids, you'd have given up a long time ago. You needed to be here tonight. Had you not come, you would be opening death's door. God says He's giving you a heart transplant and delivering you out of all your troubles. You've made you're grave for yourself and death has become your desire, but tonight, God says He's commanding all of your dry bones to live, He's calling you out of that dark and weary place because His hands are on you. He's breaking every chain and stronghold that's had your mind bound and closing every door meant for your bad." Evangelist Carr stared into Tina's eyes as she stared back into hers. "Every ounce of pain your feeling, every emotion you're going through, and every ounce of hurt you've experienced is going to be felt by these two ladies holding your hands. If you just stop fighting God and allow Him to work, you'll be delivered this night. I don't care what the enemy has made you to believe, I don't even care what your eyes have caused you to believe, I don't care what situation you've gotten yourself into, God is severing every connection you have with the devil. Everything that's killing you inside is going to be felt by these two ladies holding your hands when I place my hand on your head." Evangelist Carr moved her hand from over Tina's chest, placing her hand on Tina's forehead.

"God says it was never destined for you to die prematurely, He created you with a purpose. Woman of God, you are fearfully and wonderfully made. I don't care what you've been through, I don't care what the devil may have spoken over your life, I don't even care how you blamed and hated God! You shall live and not die, and I speak to the spirit of depression over your life, I bind you up depression and by the power of God Himself, we eradicate you right now. And I send you to the pits of hell in the name of Jesus! I command your spirit to come up out of depression! I curse the spirit of lack, the spirit of unforgiveness, the spirit of rebellion, the spirit of death, the spirit of addiction, the spirit of sickness and infirmities, the spirit of suicide and laziness, and the spirit of disobedience, and I curse it at the root! Devil, you can't have her!" Evangelist Carr began to speak with such authority that the Power of God caused Tina to drop to her knees. "God, I release your peace, your serenity and your yoke over her life right now in the name of Jesus!"

The usher that stood behind Tina helped to raise her back up to her feet as Evangelist Carr flowed under the power and anointing of God speaking in tongues as the Spirit gave utterance. "I speak to the spirit of unbelief in you right now, and I command you to line up. I command your eyes to be opened, woman of God, and I command you to see the light. I command you to see the truth! I command doubt and unbelief to die in the name of Jesus!" Evangelist Carr declared as she blew her breath toward Tina's forehead. The power of God that flowed from Evangelist Carr's mouth caused Tina to fall to the floor in a way that seemed as if she were peacefully floating to the floor rather than falling.

"Stand her up." Evangelist Carr laid her hand back over Tina's heart. "God says you cursed His name, but He's giving you a second chance. He says He's not interested in your past, He says your future is so much greater. Understand you cannot fix the past, and I want you to understand there's no perfect life! At some point, we all have to face a process for development, but it's only to pull the best out of us, and truthfully, sometimes, we feel as if God has left us, but God declared in His Word, He will never leave you nor forsake you whatever situation God puts you in, or whatever He allows, He has already strengthened you to make it through it. He knows exactly what it'll take to introduce us to something much greater than we could ever expect or imagine."

"God, I can't take this anymore. Help me, I need you!" Ida, who stood holding Tina's right hand, began crying out as God allowed every unheard thought and emotion Tina felt to be felt by Ida.

Roxy let out a blood curdling cry as she dropped to her knees as if the pain Tina had experienced and caused on herself were too much to bear. "Jesus! I need you, Jesus!" Roxy screamed as she held tight on to Tina's hand.

Evangelist Carr removed her hand from Tina, lifting her hands up to God with her eyes closed as the power and the anointing of God overtook her. She began to utter other tongues as God began to flood her ears with His voice.

"God says every filthy thing in your life is destroyed! You've always been the apple of God's eye and if you will get back in a place with Him, He will open up doors for you that no man can close, He will reveal Himself to you in such an intimate way, that you will know without a shadow of doubt no devil in hell can do the things for you that God can. God says He's calling you back because He loves you." Tears began to drop from Evangelist Carr's eyes, knowing that God loved his people so much He could look past their flaws, failures, and disappointments, and love them with a type of love that couldn't be duplicated or bought.

"Just as God restored Job's happiness, peace, family, and possessions, He's going to do the same for you. Not another day will you have to ask a man for anything, not another day will you have to beg, and you will not lose one more thing! You won't have to lay up with anyone for anything, and God's going to cut every soul tie and deliver you. When God seals it, it's done. And you can take that to the bank!" Evangelist Carr spoke. She operated in a way that let the people know she had a real intimate relationship with God. She trusted God with everything in her, and she not only believed in God, but she also knew without a shadow of doubt when God spoke, He was going to do just what He said.

"My sister, I need you to open up your mouth right now and give God a shabach praise. I stand as a prophet and the mouth piece of God, that in this praise, God is going to deliver you right now from the hand of the enemy. And I don't know what you're in the midst of right now, but God says that relationship is lethal to your existence."

Roxy, Ida, and Tina all began to let out a shabach praise as God chopped up every negative thing in Tina's life.

"Let her hands go," Evangelist Carr spoke to Ida and Roxy. "Woman of God, raise your hands." She spoke to Tina as Tina raised her hands in surrenderance. Evangelist Carr began to tap her hand against the palm of Tina's hands.

"I command by the blood of the Lamb and by the power of God that you rise up! God give her your DNA! Rise up, woman of God, and fight. I curse the taste of cigarettes in your mouth right now. Every time you get the urge to put a cigarette to your mouth, God, I command you to cause her to throw up." Evangelist Carr stared into Tina's eyes. "Woman of God, I call you out of your desolate place and into the perfect will of God. If God was able to raise up the dead and heal the sick, what makes you think God can't do it for you?" Evangelist Carr continued tapping her hand on Tina's hands as in a way that looked like she were wiping stuff off Tina's hands. "Jehovah, in the name of Jesus, I pray you strengthen her heart and give her a spirit of peace and humility, I pray everyone that encounters her sees You in her, and I pray by your blood you renew a steadfast spirit within her," Evangelist Carr spoke as she placed her hand back on Tina's forehead.

Tina fell back under the anointing and power of God. The ushers covered her legs with a shawl as Evangelist Carr continued on to others that stood at the altar.

"God loves you so much, His favors all over you." Evangelist Carr walked to Lina, hugging her.

Lina hugged her back as she began to cry.

"What do you want from God?" Evangelist Carr stepped back from Lina, looking her in the eyes.

Lina looked down at her mother who laid on the floor next to her, then back up at Evangelist Carr.

"I just want God to give me and my family happiness again." Lina smiled a smile that was trying to cover up her brokenness, as tears continued to flow down her cheeks.

"The Bible says God cares for you, so turn all your worries over to Him. God has heard your every thought, your every prayer, and your every cry. God says He's going to give you joy again. You see, happiness is predicated on what's going on around us. Happiness ties in with our emotions. If life is going good, we're happy. If this person is treating me good, then I'm happy, but if life is going bad, then we're sad. But when you have the joy of the Lord, all hell can be going on around you, and you can still smile, and your emotions won't cause you to push back from God. Situations and circumstances can take your happiness away, but when you have real joy, neither death, nor heartache, nor anything in this world can take away your joy. I also believe what truly allows us to receive this joy from the Lord is when we go through things, when we go through hurt, pain, and failures in our lives. We can truly find joy because in this, we find out that God is there when no one else is," Evangelist Carr spoke with wisdom that those around still seemed to be in amazement at the things God revealed and spoke through her.

"God is restoring you and giving you back your youth. You had to grow up fast. He says you even had to deal with abuse and rejection. But God says He has heard you and no more will you hurt, no more will anyone be able to hurt you or your family, and no more will He keep back his hand. God says no longer will you have to fight, no longer will you feel unwanted, and no longer will you have to be afraid. Whatsoever you can think of to ask for, it will be yours. God is freeing you from all the hurt and things you had to go through at the hand of others!" Evangelist Carr spoke as God filled her ears and eyes with His vision. "God, right now, I pray you fill her up even more, I pray everything you have given to me in the spirit ram be manifested in her twofold. I pray she is loosed from the imagination of the enemy right now. God, I pray you keep her and continue to reveal yourself to her. I pray that she not only has the ear and the attention of you, but that she has the heart and mind of you. Fill her with your Spirit right now and continue to lead and guide her!" Evangelist Carr laid her hand on Lina's head as the anointing of God enraptured her, causing her to fall to the floor. "I plead the blood over her life. I plead the blood over every person under the sound of my voice in the name of Jesus!" Evangelist Carr declared into the mic.

Vera and Helen sat in the pews, amused at how God was moving through someone so fresh in age.

"Just go up there and stop being so stubborn." Vera bickered with Helen, raising her hand, gently pushing her to go up to the altar.

"I don't need to go up there. Hush, people can hear you." Helen swatted Vera's hand away.

"Go before I go get her." Vera nudged Helen.

"All right, if it'll make you happy." Helen stood up, walking to the altar. Helen wanted to go to the altar, but she was afraid of what God would say to her through His prophet.

As Helen stood at the altar, God directed Evangelist Carr straight to her.

"Woman of God, lift your hands." Evangelist Carr placed her hand on Helen's heart. "The enemy is trying his best every day to destroy families. God is going to heal every issue in your life and deliver you from everything that hinders your relationship with Him. You can't hold on to anger. God got you and your family."

Helen looked in amazement at all Evangelist Carr was speaking. She had never spoken with or known about Evangelist Carr for her to know the things she did.

"God says you're stubborn." Evangelist Carr stepped back from Helen, smiling.

"Yes, hallelujah. Yes, she is," Vera shouted from the pews at the words Evangelist Carr spoke concerning Helen.

"But God loves you so much. Trust in the Lord with all your heart and lean not unto your own understanding." Evangelist Carr smiled. "And stop trying to solve everything yourself, let God work and have his way. Your daughter is going to be okay because God has her." She hugged Helen before moving along to other people.

"God, forgive us for any wrong we have done, for being judgmental, and condemning others. I pray you touch our minds, touch our hearts, and touch every area of our lives that don't glorify and bring honor to you. Let your Spirit move and keep us from evil." Evangelist Carr prayed before walking to the pulpit.

The musicians began to play as the praise and worship singers took the microphones. They sung as people continued to cry, giving themselves to God at the altar. Evangelist Carr took her seat as the praise team finished up and the people took their seats. The pastor of the house gave final remarks before dismissing service. Everyone left feeling better than the way they had come. And by the way, Evangelist Carr preached, and God moved this service was to be the talk of the town.

Tina hugged Lina in the parking lot as they got in the car. She didn't say a word as she drove, pondering on all God had spoken and done in the service.

47

"Tina, get up and go get me some bacon from the store." James shook Tina out her sleep, snatching the covers off her.

"James, stop. Go get your own bacon." She grabbed the covers, yanking them from his grip.

"Tina, don't start. Get up now and go to the store before you piss me off!" he yelled.

"You really get on my nerve," Tina mumbled under her breath. She got out the bed heading to the bathroom to brush her teeth and throw on a sun dress.

She grabbed the keys to her 2001 Toyota Corolla. To be fifteen years old, the car was in fair condition. The back windows didn't work, the air conditioner made a loud noise, and the engine over heated from time to time, but besides that, it got her from point A to point B. James had paid $1,000 cash for the car after Tina lost her car. Tina wasn't too happy with having to get something so old, but she was grateful for it.

Tina walked to her car getting inside as she started the engine to head to the grocery store, which was ten minutes away.

"Hey, Mom, good morning." Lina smiled at the sound of her mother's voice.

"Good morning, baby, what are you girls up to?" Tina held the phone to her ear with one hand, the other hand on the steering wheel.

"Nothing, Amber's mom is making breakfast."

"Sounds good. I'm on my way to the store, is there anything you girls want?"

"Umm, maybe some Oreos and chips," Lina said.

"Okay, I love you, girls," Tina said as she pulled up to a red light.

"I love you too, Mommy. Ava wants to talk to you." She handed Ava the phone.

"Hi, Mommy." Ava smiled.

"Hi, baby, what are—" Tina said before a car slammed into the back of her, pushing her car into the intersection where another car slammed into her passenger side door.

"Mommy? Mommy?" Ava panicked. "Lina, I heard a boom and big noises, and Mommy isn't saying anything." Ava shook Lina's shoulder.

"Mommy?" Lina grabbed the phone. "I don't hear anything. The call was probably lost or something." She hung up the phone. "I'll call her back after we eat." She hugged Ava.

An hour later, Lina called her mother's phone.

"Mommy, are you home?" Lina spoke.

"Hi, this is Devin Waters, I'm a nurse here at Grace Memorial Hospital, may I ask whom I'm speaking with?"

"This is Lina, and why are you answering my mom's phone?"

"Your mother was brought here by ambulance, is there a grown up available to talk?"

"I am grown." Lina ran in the kitchen where Kelly was.

"We have to go to the hospital. My mom's there," Lina said in a panic.

"What happened?" she asked the nurse on the other end of the phone.

"She was in a car accident. She's stable but in critical condition. Is there any way you can get here?"

"We're coming." Lina hung up the phone, running to get Ava and their shoes.

The ride to the hospital took about fifteen minutes. Kelly, Amber, Lina, and Ava sat in silence as they drove. They arrived at the hospital and threw valet the keys.

"We're here to see Tina Starr. She was brought by ambulance." Kelly talked to the receptionist in the emergency room.

"Yes, she's in room 19, just go through those double doors and to the right." The receptionist pushed a button, causing the double door to open.

"I hope she's okay," Lina said as they walked.

"She'll be fine. It's gonna be okay." Kelly put her arm around Lina's shoulder.

"Mama." Ava ran to her mother's bedside.

"Be gentle, try not to touch her." Kelly walked next to Ava, holding her hand. "She's gonna be okay, sweetie."

Tina was alert but in pain. Her face was swollen, the top of her head had a cut on it, she wore a neck brace, and had an IV coming from her arm.

"Mommy, are you okay?" Lina walked up to her mother as she laid in the bed with her eyes closed.

"I'm okay, baby, my head just hurts, and the light makes it worse," Tina said.

"Why did they say you were in critical condition then?"

"Because my head, they want to make sure there isn't any swelling going on. I'm okay, baby." She smiled.

"Hello, I'm Dr. Jade, we're going to take you for some more tests and a CT scan. If everything comes back normal, you'll be able to go home today," she said before walking out.

"Ugh, I don't need this right now." Tina sucked her teeth. "Lina, I need you to call James and tell him what happened."

"Momma, I'm not calling him. I don't even like him." Lina sat in a chair next to her mother's bed.

"Don't worry, I'll call him." Kelly pulled her cell from her back pocket. She dialed his number as Tina said it. "Hi, is this James? Your wife is in the hospital, she was in a car accident," Kelly talked.

"That is not his wife," Lina mumbled.

"Is she talking, is she okay?" James said.

"Yes, she's talking. They have to run some tests on her."

"Can you ask her did she at least get the bacon?"

"Are you serious, you're asking about bacon?"

"Tell him I didn't make it to the store. I was at a red light and some idiot ran into the back of me and pushed my car into the intersection. Another car ran into the side of me. The police said the car was totaled, but at least I'm alive." Tina tried to speak loud enough for James to hear her.

"No, she ain't get no bacon. Her car was totaled though." Kelly rolled her eyes, shaking her head.

"Well, tell her I don't know what she gonna do cause I ain't got no money to get her another car."

"Wow, what a jerk," Kelly said silently. "Okay, have a nice day, sir, I just wanted to call you and let you know what's going on." She hung up the phone.

Lina, Ava, and Amber sat watching videos on Amber's phone as nurses came to take Tina for more tests.

"What did he say?" Lina looked up at Kelly, breaking the stare she had on the videos.

"Oh, nothing important." Kelly looked up at the television.

"Yea, it's never nothing important when he talks." Lina looked back down at the phone.

An hour later, Tina arrived back to the room. She sat up in the bed, untying the gown. "I'm going home, everything came back normal for the most part." She smiled at Ava.

"So, what are we going to do about a car?" Lina sat on the edge of the bed.

"My insurance covers that. They'll give me a rental until the people who hit me, insurance cuts me a check to get another car."

"I'm glad you're okay, Mommy." Lina leaned, hugging her mother.

"It just seems like everything bad always happens to me," Tina said. She got dressed and waited for her discharge papers. "I'm in pain, girls, so I'm gonna go home and rest. Lina, you're in charge for dinner." Tina laid back on the bed closing her eyes.

"Don't worry about dinner, the girls can stay the night again. We'll go out for dinner. I just want you to get some rest." Kelly looked at Tina.

"Thank you so much," Tina said.

"Oh, it's no problem. I love these girls like their mine, plus when they're around, it gets Amber out my hair." She laughed.

"I heard that," Amber said without breaking stare from the phone.

Fifteen minutes later, Tina was released. Kelly drove her home then headed back to her house.

****

"I sent you to the store for one thing and you couldn't even do that right." James walked in the room as Tina laid in bed watching television.

"James, please, I'm in pain. It's not like I told that man to crash into the back of me."

"So, I guess I'm not gonna have bacon with my eggs then." He opened his top drawer, getting out a T-shirt.

"You can if you go to the store and get it yourself. You have a car, you're more than capable of driving yourself." Tina rolled her eyes. "Do you have to come in here and be so negative all the time? All you ever want to do is argue."

"This my house." James walked out the room.

"Ugh, I just don't understand what I'm doing so wrong." Tina turned the television off, closing her eyes.

****

After dinner, Lina told Kelly she wanted to go home. Her stomach was upset. All she wanted to do was curl up under her mother. She knew that wasn't going to happen, considering her mother was still in pain from the car accident. Kelly took them to her house to gather their things then headed to Lina's house. Amber was going to be home by herself the next day since she had to work, but Kelly promised to take her shopping for jeans early in the morning before she had to leave for work.

When Lina and Ava got home, James was gone. They banged on the front door until Tina unlocked it.

"I thought you were staying the night at Amber's." Tina turned, walking back to her bedroom.

"I was going to, but my stomach is hurting. I think it was something I ate." Lina kicked her shoes off laying on the couch.

An hour later, she went to her room to go to sleep. James still hadn't come home, which was wonderful to Lina. The house was quiet for a change, and everyone was able to sleep without hearing him complain about this or that.

48

"Mommy, Mommy." Ava shook Tina.

"What, baby?" Tina lifted her head up from under the pillow.

"Can I sleep with you since James isn't here?" She sat on the edge of the bed.

"He's not?" She looked at Ava. "What time is it?"

"Eight thirty in the morning."

"Did you see him leave?"

"No." She yawned. "Mommy, can I sleep with you?" Ava scooted her body close to her mother getting up under the covers.

"Well, since you're already in the bed, come on." Tina pulled the covers up to her neck.

****

Tina woke at 11:00 a.m. It was Sunday and would be a chill day. She was still in pain from the accident, but things weren't going to get done if she didn't do it. She got up brushed her teeth, then called James. His phone rung twice before going to voicemail. Tina was mad he hadn't been home and decided to handle him once he got home. She cleaned the house, then went to do laundry. Once back, she cooked homemade mac and cheese, green beans, yellow rice, a pot roast, sweet potatoes, and cornbread. She called James again. This time, he sent her to voicemail. It was now 8:12 p.m., and James still wasn't home.

****

Lina and Ava had already eaten, taken their baths and were now in their room watching television. Tina cleaned up the kitchen from dinner, made a plate for James, and put the food away. She called James one last time before getting in the shower. It was now nine thirty at night, and Tina still hadn't heard from James. She turned the shower on as hot as it would go, standing underneath the water. Steam quickly filled the bathroom mirror and walls.

"What is wrong with me?" She cried, placing her face underneath the water. "What am I doing so wrong." She turned toward the shower wall, slamming her fist into it. "Why, what's wrong with me?"

She grabbed her wash cloth from over the shower bar, soaped it and washed her body. She stood back under the water, letting the suds rinse off. "I don't understand what I'm doing so wrong." Tina turned the water off, grabbing her towel off the sink, wrapping it around her body, going to her room to lotion up and put on some pajamas. After, she crawled under the covers, flipping through channels on the television.

"Why you smelling all good." James walked in the room. He took his shoes off climbing in the bed with Tina.

"James, don't touch me. You smell like alcohol. You didn't come home last night. You haven't been home all day. You ignored my calls, and now you coming home ten fifteen at night and think you gonna layup? Not happening so you can move away from me." Tina pushed James in the chest.

"Come on, baby, why you acting like that?" James leaned in to kiss Tina.

"I'm serious, James, move!" She pushed his face away. "I'm not in the mood for this with you." She sat up.

James grabbed the back of Tina's neck, squeezing it as hard as he could. "Don't give me that attitude. All I did was comprehend you." James slurred his words.

James was so drunk he hadn't realized what he was saying didn't make sense, or that he was using the wrong words.

"Get off me, you're hurting me!" Tina yelled in pain.

"Shut up, you started this so Imma give you what you want." He pushed Tina's neck, making her fall on the floor.

"I really hate you." Tina jumped up, punching James in the face.

James jumped off the bed, tackling Tina. They both fell as he got on top of her, punching her in every spot he could.

"James, get off me!" Tina pushed with all her strength, pushing James off her. She jumped up running to the kitchen.

"I'm done with you!" Tina cried as James came running behind her, tackling her to the floor again. "I'm done, I'm leaving."

"Oh, you leaving, huh," James laughed. "This what you wanted." He stood up, walking to the refrigerator, grabbing a beer.

"Mama, let's just leave. You don't need him!" Lina ran out her room, yelling.

"Shut up and stay in a child's place!" James staggered toward Tina, throwing the beer can at Lina.

"Lina, go in your room and close the door," Tina spoke through her tears as she tried to get up from the floor. "Go now!"

Lina went to her room, slamming the door behind her.

"You really think you gonna leave me? After all I've done for you. You not going nowhere, you belong to me!" James grabbed Tina by the neck, squeezing his fingers deep into her skin.

"Stop, Stop! I can't take this anymore. I can't take you, James. I can't take this life. Me and my girls are leaving whether you like it or not!" Tina gasped as she fought to get the words out.

"I'll kill you before I let you leave me!" He let go of Tina's neck, staring into her eyes.

His eyes were blood shot red, his pupils enlarged. Tina stared back into James's eyes as if in a trance. The eyes she stared into scared her. It was a look she had never seen before.

"Stop!" Lina yelled, swinging open her room door.

Ava sat on her bed crying, rocking back and forth with her hands covering her ears.

"I hate you!" Tina jumped up, punching James repeatedly in every spot she could find to hit him. "I hate you!"

James bawled his fist punching Tina in the face and chest as if he were fighting another man. His eyes looked on as he punched her in the nose, causing it to bleed. Blood leaked from Tina's nose running down her lips on to her shirt. The sight of red liquid caused James to become irater, punching her harder and harder. Each hit sounded off as his fist met Tina's body. She fell to the floor, bawling up screaming for James to stop.

"Get away from my mom!" Lina, ran to the kitchen drawer, grabbing a steak knife, stabbing James in the shoulder.

The stab seemed to have no effect on James, as he continued to punch and kick Tina, causing his blood and her blood to cover the kitchen floor.

"Get up and fight. You want to leave, you better fight me then!" James yelled as he hovered over Tina, punching her.

The force of each hit that Tina took to the head caused her to black out. Her body jerked as James continued to punch and kick her. Lina stood in shock as she watched her mother's body thump up and down on the floor. She quickly snapped out of it, running to her room, grabbing her phone.

"He's going to kill her, he's killing her!" Lina cried barely able to get her words out.

"What's going on? I need you to calm down."

"He's going to kill my mom!" Lina screamed, crying hysterically. "He's killing her, he's killing her!"

****

It took less than ten minutes before Kelly and Monique came running in the house. Monique ran to Lina, hugging her tight.

"Where is Ava?" She looked around frantically breathing heavily.

"In the room." Lina led her to their bedroom. Tears covered her face; her hands shook uncontrollably. "He killed my mom!" She cried.

She walked to the bed, hugging Ava. "It's going to be okay, baby." She helped Ava stand as she placed her arms around her and Lina's waist, walking out the house to her car. Once Monique made sure Lina and Ava were safe, she went back into the house.

Kelly, who had just gotten off work when Monique called her, ran toward James and Tina, tasering James.

"Monique, baby, they jumped me and stabbed me." James's eyes widened when he saw her face.

Monique walked past James to Tina, checking for her pulse. She laid bruised, swollen, bloody, and unresponsive on the floor.

"Baby, her and her kids did this to me." James looked at Monique.

"Well, that's too bad." Monique walked over to James as he laid on the floor covered in blood and urine. "Look at you all, pissy," Monique said sarcastically, shaking her head. "I wore these sneakers just for you." She smiled. She kicked her leg back, then forward, kicking James over and over as he yelled out in pain. "This is for you almost destroying me. This is for Joshua!" She kicked him harder. "This is for all the pain you put those girls through, and this is for Tina!" She kicked him on his side as hard as she could. "You're a no good, manipulating, sorry bastard!" Monique kicked James harder with each word she spoke. "I loved you so much, and you treated me as if I meant nothing. You broke me down and hurt me bad." Monique's eyes filled with tears. "You fed me with lies and when I needed you the most, you abandoned me!"

"Monique, I'm sorry. I still love you," James uttered.

"Hurry up and finish kicking him, girl. Backup is outside." Kelly interrupted, looking at Monique as she listened on her walkie talkie.

"James, you don't love me. You don't even love yourself. You're incapable of loving." Monique kicked James one last time.

Monique bent down, holding Tina's hand until paramedics came to her side. She was alive but in bad shape. The injuries to her swollen head were serious enough that she had to be airlifted to a trauma hospital. James was checked out by paramedics and sent to a local hospital to be treated for his injuries. He was also informed he would be charged with two counts of child abuse, one count of domestic battery, three counts of false imprisonment, and resisting arrest with violence for giving the officers a hard time.

Monique followed Kelly to the hospital. Lina and Ava had calmed down and were sitting in the back seat of Kelly's car.

"I hope we never go back." Lina looked out the window. "I hope they don't try to take us from Momma," she whispered.

"Baby, nobody's going to take you away from your mom. I'll make sure of it." Kelly looked in the rearview mirror at Lina.

****

Tina was admitted and moved to a room once it became available. She had two fractured ribs, a concussion, a split above her eyebrow, which required ten stitches, and a broken jaw. Surgery for her jaw was scheduled the following morning. In the meantime, she was given a narcotic and was asleep from the meds. Lina and Ava sat in the room while Monique and Kelly stepped in the hall shutting the door behind them.

"Monique, why did that man say he still loved you?" Kelly looked Monique in the eyes.

"Kelly, I never told you…" Monique paused. "That man was my husband. I found out he was with Lina's mother when I overheard Lina talking to Amber about him. That's not the man I married." She looked toward Tina's room door. "I thought when I finally got the chance to be in her presence, I would cuss her out or try to fight her or something. But she's so broken, just like I was. And she didn't hurt me, he did." Monique's eyes watered. "And all this hurt was caused by him. I've never been the type to chase a man or fight over one, but he broke me to that point." Monique shook her head. "He broke me to the point of death."

"Wow, I had no clue." Kelly shook her head. "I believe God warns us to stop doing something, or to get out of something. I call it our mess. If we don't listen, He'll allow us to stay in our mess until we get sick of ourselves. Sometimes, we have to be broken in order to get sick of ourselves and our current weight or stronghold. That's the only reason you're strong enough to be standing here. You had to get sick of yourself, so God could heal you." Kelly smiled. "That lady is so frail." Kelly looked toward Tina's room door. "I feel so bad for her, and I'm so mad at myself for not noticing the signs sooner. It didn't have to come to this."

"I remember at that service when Evangelist Carr told her if she didn't leave that man, it would be death to her. Wow, she was right. He could have killed her." Monique looked down. "Dang, all I keep asking myself is how could you stay with a man who beats you or mistreats your kids? But I'm no different from her. The only difference between me and her is, he didn't beat on me. I can't believe how stupid we were for him."

"It's okay, Monique, we all have our stupid moments." Kelly hugged her. "The most important thing right now are those girls. Let's go back in and make sure they're okay. I'll keep them at my house as long as they need to be there."

****

Tina was alone when nurses prepped her the next morning for surgery. She was in a lot of pain and unable to speak because of her jaw. Surgery took about an hour where doctors wired her jaw shut.

She awoke in the recovery room still out of it due to the anesthesia. She stayed in the recovery room for an hour before nurses took her back to her room.

"Tina, I'm so sorry. I'm so sorry. I should've been there for you. I should've been there." Mitch walked to Tina's bedside as she laid asleep under heavy meds.

"Oh my god, why, baby? I'm so sorry." Mitch held her hand.

Lina had gotten Mitch's number from her mother's cell phone and called her to tell her what had happened. Tasha had also ridden with Mitch to the hospital but stopped at the restrooms before going into Tina's room.

"Oh my god, Tina." Tasha slowly walked to Tina's bedside as tears started to form in her eyes. "What did he do to you?" She stared at Tina.

Tina's face was bandaged. The only thing visible was her swollen eyes and nose and a big bandage over the eyebrow that had to get stitches. Her face was black and blue, and her ear and neck were also badly bruised. A nurse walked in to take her vitals as Mitch and Tasha stood at Tina's bedside.

"Ma'am, can you tell us what's going on?" Mitch turned around, facing the nurse.

"Hi, can I ask what's your relationship to her?"

"I'm her friend."

"I'm sorry, I can't give you information. I can only tell you she's had surgery this morning for a broken jaw." The nurse pressed a button on a machine that took Tina's vitals.

"Oh my god, why did this happen? Tina, what have you gotten yourself into?" Tasha mumbled.

"I can't, I can't see her like this." Mitch broke down, crying.

They stayed only for a few minutes. Mitch called Lina and told her to keep her updated and that she was there for them with anything they would need.

****

James sat in jail without a bond. He had an arraignment earlier that day and was told he would not be allowed to have contact with Tina or her girls. He had also had to get twenty-three stitches inside and on the skin of the stab wound he had gotten. He was still intoxicated and cussed the judge out at court. This made it worse for him and because of that, he would not be a free man to walk the streets before he was sentenced.

49

Tina was in the hospital for three days. She was getting out with her jaw wired shut and bruising all over her body. She was given information on how to function with her jaw being wired and was directed to a dietician that would help design a good diet until her jaw healed. Kelly arrived to pick up Tina around nine thirty in the morning. She had gotten word of James's court appearance and told Tina what was up when she got to the hospital.

"Tina, I'm so sorry. I should have seen the signs sooner. I'm so sorry your family is going through this." Kelly opened the passenger side door of her car for Tina.

"Kelly, it's okay, for so long I tried to hide what was going on because I needed James. I couldn't pay the bills or take care of my kids without him, so I stayed no matter what he did." Tina typed the words in her phone for Kelly to read. After she sat, she put her seat belt on. "I stayed with him because it was what I had to do." She typed the words in her phone again, then closed the car door.

"I'm so sorry." Kelly started the car and pulled off from the hospital.

She dropped Tina off at her apartment and headed home. Still in pain, Tina went down to the apartment office to talk to the land-lord. She wrote on a piece of paper everything that had happened, and that she didn't have a job, but would try to come up with the rent that was due in two weeks. They told her if she didn't come up with the rent money by the fifteenth of the following month, she would have to move out. They also told her that they were sorry, but they followed the order of the company, and it was beyond their control.

For the next four weeks, Tina sat trying to figure out how she was going to come up with rent as well as car insurance. She requested an extension on her light and phone bill so wasn't worried as much about paying these two bills. She was too embarrassed to have Lina call Aunt Berniece or Grandma Sonya to tell them what had been going on. She was losing hair from stress and was three days away from the due date of rent. James hadn't called, and his bank account had only $14 in it. Tina decided she would start packing since she had no way of getting the money she needed.

She was also scheduled to have the wiring removed from her jaw in a week in a half. She stayed in the apartment until the day of her appointment, which was also the day the sheriff was called to have her removed from the apartment.

****

"God, please help me. I don't know what to do. We're home-less." Tina cried as Lina and Ava laid sound asleep under a heap of blankets in the back seat of the car.

She was parked at the same park her and James met up at before they started dating. Beside a few pieces of clothing, all her belong-ings, and everything she and Kevin had worked for was gone. James was still in jail and the broken home they had occupied was nothing but a memory. James was still in jail, so he had no way of helping Tina out. He was also court ordered to stay away from Tina and her girls and to have no contact whatsoever with them, so she had no way of speaking to him to see if he could help her. Tina, on the other hand, had a full tank of gas and two hundred dollars. She didn't know what she was going to do or where she was going to live. Her life was crumbling beyond repair, so she thought.

The night's air had a chill to it. Tina got out the car, walking ten feet away to a bench.

"Okay, God, I surrender. I give up." She kneeled in front of the bench. "God, I'm broken. I don't know, maybe you've broken me to get my attention. I know I don't deserve you, but I'm sorry God and I..." She paused, wiping the dripping snot from her nose with her hand. "I need your help. I don't know what to do, where to go. I'm low on money. It's not even enough to move into my own. I don't have a job. I don't know. I just don't know, but my babies need you. I need you." Tina wiped her eyes. "If I were you, I wouldn't forgive me, but I know you do." Tina looked up at the stars in the sky. "It's just not fair my life had to end up like this, but I'm ready. I'm ready for change, I want to be a better woman, a better mother, a better person to you, God. I don't know how you're going to do it, but I trust you." Tina stood up, brushing her knees off. She walked back to her car, getting in the driver's seat. She reclined the seat as far back as it would go closing her eyes. "The truth is, I'm so depressed. I'm so unhappy. I know I've lied to you, disobeyed you, manipulated you, neglected the relationship we built, I turned my back on you, I disrespected the Holy Spirit," Tina mumbled as tears ran down her face. "I know I vexed you, I disregarded the anointing you placed over my life, I put everything before you, and I know it was wrong. I tried to manipulate your Word to make it fit the way I was living. I cursed you and talked really bad about you." Tina took in a deep breath, letting it out. "But it's not because of anything you did, but because I was really mad at myself. I ruined so much because of myself and my selfish reasons. I'm scared I may never get back to the place I once was in with you God. Right now, I need you more than I've ever needed you." Tina opened her eyes, looking back at her girls asleep.

She laid back in her seat, closing her eyes. Her chest rose then went down as she let out a deep breath. She opened her eyes, staring up at the night sky, so big, yet, so mysterious the way the stars shone brightly, or the way the moon never lost its face even in the daytime. She closed her eyes as sleep began to overtake her.

Early in the morning, Lina awoke, shaking her mother's shoulder.

"Mama, why we gotta sleep in the car, why can't we live with Aunt Berniece?" She wiped the crust from her eyes.

"Lina, I don't need nobody in my business, you hear me?" Tina sat up, turning her body to look at Lina. "What's going on is nobody's business and if you want to stay a family, then I suggest you keep your mouth shut." Tina yawned.

"I was just asking," Lina laid back on her flattened pillow.

"Lina, I'm sorry I didn't mean to yell. I'm just frustrated. I don't know what I'm going to do. I'm embarrassed. I'm angry that I let myself get to this point. I'm scared because I don't know what's gonna happen. I'm too ashamed to ask for help." Tina looked up through the windshield watching as the sun began to awaken. "Baby, I don't know what I'm going to do. I just don't know." She shook her head.

Tina started the car and headed to a store so she and the girls could freshen up and brush away their morning breaths. There were only a few weeks left before Lina and Ava went on summer break, and she knew they wouldn't last long sleeping in the car, especially when the summer heat hit. It was a school day, but she decided to keep the girl from school. Once finished, they went back to the park, parking in the same spot as the night before. She opened the trunk, pulling out a half loaf of bread with a jar of peanut butter and jelly. They all walked to a picnic bench where Tina fixed sandwiches.

An hour later, they left the park heading to the mall to pass time. Eventually, Tina drove back to the park as night began to fall.

"Mommy, I'm so hungry." Ava whined as they pulled in a parking spot in the park's parking lot.

"Baby, can you hold out until the morning? We just ate a couple hours ago at the mall. I have to be wise with the money we have left." Tina's eyes watered.

"No, Mommy, I'm hungry."

"Dammit! Baby, I know you're hungry. I'm doing the best I can right now!" Tina slammed her hands on the steering wheel. "Ava, I'm sorry. Mommy is not mad at you. I promise, I will try to get something." Tina got out the car.

"It's okay, Ava, just try and go to sleep." Lina wrapped her arms around Ava, rocking back and forth. "Mommy doesn't mean to yell, she's just got a lot on her plate and it's hurting her that she can't give us what we need right now." She kissed Ava's forehead.

Tina walked to the bench, getting on her knees. The night's air was still and hot. The only lights that shone was lights from cars that would pass by.

"God, please, I'm at my breaking point. I know I messed up, but please don't punish my babies because of me. I don't know what else to do. God, I need your help. Please, if not, then kill me. Please, God." Tina cried.

She stayed at the bench on her knees for twenty minutes. She walked back to her car getting in the driver's seat. Lina and Ava were asleep, so she closed her eyes humming, *What a friend we have in Jesus.* Unsure of what she was going to do, she began thinking of ways to end her life as well as the life of her girls.

At least we'll be together, she thought. She opened her eyes, staring back at Lina and Ava. "I'm going to crash my car into a tree," she mumbled as tears flowed down her face. "I just don't understand why this is happening to me." Tina laid back in her seat, closing her eyes.

She dozed off letting out the sound of snores as she began entering stage two of sleep.

****

We have a call of a suspicious vehicle, the dispatcher spoke.

"Ten four, I'm in route, I'm two mins away," Kelly responded. She had picked up a night shift and had just stopped for food when she got the call.

She pulled into the park and behind the suspicious car turning her lights on as well as her spot light. She walked up to the car flashing her flash light in the windows.

Tap, tap, tap. She tapped on the driver side window with her flashlight. "Tina, Tina." Kelly jiggled the door handle. "Tina!" She tapped on the window again.

"What, what?" Tina jumped out her sleep. "OMG, don't shoot." She stared up in a daze.

"Tina, open the door." Kelly taped on the window. "This is Officer Kelly. I'm with the vehicle, everything is okay." Kelly radioed into dispatch.

Tina unlocked her car door opening it for Kelly. Lina and Ava sat up, holding the covers up to their neck, staring at the bright light of the flashlight.

"Tina, what is going on? What are you doing out here with these kids sleeping in the car?" Kelly turned her flashlight off, leaning against the car door.

"I… I," Tina stuttered. Her eyes began to water.

"Tina, what's going on?" Kelly stared in Tina's eyes.

"We're homeless." Tina cried, her emotions overtook her.

"Come on, get out the car and talk to me." Kelly grabbed Tina's hands. "Girls, sit here. We'll be right outside the car."

"Please don't take my kids away." Tina cried as she got out the car.

"You know me better than that. No one is taking no one away. What's really going on?" Kelly closed the car door.

"I'm not working, James is in jail, so I can't pay the rent." Tina wiped her eyes.

"Why didn't you call me? This is crazy." Kelly hugged Tina. "Go to my house, you and the girls can have the guest bedroom. Stay as long as you need. You're out here sleeping in the car with these babies. Do you know how dangerous that is?" Kelly took her spare house key off her key ring, handing it to Tina. "And go get whatever you need." She handed her a hundred-dollar bill from her wallet.

"But—" Tina continued wiping the tears that continued to flow.

"Ain't no but, go to my house and get some rest." She opened Tina's car door. "I love y'all and I'll see you in the morning and put some coffee on in the morning." Kelly laughed.

Tina got in the car, starting the engine. Kelly got in her car turning her lights off backing up, so Tina could get out. She watched as Tina backed up and headed for the road. She followed behind her out the park and headed back to get some food.

****

Kelly walked into the house, the smell of fresh blueberry coffee brewing. Tina was up sitting at the kitchen table as Lina, Ava, and Amber were still sound asleep. She knew Amber was going to be so excited once she learned Lina and Ava were going to be staying with them.

"Good morning, did you get any sleep?" Kelly sat down at the kitchen table.

"A little, just trying to figure everything out." Tina got up to pour a cup of coffee for her and Kelly.

"You can stay here until you get on your feet. There is no rush."

Tina handed Kelly her cup of coffee, grabbing the coconut creamer and a spoon. She sat down at the table sipping her coffee.

"Tina, what's really going on with you? It's more than James. I mean, you wouldn't be with him after this if he was out, would you?"

"I mean yes because I need him, but I don't know." Tina blinked away, the tears she felt forming.

"How's your spiritual relationship?"

"Ugh." Tina let out a deep breath.

"Okay, this is what we're going to do. Talk as if God was sitting here right in front of you." Kelly took a sip of coffee, staring Tina in the eyes. "Tell him how you really feel."

"Okay." Tina let the tears fall. "I'm angry, I'm so angry at you God. I love you, but I just don't know." Tina let out another breath.

"Why are you so mad?" Kelly looked.

"God, I'm mad." She wiped the tears from her cheeks. "God, I'm mad at you because of what happened to Kevin. I know you didn't kill him, but you didn't save him either. My life has been hell since he died, and you haven't been there for me or my family." Tina sobbed.

Kelly stood up getting a piece of paper towel handing it to Tina.

"Tina, I just want you to know bad things happen in the world all the time. And something I learned is, God will never leave you when they happen. He didn't do it, Tina. God didn't pull that trigger and until you forgive yourself and that young man who actually did pull the trigger, you will never have peace." Kelly walked over, hugging Tina. "God can make your pain manageable."

"I'm trying, I'm trying. That young lady Evangelist Carr really walked into my life, and I know it was only because of God. But how do I really forgive and move on?"

"Tina, you just do. All I can say is pray more, speak to God more, and trust Him. I love you and I'm here, girl, always."

50

"Hey, Mitch, it's Lina. Just wanted to tell you my mom, sister, and I live with her friend. She's doing a lot better. I hope you two can work things out because she doesn't have friends these days." Lina sent a text.

Thirty minutes later, Mitch replied, "I'm so glad to hear from you. I miss you all so much. Your mom was dealing with a lot and I understand. She'll always be my friend. No worries. Text me your address so I can pop up on her."

"It's 64 Bungalow Way. And when you come, can you bring some of those chocolate chip cookies you used to buy. The soft ones," Lina replied.

"Your still greedy I see. Just kidding. Okay, love, see you all soon," Mitch replied.

****

Summer break had officially started. Lina was excited about not having to wake up early for school, but what she was most excited about was James not being in their lives. This summer, she planned on spending time with her mother as she healed mentally, physically, emotionally, and spiritually, and getting a job if her mother allowed. Amber was happy Lina and Ava were living with them. She rearranged her whole room so she and Lina could share her room. Ava slept in the room with her mother in the queen-sized pillow top mattress, which she didn't mind at all. She loved being able to curl up under her mother. Tina, on the other hand, hated being kicked in the ribs each night and waking up with a foot or hand on her neck or on top of her head. She told Ava if she kept sleeping wild, she would find herself officially kicked out the room.

Tina was applying for jobs but was having no luck with being hired. She wasn't depressed as she had been, but being jobless was starting to get to her. Kelly was at work, and the girls still asleep when there was a knock on the door. Tina was already up trying to get back in the habit of reading her word and spending time with God. She left Ava asleep in the bed answering the front door.

"Oh my god, girl, I missed you so much." Mitch dropped the shopping bags, wrapping her arms around Tina. "I missed my friend, I missed you so much." She cried as she held on to Tina.

Tina breathed a sigh of relief. She wrapped her arms around Mitch, crying. "I'm so sorry for the things I said, for the way I disrespected you, for the way I treated you."

"It's okay, I understand. I just want my friend back." Mitch continued to cry.

Lina woke up from the noise and walked to the front door. She stood silently cheering and clapping when she saw Mitch and her mother.

"Yay, yes." She balled up her fist shaking them, smiling. She threw her thumbs up when she saw Mitch looking at her. "I'm so happy you're here," she mouthed, smiling. "Did you get the cookies?" she mouthed.

Mitch laughed as she stared at Lina. She and Tina let the grip they had of each other go. Mitch wiped her eyes, smiling and laughing, thinking about Lina asking about the cookies.

"Tina, you don't understand how much I've missed you. I wanted to call you, but I figured you didn't want anything to do with me." Mitch continued to cry tears of joy. "I'm sorry, this is Avery, he works at the salon now." Mitch moved to the side, so Avery and Tina could shake hands.

"It's so nice to finally meet you. You're all she talks about." He smiled. "Honey, can we come in? It's hot out here." He wiped his forehead.

"Sorry, where are my manners, come inside."

Mitch picked up the bags and headed inside behind Tina. They sat in the living room, talking and laughing about old times. Lina hugged Mitch then grabbed the bag of cookies, putting them in the kitchen.

"Do you remember that time that lady was leaving out and slipped when she walked out the door, and her wig fell off after she tried to straighten me about my prices." Mitch and Tina laughed.

"Wait, what?" Avery laughed.

"Yes, and she had an oxtail when that wig fell off." Tina laughed.

"What is an oxtail?" Avery laughed.

"She had a rubber band for a hair tie and wanna come with an attitude trying to straighten somebody." Tina laughed. "An oxtail is when your ponytail is only a few strands of hair." Tina laughed.

"Yes, those were the good days. It hasn't been the same since you left." Mitch looked at Tina. "We all miss you." She smiled.

"Honey, what she's trying to say is, please come back. Please, no offense, but I get tired of hearing your name." Avery laughed along with Tina and Mitch.

"Tina, I told you. You could always come back when you're ready, and I miss you being around." Mitch stared into Tina's eyes.

"I mean. I... I." Tina looked down. "It's been so long since I've done hair. I don't know if I still remember how." Tina looked at Mitch.

"Well, think about it, if you want to come back, I can go over things with you. You know, help you freshen up. I know you probably just a lil rusty. It's been a few years." Mitch smiled. "I really want you to come back, Tina, so please think about it."

"Yeah, I'll be there Tuesday." Tina laughed.

"Seriously?" Mitch began to cry again.

"Yes, I'm serious. That's my passion. I feel like it's time to start doing what I love again."

"Friend, I'm so happy." Mitch stood up, hugging Tina again. "I'm telling you once you get back to it, it'll be like you never stopped." Mitch sat back on the couch.

"I hope so." Tina smiled. "So, what made you reach out to me?"

"Well, I went to the hospital when you were there. It hurt me so bad seeing you like that. I felt like I could have lost you for good, and I wasn't sure if you knew I loved you, and I couldn't say by my actions they showed I loved you. I just didn't know if you knew that. You're my real friend and seeing you like that made me realize what's most important."

Tina cleared her throat. She had never told people about the abuse she received being in a relationship with James, and she was still embarrassed that people now knew.

"I'm just glad I can move on in life." Tina smiled. "And I hope you can really forgive me." She stared at the floor.

"Tina, I never held a grudge against you. You're my friend, and I knew what you were dealing with. Enough of that though, let's forget about the past. I just want my friend back. All that other stuff is irrelevant."

"But how did you know where I live?" She looked up at Mitch.

"Your baby told me. That girl loves you so much." She smiled.

"I know she's such a strong girl." Tina looked over at Lina, smiling.

****

Tina was excited Tuesday was here. She got up early to take a shower and put on a little makeup. She put on fake lashes, did her eyebrows, and put on some foundation. Her hair was still quite thin, so she put on a soft, bouncy, curly, jet black wig. She was to meet Mitch at the shop an hour before it opened to touch up on things she had forgotten, and she was to stay late after the shop closed to learn new things. Today, she would be assisting Mitch instead of taking on her own clients. And being she had been gone so long, she would have to grow her clientele again, which wouldn't be a problem considering on a daily basis, people had to turn away because it just wasn't enough workers to fulfill the appointment clients as well as all the walk-ins who came in.

Tina kissed Ava and then headed to Amber's room to kiss Lina. She left her a note telling her she would be home a little later tonight so she could learn some stuff from Mitch and that she loved and appreciated her. She was still in a rental and enjoying the newness of the car. She got in the car, put her seatbelt on, and headed to the shop. It would take about forty-eight minutes to get there and in that time in the car, she prayed and talked to God about her life and the things she wanted out of life. When she arrived at the shop, Mitch was already there. Tina walked in, sitting in one of the salon chairs.

"Wow, it's been so long since I've been here." She spun around in the chair, looking around.

Only a few things had changed. The color was brighter, there were more mirrors, and the salon area had been remodeled to have a section where people could get manicures and pedicures done.

Mitch handed Tina a spare key to the salon before they began practicing on the mannequin. Twenty minutes later, the front door opened.

"Oh my god! Tina. My girl." Tasha ran, hugging Tina. "Are you back? I'm so happy to see you." She hugged Tina tighter.

"I missed you." Tina hugged Tasha. "I'm back for good." She smiled.

"Girl, we missed you around here for real." Tasha stepped back smiling, staring Tina in the face. "I'm not letting you go this time." Tasha laughed.

The day had started, the shop began to fill up with workers and clientele. Avery worked in the booth across from where Mitch and Tina were. Tina bounced back and forth between Mitch and Avery watching and helping them both. Around 12:30 p.m. First Lady and Pastor Sullivan walked into the salon.

"Oh my god." Tina looked as they entered the salon, quickly turning her head trying to avoid eye contact.

First lady Sullivan walked over to Tina, smiling as she hugged her. "Tina, Tina, I have missed you so much." Her eyes began to water. "How have you been?" She looked Tina in the eyes.

"I've been okay." Tina smiled as Pastor Sullivan reached to hug her.

"Hi, Pastor Sullivan." Tina smiled, trying to avoid eye contact. She quickly grabbed the flat iron off the stand to look busy.

"Tina." His deep voice penetrated her ears. "I want you to know I love you, and I'm so happy to see you." He smiled.

"Pastor Sullivan, I want to apologize for how I treated you in the past. I…" She dropped her head.

"Tina, I never held that over your head. I've always been there for you, and I still am." He hugged Tina again. "You should know me better than that. I don't care nothing about that. How is Lina and Ava?"

"They're good. They're getting so big. Lina's in high school. She'll be a junior when school starts back, and Ava will be in the seventh grade. She's gonna be twelve soon." Tina grinned.

"Wow, you're getting old." Pastor Sullivan laughed. "Well, baby, call me when you get done and I'll come get you." Pastor Sullivan kissed his wife on the lips. "Tina, my number is still the same if you ever need me." He hugged her before leaving out the salon.

"So, what are we doing today?" Mitch ran her fingers through First Lady's hair.

"I want a sew-in. I'll let you decide the style." She sat back in the chair.

Tina washed her hair, then put some stuff in it that would condition it while she sat under the dryer.

"So, we're having a program at my church for Pastor's birthday, and I would love for you all to come." First Lady talked as she flipped through a magazine.

"Me and Tina will be there." Mitch smiled, looking at Tina.

"Avery, you should come too." First Lady looked at him as he flat ironed a lady's hair.

"Uh, no, ma'am. No, ma'am." He grabbed some sheen, spraying a strand of hair before flat ironing it.

"Why?" Tasha laughed. "You said that quick."

"Come on now y'all. I'm not welcomed in places like that." He looked over at Tasha.

"What?" First Lady looked at Avery. "God welcomes everyone. Come as you are. I know you heard that before."

"It ain't God that's not welcoming, it's the people." He cocked his head to the side. "I'm a gay black male. People see that and instantly start judging me, talking about me like I'm not human. If I go to church, I want to go so I can hear from God, so I can be in his presence. I don't want to go just to feel uncomfortable the whole time, or to feel like I'm not good enough to be in the house of God, because of the way I choose to live my life." Avery continued to flat iron his client's hair.

"Let me tell you this, ain't nobody perfect, ain't nobody God, and God ain't delegate nobody with the power to put you in hell. The people should be loving you, not judging you, and it's true that's just the world we live in. But what I'm saying to you is, you have just as much right as anybody else to have a relationship with God, to be in His presence, and to experience the love of God. Because if He was that upset with you, He would have been killed you, right in your mess. Now I'm not trying to justify the way you live or the things you choose to do, all I'm saying is, it's because of His grace and mercy that any of us lives. And we all sin and fall short of the glory of God. You like men, but someone else steals, or someone else sleeps around, your sin is no bigger than theirs. It's all sin." First Lady looked at Avery with a serious look. "At my church, we don't do that. And if I find out that's going on, Imma get in it and it ain't gonna be good." She stopped at a picture of a white dress with white Chanel boots.

"I don't know. I been pushed away and preached on too many times before." Avery shook his head.

"Listen, intentional or unintentional, we are all guilty of judging someone. This man at a restaurant was with his boyfriend, and I was looking and mumbling God ain't pleased, they going straight to hell. And my husband corrected me right then and there. He said to me, and you going to hell for condemning them. Who do you think you are to decide who goes to hell? You ain't no better than them." First Lady laughed.

"What, I know you was embarrassed." Mitch laughed.

"Hmm, I was mad. I told him a thing or two, but I had to go back and apologize. After that, I told myself I never want to be someone who forgets that I'm not perfect, someone who forgets that it's not because of anything I've done but because of God that I live. The Word says, 'There is not a just man on earth who does good and does not sin'. I never want to be the type of person who is caught up in religion instead of relationship and push people away or judge someone when God called me to love. At the end of the day, winning souls is what matters, not killing them and turning them away." She smiled. "Now, if you come you can be my special guest." She looked at Avery.

"Yeah, I'll think about it." He smiled.

"And, Tina, God said the hell you've been through should have taken you out, but He has His hands on you, and He wants you to get back in that place with Him where you put Him first. He said as you become submissive and obedient to Him, He will open the gates of heaven for you." She looked at Tina.

"That lady is the real deal, she real," Mitch mumbled to Tina.

51

"There is a time for everything, and a season for every activity under the heavens: a time to be born and a time to die, a time to plant and a time to uproot, a time to kill and a time to heal, a time to tear down and a time to build." Tina sat on the bed reading her Bible. Her eyes began to water as she closed her Bible, thinking of everything she had been through the last couple of years. She closed her eyes. "Our Father in heaven, hallowed be Your name. Your kingdom come. Your will be done on earth as it is in heaven. Give us this day our daily bread. And forgive us our debts, as we forgive our debtors. And do not lead us into temptation, but deliver us from the evil one. For Yours is the kingdom and the power and the glory forever. Amen," she whispered. She opened her eyes as Ava kicked her in the side. "I am so sick of this girl and her wild sleeping." Tina shook her head. She turned the light off and got back in the bed, falling asleep.

****

"Momma, wake up." Lina shook Tina, waking her. "You got some mail here." She placed an envelope on the bedside table before walking out the room.

"Girl, you could have waited until I woke up." Tina tried to talk, but her voice hadn't woken yet. She looked at the envelope then went back to sleep.

She had been going in early and staying late at the salon all week. She was tired and since it was Saturday and she was off, she wanted to sleep in. The following week, she would be working on her own and already had a few new appointments lined up. Thirty minutes later, Lina walked in Tina's room waking up Ava.

"We're going to the mall, you wanna come?" She shook Ava.

"Yes." Ava yawned.

"Well then, get up and get ready. We're leaving in twenty minutes." Lina walked out the room accidentally slamming the door.

"That child just won't let me sleep." Tina sat up in the bed. She rubbed her eyes then grabbed the envelope off the night stand. She took her car keys ripping open the top of the envelope. It was a letter from the lawyer's office she hired after her car accident.

"We want to thank you for allowing our office to assist you on this case. If you have any questions, please don't hesitate to call us. Enclosed is a check in the amount of $17,328," Tina read. She gasped. "Oh my god, 17,328 dollars," she mumbled, looking over the letter again. She went into the envelope taking out the freshly printed check. "Seventeen thousand three hundred twenty-eight dollars. Jesus, Jesus, Jesus. Thank you, God, thank you," Tina shouted. "Thank you." She cried. "I can get a car now. I can get a house for me and my babies." She laughed, wiping her wet eyes.

She picked up her phone off the night stand calling Kelly.

"Kelly, my money came from my lawsuit from my accident." Tina smiled in the phone.

"Really? That was fast. I'm so happy for you." Kelly smiled. "What are you going to do now?"

"I need to get a car. I want to use some for a down payment on a house or something."

"Well, I'll help you any way I can. Just because you have your money, I don't want you to feel like you have to rush and move out. Take your time and find what's best for you. Do your research and look around. My home is open to you for as long as you need to be there," Kelly talked.

"Thank you so much. You're so amazing. I'm going to give you some money when I cash my check." Tina smiled. "I'm just so happy. It's been a long time coming, me and my girls have been through so much, so much." Tina began to cry. "God is blessing me over and over. I can finally live again."

"Tina, I don't want any money. I love you and your girls. All I want is for you to get on your feet and be happy again. You don't owe me anything."

"Thank you so much, Kelly, thank you. I'm so happy. Everything is just coming together in my life now." Tina smiled. "I guess I better go and find a car." Tina jumped out the bed, heading to the bathroom. "Okay, I'll see you later when you get home. Me and my new car will see you." Tina laughed before they hung up.

****

Tina visited four car dealerships, Honda, Kia, Nissan, and Ford. She learned her credit score was 786, which put her in a bracket where her interest rate as well as her down payment would be low. She headed to the Infiniti dealership picking out a dark blue Infiniti Q50, her payments would be $225 a month and her down payment $1,500. Tina had someone from the car company follow her in the rental to drop it off, while she drove her new car to the rental company. After they took a taxi back to the dealership and she headed home. Tina was so happy, she loved the jet-black leather interior, the features of the car, and most of all, the new car smell. Tina drove back to Kelly's house putting a bow on top of the car to surprise the girls when they got home from the mall. She was mind blown how God was turning her life around, even though she had hurt Him, blamed Him, and turned her back on Him. Tina sat at the kitchen table pondering on everything she had been through and the way she acted after Kevin died.

"God, I love you so much. I love you so much. Thank you, God. I just want you to know I appreciate you, and I'm so grateful that You still love me." Tina closed her eyes. "I give you all the glory, I worship you, my Lord, you are worthy to be praised." She sung over and over as she worshipped.

52

Reggie walked into the visiting room staring at the face he had seen before. He pulled the chair out from the table sitting across from the lady who repeated the same scripture.

"If you forgive men their trespasses, your heavenly Father will also forgive you. If you forgive men their trespasses, your heavenly Father will also forgive you. If you forgive men their trespasses, your heavenly Father will also forgive you." Tina stared at Reggie as he slowly took his seat. "If you think I'm crazy, it's because you made me like this." She stood up then sat back down.

Reggie took a deep breath, then let it out. He lowered his head, trying to avoid eye contact with Tina.

"You know, I held on to a lot of stuff." Tina tapped her finger on the table. "A lot of hate and anger toward you. I hoped and prayed you were tortured. You took my best friend away, my sanity, the father of my kids. You broke my heart, you broke me." Tina wiped the tears that were falling. She stared Reggie in the eyes. "And as much as I would love to wring your scrawny neck, it won't change anything."

Reggie's heart beat as fast as it did the day he was sentenced. He lowered his head, staring at the table. "I'm sorry, man, I don't know what more I can say. I'm sorry. I know I messed up. I never meant for any of this to happen." Reggie wiped his nose with the back of his hand.

"I can't hate you forever. I have to move on, so I can finally heal." Tina stared at the ceiling, tapping her finger on the table. "I... I." She let out a deep breath. "I forgive you. I forgive you for what you've done to my family." She looked at Reggie. "I have to forgive you, so I can forgive myself."

Reggie looked up at Tina, then dropped his head again. Tears immediately fell from his eyes. He wiped them with his hand, they continued to fall. "I'm sorry." He looked up, staring into Tina's eyes. "I'm sorry." He tried to speak through his emotions. "If I could take it all back, I would."

"Yeah, I know how you feel. I wish I could take so much back." Tina dropped her head. "I only pray that you will forgive yourself and find God. I forgive you." Tina grabbed Reggie's hand as he rested it on top of the table. "I want our Father to forgive me, and this is the only way. It's what's right. I'm sorry you ruined my family's life and your own." Tina let go of Reggie's hand. "It's time to move on and live life the best we can in our situation. We get one life." Tina stood up.

"Aye, miss." Reggie looked up at Tina. "Thank you. You don't know how much that means to me. And I'm truly sorry for what I did to your family. I'm not a bad person. I'm sorry."

"Thank you." Tina smiled before leaving out the visitation room.

53

It had been a month since Tina bought her new car. She also found a four-bedroom, two-car garage house that had only been built a month ago. She was scheduled to close on the house in two weeks. Tina was excited about life. The salon was booming, her clientele was more now than it was when she worked there a few years back. Her bank account was growing, and her peace and joy was evident in her health as well as her mental state.

Tina hadn't heard from James personally, but the prosecutor working the case told her he was facing ten years in prison. She felt bad knowing he had a son out in the world who would need him, and that would have to grow up without him for the time being, but she was also relieved and felt he was getting what he deserved. It was also Lina's birthday in two days, so Tina planned a nice dinner inviting a few of her friends from school as well as Monique. She hadn't seen her since her hospital visit, and she barely remembered that night so this night, she would be able to thank her personally for all she had done for her and her girls and also apologize.

****

Tina, Kelly, Lina, Ava, and Amber rode in Tina's new car to the restaurant. Monique drove her car, bringing Joshua, and two of Lina's classmates were going to be meeting her at the restaurant. Tina arrived at the restaurant following the hostess to the private room, which was decorated with purple, white, and blue balloons. A banner hung that read "Sweet Sixteen". There was a long table covered in a purple table cloth with balloons lined in the middle of the table. Another table had Lina's cake on it, and next to that sat the candy table. In the corner of the room sat a table with gift bags and gifts wrapped in pretty wrapping paper. Lina walked in smiling, spinning around, and looking up at all the balloons.

"Mommy, I love it so much." Lina grinned. "I love it." She smiled, hugging her mother.

"Baby, you deserve this and so much more. Happy birthday, my beautiful angel." Tina kissed her on the forehead.

Everyone grabbed their seats as Monique and Joshua walked in with two big gift bags and another one that read "Bath and Body Works". Joshua ran over to Lina, hugging her as Monique waved to everyone placing the bags on the gift table. Ten minutes later, Lina's classmates arrived with gifts as well. Once everyone grabbed their seats, Tina bought out the game Taboo and split the room up into even teams. They all laughed as they competed against each other. After they finished the game, Tina grabbed Monique asking her if she could step outside to speak.

"First, I want to thank you for all you've done for me and my family." She hugged Monique. "Now, I want to apologize to you as a woman for being with your husband. I would never have been with him had I known, Monique, never would I cross that line." She looked her in the eyes.

"Tina, I'll admit I was angry. I was so angry at you, but it wasn't your fault. I can't be angry with you because you had no idea. I don't blame you, I don't hate you, and I'm not mad at you. I want to thank you for being woman enough to talk to me. I love your girls, and I'm not letting James break up the relationship I have with them. As far as I'm concerned, James is where he belongs, and I'm okay with that." Monique looked at Tina.

"Monique, thank you, that means a lot to me." Tina smiled.

"Listen, I want to start fresh with you. You're a strong woman. You have two beautiful girls, and I would love to build a friendship with you." Monique smiled.

"Girl bump that you, my sister." Tina smiled, then laughed as she hugged Monique.

They started walking back in the restaurant when Monique's phone rung.

"I'll be in there. I have to take this call." Monique pulled her phone from her back pocket.

"You have a collect call from an inmate at the county jail. To accept this call, press one," the recording spoke.

Tina pressed one.

"Finally, baby, where have you been? Why haven't you been up here to see me?" James talked.

"James, I'm not your baby. What do you want?" Monique rolled her eyes.

"What you got an attitude for? I'm just trying to talk to my wife. So, what you been up to, where you been?"

"I've been finding myself, James. I'm free. I'm finally free. And I'm not your wife." Monique took a deep breath, letting it out. "I signed the divorce papers. I'm done, James. I'm done with you." Monique smiled.

"Baby, come on now. You know that's not what I really wanted. I love you, Tina. I mean, Monique."

"James, I'm done. Please don't call my phone anymore. I'm not that dumb, gullible woman anymore."

"What about my son? You gonna keep my son away from me?" His voice deepened.

"James, quit being pathetic. You kept yourself away from your son. Now that I've made up my mind, you want to come back in our lives. You're calling me because you're in jail and want someone to feel sorry for you. You're not gonna get me with that jail talk." Monique shook her head. "You messed up, not me. I loved you more than I loved myself, but no more, James, no more. God has been too good to me for me to turn back. I'm free, and there's nothing you can do to change the way I feel. It's over. Now, if you don't mind, I'm with my family."

"What family? You gonna do this to me when I really need you?" James gripped the phone tight in his left hand.

"Tina and her kids." Monique smiled.

"So, you with that hoe, that ain't your family. Why you with her?" James yelled.

"Oh, you mad now." Monique laughed. "Typical James. You played us both and now you're mad cause we talk. You want me to hate her for something you did? Not gonna happen. You're selfish, you're a nasty person, and you're the biggest manipulator I know."

"But, baby." James quickly fixed the tone in his voice.

"James, I'm not your baby. Have a wonderful life, and I'll do the same because you never loved me." Monique laughed before hanging up the phone. She put her phone back in her back pocket and headed into the restaurant to the private room.

"Are you okay?" Kelly looked at Monique as she walked through the door.

"Oh, I'm wonderful." Monique smiled. "I just want you all to know I love you from the bottom of my heart and as long as God gives me breath, I will be here for you whenever you need me." She smiled.

The waiter came in to take orders and bring everyone their drinks. After orders were placed, Ava stood up.

"I have something I wrote, and I want to say, Lina, you're my best friend. I wouldn't want to have any other sister, and I'm so happy that I have you in my life." She smiled as she pulled a folded piece of paper from her pocket. "Be grateful you have the ability to wake up each day. The ability to smile, smell the air, lift your hands, and stomp your feet. Thank God that He breathes his breath into you each day. Be thankful that God has purpose over your life and thank God He said no when the devil said yes. Be thankful you have the option to tell those in your life you love them. Problems come to make us wiser, stronger, and better. God never said troubles wouldn't arise, but He gave us a way to overcome them. So be grateful that you were able to live to make it over your problems. Be grateful because someone facing what you did didn't make it. Be thankful for grace, mercy, but most of all, be thankful God has not given up on you. Be thankful God has given us new mercies to praise Him one more day. I love you all, and I'm so happy to have you all in my life. Happy Birthday,

Lina. I love you." Ava smiled, folding the paper back, putting it in her pocket.

"Baby, that was so good." Tina wiped her eyes.

There wasn't a dry eye in the room as Ava took her seat. A few minutes later, the waiter brought out the food as everyone sat eating, talking, and laughing, enjoying each other's company.

54

"Thank you, Jesus." Tina signed some papers.

"Congratulations."

"I'm so happy. You just don't understand." Tina grabbed the keys to her new house.

"Make new memories, enjoy it." The realtor smiled at Tina.

"Wow, I can't believe I have a new home." She grinned as she walked to her car.

Tina had been buying things here and there for her new home. She had bedroom decor for her, Lina, and Ava's rooms. She had already bought all the kitchen appliances and kitchen decorations as well as all the bathroom decorations. Once she got back to Kelly's house, she would pick up the girls, so they could pick out the bedroom sets they wanted. She had her eye on a light grey sectional and planned to decorate her living room in white, grey, and gold. She would plan to officially move out from Kelly's in a week and also have her house warming the day after she moved. She was excited and felt beyond blessed to have the things she now had.

****

"Wow, this is beautiful." Mitch walked through the front door with Tasha and Avery. She bought small subs and wings with her.

"You did good. I'm so proud of you, girl." Tasha hugged Tina.

"Thank you. I'm so happy." Tina grabbed the bags from Mitch, placing them on the kitchen table.

Lina, Ava, and Amber toured the house as everyone else sat in the living room. Music played in the background as they all sipped on soda, laughing and talking.

"Oh, I want you to meet my new sister." Tina stood up from the couch as Monique walked in. "Monique, this is Mitch. Mitch, this is Monique." They hugged each other.

"This is my mother Helen." Monique smiled at Tina.

"It's so nice to meet you." Tina hugged Helen. "We've met over the phone. Now I finally get to meet you." Tina laughed.

"Baby, this is a lovely home you got." Helen smiled. "I love that picture. She pointed to a huge picture that hung over the built-in fireplace.

"Thank you." Tina smiled. "That's my husband Kevin who passed away and me and our girls when they were younger."

Kelly arrived with homemade mac and cheese and a chocolate cake.

Tina gave everyone a tour of the house. After, they all sat around the kitchen table, talking and eating. Helen stepped out to talk with her friend Mary.

"You know that's illegal." Kelly walked up behind Helen as she smoked on a blunt.

"Uh umm no, this ain't what you think it is. You the po po?" Helen blew out the smoke from her mouth. "This is to uh help my medically medical needs." Helen looked at Kelly.

"Umm hmm." Kelly laughed, walking back into the house.

Once back inside, Kelly fixed her a plate of food as they laughed at Avery's stories.

"I just want to thank everyone for coming and sharing this special moment with me. I'm so blessed and so grateful to God for blessing me and my family with this amazing home and amazing people like you. You all are my family, and I'm honored to have each of you in my life. It's so amazing to see how I had everything and lost it all. And just when I was about to give up on life because I felt like I just couldn't take it anymore, God turned everything around and has blessed me with more than I had before. I love you all, and I welcome you to my new home." Tina smiled.

"Girl, you better come on here and testify, you living your best life." Avery laughed.

"Wait, we have one more surprise for you, Tina." Kelly walked to the front door, opening it.

Aunt Berniece and Kim walked through the front door with gifts for Lina, Ava, and Tina.

"Baby, I'm so proud of you." Aunt Berniece smiled as Tina screamed, running to them, smiling.

"When did you get here?" Tina cried. "I missed you so much." She hugged and kissed Aunt Berniece, then Kim. "I'm so happy you're here." She smiled, wiping her wet face.

"I missed you so, so much, Tina." Kim smiled. "I love you, cousin. I'm so happy to see you in a different space mentally."

"It's been a long journey, a long one." Tina hugged Kim again.

Lina and Ava ran, screaming, excited to see Aunt Berniece and Kim. They hugged and kissed them, holding on to them until they knew for sure they would be staying a few days with them.

Everyone laughed as they all filled their faces, dancing and enjoying each other's company.

"Y'all trust in the Lord with all your heart and lean not to your own understanding. In all your ways, acknowledge Him, and He will direct your paths." Tina smiled as she cut the cake Kelly had bought. "I'm so happy God still loves me." She smiled. "There's truly no other side I would rather live on than God's side." She smiled.

About the Author

L isa Lynch was born in Jersey City, New Jersey, and moved to Florida as a small child. She is a college graduate. Her goal is to bring Christ into the lives of people of all races, religions, and backgrounds through her stories.

CPSIA information can be obtained
at www.ICGtesting.com
Printed in the USA
BVHW030242200819
556309BV00001B/13/P